# JAC
# TREASURE
# TRAP

A treacherous journey to uncover
a precious family secret

MATTHEW BIRD

Second edition independently published by Matthew J Bird in the United Kingdom 2021.



A CIP catalogue record of this book is available from the British Library
ISBN (Paperback UK) 978-1-7398333-0-5

Cover design by Matthew J Bird (images Canva Pro & iStock)
Printed in the United Kingdom in 2021 by Mixam UK Ltd
For further information about this book, please contact the author at
www.JackFruitTreasure.com

£9.99 in UK only

# Contents

*For my daughter, Malissa Maya, and my wife, Patcharaporn, you are the angels in my life.*

# JACKFRUIT

The jackfruit (Artocarpus heterophyllus), also known as a jack tree, is a tree species in the fig, mulberry, and breadfruit family.

The jack tree is suited to tropical climates and is cultivated widely. It bears the largest fruit of all trees, reaching a whopping weight of 120 pounds, 35 inches in length, and 20 inches in diameter. A mature jack tree can produce two hundred fruits per year, with older trees up to five hundred. The jackfruit is composed of hundreds to thousands of individual fruit flowers. The edible ripe fruit is sweet and yellow, depending on variety, and is more often used for desserts. The fruit also contains hundreds of edible nuts.

The jackfruit is the national fruit of Bangladesh and Sri Lanka[1]. It is often called *kos* in Sri Lanka and has been enjoyed as a meal or a snack for many centuries.

[1] During the 16-18th centuries, Sri Lanka was often known as the *Kingdom of Kandy*. The Kandyan Kingdom's territory typically dominated large parts of the island. References to *Kandy* within this book refer to the island as a whole.

# Prologue

Wethersby Thacker ventured into the jungle with Maylong, a young Kandyan woman he met a week earlier on New Year's Day 1631. He thought she promised him a night of passion and a prize beyond his wildest imagination.

She spoke in her native tongue and shy English too. That was enough to draw him to her, along with emerald eyes, jet-black shiny long hair, and soft glowing sun-kissed skin. She showed him her intentions with her body and drew shapes in the dirt of a key, the sun, and the moon, chattering in a language he failed to understand but longed to hear and know more. He could barely contain his hands and did not want to stop looking into her stunning eyes.

They set off by mid-afternoon from Kali in a wooden cart pulled by water buffalo. They slowly made their way down dusty and rutted paths among dense avenues of mango trees. The bone-shaking ride from the southern town took them six hours or thereabouts. That night a three-quarter moon glowed, and a sky full of bright stars lit their way. Eventually, they reached a small remote grotto, lit from the outside by simple flickering flames.

Maylong startled Wethersby by jumping from the wagon before it came to a halt.

"Come!" she teased, running. "Let go before someone sees."

Once they made their way inside, dozens of tiny lanterns smoked, and a robust fragrance of burning coconut oil settled all around. Within an inner recess was a compact sanctuary. An unnatural soft lime glow drew them deeper. The light became intense as Maylong and Wethersby shielded their eyes, bowed their heads for the lowering roof, then shuffled on dusty knees. It was uncomfortable for him; he disliked the closeness of the walls and the lack of clear air. After fifty yards or so, the vault opened, and the glimmering shifted to a golden hue.

The inner cavern felt cold and smelt musty. It was full of razor-sharp needles of rock hanging from above. To one side, a small lagoon emitted a beam from below its surface.

Without hesitation, Maylong unravelled her sarong and dived in. Wethersby, initially shocked by her lack of modesty, quickly followed her lead. The water was crisp, refreshing, and incredibly soft; it ran off their skin, not a drop would stick. They could not stand upright in its centre, although a shelf below the edge brought some relief.

Lying on their backs, they viewed the ceiling. Its colour slowly alternated in power, but there were no candles nor other distinct sources to identify the eerie lights. They lay there for many minutes, mesmerised by the cave's features.

Placing a finger firmly on Wethersby's open mouth, Maylong whispered, "No talk, rocks drop." In confident and perfect London English, she added, "the treasure you seek is all about you."

Wethersby was astonished.

Over an hour later, filled with no conversation other than romancing, they stepped out from the pool and settled down to sleep on the uneven, dusty floor. Wethersby was awoken by a dull thud, followed by a bouncing echo, but he could only see dust. Maylong stirred and wrapped her arm around his chest; he did the same, and they lapsed into sleep.

The luminescence from the water had died when they woke, so too the radiance from the ceiling. Wethersby, though, felt sure the lights were shining as he opened his eyes, but all he could see was phosphorescence in the backwash of his vision. Gradually, the pool began to flicker and glow afresh.

"There is something special in this well," she said softly.

"I know. I felt it too," replied Wethersby.

"No. Precious stones in a large box," exclaimed Maylong, her raised voice jumping off the cavern's walls. "Please, dive deep with me, and let us bring the strongbox up."

Maylong went in first. Wethersby followed. He struggled to keep up with her as his lungs tightened, and in less than a minute, he came up to guzzle air. She remained below for over five minutes more; he grew increasingly anxious. When she surfaced, at last, Maylong just smiled and breathed normally.

"Mister Wethersby, you need to concentrate and keep your breath," she told him. "Hang on tight to my foot, and I will guide you, but unless you get deep quick enough, you will not see the void to squeeze through. To bring the box out, we must move it in three stages, for it is heavy, even within water; no one can move it alone."

He smiled, dazzled by her calmness, authority, and those piercing eyes.

They plunged underwater on three more occasions until Wethersby called time; he was exhausted. He vaguely saw the small gap contour and got close on occasion but could not kick enough to swim down and get decent leverage. He could sense Maylong's frustration with him.

"It is too difficult for me down there," he puffed. "Can we have another short rest to recharge?"

"You need to practise patience and concentration," she said, resisting his request. "You can do this; you have power in your body; it is in your mind where you need to focus."

Eyes shut, they tried to relax and take a nap, but sleep did not come. Soon Wethersby unconsciously wrapped his legs around Maylong's, and they united as one again.

"See, you can concentrate when you want to, but I fear now you may be lacking some vitality," she giggled.

Maylong jumped back into the pool.

He sat up smiling and watched her dance playfully in the water. Another thud shattered their silence. Wethersby instinctively flinched as a stalactite fell to the ground. The space around them got quickly encased in dust. He felt his heart racing again but now from trepidation. As the air cleared, she got out of the water.

"This time, we must get through to the other side; you must focus and hold on. Our cave is unstable; look at the mess the rock has created and how the needles are dropping," said Maylong, pointing to the corner of the cave where the rock had just fallen. "They are shifting to our movements."

When they dived into the water together, Wethersby kicked hard and steadily. Despite his unease and sense of foreboding, he found the hollow and followed Maylong, still squeezing her big toe. After scratching himself several times along the cramped tunnel, he reached its end and rapidly aimed up towards a dull shimmer.

He broke the surface ahead of her and gasped. Hundreds of tiny lights covered the bare walls and ceiling. There was not enough room to stand upright, even for Maylong, twelve inches shorter than Wethersby. The dense musty scent was almost overpowering.

Wethersby tread water while staring at an oblong casket of milky-green and blackened jade. He was so close that his breath reached its gold key and elaborate gilded lock, making it glisten all the more. He guessed the uneven seamless box was weighty, about three feet long, twenty inches high, and twenty inches deep.

"What is innermost will take your breath away," Maylong said softly and added, "but this place is haunted."

She pointed behind him. He whirled around. Four eye sockets protruding from a pair of skulls stared back at them. Instinctively he pushed backwards, his head hitting the lock, and he scratched the back of his crown.

The heavily cracked, but intact, heads were a dark yellowish-brown. More old bones lay scattered behind, tangled together with fragments of multi-coloured cloth.

"I want to see inside the box," he said eagerly.

"Unlock it and take a look, but be quick before this air turns sour," Maylong replied.

The pungent sweet odour hit him first; the lights turned lemony. A mass of crystals lay crammed within a white sticky mess. His eyes nearly popped out of his head; he held a substantial yellow rock-crystal, overflowing in his warmed and tacky palm. After rummaging the chest, he untangled two other rocks that were more significant than the first. He counted at least two dozen smaller cut gems, thinking the principal stones may have been sapphire or diamond, but he was not sure.

"An enormous green casing, full of sweet and golden forbidden fruits. *A JackFruit Treasure!*" Wethersby pronounced as he stashed the first crystal in his pocket.

"Come on, Mister Wethersby, we must go quickly. We do not want the same fate as these two," whispered Maylong slowly as her voice echoed. "Returning is not so easy. We need to get out of the water, then dive from our knees to gain pace. You go first."

With a resounding splash, he headed back towards the passage. He struggled to pull his way through as the stone scraped along the coarse edge. He felt a searing pain across his thigh and his breeches shredding. The tunnel had snared him. He began to panic, wanting to scream.

Maylong pushed hard against his waving feet, setting him free. He rushed up to the surface and gulped hard for air.

His breeches were in tatters, the stone gone.

--x--

# 1

# Fire

A small earthen censer, shaped into a three-headed elephant, sat smoking lightly on a desk inside the musty study; his father had forgotten to quench it. Rayleigh, curious as ever, pushed the door ajar and snuck inside. He loved the smells of this room, from the old wall hung carpets and especially the coconut oil from his favourite burner. As Rayleigh reached up, his tiny fingers were mere inches from the black censer's base. Frustrated, he went on tiptoe, but still, the vessel was too far to reach. The four-year-old was determined and looked around the room to find something to make him a little taller. He saw a large green book that had fallen from a bookcase, brought it to the desk chair's base and climbed up.

To his delight, he touched the clay elephant's foot. An owl hooted from outside. Startled, he fell on his knees between the desk and the chair edge; the burner fell next to his face, its contents spilt and shattered.

Rayleigh's coal-black hair smouldered; he felt a sharp pain at the top of his forehead. Instinctively, drawing up both hands to his head, needle-like pins enveloped his palms and fingers.

Flames had covered the floor's rug, then grew sideways and higher within a matter of seconds. Rayleigh was stunned, unable to reach the door without going through the inferno in front of him. Instead, he hid behind his favourite wall carpet next to the large window.

Within minutes the fire had intensified; dense black smoke began to drop from the ceiling. Rayleigh crouched lower, his head on the floor, choking as he struggled for each breath.

Upstairs in the farmhouse, Louisa and Robert, Rayleigh's mother and father, were asleep. It was just past midnight. The blaze, in the room below their bedroom, had taken a firm hold now. The burning would have been visible to anyone looking in the direction of the house.

Feeling shards of burning rug now close to his face, Rayleigh moved slowly, crawling along the window's base just as its thick dark glass cracked, followed by two more panes on either side.

Rayleigh regained consciousness outside, some twenty yards from the study walls. Flames were rising from the broken windows. He tried to call for his mother but was unable to make a sound. Oddly, he felt no pain in his left leg as he attempted, unsuccessfully, to crawl further away. It was, though, the tingling and hurting from his hands that stopped his efforts. Overcome by his actions and smoke, he soon fell back into a deep sleep, picturing a three-headed giant charging through a burning chestnut forest.

Some distance away from the blazing cottage, Rayleigh's grandparents, Wethersby Snr and Maylong, were in bed in the estate's main house, whispering to one another.

"Oh, my darling, it is time for you to rest," sighed Maylong. "Sleep now. Let us talk in the morning about how your scar has spoiled and blackened your leg."

She kissed him gently on his forehead, only to hesitate upon seeing an amber glow from the corner of her eye.

Out of bed, she ran to the window and yelled, "*Fire*!"

Wethersby Snr joined Maylong at the window, frozen for a moment. He began to run fast, jumping down the last three stairs, landing hard, with Maylong behind him.

They were close to the searing farmhouse within five minutes. The roof was completely ablaze.

Maylong's screaming did not stop as she caught and passed Wethersby Snr on the way to the house, "Louisa. Rayleigh. Robert!"

Without hesitation, she ran through the open front door as smoke billowed out.

"Maylong. Stop. No. No. No!" he cried and watched helplessly as his wife went into the inferno.

She called his name once; her muffled call seemed to catch in the hot air and fly out of a chimney, he thought.

Then the thatched roof collapsed, and instantly all the upper windows blew out. Wethersby Snr was knocked backwards many yards by the blast of hot air.

"Maylong. Louisa. Rayleigh!" he screamed, getting back to his feet.

He frantically struggled to get closer to the door and inside, but the heat was too extreme. Running to the back of the house, he tripped hard, landing face down, his hands instantly stinging from scraping the dirt path. He turned to spot a small red foot on the ground, glistening in the house's reflection.

"Rayleigh, by the love of Christ, my boy," wept Wethersby Snr.

He put his ear to Rayleigh's mouth. He felt Rayleigh's weak heated breath, but there was no sound. Wethersby Snr looked up to the farmhouse to see flames and whitish smoke at the top of both chimneys. With his face now scorching, he dragged Rayleigh's motionless little body away. He sat by Rayleigh, wailing, knowing he would be useless inside the house. The heat and smoke were too extreme; the roof collapse had sealed the fate of his wife, daughter, and son-in-law; he would never see them alive again.

--x--

Broken glass had cut Rayleigh's left leg deep behind his ankle. He walked with a limp and would appear to drag his weak foot behind him for years after the blaze. A long fringe covered scars on his forehead. Burns to his hands healed well, but waves of pins and needles frequently plagued him.

His uncle, Joseph, refused to take care of Rayleigh. Wethersby Snr was furious with his son's disrespect. So as a young boy, Rayleigh lived and grew up with his widowed grandfather. They buried his mother, father, and grandmother next to the old farmhouse's shell within the *Thatchers* estate in Southwold, Suffolk, England. Wethersby Snr built a small memorial there a few years later.

Wethersby Snr's grief for his wife and only daughter never left him. His guilt for not venturing back into the house beset him constantly. His dreams turned on a sixpence to nightmares of the white smoking chimneys, with Maylong at the top, screaming for his rescue. His consolation was to care for Rayleigh. And all the while Joseph refused to help Rayleigh, Wethersby Snr's rage deepened towards him.

He instinctively knew Joseph's sons gave Rayleigh a rough time. Rayleigh being the youngest of the four boys, his scars and limp easy targets for ridicule, but Wethersby Snr had never witnessed their bullying first-hand.

Rayleigh never uttered a word to anyone for almost two years.

--x--

On 28th February 1685, Rayleigh's sixth birthday, his grandfather gifted him a three-headed elephant mask made from dark hardwood. It was just enough to fit and cover his face and had slits to see through. Some of his staff said it was a strange gift for such a young boy, but Wethersby Snr wanted to shock Rayleigh in a new attempt to induce him to speak. Unlike everyone else, his grandfather heard Rayleigh scream in his sleep; he kept this, and what Rayleigh had said, to himself, "*Chang, burning chang.*"

Since early afternoon, Rayleigh sat in Wethersby Snr's study, his face ashen after receiving his grandfather's gift. Joseph and his three boys were there too.

"Pa, I don't want," muttered Rayleigh, to everyone's astonishment.

He ran towards the door.

"Rayleigh, get back immediately," demanded Wethersby Snr, holding back his tears.

Rayleigh, unable to open the door, slowly walked to the desk and sat back in the red chair.

Wethersby Snr poured a little coconut oil into the elephant censor and lit it.

"*No!*" Rayleigh's scream was piercing.

He jumped off the chair. Reaching out, he almost knocked the vessel off the desk. Wethersby Snr stood calmly and moved the burner back out of Rayleigh's reach.

"Rayleigh, that is enough, be grateful for your grandpa's gift," said Joseph.

"I don't want. Never see again," replied Rayleigh as he buried himself as far back in the chair as he could.

"Rayleigh?" inquired his grandfather. "If there was one thing you could have in my study, all for yourself, what would it be?"

Rayleigh scanned the highly decorated office, turning his head around several times. He darted from mask to mask and started to feel dizzy, then vomited across the floor under the desk.

Holding out his hands, Rayleigh cried, "Nothing more, cut off my fingers, Pa," and he bolted for the exit.

His cousin, Wethersby Jnr, was first to reach Rayleigh and opened the door. Rayleigh ran outside as fast as he could.

--x--

Rayleigh hated his cousin James. For reasons he had not understood, James picked on him relentlessly after the fire. James focused on Rayleigh's restricted movement, his left leg, teasing Rayleigh by challenging him to race, playing catch. He knew full well Rayleigh could not run properly and often lost his balance and fell. And then there was the well.

On a warm summer's day when Rayleigh was seven years old, all the boys played in the main house's walled garden near the well. James had Rayleigh's head locked under his armpit and had dragged him to the shaft's edge. Despite Rayleigh's thrashes and screams, James grabbed and threw Rayleigh's simple leather shoes with his other hand; they heard a splash.

"Scarface, you must go down and fetch them," laughed James. "You know Grandpa will curse you for losing your shoes."

Rayleigh was unable to release himself from James's grip. Charles and Wethersby Jnr watched on, unwilling to help, for they knew the force of James's headlock and his filthy temper when he appeared weaker than them.

James released his hold. Rayleigh climbed up the well's wall and into the pail as James held the rope. At its base, and with little light, he felt under the well's water but could not find anything.

"James. Up. My shoes, gone," shouted Rayleigh.

There was no reply. James had tied the rope to a hook on the pit's edge and disappeared. Rayleigh remained there frightened. After some minutes, his leg and foot cramped, as they often did, and his movements made the bucket slosh around. He almost fell in. He must have passed out from the discomfort.

He next remembered lying on bare earth close to the brim, soaked through, holding one of his shoes. He could not recall being in the water nor finding his shoe. It would be one of many times that he found himself in the well at James's hands. The cramping repeated frequently. He never located that lost shoe, even on occasions when the well was dry.

It would be several years until Wethersby Jnr would intervene and stop James. Their confrontations often ended in a bloodied fight, neither gaining the upper hand nor being willing to give in until someone ended up hurt.

--x--

Towards the end of 1694, Rayleigh had developed stout resilience and self-defence against James. The boys had matching strength now; Rayleigh's increasing physique was evident for all to see.

Rayleigh worked tirelessly that year on an estate manager's land. He spent his days preparing the ground, sowing seeds, weeding, harvesting, baling, and finally milling the grains. His barley crop had the best yield across the estate that year.

Blake and his young wife were very grateful for Rayleigh's support. They gave him a neglected area to tend. He relished the hard work, rising at dawn and sleeping, exhausted, early at night, except for the monthly evening study talks alone with his grandfather.

He still had a limp. His hands were painful, but as he toiled, his imagination took over, and he mostly forgot his discomfort. He yearned to get away from Southwold and explore the foreign lands his grandfather would regale, regardless of how fanciful Rayleigh thought those tales were. He longed to visit the home of the three-headed elephant, though that made him shiver with horrific memories.

Toil, on what he called *his* acres, was most demanding after the winter. Rayleigh carted hundreds of cow manure sacks from the main barn to his field throughout spring, scattering it. Still, as he grew accustomed to the early starts and physical labour, he began to enjoy the time alone and delighted in seeing his plot flourish. The barley grew strongest, tallest, and first to a harvest of all of the Blakes' fields.

The Thacker boys, Charles and James, on the other hand, did little work or learning. Their father tried hard to school them; only Wethersby Jnr could read and write. In comparison, his brothers grew lazy, physically and mentally.

Watching his grandson carrying bales on his shoulders, Wethersby Snr straddled the old gate to the field.

He shouted, "Rayleigh, young man, it is almost six o'clock. The sun's going, and it is time for your supper."

"Pa, I will come when the last of these are safely in the barn," Rayleigh replied.

Wethersby Snr knew Rayleigh would keep going until he would barely see his hands. He had not seen Rayleigh give up during a day in the field, even during and after heavy rains. He saw a growing spirit within Rayleigh for hard graft and pride in his actions.

Rayleigh eventually came back to the house at around eight o'clock.

Wethersby Snr called out, "Rayleigh. It is time for some more adventure; let me show you."

It had been more than a month since Rayleigh had been in his grandfather's study for an evening. He had tried to enter by himself on several occasions, but his grandfather always locked the door.

As was customary, coconut fumes from the elephant burner hit Rayleigh as he entered. Wethersby Snr talked about travelling in Siam for the next hour, particularly to the great city of Ayutthaya many miles north from the Gulf of Siam's waters. Rayleigh was trying to listen to old Wethersby's story, but his mind was wandering; he had heard the stories of Ayutthaya several times before.

Wethersby Snr saw a dreamy frozen look on Rayleigh's face and abruptly stopped mid-sentence; silence filled the room.

"Young man, you have done well today. How many bales did you pin and carry?" Wethersby Snr queried.

"Sorry, Pa. What?" asked Rayleigh, then he continued, "I lost count in the dark, maybe thirty."

"Well, my man, what have you learnt this fine summer?" renewed Wethersby Snr.

Rayleigh took some time replying, "I can now defend myself against James and beat him if I want."

"What else?" countered Wethersby Snr.

"Well, barley is difficult to grow. Before sowing, I must thoroughly clear the land. Otherwise, the weeds will grow faster and higher than the barley," continued Rayleigh. "Weeding is so time-consuming and hurts my hands. I will take more time next year to tidy the field before sowing."

"And?" ventured Wethersby Snr, encouraging Rayleigh to reflect more.

"In autumn, after harvesting, it does seem like a lot of effort for such a small amount of barley. Though, my morning porridge, disgusting as it is, does taste a little better for it," smiled Rayleigh.

"Yes, Rayleigh, you have worked hard. What else did your field produce?" probed Wethersby Snr further.

"Pa, a hundred hay bales for the cows and horses for feed during the cold winter months," said Rayleigh and laughed, "and they added to my bulk. I also have a stronger bond with the Blakes now; she makes breakfast after my first hour. I have not told her I dislike porridge; I do not want her to take offence."

"And where was I talking about earlier?" asked Wethersby Snr.

"Ayutthaya, the city of temples, again, Pa," replied Rayleigh proudly.

--x--

Joseph's sons always argued and fought over many petty things. Most of their battles were over girls and women. Charles had married Rose that year. Rose was Wethersby Jnr's sweetheart; they schooled together, and he thought they had loved one another. Upon finding Charles in a naked embrace with Rose in a stream one summer's sundown, Wethersby Jnr quietly retreated, vowing eternal revenge over Charles. He never once mentioned to Rose what he had witnessed that evening. In contrast, James enjoyed the company of many a farmer's daughter from the estate without commitment, much to Wethersby Jnr's disgust and not a little jealousy.

--x--

# 2

# Death

Wethersby Thacker Snr died on 25th November 1696, leaving tantalising notes and references in his will to potential locations for the hoard he named the *JackFruit Treasure*.

The lads knew he initially found the treasure on the island dominated by the Kingdom of Kandy. However, the Portuguese were in control of the southern area where, and when, he made his discovery. He, and his grandsons, always referred to the island as *Kandy* and its people as *Kandyan*. Their grandfather had led them to believe he moved it from its original underground location. Their challenge: could it still be in Kandy or further east in Siam, or did he hide it on his return home west, in the Kingdom of Kaski or India? All four countries he mentioned in his will. The vast distances daunted them. His descriptive, yet vague, map references to possible sites fascinated them to the point of obsession, especially Rayleigh and Wethersby Jnr.

Rayleigh had his ideas too, which he kept close. He thought he knew their grandfather better than his cousins. Rayleigh spent many a long evening sitting and listening to Wethersby

Snr rattle-on about his beloved Maylong, her pool enigma with its strange lights, and his numerous adventures and near-death experiences. Ever since Rayleigh was a young boy, he had spent monthly evenings alone with Wethersby Snr. The tales were vivid and descriptive, but there were so many. Rayleigh thought he often mixed up his stories and localities just to entertain Rayleigh and maintain his interest. Or maybe his memory had become weak as he grew noticeably old, jaundiced, and frail; Rayleigh was never too sure. During their talks, he believed his grandfather had provided many clues about the casket's whereabouts.

Wethersby Snr spoke about Siam more than any other place - even more than Kandy. There was more enthusiasm for Siam when only Rayleigh was present. He used a romantic tongue that Rayleigh thought was a ruse to hide clues. Wethersby Snr was sharp, stern, and instantly to the point on the outside. In the family house, their discussions always took place in Wethersby Snr's private study and rarely with his cousins present too. As Rayleigh grew as a teenager, their evening chats became tortuous to Rayleigh, often repetitive. He tried hard to control his manner and facial expression, for he knew from experience that old Wethersby was a master of reading people.

An extensive array of exotic wares and animal heads decorated the study walls. Rayleigh was fascinated by the numerous wooden masks of strange contortions of men's faces, women, monkeys, and elephants. A giant male lion's head hung over the mantlepiece. Wethersby Snr always had a small burner lit with precious coconut oil whenever he recounted his stories to Rayleigh. The heady scent percolated his clothes, or did it just stick in his nostrils? He had grown to hate that lingering whiff.

--x--

Wethersby Snr lay on his study floor, struggling to breathe out, his body convulsing as he gained his next lungful. The flashbacks had continued, on and off, for more than sixty years; the lights, the three mega gems, the brilliant smaller stones, and the fight with Maylong after he pocketed several, including a prominent crystal. She had forgiven him for his discretion but never let him forget the impetuousness that nearly cost him his life and hers.

He rubbed his upper thigh as he had done every day. The blackness started to grow a year after their first encounter. A dark purple scar, which never healed entirely, gradually spread to cover his groin. It deepened in colour and advanced down his leg later in life. He looked at his four remaining nasty toes, his big toe now an insignificant stump.

He saw darkness in his sleep, punctured by vivid flashbacks so clear he would startle from whatever mode of sleep he could get. He thought his days were numbered ever since that day in the cave. Maylong had trusted him; he broke her faith. He should never have attempted to remove the jewels, especially the biggest that caught in his pocket and scratched his limb, for that was when his misfortunes began. He was dumbfounded to have lived sixty more years. His was a dark life, full of personal tragedy, discomfort and pain, which increased as he aged.

Rayleigh knocked hard on the study door, a first strike followed by three more taps in quick succession, his standard identifier. Wethersby Snr, unable to answer and powerless to move, clenched his body and summoned his next gulp of air. Rayleigh opened the door to see his grandfather's rotten foot lying contorted in front of him.

"Pa! What have you done to your foot? Where is your toe?" cried Rayleigh.

"My boys. Call my boys," mustered Wethersby Snr.

"But Pa, your *toe*!" whimpered Rayleigh.

Wethersby Snr said no more. Rayleigh rushed out to find his cousins. Further through the balcony, he found Wethersby Jnr in his room with Charles.

"Junior, Charles, it is Grandpa. He is calling urgently for us all now. But his foot, oh my Lord, his foot," sniffled Rayleigh.

Charles hurried out to find James. Wethersby Jnr ran to the study with Rayleigh trailing behind. Wethersby Snr was in the same position, his face yellowish and opaque, his eyes watery and huge.

"Boys, James?" panted Wethersby Snr.

Rayleigh had witnessed his grandfather often gasping for breath, but he had never seen his black leg and four-toed foot. Rayleigh placed his hand under Wethersby Snr's head.

"Junior. Water, now," demanded Rayleigh.

Wethersby Jnr scrambled out and left them.

Rayleigh was lost for words by his grandpa's appearance. He was stunned when a frail hand grabbed his arm with such a force that Rayleigh lost balance and fell into his grandfather's chest.

"Rayleigh, you can find it for me again," paused Wethersby Snr. "Hold your pride. Stay close at hand with Junior."

"But why Junior, Pa?" asked Rayleigh. "I do not understand. I do not want to share anything with my cousins."

"The journey is long. Trust me. Junior can command men. You will struggle without him," replied Wethersby Snr, slowly. "Share your riches. There is an abundance; too much."

Wethersby Snr uttered a low gurgling pitch; Rayleigh was unsure whether he was laughing or choking.

The door opened, crashing against the wall with such a force that a small mask fell and cracked on the floor. James and Charles shoved each other, and Wethersby Jnr stumbled, almost losing the cup.

"Grandpa, we are here. What is wrong with you this time?" asked James.

Wethersby Snr said nothing; his eyes firmly fixed on Rayleigh. Rayleigh's arm was still gripped tight by his hand; the pain became unbearable.

"My green book, Rayleigh. Bring it to me, you know the one," murmured Wethersby Snr.

He almost choked on his sip of water and then said, "Boys, you must all listen most carefully."

Wethersby Snr released his arm. Rayleigh got to his feet and found the sizeable green and mottled leather book from the desk and brought it to him.

"Boys. Go out and find the JackFruit. It has riches beyond your imagination," said Wethersby Snr with outstanding clarity and volume, which surprised the boys.

"But Grandpa, now is not the time to be worrying about your lost gems," said James. "Get some rest."

Rayleigh gently shook his head in aggravation. 'James is always so dismissive of Grandfather's stories of the hoard', Rayleigh thought.

"My JackFruit, it is a handsome treasure but cursed. Never be it grasped by any one man or one woman for a long haunting death will surely follow," whispered Wethersby Snr lucidly. "Do not let me down."

His rotten foot flinched. He struck James hard with his stump. James squealed as he rubbed his knee. Wethersby Snr's body shook once more while he clasped his fabled atlas. His eyes then rolled back, and he said no more.

All the boys were silent and avoided eye contact. Rayleigh blinked frequently and wiped his own eyes. For thirty minutes, Rayleigh held one of his grandfather's skeletal hands until it began to cool. He prised the green book from Wethersby's other hand.

--x--

# 3

# The Will

Rayleigh was now seventeen, James nineteen, Charles twenty and Wethersby Jnr twenty-two. They were about to find out whether their grandfather had been kind to leave them something in his will. The estate, though, had come on hard times during the last two years; earnings were down, maintenance on properties had increased, along with growing farming families.

One month after the funeral, at noon on 25th December 1696, as instructed, Joseph gathered his sons and Rayleigh in his late father's study.

Joseph's face had a curious distant expression; Rayleigh thought he was trying to cover a smile. Joseph kept quiet as he closed the door and unhooked a small black monkey mask off the wall. He untied a modest yellow key at its back, went to the main desk, opened the lowest drawer, and took out a metal box that he unlocked.

Breaking the heavy wax seal on a leather wallet, he took four pages of green-inked script and began to read aloud.

"Written on this date 25th December sixteen hundred and ninety-five, county of Suffolk, England," began Joseph.

"I name my son, Joseph Thomas Thacker, as my executor. My beneficiaries and trustees are so appointed. I hereby leave the following without condition."

He paused.

"Nine hundred and ninety-nine English gold sovereigns, minted in 1600, to my grandson, Wethersby Joseph Thacker.

Nine hundred and ninety-nine English gold sovereigns, minted in 1601, to my grandson, Charles William Thacker.

Nine hundred and ninety-nine English gold sovereigns, minted in 1602, to my grandson, James Richard Thacker."

Joseph hesitated again.

Rayleigh reasoned that Joseph's pause was to allow his sons to digest their fortunes.

Joseph continued, "I hereby leave in Trust nine hundred and ninety-nine English gold sovereigns, minted in 1603, to my grandson Rayleigh Sidney Edwards. My son Joseph Thomas Thacker shall administer the said Trust. It shall be left untouched until the day of Rayleigh Sidney Edwards' twenty-second birthday, 28th February in the year one thousand seven hundred and one. On this day, the Trust shall be released to Rayleigh Sidney Edwards in full, including all accrued interest, unconditionally."

Rayleigh was confused. Why had Grandpa allowed his cousins their vast sums now, but he had to wait over four years more?

Joseph went on, "I hereby bequeath my entire estate of *Thatchers,* including all land, buildings, covenants, debtors and creditors, to my son Joseph Charles Thacker. Save for the whole undisturbed contents of my office, which I bequeath to my grandson, Rayleigh Sidney Edwards. After this will has been read, no one except Rayleigh Sidney Edwards shall enter my study. All keys to my office, my bureau and my safe-box are to be handed to Rayleigh Sidney Edwards immediately."

Grudgingly he handed over the set of keys. Rayleigh was sure his uncle Joseph was now smiling through gritted teeth. Rayleigh reflected; only he would sift through his beloved grandfather's personal effects concentrated in this room, crammed with so many artefacts from his travels and adventures. Rayleigh thought it would take him weeks, if not months, alone. He was unsure whether to laugh or cry.

Joseph carried on, "Additionally, the following proof coins are to be bequeathed immediately to my grandsons:

Wethersby Joseph Thacker, one 1631 Gold Twenty-Shilling [marked XX].

Charles William Thacker, one 1631 Gold Double-Crown [marked X].

James Richard Thacker, one 1631 Gold Crown [marked V].

Rayleigh Sidney Edwards, one 1631 Gold Angel.

To my son, Joseph Thomas Thacker, one 1631 Silver Half-Groat."

He handed the lads each an envelope from the box, named in green ink. James immediately broke the wax seal and looked inside. His crown was in pristine condition, together with two wax seals imprinted with the coin's front and back.

Joseph continued, "I leave in Trust my one remaining JackFruit diamond within the Tower Mint in London."

"What *other* diamond?" exclaimed Charles.

"Rayleigh, what did Grandpa tell you of this?" shouted James.

"I, I have no idea. Pa only ever spoke about the one he brought back from Kandy and sold to buy *Thatchers*," stuttered Rayleigh.

"Boys, that is enough of that. There is more," said Joseph, cutting them off. "The only key to the diamond's vault is held by the warden of the Mint in London. The diamond Trust shall be released *only* to my grandson's firstborn child when he or she reaches their twenty-second birthday and without other conditions. The warden of the Mint has these same explicit instructions. Should my son Joseph die before me, my oldest living grandson shall inherit the entire *Thatchers* estate and manage the said Trusts. Should any of my grandsons die before me, their monetary share above shall be divided equally between my remaining grandsons. Rayleigh's share must remain in Trust until he, or my remaining grandsons, reach the year and day of Rayleigh's twenty-second birthday."

After the short pause, Joseph carried on, "The English gold sovereigns, mentioned herewith, will only be released to each grandson in person by the warden of the Mint in London. You must strictly guard my legacy, the *JackFruit Treasure*. A vast cache remains. I will not explain why I left it behind on my discovery journey in the year sixteen hundred and thirty-one. My remaining grandsons ought to wisely invest their monies in an endeavour to retrieve the casket. I left several clues of its resting place within the trail. After I met my wife, Maylong, and discovered the treasure in the Kandyan grotto for the first time, we advanced to Siam. Later, we retreated to Kandy, travelling by sea up the east Indian coast, along the Himalayan foothills and then across Northern India. Afterwards, we would return to England on the long sea voyage around the southern tip of Africa. The casket and its contents come with a hefty price to bear. Proceed cautiously."

He looked at the final page, which he had not yet read out loud, and said to Wethersby Jnr, passing him the sheet, "Here, make the most of this last page."

Everyone in the room was stunned and silent for minutes. A wall clock chimed twice; it was half-past noon. The four young men's new journeys would begin early the following year.

--x--

# 4

# Ye Olde Cheshire Cheese

All four lads had a competitive nature. As usual, James and Charles insisted on venturing out on their own, snubbing their oldest brother's offer of joint passage. The younger brothers intended to sink most of their inheritance into separate ships and cargo. They aimed to start their quest in Kandy, convinced old Wethersby Snr cynically wanted to send the boys on a fruitless chase, when all along, he left the casket close to where he found it.

Charles and James planned the trip to London and the Tower Mint, only informing their father the day before leaving *Thatchers*. They spent the first four weeks of the new year scheming their journey, not only to London but beyond England's shores. Their planning evenings in the *Harbour Inn* often ended in a drunken haze late into the night. They had little information for guidance, but they were desperate to leave before their brother and cousin.

They arranged for a stage to leave at eight in the morning of 1st February 1697. Carrying only a handful of possessions, they brought every penny of their saved funds and a modest gift from their father. They also took Wethersby Snr's two coins and a handful of documents.

The stage arrived at *Thatchers* early.

The driver was an odd-looking, slight fellow. An initial "Hello" was his only word, spoken at the start of their next six arduous hours. The brothers were impatient and nagged the driver to move along swiftly despite his persistent silence. They frequently stopped for the horses to be watered, fed, and rested.

The trip to London took four days, stopping at inns along the way for warm beer, mediocre food, and a rough bed.

Charles was restless. He had told Rose the trip was only to London to collect his gold coins, for he knew she would put up a huge fight, with fists, if he had revealed the truth. For a single reason, Charles married Rose not out of love but, to outdo his older brother, knowing Wethersby Jnr had been captivated by Rose since childhood. After the marriage, Charles and Rose argued over the slightest detail. They were sleeping in separate beds of late, but he could not recall if she were the first to start that argument; he had lost interest in Rose as soon as they wed, his prize secured. Charles shifted his discomfort to his task of procuring a ship and a trusted commander to take them to Kandy. He asked himself silently, onboard the bumping carriage, "Can I do this without James and his coins?"

James sat facing Charles with a big grin for most of the route. For the previous two weeks, before they set off, he spent every afternoon with Jane Bunting, a young woman who recently moved in with the Blakes as their housemaid. They spent their time together alone in the Blakes' large barn.

James laughed. "Charles, I need to thank our cousin for making such a fine barn full of hay for Jane and me. She could not get enough, the little strumpet."

"Ah, *little* brother, that time may never come to say thanks to Rayleigh and to be reacquainted with your new lady friend," replied Charles. "You have no worries. I told Rose our trip was only to London and back. I forgot to mention *leaving* England."

On that fourth day, James had been silent for some hours after Charles's revelation.

As he spied dense smoke at his window, Charles called up to the driver, "Spike, what of the blaze ahead?"

Spike reported, "That is no fire. We are getting closer to London. The fog you see is the filth of the city. Good luck."

Several hours later, they stopped and descended in a mist. It was late afternoon, grey, and overcast next to the vast river.

"Gentlemen, I have guided you to this great city and close to Blackfriars as you requested. Lodgings and taverns are ample in these parts," said Spike.

The brothers went across to the nearest inn, *Ye Olde Cheshire Cheese*, and made their arrangements for a two-week stay. They returned to the stage where Spike demanded his final payment.

Two days later, hungover, Charles and James walked to the Tower Mint, their papers in hand. After an hour, they were informed that the warden would be available to see them the next day. Disappointed, they soon found a tavern named the ***Hung, Drawn and Quartered*, and** drank a beer. They walked back towards *Ye Olde Cheshire Cheese*, stopping at other public houses along their way for more. When they finally staggered into their lodgings, they slept until sun-up.

They returned to the Tower Mint with the effects of the previous day's drinking bouncing around their heads.

Warden of the Mint, Newton, met them. He scanned their copy of Wethersby Snr's will and compared it to his text while flicking his long hair away from his eyes. The warden also examined their grandfather's death paper and their birth papers.

The warden then escorted the brothers deep below ground to a vault. They waited while he opened the treasury unseen and returned soon after with ten hefty bags on a trolley.

"Charles, these are for you. Put your mark here," said Newton.

"My, these are heavy, Mister Newton. I had not counted on that," said Charles, picking one up with no sign of thanks and ignoring his request for his mark.

He reopened the vault, returning after several minutes with another ten bags of coins.

"James, these are for you. Place your mark here," bellowed Newton, surprising James with his volume and tone.

The warden dropped a bag on the cold floor, narrowly missing James's foot.

James started to count. Newton took several steps back, his face now covered in shadow, his expression one of disbelief from the youngster's mistrust.

Newton had been Warden of the Mint for less than two years. He was brought to the position by his friend Earl Montagu. He took the task seriously, seizing on the growing problem of coinage counterfeiting. He learnt of the Thackers within his first month in office from papers handed to him. He and Wethersby Snr had never met. Newton knew the last safe box within the Thackers' vault contained a gem of immense value, for Wethersby Snr had paid a high price for the Mint's protection.

"What of your brother, Wethersby Jnr, and your cousin Rayleigh Edwards?" inquired Newton.

James brought his head up, annoyed by the warden's interruption and said, "Mister Newton, if you please, I have now lost count."

"Wethersby Jnr and Rayleigh are not with us on this trail. They will come along later. That is up to them," said Charles.

It took James fifteen minutes to complete counting in silence; the warden watched over him and the untidy piles of coins. When James had finished, he put the monies back in the bags and tried to carry them all up the stairs. The warden attempted to stop him.

"Now, laddie. I suggest kindly you think about what you are doing," said Newton. "That is a heavy load and rather difficult to conceal, do you not think? Where are you going to store all that gold safely outside the Mint?"

"That is my business now," said James, annoyed at not thinking the same thing, as he strained up the many stone steps.

Charles signed for just seventeen coins. The warden returned the rest to the vault as Charles followed his brother's footsteps.

Newton had followed Wethersby Snr's instructions to the letter. He was disappointed but not surprised by the young men's reactions. He thought greed could often control men's heads from immense newly gained wealth, seemingly gifted without effort.

The brothers returned to *Ye Olde Cheshire Cheese*. James quickly went up the stairs without saying anything to the landlord standing behind the bar. Charles followed with the other five bags. They stored the coins in James's room. Sitting together, they looked at each other for a moment and roared with laughter.

James said, "What am I going to do with all of this now, and how on earth can I keep it safe here?"

"Well, brother, the warden did try to warn you," said Charles, laughing. "Let us think about this further, but we need some more beers first."

They went back to the bar. Two hours later, they staggered to their rooms and slept until late afternoon. Then they returned and consumed more. The inn was busy that evening; the brothers did not stop drinking. A small crowd of men had formed around them, all curious yet suspicious of tales of a long voyage to Kandy. One man, John Rouse, announced that he knew a ship's captain, and they should meet George Everett in two days on the *Frostenden Nave*.

"That is early; why at seven?" inquired James.

"That would be Everett, a stickler for detail," replied Rouse. "Let us meet here, the day after tomorrow, at thirty minutes before seven, and I will take you to Everett."

James zigzagged his way to the stairs and his room. Charles remained at the bar with Rouse and the other boozy fellows.

"Mister Rouse, that be fine. Let me get another flagon for your service," garbled Charles.

Charles finally left the bar an hour after midnight and collapsed on the floor of his room.

# 5

# MASTER

James and Charles spent the next day sober, blind drunk, and straight again. They were well on their way to a second beer-fuelled session inside another tavern, less than a mile from their lodgings. It was dark outside, but only five o'clock.

"Brother, why do you mock me for taking my coins from the Mint?" probed James. "We need them to buy our boat and passage, do we not?"

"James, at times, I despair of you. *Ye Olde Cheshire Cheese*, safe as the Mint?" sneered Charles. "We do not need all the coins yet, not until we have secured our deal on a ship. Only a handful of your coins would have been sufficient to show our seriousness and worth."

Neither brother was aware of their tone or volume. A ragged, coal-dusted twelve-year-old boy sat smiling on the floor beneath another long bench, thanking his luck for overhearing the two fellows.

"Coins!" he murmured. "Master will be pleased to see some of those. I wonder how many they have. Ten, twenty or even more?"

The boy almost laughed out loud at his thoughts. He got up slowly, head down, trying not to be seen under the bench as he made his way to the open door and outside. The boy ran down an alley and into another smaller passageway before finding the concealed half-door flap and tumbled inside.

He shouted, "Master. Master. I have news of riches. Two men have coins from the Mint - to buy a ship's passage. Come quickly, I will show them to you, but I want at least one coin as a reward."

"Dick, you are always full of claptrap. Coins indeed," shouted Henry Higgins. "What colour be they?"

"Gold, of course," lied the grubby boy. "Come, Master, and have your favourite beer in the inn where the men sit. I will lead you to them but let us go quick before their coins disappear."

Higgins got up slowly, feigning interest, grabbed his heavy, full-length black cloak, and marched out of the room and into the gully. The boy walked quickly back to the raucous inn, and they sat down at a bench adjacent to the two brothers.

Neither James nor Charles had noticed the boy leaving earlier. With a slight nod of his head, Charles gestured towards the man in the long coat, who had sat facing him. James had his back to Higgins, consumed at minding the dregs at the bottom of his tankard.

Higgins ushered a server and ordered a flagon of beer; the boy got nothing.

James hollered, "Here, fill us up again."

The buxom server filled a tankard for Higgins, ignoring James's order, then headed back to the bar with her empty white pitcher.

James screeched, "Are you deaf as well as stupid, wench?"

The bar suddenly hushed; no one said a word nor moved an inch.

Higgins moved around the bench and sat next to James.

"Here, have a drop of this, ignorant peasant," quipped Higgins.

He emptied the tankard's contents into James's lap.

Shocked and slow to react, James instinctively swung his right arm towards Higgins, his elbow missing by several inches. Higgins hammered his fist into James's upper thigh. James huffed out a low groan, surprised by the power of the man in the dark coat. He hit out with his clenched hands towards the man's face, each one missing within a whisker. Charles had circled the bench. He threw a left hook at Higgins's chin, narrowly connecting the base. In a second, the young boy had drawn his pocketknife. He slashed at Charles's lower leg and ankle. Charles yelped from the acute stinging sensation and lost his balance. As Charles fell slightly forward, that was enough for Higgins to press his advantage as he drove a left, then right, fist into his eye sockets. Charles continued to fall forward, his forehead smashing on the edge of the bench; he was out cold.

James hobbled several steps away from the seat, kicked the boy in the stomach and threw a volley of punches at Higgins, but only one connected. Higgins pivoted and threw his coat at James, which covered him enough to be disorientated for several seconds. By that time, the boy had set upon James's legs with his blade and repeatedly cut, which helped sober him up, but his reactions remained clouded by the fog of the day's beer.

"Show me your coins," demanded Higgins, surprising James.

"I have no idea what you refer to, sir. You insult me by covering me with your beer, then hitting out for no reason," declared James.

"You, sir, forget your manners. You are not from around these parts, are you?" asked Higgins. "That seems obvious from your arrogance. Apologise to the lady, for she had no more beer in the jug and was returning to get yours next."

Higgins shifted his position, squaring up to James, their noses almost touching. The boy had hidden.

"Let the two of us go to *Ye Olde Cheshire Cheese* and see what you have for me," spat Higgins.

James recoiled, taking a step back and faking a smile.

"Sir, I know not where this cheese is and what you expect to find there," replied James.

Charles groaned, brought his head up slightly, shook it a little too rigorously, and then rubbed his forehead.

"James, run!" shouted Charles.

Neither of them had gotten three steps before burning pains in their legs made them realise that they were in some trouble. In any case, James's potbelly meant they would not set a record pace.

However, James swivelled around suddenly, planting his curled-up hand onto Higgins's nose just as the man's head moved towards him. The combined speed and power of the punch were enough for Higgins to instantly black out; he stood, not moving for several seconds, until he fell sideways, squashing the boy beneath him.

# 6

# Frostenden Nave

James grabbed Charles's arm and moved quickly outside. They stopped scurrying once they reached the *Ye Olde Cheshire Cheese*. James immediately went to his room while Charles stayed behind at the bar.

James returned in a couple of minutes with a bag of his coins, and both men strolled to the Broken Wharf to locate Everett's ship, the *Frostenden Nave*. It was dark, almost seven o'clock in the evening, when they found the modest single mast ship, made from substantial twisted and battered oak timbers. The brothers could make out a handful of men on deck.

They roughly pushed past a sentry and walked up the gangplank, thankful to be upon the ship's deck in relative security.

"Which one is Everett?" asked James impatiently as he spied Rouse lying half asleep on the deck.

"Captain Everett, we seek your attention!" shouted Charles urgently, surprising Rouse, who jerked up from his slumber.

The brothers' appearance was startling; both had swollen faces that shone from the firelights. Rouse thought James looked worse off, with his left eye heavily swollen and almost closed. Strange, he thought, as both men had blood-stained breeches and were limping.

"Gents, what do you want? You are twelve hours early!" bellowed Everett.

Charles was first to answer. "Sir, we are in the business to procure a ship, crew, and commander. This fine fellow, John Rouse, told us you were in that business, so to speak."

"Well, I would be careful who you describe as a gentleman. Rouse is a good-for-nothing who loves nothing better than being drunk. He does, though, recommend well. You would betta' come to my cabin," said Everett with a slight grin.

Charles and James followed Everett while Rouse stayed on deck. The captain's cabin was dark inside and smelt high of rum. Charles's partly closed eye caught several massive maps scattered on the floor.

"Captain Everett, so tell us, where was your last voyage and for what purpose?" inquired Charles.

"Well, sirs, you should introduce yourself to me first. What do you want, where are you going, and where have you been fighting?" retorted Everett.

"I am Charles Thacker, and this is my younger brother James. We have come down from our estate outside Southwold, Suffolk," Charles said carefully. "As I said, we want to procure a ship and crew and travel to Kandy. We got caught in a scrap with a cloaked man and his boy."

"Boy, you say. Looks like he got the better of both of you," laughed Everett. "To Kandy. That is a huge journey. It will take many months and is full of danger at every storm and stop along the way. Why?"

"That is our business," cut in James. "When do we set off?"

"Ha-ha," laughed Everett. "I think your little brother is getting ahead of himself."

Charles stared at James for several moments, willing him to say no more.

"My brother is a little hasty, Captain. Our grandfather visited the island some years ago. He brought back great riches," Charles pronounced. "We will do the same and more besides."

Everett said, "Charles, the ship and crew, under my command, will cost you a fortune. You do not have it. Stop wasting my time."

"Well, there you are wrong, Everett," reacted Charles. "What is your price for the return voyage?"

"I do not have the time. Prove you have funds," counted the impatient Everett.

Charles reached inside his coat pocket and pulled out a small pouch, tipping its contents on the desk.

"Here, this is a sample. We have more, many more. Now, stop wasting *our* time and tell us your price," said Charles.

Everett, controlling a grin, picked up one of the gold coins, bit on it and said, "You don't have enough. Five hundred of these to Kandy now and another six hundred to return, plus fifty-one from one hundred of all trade profits."

"No chance - that's a mugging!" interrupted James.

"Well, lad, please yourself. Find another who is willing to trust you and their ship and crew for such a modest amount. You won't find another in these parts," said Everett, now smiling.

He turned around and sat in his chair, taking hold of one of his maps and pointing at an island off India's southeastern coast.

"Here is your island; this is as close as you will get. I have changed my mind. I am no longer interested. Go. Take your handful of gold," said Everett dismissively.

"Suit yourself," replied Charles and walked to the door.

"But brother," said James and added, "can we just get on with it and make a deal?"

Charles looked directly at James with a scornful look, willing his over-eager brother to shut his bloodied mouth for once.

"Take it or leave it," said Everett, annoyed by the brothers' differences.

"Charles, let us get on. We cannot afford for Junior and Scarface to beat us to it," whispered James to Charles, out of earshot of the captain.

Charles flung back, "James, you are stupid. This money is all we have got. We don't know Everett, his crew or whether this boneshaker of a ship will last the passage to Kandy, let alone the return to England."

"But Charles, how are we to find another boat? Look around us. There are no others of this size; the big warships do not suit us and are outside our funds. These other matchsticks look like fishing boats, nothing more, and will be unable to withstand the long journey and angry seas," said James.

"Brother, do what you want with your coins. I can see they are burning holes in your pockets," remarked Charles. "I intend to guard mine rather more carefully."

James's face went deep red as he said, "Charles, going alone? Ha-ha. That is up to you. I will procure this ship and have Everett run me to Kandy."

Charles laughed, "Well, brother, you had better negotiate hard because you do not have enough, as Everett has already pointed out."

Everett slowly drew closer to the brothers, unbeknown to them, as they were engrossed in their argument.

Everett surprised them by saying, "Well, that was my first offer. If you do not hurry, my price goes up, and I may decide not to take you."

"Have a care, sir. You are almost as impatient as my younger brother. We need to decide on a single or joint passage. Please leave us for some minutes," said Charles.

He pushed James ahead as they limped out onto the plank and off the ship.

On the pier, Charles stood immediately in James's personal space, face-to-face. So close that he could smell the stale breath and blood-filled nose.

"James, you need to reign in your sour mouth. We need to negotiate with this man. What if we can get Everett, his crew and the ship for half the coins he demanded? What would you think of that?" quizzed Charles.

"Well," said James, "that would be just fine. Shall we split it fifty-fifty?"

"Again, brother, you get ahead of yourself. I am willing to concede a half share with you, but you must allow me, and only me, to cut this deal with Everett," said Charles. "Do you agree that we split our rewards from trade and all other finds, down the middle, a half each?"

James spat in his hand and responded, "Yes, brother. Shall we spit on it more?"

Charles wiped his hand on his breeches, spat into it, and slapped James's outstretched palm.

"Our deal done. Now let me conclude with Everett," said Charles.

They marched back into the captain's cabin.

Everett had not moved from his chair and greeted the brothers, "So 'boys', what's it to be?"

"Well, for a start, you are never to call us 'boys' again. Understood?" scowled James.

"Yes, James is correct there. Never," said Charles. "Your ship and you pay your crew, and yourself, from five hundred English gold sovereigns for the trip to Kandy and return to England."

"Should we wish to go further east, as far as Borneo, we will pay you an additional one hundred coins upon our safe return to England. Your share of all trade will be no more than one third. Take it or leave it," paused Charles and turned to stare directly at James.

Everett laughed, "Well, Charles, that may only get you to India and back."

Charles and James bit their broken lips.

"Six hundred coins. That includes going as far as Borneo if you wish, but no further, and forty out of one hundred for all trading and return to England. We also split funds equally for procuring all trading cargo here," snorted Everett.

He controlled his glee at such an exceptional price for his old ship and motley crew, most of which were still in their drunken haze.

"No," said Charles. "We agree to six hundred coins, but a one-third share for all trading is our limit. In that way, all three of us will be equal and joint trading partners. James and I will take ownership of this ship upon our handshake after the papers are transferred, before our departure. Agreed?"

Everett huffed aloud, "Deal!"

James went to shake Everett's hand, only to recoil when he saw his calluses.

Everett went up to Charles and said, "You should do all our trade bargaining, young fellow. We will all do fine by that."

Everett took Charles's hand tightly, then went to James and squeezed so hard that James's face went scarlet.

"Thank you, Captain," uttered James, as he moved back a step and released his weary hand.

"Everett, meet us in the *Ye Olde Cheshire Cheese* at six this evening to finalise our arrangements over some flagons," pronounced Charles. "In the morning, you will start on the ship's transfer papers. Once they are all in order, you shall collect your coins."

"Agreed," declared Everett and ushered them out of his cabin.

Charles had desperately wanted to wait and check out other options, but no similar ships were available. He had hoped there might be more, farther downstream, but was unsure. He was nervous that his older brother would be close behind; once Wethersby Jnr had worked out that Charles and James were not returning to *Thatchers* anytime soon. They had heard the best options would be close to Blackfriars. So, on reflection and all things considered, he was thankful for his deal.

At the *Ye Olde Cheshire Cheese*, Everett arrived at precisely six o'clock. Neither brother was in sight. Everett found the landlord and asked for them. Sometime later, they came down the stairs.

"Charles, the papers will take several days, five at most," said a frustrated Everett. "Now then, your timekeeping leaves a lot to be desired. I will not tolerate tardiness on my ship, even from its new owners. Having owners on a ship is unusual. We do not need confusion amongst my crew as to who is in charge. When we have readied the ship, we will address my crew to clarify from whom they take orders. By the way, that will be my officers and me, only. If either of you has a problem, you must come to me first. You must not direct orders, large or small, to any crew of my command. Is that understood?"

"Charles, I have no problem with that. How about you?" asked James.

"Fine, Everett. Just get the papers done so we can arrange your coins and be on our way," confirmed Charles.

James spied Spike in a dark corner while catching a server's arm and said, "Four flagons of your finest beer, kind wench, and when we have finished, get four more."

Everett and Spike introduced themselves, and the four men drank as the bar got fuller.

At ten o'clock, after several more rounds, James said, "Gents, I must retire now."

He staggered up the stairs to his room without paying.

Charles remained seated, wobbling on his stool.

Everett said, "Charles, I am worried about having your brother onboard. He is lively and impetuous. Do you trust him to keep his mouth shut with my men?"

"I will talk with him. Of course, I trust him," replied Charles and then shouted to a server, "Another three."

Leaving Spike and Charles slumped on the bench, Everett made his way back to the ship.

Mid-afternoon, and after the brothers continued drinking and watching their backs for four days, Everett arrived at the *Ye Olde Cheshire Cheese*. The brothers were not in their rooms; he guessed they were drinking elsewhere. Everett returned the following morning at precisely nine; the brothers were waiting for him with all their possessions and left, not expecting to return anytime soon.

# 7

# Pitching

On 23rd February 1697, the brothers set off with Everett and the crew on the *Frostenden Nave*.

During the week before, Everett and Charles had scrambled to secure cargo, still expecting to bump into the dark-cloaked man and his boy again. After several nervous false alarms, the man and his boy were nowhere to be seen, fortunately.

They planned their payload for trading, firstly down the African coast, then southern India and ultimately Kandy. Unknown to the brothers, Everett also borrowed additional funds and obtained silver bullion, which he stored in a secret space under his cabin.

The *Frostenden Nave* was a medium-sized cargo ship and suited for light conflict. There were six cannon, a modest number of nine-pound cannonballs, muskets for each man with spares, many barrels of black powder, and an assortment of long knives. Everett told James that the ship was thirty years old. However, Charles reckoned to double that again, given its odd shape, worn-out appearance and the low price paid for the lean-looking ownership documents. The deck timbers and railings were clean and free from the worm, but there was movement. The canvas sails were all tired, heavily patched, and grubby.

The weather was gentle. Progress was slow, averaging three or four knots, so Everett estimated. Two weeks into the voyage, they reached the Spanish islands off the African coast's western tip. Here they stopped for two nights to refresh supplies.

Everett's cabin was at the stern while Charles and James were given the stateroom at its bow. James thought it odd that the captain's cabin was at the front of the ship but said nothing of it.

In their compartment, the brothers were asleep in their grand chairs, as was their morning habit. Dawn had broken an hour earlier. Everett knocked hard on the door, startling Charles from his rest.

"A minute, if you may. Who is it?" yawned Charles.

"Captain," yelled Everett.

Charles opened the door.

"Man. Are you ever alert?" chastised Everett, shaking James's shoulder.

"I always hear your tones," snickered James.

"Well, we have been sailing for almost three weeks," began Everett. "Progress has been slow up to now. In the last hour, a westerly has begun to pick up our pace. You will feel the change."

"When will we reach the Cape?" demanded James.

"If I knew that, I would be a rich man. Patience is the best policy when sailing. We have a very long way to travel and many uncertainties at each stop," said Everett sarcastically. "So, gentlemen, in truth, what takes you to Kandy, apart from this fine ship?"

"As I said back at Blackfriars, we are following in our grandpa's search of trade and riches," said James.

"Well, sir, you can find that aplenty in southern Africa. Our ship is of modest size and can only carry a limited weight and volume. Its timbers below water, while well tarred, have witnessed many big storms. As you know, she constantly aches with pain," stated Everett. "With what riches do you expect to return to England?"

"Gems," said Charles. "Kandy is well known for its gemstones, star sapphires and rubies. These are what we seek."

Everett's expression changed to scorn as he said, "Well, that's fine, but how do you expect to pay for them? The main currency in Kandy is silver or gold. Your English gold sovereigns will only bring you so many rocks, and especially now the Dutch have muscled in on the Portuguese, taking the best pickings."

Charles shook his head while looking directly at James.

James's seasickness started as they sailed along the English Channel, despite the gentle sea. He kept himself in his forward quarters and away from the crew for large amounts of time. Captain Everett suggested he would be better off on deck, watching the horizon and steadying his head and balance. Still, James was stubborn and refused to take any notice. His sickness worsened as the ship picked up speed, and he began to lose all sense of balance. Despite a fever, he slept solidly, though, much to the annoyance of his brother.

James shed many pounds in weight during the first month. He was always tired and found it challenging to eat, even the fresh oranges they picked up from the Spanish islands. His vomit was a mixture of orange and deep green. His stomach ached, and he regularly coughed, making his stomach burn more, inducing more sickness. He hated his new routine.

Charles awoke to the ship rolling and pitching violently. He had had a difficult night sleep, often waking, dreaming of a dark cave with flashing lights and green naked women swimming in a pool; he felt sure his dreams were in brilliant colour. His fantasies had been similar during most nights of the voyage.

Thrown upwards, he hit the low ceiling and bounded out of his hammock, landing severely on his back against the floor. He knew he was in trouble as a penetrating pain, unlike anything he had experienced before, immediately racked his upper leg and down to his toes. He was able to move his legs; at least that was positive, he thought.

“James, wake up Brother, I need help down here,” hollered Charles.

James stirred, and after a pause uttered, “Oh Brother, you have made us wake from a wonderful vision; there were bare wet ladies everywhere.”

“Were they green by any chance?” scoffed Charles.

James jested, “Brother, they could have been any colour you like.” He then muttered, “That’s weird.”

“James, now give me help,” replied a perplexed Charles.

“Why are you sleeping on the floor?” asked James. “You look rather uncomfortable.”

Charles’s patience with his brother was low at the best of times. He tried to sit up, but the pain through his left leg hit him again, and he fell back in agony. He needed his brother’s aid now, not knowing if he had done any significant damage.

“James, turn me over slowly and take a look at my back,” said Charles softly.

James rolled off his hammock just as another crashing against the bow rocked them. He roughly turned Charles onto his stomach and lifted his shirt as Charles winced.

“Brother, I see nothing other than your tanned back and flabby sides. What’s up?” offered James.

“I cannot sit up. I have shooting pains through my leg here,” cowered Charles, holding the top of his thigh.

"Wait, I can't hold," exclaimed James.

His sick missed Charles's leg by a few inches.

Wiping his mouth, James looked again at his brother's back and poked the base of his spine where there was a recognisable lump.

Charles let out a roar, "James, for hell's sake, have a care."

"Oh, is that the spot?" laughed James. "Let me try sitting you up straight."

"No, James. Go and get Everett," shouted Charles, just as the captain entered.

Everett mocked, "Well, how was your night's sleep, Thackers?"

Charles raised his chin off the floor and looked up, straining his neck, and stressed, "Captain, I need help here, unable to sit. Shooting pains down my left leg. Please, take a cautious look."

Everett prodded the same spot as James had done a minute earlier, only harder. Charles let out a scream and instinctively rolled over. The pain from his leg pulsed again.

"For the devil's sake, man," he yelled.

Everett laughed, "I see nothing wrong with you, except for all that beer padding around your sides."

Charles could not walk more than half a dozen steps for three weeks, racked each time he sat up or put weight onto his left leg. The brothers barely left the stateroom for a month.

--x--

# 8

# Tower Inn

Leaving *Thatchers* on Rayleigh's eighteenth birthday, 28th February 1697, was a solemn affair. His uncle Joseph said nothing to Rayleigh as three stages approached the driveway; it was early. Another seventeen men were waiting too: all well known to Wethersby Jnr and Rayleigh; young, hard-working fellows from their estate's families. Southwold greeted the quest disapprovingly, especially among many local girls who reminisced about future slim pickings.

Wethersby Jnr had earlier agreed with Rayleigh to invest a modest sum by hitching passage on board the *North Cove*, commanded by William O. Boyce. They were in for a long ride south to the African Cape and northeast to India's upper west coast.

Wethersby Jnr would separately pay each of his men an adequate sum. They were all promised, in writing, a combined half share of the profits for whatever goods they could bring safely home. He thought that would be enough to keep them interested during the return journey, but not too little that they may jump ship at the nearest whiff of a better deal.

Wethersby Jnr was privately nervous as greed could set in, and men could begin to disappear, especially while returning. The deal was conditional on both Rayleigh and Wethersby Jnr returning to England in one piece. The two knew they would need to be on guard should their fortunes be realised. Wethersby Jnr offered Rayleigh a forty-ninth from one hundred of the remainder; Rayleigh gratefully accepted.

They were waiting for Wethersby Jnr, who was shouting to only himself from the top of the grand staircase, “Where are my glasses?”

He came bouncing down the stairs, and tripped on the third-from-last, somersaulted and somehow landed back on his feet, grinning but still without his glasses.

“I shall get new ones in London before we set off,” he exclaimed.

“Stop wasting your money and take greater care of your possessions. How many times have I told you, Junior?” berated Joseph. “Go up and find them.”

Wethersby Jnr duly climbed the stairs and went into his room. Rayleigh followed.

“Cousin, come on, we need to be ready. Let me help,” Rayleigh said, as he got on his knees and looked around under the bed.

“Here they are. But these glasses are smashed,” said Rayleigh.

“I know Rayleigh. That is why I could not find them and will buy new ones,” said Wethersby Jnr. “Let us pause for some minutes; there is no rush. It is going to be a long time until we see this room and house again.”

“It will, but I’ll be glad to let this place go, and when we return, I shall make some changes,” said Rayleigh.

“Oh, is that right young man?” laughed Wethersby Jnr. “What makes you think you will make commands of my father?”

"For one, he is not *my* father. And for a second, we will have brought back the JackFruit," stated Rayleigh. "Riches will triumph his seniority."

Wethersby Jnr was stunned for a moment, then said, "Why you may be right, but in the meantime, we need to travel the world and back. I suspect *if* we return, and *if* we return with the treasure, you may be right. Now, let me take those off you and let us get on the stage."

They laughed as they came down the staircase.

Joseph hugged Wethersby Jnr tightly and cried softly, "My first, and now my last son, come back in one piece. Draw your sword, not in anger, only in defence. Do not let Rayleigh distract you on this quest; he may know more from the old man than he lets on, so keep him close but never trust him. Bring the treasure to me. Bring me back a grandson too!"

"Why, Father, I will need to find a wife first," replied Wethersby Jnr.

"Charles, well, he left without that deed done. And James, he just wanted fun in the Blakes' barn with their maid or the next flossy who knew no better," said Joseph. "Bring your young lad back before Rayleigh."

Wethersby Jnr never understood why Joseph had not bought Rayleigh up alongside his brothers. He had often witnessed his father's scorn towards Rayleigh, but this one was the ultimate low. His selfish father had never helped Rayleigh in any way, always putting him down.

The seventeen other men were hanging on patiently. A dozen had already climbed aboard two of the stages; the others waited while the two men climbed in the coach, and then off it went. Wethersby Jnr looked out of the stage window towards the house. His father had already gone back inside. All the other men's fathers, mothers and siblings were gone too.

Wethersby Jnr called to the driver, "Sir, please ride us carefully to Blackfriars. Do not lose sight of the other two stages, front and rear; we must ride as a caravan. What do you go by?"

"Spike," responded the driver. "I took your brothers there too."

And with that, he said no more for the rest of the day.

Rayleigh and Wethersby Jnr tried in vain to strike up conversations with Spike to pass the time. They wanted to learn more about Charles and James, where they lodged, when they sailed and their ships' names.

They were relaxed about their arrangements. Wethersby Jnr corresponded letters with William O. Boyce and broadly agreed to their joint adventure and crew terms. He sent his first letter on 28th December 1696 after seeing, by chance, an advertisement in The Times.

Wethersby Jnr had agreed to finance their handpicked crew from Southwold, with Boyce topping up their 'pay' with food and provisions. However, Boyce had stipulated he would vet each of the team before allowing them on board.

The four-day trip was uneventful. Wethersby Jnr was bored already by the third day. Spike continued to say very little; he stayed at the head of the three coaches, knowing the route like the back of his hand.

Rayleigh laughed at Wethersby Jnr's stern look and asked, "So Junior, if you are bored after three days, how are you going to handle months at sea?"

"Ah, young man, now I love the sea, but I cannot stand rattling around in this godforsaken coach with a driver who will not speak," stated Wethersby Jnr.

Rayleigh let out a roar. "Junior, have you not forgotten? The sea journey to India is just the start. We have that great continent to traverse. This little coach is luxury compared to the transport we may get later, on top of camels and elephants."

Wethersby Jnr said nothing more, his self-doubts urging him inwardly to turn back, but he could not now.

They arrived at London's outskirts around midday; however, the sky was already darkening, and a dense brown fog enveloped them. By the time they stopped alongside the River Thames near Blackfriars, it was dusk-like but still only four o'clock, according to the chimes of a giant clock nearby.

Spike opened their door and said, "Sirs, your carriage has arrived safely. Do you wish to lodge in the same tavern as your brothers?"

Surprising himself, Wethersby Jnr replied sarcastically, "Well, that would be interesting, but no. I fear those drunkards left behind some trouble for us to pick up. Please take us to a modest establishment close to the Tower, for we have a meeting there tomorrow morning."

Spike moved the coaches along to the *Tower Inn*, where Rayleigh and Wethersby Jnr set about agreeing to terms for a week's stay.

Before their London arrival, they had decided how much time they needed to sort out their finances. They would meet Boyce and confirm all the written arrangements, along with Boyce spot-checking the Southwold men.

The inn was comfortable enough. They shared a room overlooking the Tower and the river, despite fog obscuring the view.

The cousins walked the short distance from the *Tower Inn* to the Tower Mint entrance in the morning. Their meeting with the warden of the Mint started promptly.

Newton arrived precisely at nine and greeted the men. "Welcome to my rather grand establishment, The Tower Mint, gentlemen. Which of you is Rayleigh? Come this way if you would."

"That is I, and this is my cousin Wethersby Jnr. Thank you, Mister Newton, for agreeing to see us," said Rayleigh as they walked inside and down some steep steps. "We only know of the arrangements made by our late grandfather. How long ago did he make arrangements with you?"

"Rayleigh, that would have been over fifty years ago. I, however, only found out about its more recent provisions last year when I gained this position. The previous warden, Overton, took care of matters before his predecessors. Wethersby, I met your brothers not long ago. They appeared rather impatient; James took all his coins with him on his first visit here," grimaced Newton.

"Mister Newton, my youngest cousin always tends to react without thinking. So, apart from our small hoard of coins, what else have you stored here?" enquired Rayleigh.

"Thank you for showing interest in something other than your own. Here, we have coins in quantities beyond comprehension. I am in the process of issuing new coinage to stop counterfeits. Too many are clipped or otherwise fiddled. So, we have a mix of both newly minted and old coins in various states of disrepair, as well as hordes of fakes. It is my mission to rid this country of fraud and clean our money for King William III. Not for those who have made money at his and his predecessor's expense," said Newton grandly, barely pausing for breath.

Rayleigh expected that he repeated this statement many times, word for word, not only to visitors but to anyone in high authority and influence.

The cousins stayed with Newton for an additional hour.

"Do not worry, Rayleigh. Your coins are safe here. They are going nowhere until you return on your birthday in four years,"

Newton promised and added, “as for your grandpa’s other Trust, when that time comes, it too shall be released.”

The cousins headed back to the *Tower Inn* to discuss their plans again before meeting William O. Boyce. Wethersby Jnr had withdrawn a chunk of his coins. Despite his prior written agreement with Boyce, he hoped to keep some coins as extra security.

They drank two beers each before retiring, leaving their men in the tavern to drink some more.

Wethersby Jnr said in passing, “Now men, behave yourselves. No fondling the locals nor getting hungover. We will soon be on our way. You must be sober for the meeting with Boyce in two days; make no mistake.”

# 9

## North Cove

The morning of their meeting with Boyce, the cousins were up well before daybreak. They walked outside in greenish haze and through narrow alleys as they followed their noses for yeasty bread and into another side street. They gorged themselves on the hot treat, covered in beef drippings.

As they stuffed their mouths as quickly as they could eat, unable to say anything, they walked along the river and back towards Blackfriars. They located Boyce at the Paul's Pier Wharf, arriving earlier than planned, and boarded the *North Cove*. After brief introductions, Rayleigh offered Boyce a loaf.

"Young man. That will do very nicely. Thank you," said Boyce. "Where did you find this fine bread?"

"A small bakery just by the Tower. We got up early. It had just left the oven," replied Rayleigh. "It does for a fine, if simple, breakfast, don't you think?"

"Indeed. You have an excellent nose for flavour. This dough is some of the best in all of London. I pray though it may be some of the last for a considerable time for us; more simple fare we will consume for months," said Boyce.

He struggled to talk without dribbling and spitting dripping out of his mouth, savouring every morsel.

The men spent the next three hours reaffirming their plans for the journey. Boyce, though, was seemingly distracted in wanting to see the cousins' men. Wethersby Jnr thought he knew why; after all, the crew would take commands only from Boyce and his officers, and that was the deal for which Boyce was clear. Rayleigh wondered, though, what would happen during disputes since 'their' crew were being paid by Wethersby Jnr, except for food. Rayleigh worried the arrangements could get too complicated but said nothing more out of fear of showing a lack of commitment. Nor did he want to show Boyce potential kinks in the cousins' solidarity, and not to Wethersby Jnr for that matter.

They agreed to a fixed price; Boyce was adamant there would be no compromise. However, Wethersby Jnr held back sixty coins, maintaining additional risks with a single fee given the journey's length and uncertainties. He explained that they intended to go further than western India, overland to the east, so they did not intend to return to England with Boyce. The captain would be free to do whatever trade he wished once they went their separate ways. All three men were satisfied with the arrangement.

Unbeknown to the cousins, Boyce had already decided that this was his last complex journey. He would sell his ship upon return, regardless of whatever bounty or treasure returned with them.

Boyce knew of the other Thacker brothers' departure, not a month earlier. In *Ye Olde Cock Tavern*, he had overheard George Everett boasting of riches in Kandy. Boyce detested the man and the newly moneyed brothers who carelessly bought Everett's worthless worm-ridden boat. Boyce suspected the cousins in front of him were hiding part of their journey;

although he had so little trust in Everett, he was unsure who was pulling him in.

At seven the following morning, seventeen men, Wethersby Jnr and Rayleigh, arrived at the *North Cove*. One by one, each of the Southwold men went to meet Boyce.

Boyce asked the same four questions to each of them.

"You join my crew, as my crew. You take command from my officer here or me and no one else. Especially not from Wethersby Thacker nor Rayleigh Edwards. Is this understood?"

"Yes," they each replied.

"How is your health?" asked Boyce next.

Each man answered either, "Well," "Good," or "Fine."

Boyce's last two questions were, "What is your age?" and "What do you go by?"

Sitting beside Boyce, Officer Peck wrote down each man's name and age in a ledger and placed two ticks against each of them. The sheet was filled with nineteen titles by the end of the parade. Wethersby Jnr and Rayleigh were at the top, along with the word Ahmedabad. Not one of the men had coughed despite the confines of the captain's cabin and the smoke that filled it.

Boyce was pleased with the men. They all appeared healthy and burly. He doubted whether Wethersby Jnr would bring any who were unwilling. Or whom he thought did not have the physical and mental strength for the long, uncertain journey ahead.

At daybreak, 10th March 1697, the *North Cove* departed from Paul's Pier Wharf. Rayleigh insisted on visiting the bakery for the last time at five that morning before leaving. He and Wethersby Jnr struggled to carry the many hot loaves and lard while trying to stuff themselves as they returned to the quay.

The first half of the passage was tough, despite several calls to anchorages. Officer Lawson Peck, known merely as Peck by the men, had generally been in a foul mood, stomping about the deck. He ranted about the men's and the ship's cleanliness, barking his orders so busying the crew. That morning, early in April, Rayleigh was again enjoying the fresh sea breeze and spray on his face.

"… But it is a handsome treasure, cursed. Never be it grasped by any one man or one woman, for a long haunting death will surely follow…." Old Wethersby's last words were playing on Rayleigh's mind again, "Why, man or *woman*?" he pondered.

Rayleigh had been continually reliving those moments, trying hard to remember his grandfather's stories, convinced that he had shepherded him for many years. But Wethersby Snr's directions were often vague and so full of improbable confrontations. Rayleigh worried he had not listened well and missed signs that they would soon need.

The sea was building a good swell. Ahead, the sky was darkening and moody. Soon the wind picked up yet again, straining the giant sails as the ship picked up speed, misting even more on Rayleigh's frowning face.

"Rayleigh, cut loose that rope by your feet before you swing up the staff," bellowed Peck.

Rayleigh, startled, moved to the port side, checking no ropes were near his feet. But he tumbled hard near the edge as a rogue wave sharply buffered the bow, his foot catching severely on a protruding plank. He somersaulted twice over, and his head smacked a corner railing.

"Ray-, Rayleigh get up," he could hear Peck say.

Rayleigh had fallen in a heap and was struggling to focus, seeing three Pecks. He tasted metal. Then the pain caught him.

His weak foot was a tangled mess. He rubbed his forehead and passed out again.

He came round, staring at their compartment's ceiling. His head was throbbing, spinning and pressured inwards. Rayleigh's hand went to his skull, feeling a damp cloth. He looked down at his strapped foot, browned from his blood and twice its proper size. He sat up delicately and prodded his foot, wincing as he felt nothing. Touching where his big toe should have been, he pressed down only to sense bindings.

"Cousin, what in heaven's name happened to my *foot*?" screamed Rayleigh, making his head pulse more.

Wethersby Jnr got up from his chair and stood over Rayleigh.

"Cousin, you will live. There is a nasty gash to your head, but your big toe is overboard; it had snapped almost entirely. Thomas cut to relieve you of it. That is for the best, young man," declared Wethersby Jnr, calmly.

Before Rayleigh could say anything more, Wethersby Jnr went to his desk, poured an imposing shot of rum, and handed the clay cup to Rayleigh.

"Drink. This will put more hairs on your chest for your women to get tangled in," grinned Wethersby Jnr.

"I am not sure if I should thank you for giving my toe to the sea, cousin?" asserted Rayleigh, trying not to laugh. "Oh, my head is banging. Get more rum."

--x--

For seven nights, Wethersby Jnr kept a watchful eye over Rayleigh. Thomas came to change his bandages every morning. Rayleigh's eye sockets had first blackened, then turned purple and were now yellowish. An unpleasant smell from his foot, a mixture of rot and rum, commanded the room.

Rayleigh began to feel some of his toes again, an acute, dull pain, although he had not tried to stand up. The new deep-rooted aching would last for many weeks as he gradually learnt to walk without falling over, though his balance was off.

# 10

## Green-inked plots

The voyage to India took almost two months, after numerous but fleeting stopovers down the west African coast and Cape Colony, most of which were uneventful.

At Cape Groot, they ventured inland for some days to hunt freely, returning to the ship with their spoils.

They collected a mass of goods for trading and some, Boyce hoped, for return to England. Rayleigh despised killing magnificent animals despite their worth, especially the slashing of ivories from seventeen immense elephants and rhinos.

The passage had been surprisingly smooth, except for the 'toe squall', as Wethersby would call it, and getting around Cape Peninsula. Here, the heavy sky whipped up a monstrous sea with waves cracking over the bow's oak timbers; the storm was relentless for three days and nights. Most of the crew were sick from the sea.

Rayleigh, notwithstanding his foot, was growing tougher. He relished skimming up the tall masts, often winning the climb almost one-handed, settling in the rigging for the sea breeze to whip back his braided queue and spray his face. The scars on his upper forehead were less noticeable now, despite the sun's rays penetrating them to a wet shade of pink earlier on. Despite the hardships on board and lack of proper water for washing, he took considerable pride in his appearance. He remained clean-shaven despite nicking the same spot on his chin each time. All exposed skin, upper body, his face, and below his knees turned a dark golden brown. He was lean, fit, and muscular for his eighteen years. He hid his dizzy spells that often occurred while merely walking along the deck, but up in the rigging, he never once lost his sense of balance.

By contrast, Wethersby Jnr attempted to keep out of the sun for large amounts of the trip. There was no escaping the Indian ocean, though; he, too, had taken on a weathered look with wrinkles on his head, cracking and beginning to ooze.

--x--

An old pressed and greened calves leather skin provided a broad base for the atlas and notes. Several maps, when unfolded, measured three yards wide and two yards deep.

Rayleigh had laboured over 'his' atlas. A year or so before Wethersby Snr's death, he meticulously copied his grandfather's maps, despite them being threadbare and over sixty years old. He had allowed Rayleigh sight of the charts on most occasions during their monthly study sessions. Rayleigh was not permitted to make copies within the study despite his frequent requests. Instead, from memory, he lightly traced each area. He reconfirmed each time Wethersby Snr allowed him to see the original maps and eccentric green annotations.

Since his death, Rayleigh had marked his grandfather's original book from memories of their evening study discussions at *Thatchers*, using his same green ink.

Rayleigh was unsure why he persisted, other than to try to bring the stories to life, even if he did not believe all of the yarns old Wethersby recounted.

He had also made marks and added place names on the map as Wethersby Snr described them. He often asked his grandfather to point to the place on his plan. After Wethersby Snr's death, Rayleigh would often wake in the dead of night, recoiling from another vivid dream of a mysterious place, and would make another note on a map.

Alone in his cabin, Rayleigh was amazed at the details he had covered. He worried, though; so much of what was labelled came from his recollections. How accurate could they be? All his markings were in the same green ink; he could not distinguish what was original and what he had added. Then again, how much of what his grandfather told him did Rayleigh honestly believe?

Carelessly, the book slipped from his hands and dropped with a thud and a click on the floor. To Rayleigh's amazement, a sliver of metal protruded from the binding. He pulled it, and out fell a small and merely decorated silver compass. It felt cold to his touch as its needle spun and settled. He twisted its base and lined up one needle north; the other pointed due south.

Rayleigh had kept the atlas and compass onboard a secret. Carefully he folded the parchments and placed the book back under a wide floorboard. Rayleigh secured the small flooring gap with a slither of wood and moved his bed so that one leg sat over it. He felt the time was near to reveal the maps to Wethersby Jnr, who, after all, had supported Rayleigh's adventure. They had come so far already. India was but a week away if Boyce's calculations were correct.

One aspect intrigued and worried Rayleigh; there were many wild differences in Boyce's maps' land outlines compared to his own. Rayleigh presumed this was due to his poor tracing ability. However, Boyce said he had seen other plans with different northern India and southern Siam and Malay coastlines. Still, Boyce confirmed that his onboard maps were less than a year old. Rayleigh's trust in his beloved book dwindled despite the many hours and days he had laboured over it.

He had just finished positioning his bed as the door flew open from a gust of wind. His cousin fell through the open door and collapsed in a heap in front of him.

"My, this wind has come out from nowhere. There are hardly any clouds in the sky," said Wethersby Jnr breathlessly. "Blew me right off my feet."

Several weeks earlier, Wethersby Jnr noticed a new crack in the floor near Rayleigh's bed, and a small piece of wood was in a different place. He thought he might be hiding something, and now he finally spied what it was; Wethersby Snr's old giant green atlas. He wondered when, or even if, his cousin would come clean and reveal the plot. Rayleigh had not noticed his cousin's unusual behaviour or the glint in his eyes. He decided that evening he would tell his secret. However, he would never allow Wethersby Jnr to know to what extent it had come from his imagination.

"I suggest we secure the stateroom again in case this wind worsens. I see how unsteady you are on your feet. It is usually me who cannot keep my sea legs," laughed Rayleigh, as he tried to covertly wipe some dust with his feet over the board.

That evening, the wind stalled, the sails slackened, and the ship barely moved forward. Most of the crew were lying on the main deck, appreciating the cooler air. After the wild ride they had had all day, many on board were relieved to sit undisturbed. Rayleigh was fretting on how to divulge the book to his cousin.

"Junior," said Rayleigh quietly, "I need to show you something in our cabin. It is important."

Wethersby Jnr stood up eagerly and was first to the door of their compartment. Inside, Rayleigh went to his bed, moved it to one side, slid a metal spike into the boards and prized one open. He took the atlas and offered it to Wethersby Jnr.

"What is this, bedtime reading?" asked Wethersby Jnr sarcastically, as he opened the book, surprised by the intact pages.

"Here, Junior. Boyce could use this," said Rayleigh handing the compass to his cousin.

Wethersby then read the atlas's inscription:

***"To Rayleigh.***
***Follow my footsteps, not my hands.***
***Seek green senses, not yellow pearls.***
***Let this always point your direction.***
***Wethersby Longfellow Thacker.***
***28th February 1689."***

--x--

From the foot of Africa, they sailed northeast to the island of Mauritius, pausing for a week for fresh provisions and recovery.

From there, Boyce successfully navigated his way to the Indian northwest coast. His huge maps, drawn only a year or two before, trusted compasses, and an uncanny instinct, provided essential guidance.

It was his fourth journey along a similar route in the past dozen years. Each voyage was unique, with a different crew, weather, and people they came across at each landing. For days, as they made their way carefully along a wide river called Sabarmati and well before they arrived at Ahmedabad, the bone-dry heat had intensified.

--x--

# 11

## OUT OF TACK

James had drunk a dozen or more flasks of rum from his secret stash in the course of the last seven days and nights. The seasickness had gotten worse - his retching painful, hot, and stale. Surges of bile frequently rose from his stomach, straining his chest, causing him to double over. He had difficulty eating what little food he got given; nothing would stay down. He felt increasingly fragile. The smell of sunbaking mackerel wafting in waves through the cabin amplified his discomfort; James detested fish.

Captain Everett was anxious. The stores were dwindling rapidly, so he had begun rationing the previous week. The crew desperately needed nourishment. They took to foraging, using simple poles and ragged nets, at first casting off small precious chunks of stale green tack, then tiny fish to lure larger fry. They were unsuccessful, and the men now ate the tiddlers rather than risk losing them as bait. How much longer could they endure their famine?

That morning, several weeks after they set off from the island of Mauritius, Charles had been gingerly walking the deck. He sat down next to Henry, who had just cast a small net, holding two rope ends in one hand.

"So, Henry, how is our luck today?" asked Charles.

"Sir, it is a fine day, a tad too hot for my liking," returned Henry, rubbing his face with his free hand, then pointed. "We can all but try to catch something. Look!"

Charles could only see the greenish-dark water ahead of them, unclear where Henry was directing his eyes. Perhaps thirty yards away, the water began to froth, then the V-shaped tail of a substantial whale broke through the surface, then padded the water with a giant splash.

"Mister Charles, we are saved. See, he is fishing," exclaimed Henry with a huge smile, still pointing towards where the whale had risen, almost losing his rope grip.

"Henry, unless we catch some of those fish, there will be none left. Look at the size of the beast," cried Charles.

The whale's enormous gaping mouth rose out of the water, where tens of tiny fish darted out between its gums.

Most of the crew now joined Henry and Charles and tossed more nets into the water. Two traps were gone as the lines tangled and snapped in their haste. Henry and Charles pulled their net in slowly, gathering what they hoped was their next raw meal.

The whale disappeared. The net contained four finger-sized fish. The crew brought up the remaining nets; those too held a mere handful of small fish. Overall, there was one for each man and a couple of spares.

Charles saw James coming towards them, his face pale, with some spit dangling from his mouth.

"Brother, is that our dinner?" chuckled James.

"No, James. You will only bring them up," replied Charles.

All the clean water had gone, so too the whale's loose fish and the last of the ship's salt pork, hardtack and rum spirit.

Captain Everett had maintained a small reserve for himself, his officers and the Thackers, but even those supplies were low. It was a desperate time onboard. The officers demanded limited effort from the men, for they had so little energy other than to bemoan their predicament.

Everett could not understand how he had gone off course; the northeast winds were favourable, after all. But the Indian ocean was vast, and there were so few land spots to confirm positions. He estimated the distance travelled from the strength of winds and marked intervals on his many maps. They should have been upon the Indian southern coast in the last two weeks, perhaps even as far as Kandy. The supplies they bargained hard for in Mauritius gave him a cushion of a month from his initial estimates. A clock was itching inside his head for every day they had not spotted earth or another ship. He assumed he was too far south, so he had steered the vessel on a northeast bias during the last week.

He stood in his cabin at the stern, with the most extensive maps on the floor, scratching his temple.

A knock on the door was followed by, "Captain, it is me, Charles."

Everett opened the door and ushered Charles in.

"How many more days until we reach Kandy?" demanded Charles.

"Come now, Charles, as I have said before, we cannot be precise about these things. This sea is huge, as was that last storm. There are few islands in our path, and they are tiny, see here," said Everett as he got down on his knee, pointing to an area to the west of the Indian coast.

Charles joined Everett on the floor, studying the heavily creased map; his eyes followed where Everett had plotted their journey so far.

"I judge we are this close to the islands of Maldives, perhaps two or three days away. See, this island group follows a north-south line; we should come across them easily," lied Everett. "Stores are lower than I wish, and yes, the men are restless. At least we have enough food in my cabin to last us the next couple of days."

"So, you say we are close to land. How can you be so sure, Everett?" challenged Charles.

"Well, sir, I have commanded this ship for many a year and before that learnt my craft from the best in the Navy," replied Everett defensively. "When we arrive, you shall see I am right."

Charles had heard these exact words two weeks before and was convinced that Everett did not know where they were. The colossal week-long storm had pushed the *Frostenden Nave* hard from behind. Charles was perplexed; how was the ship being steered? How did Everett know how far they had travelled and in which direction? Charles looked again at the map, pondering Everett's hand-drawn plot. To the south, an area of nothingness on the paper.

"Captain, well, we shall see in three days. If you have not found us land by then, I shall reduce your fee; for James is very sick, and I am famished," declared Charles.

"A deal is a deal, sir. We agreed to nothing about the length of days. Do not talk to me with your foolish threats; you are beginning to sound like your brother," retorted Everett.

The resounding thud hit close to the ship. Everett scrambled up and out of the door without another word. Outside in the mist, he saw nothing ahead or behind them.

One of the crew shouted from the crow's nest, "A ship's mast, north by northwest, five hundred yards, perhaps four."

Whistling and then another great thump followed. The big splash to the starboard was close enough to shower water over the deck. Another one followed in ten seconds, hitting and splintering the stern's railing and part of the bridge. Wood chips flew in every direction.

Two more cannonballs hit them soon after. Blown off his feet, Everett crashed backwards into Charles; they both landed in a heap below the main topmast. The back of Everett's head banged hard against Charles's nose and smashed his bridge. Charles squealed, holding his face as blood poured from his disfigured snout, before losing consciousness.

"Captain, are we to fire back?" bawled one of the crew.

Everett could not respond. He was out cold, knocked out from bouncing off Charles, landing head-first on the deck.

An officer named Clark came to them; they were breathing, but both were non-responsive. Clark went immediately below deck, finding only three crew by two cannon.

"Ready them now. Let me see the angle and fire when I command," said Clark.

"They are ready," said one of the gunners near to a cannon, holding a three-foot-long linstock, with the match smouldering.

He touched the cannon before Clark ordered, and a large plume of smoke covered the inside. The gun moved backwards, squashing Clark under one of its wheels. His skull instantly cracked open, showering the artilleryman with pieces of bone and matter.

The brief but fierce skirmish between the two ships was over within fifteen minutes. The invaders outgunned the *Frostenden Nave*, quickly smashing two of its four cannon permanently out of action, with the others facing the wrong direction.

The smaller ship came alongside. Hooked ropes were thrown, catching on the railings as the two boats drew together. Men seemingly flew through the air, boarding the *Frostenden Nave*; others used planks to cross the narrow void.

Despite one well-aimed musket volley, which dropped several men between the ships, the skilful invaders' swords were no match for the ill and starving men. Many bodies dropped lifeless on deck; their necks cut to the bone.

Everett came round, blood trickling from a deep cut between the bridge of his nose and upper lip, his mouth nearly closed from swelling. He looked up to see strange men in colourful gowns standing over him; he thought he was still dreaming. He tried to shout out, but nothing came, then he cocked his head to see Charles laid out cold.

A pool of blood covered the deck behind Charles's head; his nose smashed and contorted.

The remains of Everett's crew gathered on deck, roughly in a line against a railing. The colourful foreign men each had a long-curved knife in one hand, and some carried two. Everett made out one of the new men dragging James, his sword at James's throat. The marauders laughed as one teased James, repeatedly nicking skin on his bare arms, the knife slicing through effortlessly as James screamed in agony.

"I beg you, stop. What have I done to you?" pleaded James.

"Silence," demanded the man.

He withdrew his knife from James's arm and pocketed it into its sheath.

The man was short, perhaps only four foot ten but weighty around his middle. His swift wrist had opened James up like a kipper. James coughed, dribbling some vomit, then heaved violently, spraying onto the man's skirt. The short man's face reddened as he grabbed and swung his sword down James's head, slicing off his left ear instantly. James fell forward, unconscious, smacking his jaw on the deck and expelling a tooth.

"Who is next to spit on my cloth?" laughed the man at James's ear next to the quarter rail.

The man picked up the ear, unsheathed a smaller knife he carried, walked over to the mast, and stabbed the ear onto the pole with his blade.

"Who leads this plague-ridden ship?" said the man, his eyes staring at Everett.

After a short pause, Everett mused, "Do you mean our one-eared Captain James? By my reckoning, he cannot hear you now."

Sitting next to James, one of Everett's crew let out a short cackle, at which the short man spun around, his sabre slicing the man under his jaw. The head wobbled briefly and dropped to the floor; a jet of blood gushed out from the quivering neck, spotting all over James and another crewman.

Arching his spine and bending his head backwards, the man roared, "Who's laughing now?"

Everett knew to keep his mouth shut on this occasion, willing James to wake up and spout off. But neither of the Thacker brothers stirred from their injuries.

The unusually dressed pirates began to tie up each man, leaving James and Charles to the last. Then they started to ransack the ship, quite randomly, Everett thought and hoped.

Over the next hour, numerous knives, muskets and a few barrels of black powder were laid out in front of the prisoners. They amassed precious maps from the captain's cabin, his compass, candles and hammock, and all the while, the attackers laughed and barked. Still, the brothers had not moved.

The Thackers' compartment got trashed. Everett could hear the men calling to each other in a foreign language he had listened to before but knew not what they said. They found the only food in the captain's compartment, along with two almost empty barrels of water from the Thackers' hovel, much to

Everett's surprise. He remained silent throughout, desperately hoping and praying that his silver stash and the Thackers' gold remained undisturbed.

# 12

## OVERBOARD BOUNDER

A modest cargo of goods was thrown overboard, most barrels sank to the deep, apart from a half dozen that bobbed in the slight swell.

The *Frostenden Nave* crew members were led singularly along a plank onto the smaller boat and bundled down two hatches. In contrast, the small man who had sliced off James's ear carried and dropped him down the second hatch. Charles was less fortunate.

The short man came back just as Charles roused.

Charles shouted, "What? Get your filthy hands off me. Do you know who I am?"

"That doesn't matter. Let's see how well you can swim and how long you can fend off sharks," laughed the man as he grabbed and cut the rope around Charles's wrist.

Charles was screaming, his lungs strained, and his head thumped as he was carried by four men, squirming like a feral cat, "I beg you, No!"

He went overboard. Slowly, the current took him away. He stopped trying to swim towards the ships and switched to catch up with the floating barrels. After twenty minutes, Charles was utterly exhausted, but at least he had one cask between his legs. Lying on his back, trying to conserve energy, he could make out that the two ships had moved away from one another. The *Frostenden Nave* was now well alight; smoke belched and drifted towards Charles's position. He was moving further from the ships. Soon, the smoking stopped.

Charles assumed that their vessel had sunk with the remaining gold coins and whatever Everett had tried to hide under his cabin floor. He had come across Everett late one evening, forgetting to knock. He noticed Everett's sleight of hand, more accurately his feet, as Everett tried to conceal shuffling a large rug back into its previous position.

Charles drifted in and out of consciousness for the next day and night and only swam as he spotted and gathered three more barrels. It was a struggle to open and keep the casks from drifting off.

Two were empty, but in the last one, he was amazed to find one whole bar of hardtack and a small piece; someone on board had been deceitful. However, this would sustain him, for the time being, at least, he thought. How had the invaders missed it?

The pain in his face was relentless. He felt his nose as it moved effortlessly around a large open wound; his hands dripped red.

For most of the time, the sea was gentle, with only an occasional wave washing over him as he balanced the barrels between his arms and legs. Early on the following day, he adjusted himself. His arched back had one barrel below it, his head rested on another, and the last barrel was under his knees. His arms were, thankfully, free. In the process of that hour, he had almost lost all the barrels.

The sea was surprisingly warm, but he felt cold now, despite most of his body being out of the water. Charles had never felt so lonely and weak.

He nibbled at the tack biscuit, washing down the stale powder with seawater. The sun's rays burned his exposed skin, especially on both knees and his ruined face. He was incredibly uncomfortable but alive. He talked to himself in his head, not wanting, or able, to move his facial muscles, wishing he had never left Rose and the security of *Thatchers*. The hours ticked by, and another night fell. He fought sleep again. On the fourth day, he finally faded and began a deep sleep.

Charles woke to the blistering sun beating the back of his head. It took several moments to realise he was no longer moving. However, he heard and felt gentle waves lapping his feet. Spitting out coarse grains of sand and strands of seaweed, Charles shifted his head to see a barrel immediately in front of him. He cracked a smile before the barrel disappeared, and he faded back into nothingness.

Charles nursed his pounding headache for three days. He searched the shoreline in search of an easy meal; he found nothing.

It took him an hour or so to encircle the island. The sandy beach was an almost continuous circle, except where the rock cliff came down directly into the sea. He looked up at the outcrop and paddled around the waist-high water nervously. The sea was unpredictable even when the tide appeared to be out, the surge at his feet always trying to pull him out to sea. Above him, he watched the top of the cliff where large black seabirds squawked on their precarious nests, clinging to the steep edge. He could only think of their eggs. He was delirious. Laying back on the sand, he slipped into a broken sleep.

A wing flapped and woke him. The bird's red eye blinked as it pecked at Charles's leg. He felt nothing but tried to let out a scream. His mouth was so dry he croaked instead, feeling razor-like pains travel from his stomach; he gagged. The crow-like bird ignored him and pecked more flesh before he summoned the energy to swat it away.

Charles caught the crow on its beak, and it dropped like a stone. Dead. For the first time in many days, he felt lucky; until he looked at the holes in his leg.

"Food. Thank you," said Charles aloud.

He rapidly plucked some of the feathers, tore off its legs, and shoved a piece in his mouth. Dark vomit showered onto the white sand, and his head pounded more. He threw the carcass in a fit of rage into the sea and cried. Several more birds encroached on him, seemingly waiting for him to drift off again. He stood up, dazed, and walked into the sea, cleaned his mouth, puffed out a feather and vomited again. He ignored the pain from his bleeding legs.

The sea was warm, incredibly salty, and full of multi-coloured fish. He scooped up some water in his hands, only to see the fish disappear back. The slippery fish kept darting out of his palms. Eventually, he caught one and swallowed it whole. Over the next two hours, he ate three more. His head was swimming, even though he stood still. His dizziness grew worse, as did his hunger and thirst.

Charles slept on the beach above the tide mark. He woke, itching. His thighs had new long scratches; he guessed from his sleep. Red swells covered his exposed skin. He ran into the water to try to soothe his discomfort and to go hand-fishing again. After fruitless attempts, he returned to the beach in search of something to aid his efforts. He circled the island afresh. He found a large conch shell, about ten inches wide, but little else. There were no trees and very little vegetation, except near the cliff's top where the raven-like birds nested.

Patiently and unmoving, he kept the shell underwater, waiting for a fish to enter. After snaring one, he spilt the contents on the beach and devoured the slippery fish.

"I hate fish," Charles exclaimed, but there was no one there to hear him.

--x--

# 13

## Once a Bully

James came around within a room in darkness. A horrid stench clung inside his nostrils. He tried, without success, to gag. He struggled to stand, but thick ropes around his ankles disabled his feet; rope around his wrists had cut his skin.

Disorientated, he yelled, "Help me!" and immediately regretted his words as intense pain shot through his head.

With difficulty, he reached to feel a sticky mess where his ear once was, then blacked out again.

For an unknown number of days, James drifted in and out of reality. His brief awakenings in the darkness left him petrified. He was parched and starving; he could not remember the last time he ate or drank. But the warm smell that buzzed all around him was appalling, and he gagged three or four times each time he stirred. One thought repeatedly went through his mind, being thankful for his fat, though much reduced, around his belly. It was the only time in his life he had considered that.

"Bring him up now, then put him in this cage," the short evil man shouted to a couple of his men.

He pointed to a slatted wooden box on the deck, barely four feet on each side.

They carried James out of the festering pit, still comatose, and bundled him into the small cage.

"Now, leave him in the sun and let's see how he likes burning," mocked the short man. "But be sure the birds do not peck at his eyeballs, for he can still hear, and we do not want him blinded, then he will fetch nothing. Or you will see my knife. Get him something to drink and untie his hands."

"Yes, Mister Solroy," echoed both men.

They fetched a small jug half-full of water, left it inside James's box and cut the rope around his wrists.

James shifted and opened one eye to a flash of white light. After some minutes of squinting, he began to take in his surroundings, spinning slowly around the confined space.

There was no sea in sight; was he hallucinating? The box was uncomfortable in the heat, but James was thankful that the terrible smell was no longer around him. He looked down at his free hands and gingerly held the jug to his mouth. He choked on the first gulp, spraying water. James slowly brought his tongue to the edge of his mouth and flinched as it wet his cracked lips. Looking ahead, he saw many men, perhaps forty, all dressed in similar multicoloured robes; two were staring at him.

Another couple of men passed James, carrying the remains of one of his shipmates, David, whose arms and legs were bound to a large pole. The stink was unbearable. David must have been dead for a week or more, guessed James, as he looked away and gagged once more. James mused that David had been keeping him company as he flashed back to the dark compartment and the same stink.

"Where am I?" muttered James to no one, and no one answered.

The rope around James's ankle bones was biting deep now. His wounds went from dry to wet and dry again within the space of a few hours as bursts of humidity followed the relentless heat. He felt his skin burning and only had the sun for company. He had no idea where he was, except inside a cage.

The cart, pulled along by four men, bumped along a well-rutted track. James looked around for other signs of life but could see only an endless expanse of red-brown soil, sand, and the occasional short palm tree. He knew from the angle of the sun on his back that they were heading east. James had repositioned himself, so that one side of his head avoided as much direct sunlight as possible, for the swelling around where his ear once was, was hefty. The whining pain was unbearable, so much so that he could not stop poking and prodding it, despite the extra pain that brought. He imagined his missing ear was moving.

His small clay jug was partly filled with water twice a day by one of his captors, but he had nothing to eat. He slept and toileted himself where he lay. He had stopped smelling his stench.

Behind him, there were six other carts and cages with men from the *Frostenden Nave*, Everett in the last. One of the crew, Stephen, was in a cell next to James; Stephen never spoke, despite James's whispering.

"Stephen, talk to me, man," said James softly.

Stephen's eyes bulged, appearing twice their usual size, as he sat motionless, for fear had taken hold of his senses.

On the third day, late in the afternoon, James was woken by a heavy judder and voices shouting from a distance. He saw a large wooden hut with a roof covered in dried palm leaves.

Two of his four captors went inside. They came back within an hour, untied James's ropes, grabbed and dragged him out, whereby he dropped heavily on the sand.

The short fat man with the deathly sword action hailed from the hut, "Omani, you will see my sword across your neck, should you drop him or any of the others. Now, leave him and bring them all out here."

James spent two more weeks in the hut. He only saw a captor briefly in the morning, who gave him several small pieces of coconut and filled his water jug by half. James was very sick and weak. His head endlessly thumped, and he slept only when utterly exhausted. He would regularly wake during the day and night.

As he lay on the sandy earth, his mind drifted deeply to Southwold and his last conquest, Jane Bunting. How he wished he were there with her now. James got bored quickly with his girls and women. The thrill of the chase and the allure of that satisfaction outweighed any lingering attachment. Perhaps Jane was different; he was not so sure now. He was thousands of miles away, at a place unknown and in dire need of food, grog and attention for the festering wound on the side of his head.

The resonant high-pitched ringing in his head was constant and growing louder each day.

"I am going mad," he murmured, as he lay shaking. "Where in hell's earth am I. When will I see my brother again?"

Despite all his usual cocky charm, James was frantic. He had spent his inheritance on a shipwreck, somewhere amid the Indian ocean; he had even lost his 1631 gold crown. Then he thought about his appearance.

"Would the women of Southwold, or anywhere for that matter, want a man disfigured so?" he asked himself.

Finally, reality struck him. How was he to escape the hut, and what lay beyond it? Would he ever have the company of a woman again? He had lost all hope. He despised his grandfather's legacy. He wished he had never set foot onto Spike's Southwold stage to pursue a treasure he did not believe existed now.

"Old Wethersby, what have you done to your grandson? Look at me now. It is all your fault," he said in a murmur. "My coins are all gone, so too is my ear and front teeth. What more do you want from me?"

He lay awake that night, hot and sweating, wishing for the ringing to stop. But it did not. His earhole continuously oozed yellow-green pus, and he felt sure that his lost ear was still there, moving. James wanted to eat and drink anything. He had not toileted for more than a week.

His shrivelled stomach, with folds of fatless skin, wobbled as he shifted his weight, trying to get comfortable without siding on where his ear once was. He lay on his back, coughing hard; with each one, his pains drew a cringe, and his head pounded more.

James woke from a shaft of daylight coming through the timbers, seemingly aiming for his left eye. As he blinked, the door of the cabin was unlocked and in came the short man.

"It is time. We will go to the market to sell you now that another boat has arrived with potential buyers. You are lucky they have come, for we usually see only two or three boats every year here," spoke the man. "Get up. Here, let me cut those ropes from your wrists and ankles."

James sat up slowly and outstretched his arms as the man cut the rope, then did the same around his feet.

"Now, get up and put this cloth around your waist; no one wants to see that shrivelled piss shooter," laughed the man.

Outside, the sky was a brilliant blue, and it was already hot despite the sun being up, he guessed for only an hour. James wrapped the red and blue patterned cloth around his waist, struggling to fasten it. He wanted to get away and run but had little strength, so he resigned himself to follow instructions, for he did not want to lose his other ear or something even worse.

He climbed into the cage, two men sat with him, watching him closely. His pains grew more assertive the further they ventured, as did the ringing in his head. The track was primarily sandy and well rutted, making progress slow. There was little cover from the sun; only an occasional group of palms provided shade. James began to sob quietly, tasting his salty sweat and tears.

When the sun was directly overhead, the cart stopped at the edge of a half-moon shaped beach, about a mile long. Out in the water, he saw a small ship and did a double take.

"The *Frostenden Nave*, surely not? It burned and sank," whispered James.

He could not believe his eyes and blinked several times slowly to try to refocus. He was sure it was his ship.

Another colourfully dressed man, who he estimated was over six feet tall, bought James at the market. The tall man bought four other men, including Everett. James had no idea how much he paid; no one spoke English. Although unspoken, through their stealthy yet friendly demeanour, James reasoned the lofty man and Solroy had known each other forever and a day.

Hands roughly tied, the five men staggered to a sizeable, caged cart and were pushed up one by one. A wooden cup and a pail of water awaited them; they drank it all eagerly. Two other men and the tall man sat upfront while six skinny men grabbed ropes and started to pull the assembled wagon.

They arrived on another half-moon-shaped white sand beach lined with many tall palm trees about an hour later. James tried to readjust his eyes; the beach was a fabulous pristine sight; however, he quickly came to his senses as the cart jolted to a stop.

"Off," the tall man said, looking at James. "Tell me, what happened to your ear?"

James was stunned again.

"You speak my tongue," he said to the tall man.

"Yes. Answer my question," the tall man demanded. "If you ever ask a question and refuse to answer mine, you will lose another piece of your body. Make no mistake."

"The short man cut it off," stated James. "Yes, I will do as you say."

"Good. My name is Ohama Boyce, and you may call me only Ohama," said the tall man. "What is your name, and how did you get here to these islands?"

All five men were now out of the cart. One of the other men cut off the ropes around their wrists.

"James Thacker, from Southwold England. We came on the *Frostenden Nave* commanded by George Everett, headed for Kandy," said James.

"My goodness, man. You were way, way off course. Unless you intended to stop at these fine islands before heading to southern India?" replied Ohama.

"The Maldives. These are lonely islands," said James.

"You have no idea, do you?" snorted Ohama. "These are the British Indian Islands. We're over *six hundred* miles due south of the outermost Maldives and about twice that to get to Kandy."

"Oh, Everett!" retorted James, "Master of the seas."

Everett said nothing, controlling his physical response and pretending not to hear the conversation. He was astounded they were so far off the course he had carefully navigated. How could he have miscalculated so seriously, he wondered?

James was still in shock, not from his wounds but the man in front of him, speaking English and treating him with a level of respect James had rarely experienced. James was confused, though. Was it his ship off the beach he saw two days ago? He swore it had gone up in smoke and to the ocean's depths.

His headache was no better. Pus occasionally dripped from his ear, down his cheek and into the corner of his mouth. It was such an awful whiff and taste. He observed his reflection at the water's edge; the sea was a dead calm. He could vaguely see a blackness around his left earhole. It was almost dry to the touch now, although inside was soft, spongy, and tender. The cut wounds had healed, but the ringing in his head was almost deafening and distracted James from just about everything. He could not remember sleeping for many days; he was utterly exhausted.

Later that afternoon, James and Everett were sitting on the beach with no one else around. James gently washed for the first occasion in goodness knows how long; the water was warm, crystal clear but tasted of salt-pickled herrings. It mattered not; he welcomed the freedom Ohama had given him and the other men. Still, they talked in a whisper.

"Everett, regardless of your awful sense of direction, did you recognise our ship in the market's beach?" said James, laughing at first.

"Well, that ship was some distance out, but yes, I believe it to be the *Frostenden Nave*," answered Everett.

"But how? I saw it flamed and bellowing," said James.

"Me too," continued Everett. "We'll know for sure when we see it again. Ohama seems reasonable, we need to encourage him to show us, but I fear we need to bargain some away."

"We have nothing to bargain with now. Everything I owned was either on that boat or is *that* boat," snapped James.

"Ah, I would not be so sure about that, my deafened friend," laughed Everett.

--x--

James's teeth were rotting. A large abscess had formed at the back of his jaw, opposite his lost ear. He was finding it difficult to talk through the pain and swelling. He slept on his back, not wanting to put any pressure on his bulging neck. He felt with his tongue a jagged tooth and a newly erupting one behind it. He set off pains that racked his whole head and through his old earhole.

He was angry; he felt minor discomfort from his missing ear, and now this.

"When will my pains go away?" he kept asking himself.

James spent his time wandering along the beach, from one end of the crescent to the other; its beauty now lost on him.

"Where is Charles? Had he survived the pirates, and if so, where is he now?" said James aloud.

He had no answers; neither did his new owner.

"Just get me to Kandy," he mentioned that evening.

Ohama pretended to ignore him.

He had seen James's face grow red whenever he goaded him on.

"And for goodness' sake, please help me with the pain in my neck," continued James.

Again, Ohama just sat, saying nothing.

As James stood, the fermented coconut liquor they drank took a firm hold; his legs folded. His reactions were not quick enough for his hands to protect him, and he fell flat on his face. His head clipped a rock. Another tooth went flying out of his mouth.

"For the love of God, why me?" he screamed as he spat out a sticky stream of blood.

Ohama did not move, but he worried that his market purchase was going mad, although he knew he was partly to blame for that.

The pains in James's head and swelling around his neck slowly drifted away over the next two weeks. A large green and deep yellow bruise covered one side of his collar. The spot where his missing teeth once were, remained tender. He had taken to moving his jaw to one side as he could not and did not want any food trapped inside, as that sparked the dull lingering pains again.

--x--

# 14

## Por, Charles?

His tedious routine of fishing, walking, waiting, and sleeping lasted four weeks. His skin was now burnt from exposure to the sun and cracked from seawater and salty air. With his shirt and breeches shredded and the soles of his feet raw, he felt hot sand sting through his holey boots. Charles had no protection from the elements despite frantic searches around the island and painful cliff climbs. His earlier headache had reduced, although he often woke before sunrise, still throbbing.

The woman and four men found him lying face-down on the sand. A man poked Charles's back with a stick. His body flinched, then he waved his arms behind his back. But at least he moved. The men grabbed him roughly, carried him to one of the kayaks and knotted his hands before Charles realised what was happening. He sat quietly in shock. The woman climbed in and sat facing him. She placed her stick firmly in Charles's groin and cracked a toothless smile. Charles remained dead still.

The woman constantly scooped water from the canoe as waves repeatedly covered them despite a fearsome amount of rowing, pausing only to ride down the most significant waves. After a jarring three hours, they approached the coral-fringed island. Despite his precarious position, Charles could not hold his smile on seeing people on the beach waiting for them. Shouts went back and forth in an unknown language, then a cheer.

Charles's head pains restarted.

"Finally, I will eat something other than raw fish and not take hours catching it," he muttered under his breath, only for the woman to smack his face hard.

They drifted over the reef, and a breaker took them onto the shallow beach. The old lady finally removed her stick and pushed Charles off the boat. His legs buckled. He fell headfirst into the water, somersaulted, and landed face up in the water.

The lady cackled loudly, and the man rower said, "I would get up if I were you. She has a filthy temper and does not tolerate weakness."

The leg tasted fantastic, steeped in a porky broth. Charles devoured the beast and rice in seconds. After the hiccups stopped, he belched loudly; the old lady giggled with pleasure.

"More?" he pleaded, and the woman slapped some more rice on the banana leaf along with a slab of pigskin.

Charles did not stop eating for an hour. His regular burps were the cause of great laughter between the males too. The big pot continued to bubble away, but now it was only half full. The woman had just one plate of food herself and was surprised by the volume Charles tucked away.

He felt energised for the first time in over a month and thanked the lady profusely. He could hardly believe his luck. His first impressions misguided him; he had expected a rough time from the savages. The small troop of villagers had welcomed him. They were fascinated by his long black hair and scruffy beard and continually touched his features. However, she kept her stick close to his leg the whole time.

Charles was beside himself to be off his tiny island; he had given up all hope. His only comforts were in his dreams of Rose; he would often wake in a sweat. He could not understand why his thoughts were of the wife he did not love. She was so far away now.

"How would you react if you saw me now, nearly at death's door?" he said aloud. "I know you hated any signs of a beard too."

He slept in a small hut made of hardwood branches and palm leaves; it was simple, but the shack was a luxury compared to his island, where he had no shelter. He did not care for the masses of tiny flies buzzing around the hut and zeroing in on his ears; they stopped his sleep despite his exhaustion. The sun streamed through a crack in the door; the sunbeam touched his eyelids and woke him. He instinctively scratched his face but did not stop itching, his skin red-raw.

One of the men gave him a water bottle which he had finished during the earlier hours. He started to panic now, not knowing how long the hike around the island would take him. He walked for what seemed like miles. The land was almost flat, a complete contrast to his island. A narrow strip of sand circled it. Countless coconut palms fringed the beach. When he ventured slightly inland, he found a tangle of trees, appearing to have their roots growing from high in the air and spreading down into the sand. Then he found a small stream, and with a broad smile, replenished his flask. The water tasted like nectar; sweet and lightly salty; he undressed and lay in the shallow water.

He resumed his trek. Within an hour, he found the village again. The stick lady was waiting for him and cracked it across the back of his legs. He yelped; his legs buckled, and he sank to his knees.

She waved the cane towards him and shouted, “You will not wander off again. Now, pleasure me.”

Laughter rang out behind him as she led him back to the hut. Physical contact was the last thing Charles had in mind, but he had little choice. She stripped him of his rags, pushed him on the floor and jumped on top of him. Less than fifteen minutes later, they came out of the hut.

One of the men, who found Charles on the island, patted him on the shoulder and said, “Well, man, you should be so lucky. That has not happened around here for a long time. Por has taken quite a liking to you. You will be married before you know it!”

Charles ran out of the makeshift hut and paddled into the sea. There was nowhere for him to go, he knew the island was more extensive than his last one, but still, it was small. Finally, he rested and looked up at a partly black and blue sky; the sun would rise soon, he thought. Charles saw nothingness.

“Where on God’s earth am I?” he questioned aloud. “What was I thinking, leaving the safety of Southwold, my wealth and wife? I do not care for the JackFruit and its alleged diamonds. Grandpa, you have set me up, sent me on a wild chase to nowhere. There cannot be more treasure; you took it home for yourself.”

But Charles had countless second thoughts, “Why did you place the second JackFruit diamond at The Mint, Grandpa? Why leave it to your grandchild that has not been born yet?”

Charles was thoroughly confused, unsure what to believe. “I am going mad. What clues did you leave for us, old Wethersby?”

He thought about his grandfather’s dying words, unsure if he had remembered them all, saying them to himself, “Cursed. Never let one man hold it. Old Wethersby, I am sure you merely hid the JackFruit in that Kandyan cave where you first discovered it.”

He kept swimming, unaware of the woman, Por, in the water behind him, listening to his every word.

As Charles weakened, physically and mentally, Por increased her rituals. He thought he could bear the pain no more, but it intensified. His wrists and ankles were red-raw from the iron cuffs, swollen; flies laid their eggs in his wounds.

She giggled at his discomfort; it spurred her on to be extra cruel. She enjoyed her favourite leather whip cracking across his chest and groin as she demanded his arousal.

He tried desperately to detach himself from her rites, sometimes entering a trance-like state. After another lashing, he would come round, thinking he had been in the *Thatchers'* well, in place of his cousin.

He lost track of the weeks and months of his confinement.

Por had been playing with him again, screaming, waiting for him to blackout, but he resisted and laughed instead.

"Woman, when will you have had enough?" he griped, longing for it to be over before she had truly begun.

"After you and all of your clan are dead," she replied ominously. "Now shut your mouth before I stuff it for you."

He tried to lie still while looking at his wrist move as another tiny maggot broke out.

"You may be right there, but then you will lose my pleasure," he chuckled.

He fell into the *Thatchers'* well once more. Only this time, Por was there with him, her blade above his head. She cut the rope. He dropped into the water. Rayleigh's sandal floated to the surface. Charles grabbed it as a searing pain burned him across his forehead. He lay there, his eyes bulging. She stood over him, holding her shoe, and whacked it across his head.

“Stay awake, or you will receive more strokes,” she shrieked.

That night he vowed to escape her clutches.

“But how? I have so little strength left in me,” he murmured.

Early one morning, Por came to his hut and shook him violently.

“Get up. The wind has changed. You and I are leaving this place,” Por whispered.

‘But, what?” he yawned in reply.

“I want your child to grow inside me surrounded by beautiful things, not a worthless hut on a useless beach. But she may never know her father if he ever resists or fails to satisfy me again,” she said.

They drifted in the current for three days, Por prodding him gently to maintain a rhythm with the oars, but he could barely move. Por’s demeanour seemed to have changed, he thought. He studied her carefully.

“You must be over sixty years old, judging by your wrinkled, pot-marked skin and deep-set yellowed eyes. But your strength, I know rather too well. Surely you cannot be nurturing a child?” he said in his head, over and over.

“Another day or two, and we will arrive,” she lied.

He scraped another notch on the inside of the boat. Seventeen days. Several days before, he had begun to go senseless, unable to control himself, shaking violently. There was no food or water left. He fell back into the *Thatchers’* well, finding Rayleigh holding his missing shoe. When he woke, the sky had started to lighten ahead of him. She lay next to him, cold. Por was dead.

--x--

# 15

## Oasis

Rayleigh asked, "Junior, are you certain this is the place? Who can surely survive for more than a few days exposed to this heat?"

"Well, young man, by the looks of you, you will do just fine now. But our team may struggle, so we must protect them," replied Wethersby Jnr.

"Agreed," said Rayleigh.

"This great desert-like city, Grandpa would often say, shields a channel where a temporary river runs. See now, it is dry," continued Wethersby Jnr, as he pointed towards a large palace with giant entrance domes and some huts to its left.

Rayleigh was unconvinced. Was this the place their grandfather repeatedly talked about as the last point of his Indian journey? He never mentioned this grand palace.

Wethersby Jnr, eyeing Rayleigh's dismissive expression, went on, "Boyce told me that building the Azam Khan Sarai palace started around 1636. That was several years after Grandpa had left; he never knew of it."

As they neared the old jetty, Rayleigh helped Wethersby Jnr throw a thick coil of rope, at first missing the boys on the pier. The second was successful as one of the lads skilfully caught it with his foot and guided the twine around a solid looking post. Rayleigh wondered how long the dock could last, but his mind soon switched in the direction of the palace as a white puff of smoke rose from its inner wall, followed by a dull thud.

"What on earth are they doing, Junior? There are no other ships to be seen, and they did not launch upon us earlier," Rayleigh exclaimed.

"Captain, if I may, why do they fire cannon?" asked Wethersby Jnr.

"It must be noon," laughed Boyce, handing the silver compass to Rayleigh.

Sultan Aurangzeb and a large entourage welcomed Rayleigh, Wethersby Jnr, their motley gang and Boyce by the pier as they disembarked. Boyce was amazed to see the sultan himself greet them first. They had met on the last two visits to Ahmedabad, but never upon arrival, usually only after considerable persistence in obtaining a meeting in the Azam Khan Sarai palace.

Upon seeing the sultan, Boyce said to the cousins, "Be aware, here is Aurangzeb himself, the most powerful and richest man in all of northern India. Let me do the talking. Do not say a word unless asked first."

Boyce was both humbled and somewhat wary as to the sultan's motives. Then again, Boyce was sure Sultan Aurangzeb had made a very handsome profit from their last exchange of southern African ivory and a mountain of silver. Boyce made a fortune too, but not on his preceding journey. Indeed, that had nearly cost him his ship. Pirates almost overtook them in a sea-fight two days after leaving the Indian coast.

"Welcome again, Mister Willy," said the sultan, as he bowed his head but never took his eyes off the men in front of him.

"Your Majesty, *Assure Grab*. Thank you for your most dignified welcome," replied Boyce.

He was sure Sultan Aurangzeb did not understand his nickname fully; perhaps neither did Boyce understand his.

"So, who are these new men with you? Your names?" asked the sultan.

"I am Rayleigh Edwards. Here is my cousin, Wethersby Thacker Jnr. We come from England to trade in your fine country," declared Rayleigh, before Wethersby Jnr opened his mouth.

"What happened to your foot, young man?" inquired the inquisitive sultan.

"Two accidents. One when I was very young, and another onboard our good ship, just a few days out of England. I tripped on the deck while a storm raged," replied Rayleigh proudly.

"You should watch your step, now," the sultan remarked, much to Boyce and Wethersby Jnr's amusement.

"Yes, Your Majesty, I intend to, especially around these parts, for you never know who wants your back," noted Rayleigh and let out a belly roar.

The sultan immediately feigned surprise and anger. Within several seconds he too roared with laughter, much to Boyce's relief.

The crew, save a skeleton staff for security, and the sultan's company, slowly moved towards waiting elephants and their mahouts. Once the sultan's elephant had knelt, he quickly climbed and sat on his throne-like golden chair and shouted to his mahout to set off quickly. Before the last of the crew had taken their seats, the first elephants were already out of sight. Rayleigh had counted at least twenty animals, each carrying up to four men.

As they sat together holding on tightly, Rayleigh asked Boyce, “Where are the women? I have seen not one since our arrival.”

“Do not worry, young man. Soon we will have the pleasures of the sultan’s harem, I hope,” grinned Boyce. “Be careful though, do not make eyes at the sultan’s favourites, for he will have your head off before you can blink.”

“How many women are there in his harem?” asked Rayleigh. “How do we know who the sultan’s chosen ones are?”

“I have only seen inside one large room with perhaps thirty concubines, but I lost count from so many distractions,” replied Boyce.

Then Boyce’s demeanour changed to a scowl, and he cautioned, “The point is that we do not know who the sultan’s darlings are, so best wait until invited by one. Take great care. But I am getting ahead of myself. This visit may be different from my last.”

They stayed in luxury within the palace for a week, exploring the fascinating city every day, before readying for their next move east, never seeing inside the harem.

Wethersby Jnr and Rayleigh parted company with William O. Boyce and his ship with fond farewells and the promise of meeting one day again. They never asked, nor were told, what name his ‘O’ stood for. As agreed, back in the *Tower Inn*, they estimated the *North Cove’s* cargo holds and split it. However, Rayleigh and Wethersby Jnr were less bothered by the trade's accuracy and far more concerned about keeping the weight of the remaining items as low as possible for the long desert trek ahead.

The cousins' journey into the interior started well. Their caravan plodded over gentle dunes mixed with low-lying grasses and an occasional short tree for five days. Of the twenty camels, Rayleigh and Wethersby Jnr shared one; theirs seemed to take an instant dislike to them, regularly gargling, hissing, and spitting. It also had the habit of mounting another male camel ahead of them, bringing on much-welcomed laughter from the cousins and the rest of the team.

Rayleigh and Wethersby Jnr took turns sitting on the leather saddle on the single-hump animal. Before the first day was over, they retreated to rest on bales in the wooden wagon behind the frisky camel to ease their newly bruised backsides. They saw only a handful of other people and animals and slept in the open air; nights were slightly less hot than daytime.

On the sixth day, the wind picked up gradually after midday, and by sunset was a raging storm. Sand covered them, stinging their eyes and faces even when covered in colourful cloth. The camel train's pace slowed. They did not stop until it was impossible to see the unlucky camel ahead of them. The xiansheng, the caravan's leader, directed the putting up of makeshift tents by covering groups of four wagons before last-light and before the lightning began.

While assembled under canvas, brilliant sparks lit the sky above; there was no thunder. Rayleigh felt exposed for the first time since he was on the *North Cove* in a raging storm. He was unsure of the terrain around them and worried that they were the highest point. Lightning continued for what seemed like four or five hours, the bolts getting closer, then retreating, only to come at them again. They had a restless night, even after the flashing sky had died down.

Rayleigh woke, rubbing his eyes in wonder. The covering over his head had gone; he saw only a towering mound of sand.

He got up quietly, stumbling over the xiansheng and his puller, and walked out of their pit. Rayleigh was curious about why the sky was bright, but he could not see the sun, only sand.

The dune ahead of him was immense and steep. Rayleigh was eager to see how high it went and what was beyond. He knew they needed to head in an east by northeast heading, and the dune was standing in their way; it appeared endless to the north and south.

"My, how are we to navigate over or around this?" asked Rayleigh. "It's a monster."

He grappled with the sand under his feet and slowly made his way up the dune in a zigzag pattern. When he tried to go vertically up, he fell backwards, often falling further than where he had started. Rayleigh was tired by the time he got halfway. Below him, the four groups of wagons and all the camels had shrunk. He could barely count the camels individually despite their natural size. He kept on moving for an hour before reaching what he had expected to be the top of the sand mountain.

Open-mouthed, Rayleigh sat mesmerized by what was ahead of him. Dune after dune after dune and no vegetation; the vastness was a wonder. Then the realisation of what lay ahead of their caravan hit him.

"How can anyone find their way through? The sands must constantly shift, too," Rayleigh wondered aloud before he caught himself doing so.

He sat on top of the dune for an hour, tired and yet exhilarated by the emptiness ahead. Strangely, his compass needle did not stop spinning. He failed to hear the shouts from below.

Wethersby Jnr panicked when he could not find his young cousin in the tent nor around the camp.

His shouts of “Rayleigh, where on hell’s earth are you?” went unanswered.

He then spied the shifted sand marks at the dune’s base and watched as they snaked and wiggled their way up. There were no visible footprints, but he assumed that was how Rayleigh had gone, adventurous and curious as ever, and nowhere in sight.

Rayleigh sat and recalled one of his grandfather’s study sessions.

Wethersby Snr had said, “Rayleigh, the vastness of the northern Indian desert is shocking in its beauty and isolation. When a low sun catches the dunes’ tips, it is beautiful beyond comprehension. Still, when amid it with only provisions carried by camels, it can be a horrible place. Certainly, no place to hide any treasure, for the sand will shift. However, a rare oasis formed from springs could be a different matter. Oh, those oases, sometimes they are real, but others are figments of your imagination. Desert fever, they call it; madness would be a more fitting description.”

He caught himself rolling backwards and gaining speed; either he had fallen asleep or had another of his dizzy spells. He could not control his speed but managed to tuck in his legs and arms over his head. He closed his eyes as tight as he could. After what seemed like many minutes, Rayleigh eventually slowed and came to an abrupt halt.

Wethersby Jnr could not contain himself as he bent forward, howling with laughter upon seeing Rayleigh falling down the vast sand slope. The two of them were barely twenty yards from one another after Rayleigh stopped. Wethersby Jnr heard his screams when Rayleigh was about halfway down.

Rayleigh let out a giant roar. “For pity’s sake, Junior, help me, but slowly. I am not sure what I have broken. Everything aches, everything.”

“Well, young man, I suggest you try to unravel yourself first and lay on your back, then I will assist,” replied Wethersby Jnr, still laughing.

Slowly, Rayleigh moved his arms away from his face, then shifted weight onto his backside while unlocking his knees and straightening his legs.

“That was not so bad,” muttered Rayleigh. “Now help me up, Junior.”

Wethersby Jnr roughly grabbed Rayleigh’s outstretched arms and instantly pulled him up to his feet.

“You will live, Rayleigh. Now let us get going,” he hooted.

“But these dunes go on forever,” said Rayleigh. “I fear the caravan leader, Omar, knows not where to go.”

“Relax, Rayleigh. We rested from the storm by this huge sand mountain, and neither of us saw it, did we? If we had not stopped here, I am sure the sandstorm could have covered us from head to toe, and we’d be lost forever. Let us give Omar the benefit of the doubt that stopping here was not just a stroke of luck,” answered Wethersby Jnr.

He patted Rayleigh hard on his back, which covered them in a cloud of fine yellow dust.

“These dunes are never-ending, Junior. It will take weeks to get through them. It would help if you looked from the top. I will instruct Omar to have the caravan wait for you,” said Rayleigh.

“No, we need to get going. While you were tumbling down the dune, everyone woke and are now ready to set off again. There is no time for more climbing. We will see the desert ahead of us all in good time, Rayleigh,” replied Wethersby Jnr.

“Do we have enough supplies to sustain us?” asked Rayleigh. “I saw no vegetation, no sanctuary, no water.”

"Think about this. We stopped at the height of a sandstorm; this dune protected us. If Omar can navigate blind, we should have confidence that he knows where to find the next oasis and can seek it with his open eyes," stated Wethersby Jnr.

He turned and marched towards Omar and jumped up into their cart.

"Omar, we should go before the sun is too strong again. How long until we come to water? I could do with a wash," grinned Wethersby Jnr.

"Get your cousin onto his wobbly feet. It will be a week more until we wash. I advise you not to climb these dunes, for the sand can swallow camels alive, along with men and women. It is effortless to lose your sense of perspective in the desert. Tell him not to venture off on his own again, or I will proceed without him next time. Understood?" decreed Omar.

The train did not stop all day. The queue of camels, carts and men set off with the sun directly ahead of them, half-masked by a dull brown sky that thankfully held off the worst of its rays. All they saw ahead and behind them was dune after dune. As they snaked around one mountain, another would appear.

Omar would stop the camels about an hour before the last light, giving him and the men enough time to set up their camp. For one more week, this was their routine. The evenings were surprisingly cool; only once did they find enough material to keep the fire alive, after cooking rice, for the pullers to stay warm. Everyone from Southwold welcomed the cool evenings.

Supplies of dried meat, rice and water were going down rapidly, thought Rayleigh. Their frisky camel even seemed to tire from two weeks of fruitless effort. 'Humpy', as Rayleigh had nicknamed him, became even more challenging to handle. He failed to go in a straight line and often turned his head towards Rayleigh and Wethersby Jnr, spitting at them and gurgling from the depths of his giant belly.

On their fifteenth day in the desert, the dunes started to thin out and were much lower in height. The camel pullers were excited to see more than a few hundred feet ahead of them. Their initial excitement was short-lived; they could now see just sand for many miles.

At around what must have been mid-afternoon, given the angle of the lowering sun, the constant silver shimmer on the horizon gave way to palms and a camel, or so Rayleigh thought.

"Look there, Junior!" exclaimed Rayleigh as he pointed to the distance. "Palms, everywhere. See, I told you old Wethersby's green map would find us water."

Wethersby Jnr did not look forwards. It was the third time that Rayleigh claimed he pictured palms in so many days. Wethersby Jnr had one of the maps outstretched on the wagon's base anchored by rounded stones. His middle finger lay on one mark, an 'O' with the letter 'Y' inside it, one of two similar symbols in this plot section.

"We could be anywhere. The accuracy of this map is highly questionable, given the modest distance we have travelled since leaving Ahmedabad and the scale of the desert," said Wethersby Jnr.

"Water!" shouted Fredrick from the wagon behind them and added, "I see trees too."

Wethersby Jnr could scarcely believe what he heard as more shouting rang out. He saw nothing but sand and silver waves ahead of him. He folded the map slowly and carefully, tucking it back into its leather wallet, and joined Rayleigh looking forward, holding his hand above his eyes. Omar said nothing; his broad smile showed his rotting yellow and red-stained teeth.

As they approached, Rayleigh watched the palms disappear, saying, “Where did they go?”

The disappointment, and building desperation, after another false sighting had worn Rayleigh down mentally. Physically he was well enough, his early travel wounds now all but healed, and his dizzy spells were much less frequent. He ached from the buffeting of the cart; his legs bruised in many places. He had taken to sitting on the camel’s saddle for prolonged periods despite the discomfort to his backside. It relieved some of the boredom, and importantly, gave him a better view of the horizon.

Their camel had given up his futile quest and had settled down to a constant pace, rocking Rayleigh gently back and forth. Rayleigh felt sure the animal was happier with him on his hump.

“You are a strange beast. How do you not eat or drink for so many days?” Rayleigh asked of the puller, and the camel blubbered as if by way of an acknowledgement.

The caravan had been plodding the sand for nearly twenty days with no end in sight. The sun had got, if anything, more potent in the last two days. It led Omar to wake them and set off before sunrise, pausing for several hours on either side of midday. He would always stop about an hour before sundown to set up camp afresh.

Fredrick suddenly shouted, “Trees at three o’clock.”

Wethersby Jnr jumped to his feet and cried, “Yes, I see them too. Rayleigh, what do you think?”

“No, nothing more to see from up here, just silver streaks in the sand again,” moaned Rayleigh, rubbing his eyes to refocus. “But, maybe, just maybe, Fredrick is right this time.”

The caravan made its way towards the mirage ahead. As they drew closer, the palmtops disappeared briefly, only to reappear more vivid than before. The camels' pace quickened, so too their drooling and bellowing.

About five hundred yards from the sanctuary, Wethersby Jnr jumped from the moving cart, falling clumsily. Picking himself up, he ran hard. Most of the other Southwold men followed.

Rayleigh shouted, "Stop this beast."

Omar ignored him.

Rayleigh was almost thrown from his saddle as the camel started to gallop, then ran hard. They soon reached the edge of the refuge. High dunes partly encircled the palms, Rayleigh counted at least forty stumps and looked in awe at the palms' height and the fruits dangling from below their tops.

The pond was modest, perhaps fifty feet across. All the camels were drinking steadily. Rayleigh sat in his perch, smiling; he could not get down unaided unless the camel buckled its legs.

The men laughed and shouted as they approached the camels, sinking to their knees at the water's edge, cupping their hands and drinking heavily. The water was brackish yet sweet; it mattered not. The men stripped bare and plunged in. Omar stood at the edge and strained on Rayleigh's camel chain; it dropped onto its front knees allowing Rayleigh to clamber off; he joined the rest of the men.

A sizeable fire burned in the middle of the camp circle Omar created from the wagons. Orange embers smouldered and slowly consumed the palm trunk.

"Omar. How long are we to stay in this beautiful spot?" asked Rayleigh.

"We should rest the animals and ourselves for another day and night. Apart from the palms and water, there is nothing else to keep us here. We have another week of shifting sands before we reach the next haven. It is smaller than this, obscured in a large gully, so is easily missed," smiled Omar.

"Do we have enough food for another week or more?" asked Rayleigh.

Looking up, Omar pointed at the round green-black balls high up in the nest of a palm above their heads and said, "Maybe, if we can harvest some tan from the tall palms. It is not easy to collect but very sweet to eat, rather like young coconut. We are lucky, for the tan are ripe for only two months of every year. You shall see in the morning."

Rayleigh thought the orbs were like blackened coconut. Although, these palms were taller than any he had seen back in Ahmedabad and on the island of Mauritius.

All the animals and men slept solidly that night, except Rayleigh. His mind kept returning to Omar's words about the next oasis being a week away. Consumed, he studied the oversized green atlas page, trying to remember whether he or Wethersby Snr had drawn the three tree symbols. The last sign was much further away than the other two; indeed, remoter than the first one at Ahmedabad.

"Could Pa have stashed some of the gems here?" he asked himself. "Surely these moving sands would make it hard to conceal or impossible to find again? There are no clues on the map either."

He closed his eyes as he tried to remember one of the evening stories. His mind was blank; he could only see stars behind his darkness.

He woke sharply; it was still dark. The only stirring came from a grumbling camel. He lay on his back, studying the brilliance of the night's sky and its magnitude. Never had he seen so many stars in all his life. The tiniest sliver of the new moon was barely visible close to the horizon. The sky began to turn from black to deep blue at the top of the camp's dunes. Then it came to him. In the month of his harvest at the Blakes' farm, they talked about the ageing chestnut tree in the field where Rayleigh would often lie beneath. His grandfather recited how he dug around the base of a large desert tree with green, shallow roots and found a hidden box.

Rayleigh walked around the oasis in the morning, secretly hoping to find a collapsed palm and root for scrutiny. However, the only one he found had been firewood from the night before. He guessed where it had fallen and kicked at the sand for fifteen minutes, out of sight from the camp.

He found nothing other than small pieces of root wood, despite digging down several feet. There was no remaining stump. The other palms appeared healthy, upright, and all were very tall; he thought it odd that there were no young trees.

Walking back to the wagons, he found Omar and asked him softly, "How old do you think these trees are?"

"Mister Rayleigh, I expect they are sixty years old, maybe more," replied Omar, pointing at one of the tallest palms. "Look at that big one; it is probably one hundred."

Rayleigh nodded his head and probed, "Why are there no young trees?"

"Palms. Well, the sand is fine and bone dry, except around the water hole. These fruits are tough and firm, and unless they drop close to the water and do not dry out completely or get waterlogged, they have a chance to sprout. Even if they shoot, they need some water to survive. The water comes and goes from here, for I have never seen the pond the same size," responded Omar, enjoying giving Rayleigh a lesson.

"I expect the pond was much larger when many of these palms took root. See how many are the same height, with all set back from the biggest pond ring," continued Omar.

"What ring?" Rayleigh asked.

Omar got up and walked towards the pool and said, "Look here at these small pieces of wood; watch how they roughly circle the pond. And can you see where the water's rim was before we arrived?"

Rayleigh nodded as he walked closer to the edge; he spotted another ring where the water had retreated about one foot.

"Did Pa bury some of his treasure out here, and if so, why?" he wondered.

Rayleigh woke early again.

Wethersby Jnr stood over him and said, "Rayleigh, I have never heard you talk in your sleep before. What is *burning chang*?"

"I have no idea, Junior," lied Rayleigh, concealing his nightmare.

It was the first time he remembered his vision since he was a boy. He got up quickly, his face and body wet from sweat, ignoring Wethersby Jnr, and walked into the pond. The water was instantly refreshing and helped Rayleigh hide his mannerisms. Wethersby Jnr followed him in.

The caravan continued its journey northeast for eight more days; the euphoria of the previous shelter was now a distant memory. Boredom set in again. Rayleigh counted the days.

"One week until we reach the next sanctuary, Omar promised," said Rayleigh. "We are in the middle of nowhere with only sand and an occasional snake for company, other than this troupe. He is late."

"Come on, Rayleigh," replied Wethersby Jnr, "There can be no truth out here. There is never a path; the sands shift. It is best to think of this as more of a meander. From the sun's angle, we are heading northeast, towards the castle in the sand, just as the sultan explained to us."

The compass needle kept spinning.

# 16

## Second palms

The endless greyish-yellow scenery, the lack of green grass, trees or, for that matter, anything but the sand had made the cousins slightly delirious. They ached for variation, yet they had enough water and dried food, plus a few tans. They were not hungry but wanted something more.

That evening the men were restless, and the camels blubbered constantly. A wind had begun to rise from the west, and the sand was shifting again. Soon the wagon wheels were half submerged. The wooden carts partly shielded the men, and they had their faces covered. More tiny particles peppered and stung their skin through fabric masks.

Omar signalled to one of his pullers to see to the camels. He came back after fifteen minutes, visibly shaking and exhausted.

He muttered something, barely audible in Hindi, and was immediately struck with a large stick and let out a yelp. Omar struck him ten times in all until the man collapsed and passed out. The sand blackened around him from blood oozing from cuts across his back and legs. The camels continued to grunt.

The storm shrouded the camp completely that night. Wethersby Jnr had his arms over his head and crouched behind Rayleigh. Like a pack of wolves, a strange and eerie howling increased to where Rayleigh felt his eardrums were going to burst.

Wethersby Jnr shouted, "Why did we take your bait, Grandpa?"

Rayleigh missed his words.

None of the men slept well that night. Rayleigh convinced himself that he had not slept, rising that morning, covered in dusty sweat and utterly exhausted. The wind had eased, although the sand still moved. The temperature was fresher than at any time since the caravan set out.

It took over two hours to dig out the wagons and get moving once again. Despite their difficult night, the camels seemed to pick up their pace; Rayleigh and Wethersby Jnr grimaced as their bruised backsides shouted out for the punishment to stop. Rayleigh imagined their camel had purposefully started to run.

Rayleigh came round, seeing Wethersby Jnr's face at ninety degrees, silhouetted by the sun. Dazed, Rayleigh tried to lift his head, but he could barely shift an inch.

"Best not move, Rayleigh, for you had a terrific fall from our wagon," said Wethersby Jnr, almost laughing. "Try to keep still for some minutes more while we find what, if anything, you have broken or lost this time."

As Wethersby Jnr budged, the sun blinded Rayleigh with its glare. He lifted his head, instantly regretting the movement. A deep pain rose from the middle of his back to his neck and out of his nose. He winced, his eyes tight, mouth open and teeth clenched.

"How, Junior?" sighed Rayleigh.

"Our camel decided to go off copulating again, jolting the wagon as the cart bounced into a rut; it sent you flying. Look at our wagon. I think you will agree it came off worse for the experience," laughed Wethersby Jnr.

Rayleigh coughed as the pain rocked him once again. He lay in the sand for thirty minutes, unwilling to shift and flatly refused to be touched.

When he did get to his feet, unaided, Rayleigh saw that both wagon wheels had splintered, their rims broken in at least four places. It would be going no further with them. The frisky camel sat motionless, his chin resting on the sand with its legs splayed out. For a moment, Rayleigh thought the camel was dead, but it let out a low sigh and hiss.

By late afternoon of the tenth day since leaving the oasis, Wethersby Jnr surmised that they had travelled for at most thirty miles. Rayleigh's fall and the fruitless efforts to mend the wagon delayed them considerably. They stopped for the evening and began to make camp. The wind was no longer blowing. Rayleigh was barely moving, although thankful the caravan had stopped.

He and Wethersby Jnr were sharing separate wagons now. James had been caring for Rayleigh at his request, while Fredrick joined Wethersby Jnr at the head. Rayleigh slept heavily that night and again woke full of sweat. His back was sore, but the shooting pains had gone; his previous boredom, forgotten.

Two hours of travelling later, and the camels unexpectedly began to canter. Rayleigh felt the wagon shudder as he remained lying on the wagon's board. James gently knelt on his legs as Rayleigh held onto ropes with both hands. They slowly rose an incline. Soon they were coming down the other side, and screams let out as the wagons' pace quickened.

"Sanctuary. Trees. Water," he said.

The caravan rested after the animals and men had gorged themselves on crystal clear yet slightly salty water. Most of them were asleep, the wagons again covered in canvas.

"It must be only midday," whispered Rayleigh.

He slowly walked around the water's edge, his hand shielding his eyes. The pool was no more than half the size of the previous oasis.

The palms were set back further; they were the same type and height as those growing at the last pond. In their centre crowns hung familiar large green-black tan nuts.

Rayleigh traced a faint watermark close to the palm's stumps and followed it around the pool. He stopped at a fallen palm; its branches entangled in the stump of another. He guessed it must have been one of the tallest before it dropped. A large mound of sand sat at its base; tiny twig flecks surrounded the pile. Rayleigh started to rub his feet into the sand, kicking it away. Over thirty minutes, he slowly and painfully exposed the embedded stump, and with his hands, continued to move as much of the sand from within it as he could.

He sat next to the stump, exhausted and unable to speak, spellbound, for an hour. Rayleigh eventually passed out. A small bluish-silver casket lay glistening in the sun, half-buried but firmly stuck within the root's base.

Wethersby Jnr patted Rayleigh's slumped shoulder. The shooting back pain returned.

Clenching his teeth, Rayleigh said, "Thank you, Junior. Now please, will you stop creating my pains. Look here. Fetch a shovel and a pick with stealth."

Dumbfounded, his cousin started to scratch with fingers around the shiny casket; it did not move. He returned with a hatchet and an outstretched arm.

Rayleigh said with authority, "This one is for me to uncover, Junior. Hand it over."

Wethersby Jnr reluctantly gave the axe to Rayleigh, shocked by his tone. Rayleigh tried hard to prise the box by gently chopping around it, not wanting to make too much noise to avoid a gathering. After several minutes he had it out of the root in his hands.

A blued silver box, crushed in its centre, so much so that the top and bottom were almost touching. One corner had buckled.

Rayleigh stared at the box, trying to remember his grandfather's words, or had he dreamt them? He was no longer sure. Wethersby Jnr stood over Rayleigh, shaking his head.

The once ornate box was about twelve inches wide and six inches deep. It had no lock nor apparent seams.

"How did you know, Rayleigh?" asked Wethersby Jnr curiously. "There is nothing on the green map."

"I remember Grandpa telling me one evening, maybe three years ago, I am not exactly sure," reacted Rayleigh, smiling. "Let's get it open."

They spent ten minutes trying not to smash the box. The axe added several more dents, clearly too big for the task. Wethersby Jnr went to his wagon and brought back a short, curved dagger. Using the tip, he tried in vain to dislodge the casket but nicked himself in the middle of his hand.

"Junior. Let me try again," requested Rayleigh.

The dagger was razor-sharp and surprisingly heavy. Rayleigh dug into the broken corner and twisted the knife gingerly as he held the box with the base of his four-toed foot. The blade suddenly slipped, narrowly missing his stump, the box flew in the air, landing back in the palm pit.

Fetching it, Rayleigh saw the box was almost in two pieces; a brown parchment poked out of it. His hands trembled as he carefully removed the animal skin, sat down next to Wethersby Jnr and read out the faded manuscript.

*"You have done well to find me.*
*You have travelled far. Are you ready for more?*
*For there are many clues to uncover before discovering the prize you seek. A fortune cursed.*
*Take those around you who want their hands burnt first.*
*But remember my words, that I have not yet spoken; haunting and all that.*
*Plot your course. Continue to the airless hills.*
*You understand the way already.*
*Wethersby L Thacker 5th November 1632."*

Both men could scarcely believe the words written in their grandfather's scripted hand. Even the ink had a green tint.

Omar sat smiling, watching the two men, taking in their words. He was confused upon hearing what Wethersby had written.

He muttered, "But Wethersby had not been born. This note is more than sixty years old. It is such a small object; I nearly missed the sanctuary, after all. And anyway, how did Rayleigh know where to look? What and where next?"

Omar crept to the camp and ordered the pullers to quickly fill all the pots and ready the camels and wagons. He told them they were not staying overnight.

"Onward to Jaisalmer, the castle in the sand," he shouted.

The cousins returned soon after, seeing men approaching them with water pots; Rayleigh was confused by the dismantled camp's sight. They found Omar.

"What is going on. Surely we need to rest at least one night?" Wethersby Jnr probed.

"No!" Omar replied and said nothing more to the cousins.

They travelled all night, for once. Rayleigh thought it wise to do so. The sand was virtually flat, the vast dunes gone, and a cooling breeze was enough to refresh them, yet not enough to blow sand into their nostrils again. Rayleigh was exhausted, and his dizziness returned, his right hand both numb and painful from pins and needles. Bitterness from his nausea began to build. His self-doubt for maintaining the journey returned once more. The constant grinding of the wagon's movement on his bruised back he ignored; numb like his hand, he thought.

The train snaked through the desert for another week, stopping soon after midday and sheltering under canvas from the worst of the sun's rays. The whole troop slept through until sunset when the caravan would roll forward anew. They had not met another soul. Then again, Rayleigh thought, how could anyone see another party unless they stumbled directly upon them? While the wind had kept at bay, and the nights were brilliantly clear, it was a gruelling part of the trek. Omar would often gaze to the heavens, shaking his head briefly.

Rayleigh lay on his back, wide awake. He made out the moon's crescent low on the horizon, despite the sun having another couple of hours to set. He watched as the moon rose gradually, and the sliver became brighter after the sun eventually went down.

Rayleigh's thoughts transported him back to the Blakes' farm in Southwold and his barley hay barn. Every fourth week he would finish his work early, creep into the barn to watch the new moonrise, much like now, except the stars were aligned differently. He laughed at the thought, as many an English dusk would be cloudy. He was often unable to see his favourite regular event, but here in the desert, it was crystal clear.

The camp stirred, and soon they were bumping along the invisible track ahead. Rayleigh noticed Omar correcting the camel's direction, keeping the new moon in sight ahead of them. For another ten days, their routine continued as the moon's rays gradually lit up and sparkled off the sand.

The elongated shadows from the camels and wagons appeared to snake and wander over the dunes, catching their different heights. The silhouettes shortened as the nights wore on and then lengthened until the moon was low and yellowed and disappeared altogether. Rayleigh began to realise that he enjoyed a new moonrise and a crystal-clear full-moon night more than anything else. Those evenings took his mind off the arduous trip, so much so that he began to relish them, not only for the cooling dry air.

Jolting him from his thoughts, Wethersby Jnr slapped Rayleigh hard on his back.

"Junior, are you intending to give me a permanent injury?" laughed Rayleigh with a grimace.

"Cousin, what do you see in the sky? You are always looking upwards," asked Wethersby Jnr, whacking his hand again on Rayleigh's shoulder, ignoring the younger man's pleas.

"It fascinates me, that is all. Do you not see the magical beauty in the night's sky? Now even the moonlight is so strong it creates a giant camel's shadow. Look!" burst out Rayleigh, pointing left at the snaking image.

Wethersby Jnr pretended interest. He was desperately restless, bored, and hungry for fresh food. These nights were drawn out for him, seemingly increasing in length, despite their real shortening nature.

"Now stop testing me with your slapping. You are starting to act like your youngest brother," continued Rayleigh.

Wethersby Jnr went bright red, not that he knew it, nor could Rayleigh see either. He never heard Rayleigh mock him so and just sat speechless, lifting his head towards the moon.

Another night and half-day travelling along the sands ended after they cleared the summit of a small hill.

Fredrick let out a cry, "A huge castle, two o'clock!"

"Jaisalmer," shouted Omar and added, "the castle in the sand."

Ahead of them, Rayleigh could hardly believe his eyes. A castle, just like old Wethersby and Omar had promised. The city walls stood frighteningly tall, ornate in their design, even from a distance. Small archways covered the top along its width, a massive gate in its middle.

It took what seemed like an eternity for Wethersby Jnr to reach the gate; in reality, it was barely half an hour.

Oddly, Rayleigh thought, there were no people to greet them before the gate. Instead, Omar drew a wooden mallet from a recess, knocking it hard against the giant door three times. Nothing happened. He hammered twice more.

Resting for a week, they feasted on semi-dried dates, spicy goat stews and dried camel meat while admiring the heavy sandstone walls of the numerous city buildings. Wherever they ventured, the whites of children's and adults' eyes never left them. Several of the Southwold men begged to stay longer. Wethersby Jnr soon stopped their bickering, reminding them how far they had come already and what riches remained undiscovered. None stayed behind.

--x--

A heavily creased plot from the atlas, unfolded again, flapped in the wind on the wagon's deck. Wethersby Jnr worried that it was becoming damaged and problematic to read in places; some symbols were wearing away at its folds. Making a decent replica had been out of the question, or so he thought. But it was massive, heavily detailed and the only copy they possessed. They carried a small quantity of writing material; goose quills and several pots of stinking green ink, but they found no suitably large parchment in Jaisalmer.

As the convoy plodded along the grains, the sun beat men into delirium. The wind continued to blow sand horizontally and into tiny seamless cracks of their masks and faces. Wethersby Jnr's mouth was bone-dry, his tonsils like a sabre's edge, his eyes virtually closed, raw from inadvertent rubbing.

Earlier that morning, Omar pronounced that they were a mere two days from the major city, Jodhpur. He vividly described the walls of the grand palace and most other modest buildings painted in vivid blues and white.

"It is like nothing you had seen before - like a giant waved island in a sea of sand," he reminisced.

Wethersby Jnr desperately wanted to find parchment and begin copying the plot before it was too late. He thought the smudged emblem next to the name '*Jodhpur*' could be another oasis or something more sinister.

"Maybe it is a cutlass dripping green blood?" he whispered.

Frowning, Rayleigh asked, "Junior, you have been mostly quiet these last days. What have you been thinking?"

Wethersby Jnr froze, staring at the dagger's mark.

"Junior?" repeated Rayleigh.

The island rose, then sand swallowed it yet again. Ten minutes later, an outline of a vast blued fort became more evident through the haze. Rayleigh was surprised how close to the city they had come. As the group moved slowly forward, the prodigious settlement's outline grew broader and more profound. Before reaching the city's tall brick wall, and unlike their silent arrival at Jaisalmer, a cluster of welcoming children came running to them.

"Food. Water, masters," they screamed.

Omar drew a long knife, waving it above his head, scattering the children from the hooves of his camels.

Rayleigh reached down, his open water container in hand, and gave it to a young girl nearest to him.

"Here is mine. Sorry, no more," Rayleigh croaked.

The girl's smile beamed as she snapped the leather bottle from his hand and gulped down a mouthful before her friends quickly swamped her. In the melee, the flask dropped to the ground and emptied. She forced herself upon one of the taller boys, pushing him hard to the earth, and clutched the soiled bottle from the floor.

"Thank you. My apologies, mister," she begged, reaching up as she handed back the canteen.

Rayleigh studied the girl for some moments. She was, he guessed, ten years old. The sunlight glistened off her short jet-black hair, all the while her dark green eyes fixed on him. Her smile captivated him, along with her feistiness in front of the group of mostly boys. He smiled broadly towards the girl and nodded as Omar moved the caravan forward and through the gates.

# 17

# Mister Wethersby

An overriding smell within the inner walls took Rayleigh by surprise; he choked continuously for several minutes. A spicy, pungent odour and light smoke had surrounded the procession. Many of the Southwold men joined Rayleigh in the pepper frenzy.

Rayleigh's throat became so hoarse that he could not swallow. A painful and warm lump in his throat began to move, settling in the middle of his rib cage. He jumped from the wagon, holding his hands to his chest. He tripped at the back of the camel train, stopping in front of the water girl, his face red, unable to speak.

She smacked his back with such a force that Rayleigh slumped to the ground, surprised by her strength. He coughed again as phlegm shot from his mouth, and a droplet of blood dribbled off his lips. He was breathing from his nose but in agony from heavy pressure inside his chest. His eyes bulged. She saw his bloodshot eyes as he tried to speak, but no words came out.

"No talk," she said softly. "Come over here quickly, away from the cauldron."

A short old lady, with a heavy bent back, offered Rayleigh her hand. They crawled thirty feet before he stopped, gasping for breath once more. He took the cup of steaming liquid and brought it to his mouth. Hesitating, he looked to the girl, who smiled and nodded. Rayleigh smelt honey as he then sipped at the sharp yet sweet tea, wincing as he swallowed as gently as possible. He drank the warm liquid slowly from the cracked cup, each mouthful lightly soothing his throat until it was empty.

"Thank you," he managed, bowing to the hunchback. "More, please?"

The lady shuffled away, and within a minute, had returned with more. He drank slowly, trying not to scald his lips. The lump in his chest had mellowed somewhat by the time he finished the second drink; he felt relaxed and calm, although wheezing heavily.

"At least I can breathe," he muttered and smiled towards the hunched old lady.

"Great-grandma Gooty, what do you think of him?" asked the little girl. "For he is very handsome for an odd-toed boy. I will get my ma."

"You look rather familiar," asserted Gooty. "But that was a long time ago, and my memory's shot. Never mind."

"No, carry on. What is it?" posed Rayleigh.

"Do you know Mister Wethersby?" tempted Gooty.

A beautiful young woman held Rayleigh's head. He had been lying on his back for over thirty minutes, having passed out after hearing the old lady. Wethersby Jnr knelt next to him. The old lady and child had disappeared.

"But who are you? How do you…?" he slurred, then fell back into a deeper sleep.

Two days later, Rayleigh woke. He looked around the small, red-bricked room, disorientated. He lay on a cold floor covered in brightly coloured mosaic tiles of whites, blues and dotted with orange. The young woman lay on a cloth beside him, asleep. He swallowed, instantly regretting it. His mouth was scorched; Rayleigh thought daggers were poking at the back of this throat.

They left the room and walked outside; the older woman soon joined them. Rayleigh could not believe his good fortune. He had never considered himself lucky.

Jodhpur was a vast city of wonderful blue painted buildings, minarets, and the fort. The intense heat, though, seemed worse than in the desert, thought Wethersby Jnr.

Rayleigh gently asked the old lady, "Mister Wethersby, that is a strange name. How did you come across this man?"

"Ah, you know him. I can tell from your wide eyes. Yes, we met fifty or more years ago, I am sure, on this very street. We drank tea," replied Gooty, her eyes widening.

Rayleigh sat stunned, willing the lady to continue, but she stopped.

"What did he look like?" probed Rayleigh.

"Mister Wethersby had long black hair. He was tall and handsome, very much like you two. Are you brothers? Who is Mister Wethersby to you?" asked Gooty.

"Seeing as very few people go by that name, I say the man you met all those years ago was our grandpa. I am Wethersby Junior. This is my cousin Rayleigh Edwards," smiled Wethersby Jnr. "How fortunate we have met each other. Indeed, this is fate."

The two women and men strolled to an open charcoal cauldron, bubbling with a brown liquid.

"Chai? Please try more, Rayleigh. It is sweet, tasty and will soothe your throat," said the young woman. "I am Mayling."

They locked eyes for the briefest of moments; Rayleigh tongue-tied.

At first, the chaiwallah poured tea from a clay cup held high into another cup arranged at her waist. She repeated the pouring process three times, without spilling a drop, before offering one cup to each of them.

"This chai is good," exclaimed Rayleigh. "So sweet."

"Please tell us about Mister Wethersby," said Wethersby Jnr, as he jerked Rayleigh with an elbow.

The men listened, sipping their tea slowly, trying to make it last forever, as the old lady recollected the encounters with their grandfather.

"Mister Wethersby travelled with three others, two young men and a woman. They were heading west to the great ocean for passage to England," Gooty began to tell her story. "Mister Wethersby looked yellow and sick. He kept scratching his leg and looking down at his calloused hands. He rambled on about lights and ancient rock pools. I did not understand everything he said, nor can I remember every word now, for this was a long time ago."

They occasionally nodded as the old lady continued, "He spoke about a huge jackfruit he found around a shrine in a southern Kandyan city. He said it contained riches beyond imagination, but that it was an evil discovery, the substance of nightmares."

She paused regularly to take her tea. When all their cups were empty, she asked for more chai.

She then spoke again, this time more slowly. "Mister Wethersby's eyes lit up whenever the woman, Maylong, spoke. She was born in Kandy. He said they were to be married in England. She wore a simple yet heavy silver chain around her neck with a huge saffron stone lying between her deep valley.

The sun followed the jewel; its reflection blinded me countless times, for it was hard not to stare at its beauty. It appeared to be a chiselled piece of old round glass, cut into a thousand tiny faces. All men viewed the beauty; perhaps they were eying what lay next to the stone too?"

The old lady, Gooty, talked for another hour. They each consumed three more cups of tea. Rayleigh was feeling better. He was not sure whether that was the tea, the story of his grandfather, or being in the presence of the beautiful Mayling. He kept shaking his head.

"This is such a vast continent and city. Your child found us, and we found your grandmother and now you. How is this possible?" asked Rayleigh as he touched her hand. "You have a remarkably similar name to my grandma."

Mayling did not answer. She shifted on the mat, faced Rayleigh, smiled and kissed him quickly yet softly. Rayleigh's heart raced, unsure of what to do next. She kissed him again; this time, she did not let go of his lips. Slowly, Rayleigh raised his hands and touched her cheeks.

Gooty desperately wanted to share her story, but she was concerned that the two young men might be imposters. She needed to identify that the men were truly Mister Wethersby's grandsons, but how? They seemed too young, she thought. Was it possible that Mister Wethersby could still be alive? She so wanted to divulge her blessed secret.

Rayleigh and Mayling continued caressing. He had never been so close and intimate with a woman; indeed, he could not think of anyone more beautiful. Rayleigh stopped suddenly, surprising Mayling.

"Yes!" Rayleigh suddenly blurted out. "That is where I have seen you before, but it was so long ago. The painting of you no longer exists, burnt like everything else in my father's room."

"What is it, Rayleigh? Who has burned?" whispered Mayling.

"Ah, it is nothing. I just had some thoughts of my home in England many years ago," said Rayleigh.

"Having strong memories is a good thing. Please let me know what happens in your dreams," reacted Mayling.

"My mother and father died in a blaze when I was a boy. Our grandma, Maylong, perished too. You remind me of her - the shape of your nose, your long silky-black hair, and especially your emerald eyes," continued Rayleigh.

"Your grandfather, Mister Wethersby, is he still alive? He would be more than eighty years now. And you appear so young to be his grandson," asked Mayling.

The knock on the door interrupted them. She got up and opened it for her mother.

Gooty beamed, "I brought you some more sweet chai."

"But Grandma, surely you can leave us for another hour?" said Mayling, winking.

"Come, children, drink your tea. Mayling, let young Rayleigh rest now, for those smoking Portuguese hot peppers can take a toll on one's throat. This afternoon we should take the cousins for a tour of the city and close to the grand fort."

"But Grandma," pleaded Mayling softly.

"Come now, Mayling," insisted Gooty.

The women left, leaving Rayleigh to sip his tea. His sore throat was no longer painful; Mayling had distracted him.

"She could be my sister," he thought aloud. "She is, was, the image of my grandma, the portrait in Robert's study."

Once they were in the street several hundred feet away from where they left Rayleigh, Gooty urgently asked, "So, what have you found out?"

"He's a great kisser, inexperienced but shows respect and promise," laughed Mayling.

"Child, do not mock me. What has he said about Mister Wethersby? You had plenty of time to ask him," declared Gooty, her voice rising impatiently.

"You stopped him from telling me, you and Mother's chai," giggled Mayling.

"We must be assured that Rayleigh is the son of a son, or daughter, of Mister Wethersby. Only his clan may share the family secret," said Gooty.

"But Grandma, surely you can see from his eyes and hair, and indeed his cousin's name is the same. How many Wethersby Thackers can there be in our world? Having two, visit this city; that is surely beyond coincidence, do you not think?" asked Mayling.

"But I must know what they recognise about the JackFruit. It would help if you did not ask directly but prise from him gently tonight," demanded Gooty.

"You mean, we must know?" retorted Mayling.

"Indeed, we must," said Gooty, as the little girl ran towards them and hugged Mayling's legs.

The women returned to Rayleigh at midday. The little girl immediately jumped on his lap.

"This is my daughter, Freya," smiled Mayling.

"Yes, I see the resemblance," said Wethersby Jnr. "She is beautiful, adorable."

Mayling blushed. Rayleigh clenched his fist, only for Mayling to come to him, stroking him gently on his shoulder. Rayleigh was livid, but her touch softened him instantly. Freya held out her hands and jumped to her mother, almost falling, catching Mayling unaware.

"Let us go and explore our beautiful city. We will show you some of its secrets," said Gooty.

They spent the afternoon walking close to and around the grand fort. Rayleigh marvelled at its enormous walls and the contrasting delicate detail within its design. Freya's friends joined them without the boy she pushed to the ground the day before. The twenty or so children took turns holding Wethersby Jnr and Rayleigh's hands; there was no scuffling.

Gooty brought them back to the narrow passageway just before nightfall, the children disappeared, and Rayleigh bought more tea. She led Wethersby Jnr and Freya away through another alley and doorway. Mayling bolted the door and checked it twice.

She unravelled her clothes slowly, standing not ten feet from Rayleigh; candles lit his eyes and her silhouette.

"Wait," she said, surprising Rayleigh.

"I, I do not understand," he said.

She disappeared into the other room; Rayleigh could hear splashing. He went in, curious as ever. She was waiting and instantly showered him with a pail of water and giggled wildly by his surprise.

They bathed together, then united on the wet floor, then cleansed again.

For several hours they slept in each other's arms, only to be woken by stray dogs howling in the alley. They smiled together, and they united as one again with an eagerness and intensity that astonished them both.

Late at night, they began talking about their families, of a secret hoard, the JackFruit, and warm yellow stones. Rayleigh could not remember who mentioned the treasure first, for he had come over in another hot sweat simply by staring into Mayling's hypnotic eyes.

"They have come in search of the JackFruit crystals. Rayleigh told me so last night," Mayling said to her grandmother as they sat with the chaiwallah.

"Ma, when are you going to introduce yourself? For they recognise your chai already," begged Mayling.

Gooty and her family sat around the chai cauldron with the cousins. She spoke slowly but with authority, reliving the encounters with Wethersby Snr. Rayleigh and Wethersby Jnr were left dumbfounded on hearing her revelations but suspicious as the story seemed too good to be true.

"How can this be?" thought Rayleigh, realising his fleeting romance with Mayling was probably over; she was family now after all.

Wethersby Jnr interrupted Gooty, "I cannot believe you and our grandma were twins. That is astounding. How can you prove this? You do not look alike."

"But my granddaughter?" countered Gooty.

"There is a resemblance. I think you and I need to discuss this in private, Junior," acknowledged Rayleigh as he winked towards his cousin.

"Not yet, Rayleigh, not until I, rather we, see proof that these women are indeed part of our lineage," answered Wethersby Jnr.

Gooty suddenly got up, grabbed Mayling by the hand and ran into the hut. They returned after ten minutes. A necklace hung around Mayling's neck; a large teardrop-shaped yellow gem at its centre sparkled in the sunlight.

"Quickly now, take a look but do not let anyone else see, for we have kept this hidden for many years," demanded Gooty. "I believe it should satisfy your curiosity."

Wethersby Jnr was stunned. He thought, "Could it be one of the JackFruit gems here in Jodhpur, with a heritage we never knew? It must be worth a fortune."

"Why have you not bargained this? It must be worth an uncountable number of rupiya?" asked Rayleigh.

"Trust me, I have thought about doing so many times; each time, I came to the same conclusion. Once this leaves our hands, it is gone forever," said Gooty. "This is our family's legacy. If we had sold it, how would you have the confidence now to accept us as your kin?"

"Mayling has a fair point, cousin," said Rayleigh. "What do you say?"

"I think you and I need to have that conversation now," said Wethersby Jnr, firmly.

Rayleigh locked the door and laid out the atlas's map on the floor of the hut. He studied the plot around Jodhpur; the green symbols were hard to see and harder still to decipher.

"Junior, there can be little denying we have found our first JackFruit gem. But we have found something else so exceptional, do you not think?" posed Rayleigh.

"Indeed, we have. But your interest in Mayling needs to change promptly. Agreed?" responded Wethersby Jnr.

"Yes," was all Rayleigh could muster.

"But the chaiwallah, she bothers me. What do you make of the mark on her chest?" asked Wethersby Jnr.

"That reminds me of how Grandpa's leg looked," uttered Rayleigh, looking down at the chart again.

"And what about Mayling? Any interesting features?" asked Wethersby Jnr, with a wry smile.

"She is... perfect, not a blemish," reacted Rayleigh, desperate to change the subject. "What are we going to do now?"

"Let us study the plot again and ask them more questions later. They are probably as sceptical of us as we are of them," replied Wethersby Jnr, still smirking.

"Yes, and find out about their men too," remarked Rayleigh.

The green plot's route came to a place marked Fatehpur Sikri with an arched gate symbol alongside. It seemed too soon to be leaving Jodhpur and their newly found family. And what would they do with the stone? It was not theirs after all, though it would bring great fortune to the household.

"Men. They each made one baby and left us before the birth," said Mayling, stroking Rayleigh's hair.

"What has your grandma told you of Mister Wethersby and his adventures across India?" asked Rayleigh.

"Very little. Mister Wethersby talked more about the Kingdom of Kaski and Siam; his favourite Indian place was Fatehpur Sikri," she replied.

"Fatehpur. Is that here in India?" faked Rayleigh.

"Yes. It is a small but wonderful palace, a great place to shoot elephants. Fatehpur Sikri is not far from the city of Agra and its palace of lost love," Mayling smiled.

"What about the JackFruit?" probed Rayleigh.

"You better ask Gooty. She would never tell me what she knows, but I know there is more than one stone; she occasionally talks in her sleep," chuckled Mayling.

Rayleigh remained relaxed in Mayling's company; his passion extinguished despite his deep longing. He desperately wanted to know more about his new family but was torn; should they stay or travel onward?

"But this amber stone has brought nothing only misery for us. Look at my poor mother, Mari, incapable. She sells good chai, yes, but it is barely enough to survive, especially during drought. The growth has spread too; it now covers half of her chest and continues around her back," said Mayling. "Grandma Gooty has it too, but you will never see where."

"Now we have found each other, you should trade the stone and free yourselves. I am sure the maharaja would offer you great riches," he said.

"Rayleigh, that is Gooty's decision only. For us children, we have played with the stone, but she is its owner. She may never be apart from it, for her love of Mister Wethersby," she said softly.

Rayleigh offered his hand, but she refused his touch.

"He is dead," said Rayleigh.

# 18

# Young Maharaja

The revelation of Wethersby Snr's death shocked Gooty. She cried and howled for three days and nights, refusing food and even chai.

Wethersby Jnr and Rayleigh discussed their next move. They agreed they would leave Jodhpur after dealing the crystal with Maharaja Ajit Singh.

Finally, Gooty came out of the room and into the foul air outside.

"You must take Mayling and her daughter Freya to Kandy. They belong there now. Mari and I are too frail for such a journey," pronounced Gooty. "There is another precious find before reaching Kandy, on a mountain in the Kingdom of Kaski; Fatehpur Sikri holds its key."

"We are not leaving here until we know you are safe and the gem bartered," stated Rayleigh. "The journey is no place for a young woman and girl."

"Rayleigh is correct," added Wethersby Jnr.

"If you take Mayling and Freya, I will sell the wretched pebble, and you will help me get a fair price from the maharaja," pronounced Gooty. "Let us get on with it, shall we?"

Caught by surprise, Wethersby Jnr nodded instinctively.

Mayling howled, "No! I cannot leave my ma."

"You will do as I say. Do not argue. Know your place," said Gooty and smacked Mayling's face.

Rayleigh reacted first, grabbing Gooty's other hand just before it too hit Mayling. At the same time, Wethersby Jnr caught Mayling from falling over.

Blood oozed from her nose; red spots covered Wethersby Jnr's white shirt too. Rayleigh's fury was tempered only by his cousin's firm hand on his shoulder. Mayling covered her mouth with her hand and sobbed gently.

The door burst open.

"Mother! What have you done to my child now? Leave my daughter alone. Never touch her again," shouted Mari. "Let us sell this tearful stone and eat well tonight."

Rayleigh and Wethersby Jnr were stunned. It was the first occasion they heard Mayling's mother speak. Wethersby Jnr thought she had an enchanting although rather fearsome voice, much like his dear grandma.

"How are we to approach the maharaja?" asked Wethersby Jnr, trying to calm the atmosphere.

"That is a good question. It would not be easy for our caste to approach the fort. However, those inside are more likely to listen to a foreigner and allow an audience with you," said Gooty. "I suggest that you go with all your men but take no arms. No swords, nothing. You must show your vulnerability."

"You mean to say we should take the teardrop but have no protection?" said Wethersby Jnr.

"Yes," said Gooty.

"What do you want for it?" asked Rayleigh.

"I have thought about that question for many years. I am unsure what type of stone it is. A diamond in my dreams, maybe a sapphire or most likely a piece of sun-coloured glass," replied Gooty. "Nobody must know it is mine nor that it has been here for more than sixty years. Understood?"

"I need to see it again," said Rayleigh and added, "for if it is a gemstone, it will be tough and nearly impossible to scratch. At least try first, for we cannot afford to be embarrassed in front of the maharaja. Our grandpa told me how to check for gems when I was a lad. He showed me with one of his modest star sapphires. Fetch me your whetted knife, Junior."

"Go. Come back in ten minutes," addressed Gooty.

He put the blade close to the stone. Rayleigh looked up at Wethersby Jnr and then to Gooty, seemingly asking for permission before touching one of the crystal's faces. He tried to scratch it, again and again, pressing down harder each time; nothing. He could see no mark.

"It is as hard as iron," exclaimed Rayleigh.

"Iron would score if you tried that," snorted Wethersby Jnr. "Try again, and let me see too."

Wethersby Jnr went to find the Southwold mob. Rayleigh stayed behind to watch over the women. He played with the young girl, Freya.

Wethersby Jnr returned with ten men.

"I could not find the remainder of the crew," said Wethersby Jnr. "I have explained to this group what we intend to do. A dozen of us; that should be enough."

"Did you make it clear there are to be no weapons taken into the fort?" invited Rayleigh.

"Yes, but we must check them. We know from previous experience that some will feel uncomfortable without pocketknives," responded Wethersby Jnr.

"Team, it is vital we go into the fort weaponless. Is that understood?" demanded Wethersby Jnr. "Now, line up and strip to your breeches."

The surprise on the men's faces said it all. Fredrick was first, throwing his knife towards Rayleigh's feet then removing his clothes and sandals. The other nine men followed suit; young Thomas threw two. Gooty took the knives, Mayling sniggered, catching Fredrick's eyes for a little longer than necessary.

"My crew, I have told you all before, I am not in the habit of repeating myself. When I give you an order, you will obey me or face the consequences. Do I make myself *clear*?" retold Wethersby Jnr, then he added, "Now, remove everything."

Fredrick's face and neck went bright red. Two more knives fell to the floor. Within a minute, ten men stood in the line, naked. All showed heavily tanned contours around their arms, legs and neck, their unexposed skin a pure white. They were all lean and visibly fit and a touch embarrassed. The women wandered slowly back into the hut, giggling.

The posse arrived at the fort gates just before eight o'clock in the morning; early enough thought Wethersby Jnr. They went through a large painted orange door, Mayling and Gooty followed. The women had argued steadfastly to come to the fort; they had lingering doubts and did not want the necklace to leave their sight until payment.

The imposing room's ceiling glittered with gold leaf. Large carpets hung on the walls and the floor; there was no furniture. They waited in the hot, airless room for three hours. As the bolt moved and the door opened, Fredrick fainted. A short round man entered with two guards carrying pikes.

"Show me what you have brought to trade that you think fit for a king," said the fat man after the guards closed the door.

"No. Only Maharaja Ajit Singh can see this," replied Wethersby Jnr. "We have come a long way, from England, knowing the maharaja has a passion for great jewels. He will not be disappointed, although he will be digging deep to lever this one from us. Bring him to us, and do not keep us waiting any longer in this sweatbox."

"You do not understand. It is you who will go to see the maharaja, not the other way round. Now, wait," said the rounded man and left quickly before Wethersby Jnr could respond.

Maharaja Ajit Singh sat in an oversized golden chair, perched upon three steps. The chair glittered in the candle lights that filled the palatial room. Ornate red, blue, and green patterned carpets covered the floor and walls; the shutters were closed. The maharaja was close to twenty years old. He wore a white and grey cloth, and a white headscarf covered his dark hair. He bore a young wispy beard and moustache. Two large crystals in gold dangled from his ears, and a big pearl necklace dominated his chest. Two guards, covered in white cloth and a red sash, stood on either side of the throne, long sabres by their flank.

The approaching guards dropped to their knees as soon as they entered the chamber. Rayleigh and Wethersby Jnr remained standing; their heads were lower than the maharaja. The round man turned to the people, motioning with his arms for them to kneel.

"Sit," said the maharaja in a softened tone. "Make yourselves comfortable. I do not bite."

Silence filled the room. The two men remained standing. The maharaja's guards looked at each other, poised to remonstrate with the cousins.

"Your majesty. Thank you for lending us your audience. We have come a long way and bring you great riches," announced Wethersby Jnr.

"What are your names, and why have you come here from England?" bade the maharaja.

"My name is Rayleigh Edwards, and this is my cousin Wethersby Thacker Junior. These men are from our crew, these women our family too," declared Rayleigh.

"And why come here?" repeated the maharaja, nodding slowly.

"We come to trade. We have something extraordinary for you. It will cost you a small fortune *and* a unique arrangement," said Wethersby Jnr.

The maharaja's face contorted from a stern look to one of surprise. No other foreigners had ever been in his presence. Never had anyone interrupted him while he still had questions.

"What is so special? When will you bring it to me, whatever it is?" exclaimed the maharaja.

"A simple, unbreakable crystal; golden like the sun that glitters greater than your throne, more rigid than the finest forged steel. It will bring tears to your eyes," revealed Rayleigh. "It is here."

"You had better show me, then," laughed the maharaja, his eyes widening.

Mayling passed the brown bag carefully to Rayleigh, surprising the maharaja.

"Who are these women?" he asked.

Ignoring his question, Rayleigh got up to his feet, handed the bag to the maharaja and stepped back without losing eye contact.

The maharaja opened it. His chin glowed brightly, and his eyes almost burst out of his skull. He placed the bag on his lap without saying a word, removed his pearl necklace, and replaced it with the silver chain holding the giant gem. He beamed.

"It is inexpensive for you," said Wethersby Jnr.

"Well, I think I will simply take it and give you my pearl chain in return," smirked the young ruler.

"No," declared Rayleigh softly with a wide smile.

"I need to see it out of its mount and have it weighed," conveyed the maharaja, surprising Rayleigh with his directness.

Rayleigh looked back towards Gooty; she nodded.

"I guess it is more than two ounces. We know it is pure and unblemished. You and I should remove it together," said Wethersby Jnr.

"Anat. Get my jewellery-set this instant, and fetch Taantrik too," said the maharaja to the short, rounded man, who crawled back to the door and disappeared.

Ten minutes later, he returned holding a large silver box, along with an older man who wore nothing other than a loincloth and a small gold medallion.

"I said instantly. Do not cross me," said the maharaja staring at Anat.

The maharaja set to work and removed the yellow stone from its silver mount, aided by tweezers. Wethersby Jnr scrutinized his every move. It came away from its support with a click. The maharaja stood up, held the gem in the air, then walked up to a candle to carefully examine the treasure.

"It is a magnificent specimen; flawless. Now let us see how it scratches," said the maharaja as he returned to his throne. "Taantrik, prove to me this is indeed a diamond."

Taantrik stood, grabbed the stone, the silver casket and a nearby candle. He sat down with his back to everyone except the maharaja and Wethersby Jnr. He fumbled around in the box and began to try to scrape the stone, shaking his head as he did so.

"Master, I cannot scratch this monster. It has though flaked everything in your box. Look!" exclaimed Taantrik. "A sun-kissed diamond. You must have it."

"This will be the *Star of Jodhpur*, and more importantly, the whole of India," stated Rayleigh and added, "Let *me* hold it now. How much does it weigh?"

The maharaja handed the diamond to Rayleigh, who instantly threw it in the air. The horror on Gooty and Wethersby Jnr's faces made Rayleigh laugh; Mayling gently put her hand on his arm and shook her head, smiling.

"Yes, it must be at least two ounces. Here, Junior, what do you think?" invited Rayleigh, passing the stone to his cousin.

Wethersby Jnr imitated weighing it in his right hand.

"Maybe even three, Rayleigh," feigned Wethersby Jnr. "It is worth more than Maharaja Ajit Singh can afford."

The maharaja belly-laughed and stuffed several candles out.

"I am interested. It is a fine jewel. What do you want for it?" asked the maharaja.

"At last," thought Rayleigh. "The price."

Neither Rayleigh nor Wethersby Jnr spoke; Gooty broke the silence, as they had agreed.

"We have three demands in exchange for this precious jewel," she started.

"Firstly. My daughter and I will live here in the fort with you for the rest of our lives. Not as your wives nor your slaves but treated with utmost respect and dignity. We will be watered, fed and clothed well, and you will protect us," said Gooty, pausing.

"Second. You will gather one hundred strong men and many animals to trek towards Agra and onward into the Kingdom of Kaski. Wethersby Jnr will lead them, but they may not come back," she asserted.

"And thirdly?" inquired the suspicious maharaja.

"My weight, in gold," concluded Gooty.

The room was quiet and still for several uncomfortable minutes.

A mammoth laugh from the maharaja astounded everyone. Rayleigh flinched, his elbow narrowly missing Wethersby Jnr's face. The two women remained steadfast.

"Is that all?" pitched the maharaja and continued laughing, although he was not smiling. "Your demands are fair and reasonable, except the gold, of course. That is preposterous."

"So be it," said Gooty. "Wethersby Junior, Rayleigh, I told you so. Now let us go from here and stop wasting Maharaja Ajit Singh's time and ours."

They all stood and inched backwards towards the door. The guards did not move.

"Wait. You are rather hasty. Let us bargain," said the maharaja.

They returned and knelt again.

"Yes, you can stay here. I will give you fifty men and animals for the trek. No gold, though," stated the maharaja.

"No," said Gooty.

"Sixty?" he offered.

Gooty shook her head. "The gold, it is a small price to pay."

"How much do you weigh?" he asked.

"Enough. Show me, and only me, what riches you hold," she said, surprising the cousins.

The maharaja tried to outstare Gooty but blinked too soon.

"If you insist. You will not be disappointed at the volume, perhaps the colour," said the maharaja getting up.

He took Gooty's hand and led her out of the door; the guards remained unmoved. The room went mute again.

After an hour, Gooty returned to the room. The maharaja was not with her.

"He loves silver rather than gold," she declared. "What shall we do?"

"I suggest we leave and let the maharaja stew on our offer," said Wethersby Jnr.

"I think we need to ask Gooty what got offered," smiled Rayleigh, as he winked at Mayling.

"He offered me, us, ten times my weight in silver bars. I have seen them and more too. He did not show me any gold," said an exasperated Gooty.

"From my knowledge, before leaving London, gold is worth a hundred times silver, pound for pound," said Wethersby Jnr. "The maharaja would be getting the diamond for a tenth of the price."

"And your weight?" asked Rayleigh.

"About one hundred pounds, but I will need to feast before he inspects me," laughed Gooty.

"A thousand pounds in silver is huge, do you not think, Junior?" blurted Rayleigh.

"Yes, but it's not worth as much as gold. Significantly more in silver will be far harder to carry too. Gold would be so much easier for us all," said Wethersby Jnr steadfast.

The Southwold crew were restless but also deeply curious about the ongoing bargaining.

"What should we do, Grandma?" asked Mayling.

"Demand fifty," interrupted Wethersby Jnr.

"The maharaja did say he *needed* the diamond, and he has never seen one like it, neither in size nor such a rich deep colour," said Gooty.

"Yes, and remember that we hold the diamond. He will have to reward us if he wants it," said Rayleigh.

The door opened, and in walked the maharaja with four more guards. They all waited for him to speak.

"Well, what is it to be? Do you accept my offer?" asked the maharaja.

"Please may you repeat it in front of all of us to avoid any misunderstandings?" asked Wethersby Jnr, surprising Gooty.

The maharaja went bright red. Although his mannerisms were unruffled, Rayleigh noticed a slight recurring twitch by the maharaja's mouth. Rayleigh sensed the maharaja was outraged by Wethersby Jnr's request. A lack of trust, perhaps?

The maharaja repeated what he had told Gooty. Wethersby Jnr shook his head impassively.

"Let us come to an understanding. Gold is worth a hundred times more than silver. Agreed?" stated Wethersby Jnr waiting for an acknowledgement.

"Not in these parts. Ten times," replied the maharaja.

"That may be so, but in these parts, this diamond is worth considerably more. We need fifty times Gooty's weight in silver. One hundred men and animals for our trek and the care of the women here," stated Wethersby Jnr, holding up the yellow gem.

"My final offer is thirty times this woman's weight. Seventy-five men and animals. And the two women's safe care here," roared the maharaja. "Do not ask for more, for I will reduce my offer."

"May we have some moments to confer?" asked Wethersby Jnr. "In private, if you may, and no guards."

"As you wish. Anta, take all these people to the orange room and bring them back when they are ready," said the maharaja, without emotion.

Anta led them back to the antechamber. He and the guards remained outside by the door.

Rayleigh was first to speak. "Gooty, you have held one of the JackFruit stones for sixty years. What do you say to the maharaja's offer?"

"I know what I want; safety. The stone has brought nothing but pain and misfortune, especially to my daughter. While I have lived a long life, there is little time left for me now, apart from seeing my daughter smile and be well-fed," said Gooty. "You get your men and animals. I want you to take half of the silver with you and Mayling. Then, when you reach Kandy, I want you to trade it for property so that Mayling and Freya may live comfortably for the rest of their lives without fear. If it can help you to find the second stone in the Kingdom of Kaski, then use it for bargaining, but you must keep this promise to Mayling."

Wethersby Jnr smiled as he listened to Gooty. He worried about the journey ahead, the risks of carrying such a heavy payload and a new, but welcome, mob of men - could he trust them? And taking an attractive young woman would be full of challenges to keep her safe from them.

The Southwold gang sat mesmerized, with the silver scale to carry, the distance to the Kingdom of Kaski and an even longer journey to Kandy.

"I agree," said Wethersby Jnr and added, "but are you going to accept the maharaja's offer?"

"Yes," replied Gooty and continued, "if Rayleigh agrees too."

"I do, and I want to hear Mayling's opinion too," said Rayleigh.

Mayling raised her head; a single tear rolled down her cheek, and she said, "Yes, Grandma."

"Good, let us seek written agreement with the maharaja, then quickly leave before he changes his mind," gestured Gooty. "He has not met his new *mother* yet."

Wethersby Jnr, Rayleigh, Gooty and Mayling returned with Anta and the guards to an empty throne room, leaving the rest of the gang behind to perspire.

Maharaja Ajit Singh entered.

Gooty nodded. "Yes, we agree. Please can you have the agreement written, marked by us all?"

"Of course. Now let me have my prize. The diamond," said the maharaja.

"Would you rather not weigh me first?" cackled Gooty, and the room erupted in laughter.

They left the fort and returned to drink chai together. Gooty told her daughter she would be going to the citadel and never coming back to their hut.

"My chai pot is coming with me," is all she could say.

Gathering their few possessions into a small cart, they returned to the fort the next day. Guards ushered them to the throne room, where Maharaja Ajit Singh was waiting.

"Who is this?" he asked.

"My daughter, of course," replied Gooty. "Do you not see the family resemblance?"

"But…" his voice trailed off, then he continued, "Here are the papers for your marks. Please cross them all."

"Thank you," said Gooty.

"Mister Wethersby and Mister Rayleigh, I will ready your soldiers, elephants and camels. When do you intend to leave my fine city?" said the maharaja.

"A week from today, leaving at sun-up. We will also be taking some of the silver and needing five horses," replied Wethersby Jnr.

The young maharaja nodded; his mouth twitched again.

# 19

## Lost Chai

Thursday morning, 22nd August 1697, came and went. The maharaja had seventy-five soldiers, thirty camels and a dozen elephants, but no horses, ready in the blue fort's grounds. Gooty's daughter, Mari, had disappeared.

Rayleigh, Fredrick and Mayling had searched countless alleyways all morning. The heat was unbearable. They were resting briefly under multi-coloured cloths covering one of the passages. The sad figure of Mari, pushing her chai pot cart, came clattering along the hard-baked track.

"Where have you been, Ma?" gasped Mayling. "You are keeping the maharaja and everyone else waiting."

"Selling chai, like I do every day," replied Mari.

They walked back to the hut. The Southwold gang were outside sweating; they could not see Wethersby Jnr.

"Our captain is out looking for you," exclaimed Jack. "Gone for more than an hour now. Told us to stay put."

They waited while Rayleigh strolled up and down adjacent passages, not wanting to go too far. He soon lost his sense of direction; another dizzy spell hit him. Wethersby Jnr found Rayleigh slumped on the dirt next to a small temple entrance.

"Rayleigh, where are Mayling and Mari?" he asked.

He patted Rayleigh's shoulder, and Rayleigh jerked.

"Junior, finally you are here," said Rayleigh groggily. "Let us get back to the women and our crew, then march to the fort without delay."

"Are you feeling alright, young man?" asked Wethersby Jnr.

"Too much sun; the heat is insane this afternoon. You can lead the way from here. Slowly, please," said Rayleigh.

The two cousins caught up with their crew, the women and the girl. They set off to the fort with Mari's trusted cart.

Inside the main gate, a rush of activity welcomed them; men in ragged green uniforms scattered all around. The group of camels spat and snapped, and the chained elephants trumpeted.

Anta was waiting. He looked up to the sun and shook his head.

"Maharaja Ajit Singh is not in the habit of being kept waiting. This way," he bellowed. "Leave your men here."

The maharaja's chair was empty. A tidy pile of wooden boxes sat next to the throne.

The maharaja slipped into the room unnoticed.

"Here is your silver. How much of it will you take on your trek?" asked the maharaja and added, "I will keep the rest here, in my treasury."

Everyone in the room looked around but could not see him.

"I am here," he said, appearing from behind the chair's platform, and sat down.

"I will keep one-thousand-pound weight here. The rest, Mister Rayleigh and Mister Wethersby will take for their expedition," shrieked Gooty, surprising the maharaja.

He had never heard anyone approach him with such a tone before.

“So be it. Return twenty boxes to my treasury at once, Anta. Show Gooty and her daughter to their quarters after they have said their goodbyes. Please give me the diamond now, Gooty,” said the maharaja sternly.

Gooty got up and handed the maharaja the stone.

“And the necklace,” he said softly.

Mayling refused her grandmother’s embrace. Mari turned away from Mayling, ignoring her too.

“Do not worry, Gooty. Mayling and her daughter will be safe with us. We will keep our promises. Thank you so much,” said Rayleigh.

The two women left the room.

“Will we ever see them again?” asked Rayleigh.

Wethersby Jnr said nothing.

The pile of wagons, soldiers, animals, and the Englishmen rode out of the main gates. A large group of people watched and cheered as they went. Children ran alongside until they were exhausted. The troop were soon heading into brown hills. The blue hues of the city, and their trusted friend Omar, disappeared behind them.

Wethersby Jnr had insufficient time to introduce himself to all the Indian soldiers; however, their leader soon became apparent. A chubby man sat on the camel’s hump behind Rayleigh and Wethersby Jnr, flapping his hands furiously, often turning, shouting to those behind him.

The convoy continued for five days. Wethersby Jnr soon exerted his authority, waving off the soldiers’ leader’s attempts to stop early on the first and second nights. Once they went through the first set of short mountains, the terrain was easy. It became sandy, flat and with light vegetation. It felt like the outskirts of a desert to Rayleigh, but here the undergrowth continued. It was scorching, though; three soldiers had already collapsed, halting the caravan for their revival.

Wethersby Jnr rationed the water within the first week, although Rayleigh thought they were carrying too much. But their biggest fear was the solid wooden boxes, coupled with the procession's size. Wethersby Jnr split the Southwold gang into four groups to always guard the silver wagons. One man could carry a box for a short distance; Rayleigh wished for more substantial crates.

Rayleigh's fears were realised on the eighth moonlit night when six soldiers tried an escape with a camel and cart. The small group had travelled about a mile before the others surrounded them.

The stout leader executed them on the spot; their bodies left for vultures to feast. A camel took the cart, and six heads, back to the camp. A long, firm stick, anchored to the ground, held each crown. Mayling spat at them before covering her daughter's fascinated eyes. Every night, the skulls came out, rotting and stinking; the grotesque sight was a bloodied prophecy for the convoy to stay in line.

They reached the city Pushkar and stayed only one night after replenishing the water pots and food supplies. Two of the Southwold crew were missing at daybreak. Wethersby Jnr was furious when Jack and Fredrick meandered back to the camp. He scowled them in private before the expedition set off again.

--x--

# 20

# Lightning repairs

The *Frostenden Nave* rocked silently in the bay, a heavy swell straining its anchor. Ohama took Everett to inspect the damage caused by the pirates. Approaching the hull, the odour of charcoal struck them. As they rounded the bow to the windward side, they gazed awestruck at the long gash, a gaping hole of about thirty feet. The gap was, fortunately, above the waterline. Everett pinched himself when he saw the nameplate close-up, despite the opening taking some of it, '…*den Nave*'.

After climbing the steps, they stood on the blackened deck. The flames had consumed the ship; that was obvious. Everett spotted only light pitting on exposed timbers. The canvas sails had gone; fortunately, so had the swashbucklers. Ohama knew that they would be back, but it was a long way to the southern Maldives.

"We have about a month. There is not enough to sustain us here, and the pirates will return, that is for sure," said Ohama.

Everett was not listening. Instead, he focused on wanting to get into his cabin to confirm that his stash had been undiscovered.

Mending the giant timbers took three weeks. They only had palm trunks to patch the massive hole. Everett expected the repairs would not last long at sea. The patching-up, though, was out of necessity until they reached firmer land and hardwood.

The crew scrubbed the top deck and down below; Everett insisted he would clean his cabin alone. Out of sight, he carefully prised several floorboards and smiled for the first time in a month; his coins and silver were untouched. Then, he quickly replaced the planks and rubbed their edges with charcoal dust to disguise their movement.

Everett searched Charles and James's cabin next, carefully tapping each baseboard for signs of movement; they were firm, he found nothing. Most of the modest furniture was scorched. On seeing Charles's favourite blackened cream shirt, he stopped to wonder about the man's fate. Had he by some stroke of luck found land or been eaten by sharks or giant squid? His brother had, after all, not asked after him.

"How are we for a sail?" asked Ohama.

"We must repair the canvas. There is some below deck, heavily charred," Everett replied as he walked down the steps focused on Ohama. "Give me help and let us see what we can make from it."

They took the canvas back to the beach and inspected it more closely. The immense cloth ends were seared but remained remarkably intact along their length. One had a hole running through it, which repeated itself when the canvas was outstretched.

While a team knocked up the wood repairs, another mended the canvas under Everett's watchful eye. He barked his orders, much to the surprise of Ohama, who looked on. Together they inspected the work at the end of each day.

Satisfied that the repairs were strong enough, the sails were returned to the ship and roped up. They only had one mainsail, about half of its standard size, and another one much smaller still. The patchwork was a sight to behold. Everett thought it looked rather like a skull, but there were no crossed bones. Ohama wondered if it would hold in a stiff breeze, let alone the gales they could expect.

Ohama distracted James and got him to work on his land area, despite James's protests. The corn he sowed eight weeks earlier was tall now, although carpeted with tall seagrass in one spot. Ohama harangued James for his passive attitude, but that made no difference to his work ethic. Burnt skin peeled off James's shoulders and nose. The temperature had remained hot and mostly dry. There was little protection from the sun, other than the palms and the makeshift huts. Rain showers had been occasional and a welcome relief to stock up their water supplies and wash away the sand that seemed to get into every joint.

James had begun his morning with his usual walk along the beach, daydreaming of vast piles of coins in his room at *Thatchers*. He flicked back and forth in his thoughts and to the island. Black clouds loomed on the western horizon. As he reached the end of the moon-shaped beach, he stopped and watched the approaching cloud bank heading towards the island. For the next hour, he waited on the rocks. Half the sky was dark and foreboding; the other sunny and blue. The horizon had disappeared in front of him. A wall of mist crept along the sea to the beach. Overhead, dark grey and black clouds bubbled. The wind hit first, then the rain.

Although barely able to move, James fell into a gully within the rocks. Now protected from the worst of the wind, sheets of rain punched him; drops the size of acorns, he thought. He knew he had to move as the waves began to break over him. The intense wind blew him over. He scraped his knees hard on the beach. Disorientated, he continued to roll before a palm stopped him. He tucked his arms around the stump and held on as if his life depended on it.

James was thrown sixty feet through the air, and he landed in the water. He briefly sizzled like a hog on a spit. Ohama saw a fork of lightning struck the palm, not knowing James had been under it. A clap of thunder and a shudder instantly followed. Everett was cowering under another coconut palm and saw a smouldering shape ark through the air and land at the water's edge.

Everett ran as fast as he could; sheets of rain hit him as he struggled to put one foot in front of another. He fell forward as the rain stopped. The smell hit him first; pig. James lay still, his eyes wide open, teeth clenched, and his mouth crooked to the left.

"James, James, open your eyes, man," Everett shouted and shook him hard.

James did not move or say anything.

Everett ran to the surf too, and the two men carried him to one of the small huts. Ohama was waiting, perplexed by the sight of James.

"What has happened to him now?" shouted Ohama.

Everett watched over James during the daytime but fell asleep for parts of each night. Everett took to dripping a watery fish broth into James's mouth, often missing and making a mess, as James did not take to it.

He arose from his coma after eight days; his eyes flickered, and he let out a low groan, "Water, I need water."

"Wait a minute," responded a surprised Everett. "You had us worried there."

Everett fetched a cup and sat James up on the reed-mat floor.

He sipped at first, then tugged it quickly. "More, Everett."

Everett left the hut and found Ohama. They brought back two large jars; James was laughing, surprising them.

"Well, it is great you have a sense of humour. You took one hell of a bolt. Everett saw you flying through the air after it hit," said Ohama.

"What?" responded James. "I remember Charles going overboard. How did I get here?"

Everett recounted the last couple of months.

--x--

# 21

# Nerway

The uneventful monotonous terrain strained Rayleigh's patience. His foot was tender again, that after he whacked it on one of the cartwheels the night before, he thought he heard a bone crack.

Spinning his head and body around in the wagon, he made out a bunch of small trees in the distance of the otherwise simple vista. A dust storm was coming at them from his left. Mayling snuggled next to him, smiling. Freya had taken to ride with Wethersby Jnr in the cart ahead, sitting in his lap.

A huge shout rang out from behind, "Have a care, dust devils, at nine o'clock."

Out of the approaching cloud of sand came half a dozen yelling horse riders at full gallop.

The long caravan quickly formed a circle, with the animals on the outside and the silver in the middle. Half of the soldiers drew spikes; others pulled bows back. The Southwold gang held their swords and primed muskets firmly.

Arrows flew above their heads towards the approaching marauders. Three horses tumbled over, squashing and killing their riders instantly. The remaining two equestrians reined back, but momentum carried them forward. Rayleigh saw the whites of their eyes now; they were too close.

From behind the mounts came a sky-full of arrows. They started to land ahead of the wagon circle; others made it over. Mayling screeched wildly as a shaft went through her calf. An Indian soldier cried out, clutching an embedded arrow in his stomach, stumbling as he fell backwards.

More arrows flew beyond the riders as another gang came running forward, aiming for the wagons. They cut down three of the maharaja's soldiers.

"Hold your ground, men," shouted Wethersby Jnr. "Rayleigh, see to Mayling and muffle her cries."

The soldiers' commander ignored Wethersby Jnr's order and came out of the circle, howling, waving his curved sword aloft while running directly at the horses. He punctured one of the rider's legs, leaving a partially severed foot dangling and the man screaming in agony. The leader ran at the other rider and performed the same manoeuvre, slicing across the man's ankle. The rider screamed out as he fell, clutching his stump; the leader finished him, swiping at his neck. Three men on foot came towards him; he swiftly slashed them too. One tripped heavily, falling on his sword and twitched violently as the blade speared through his middle and out of his back.

Their one-man army continued. He lurched forward, swinging at the rabble with deft precision. Rayleigh admired the man's skill, strength, and courage, as he watched yet more of the bandits dropping dead to their knees. Another volley from the wagon's archers caught the last of the invaders.

The bloody commander stood over the still-alive rider and spoke to him, "What is your name?"

The look of surprise on the man's face defied his fear.

"Lucknow," he said as the swordsman stood on his bleeding leg.

"And who is your controller?" demanded the leader.

"Maharaja Ajit Singh," said the injured man.

"Liar. Try again, one time only," said the wary chief.

"But, but I speak the truth. We left Jodhpur and followed your group from a distance," he begged. "My orders are to kill the Englishmen and return with silver and the girls."

"Jodhpur? Silver? Impossible. We have never met before, and now you will meet your maker," feigned the swordsman as he twisted his blade into the man's thigh. "Tell me the truth, and I might spare you."

"But you have your orders too," implored the desperate man.

The commander acted in a frenzy. The disfigured rider was now unrecognisable and lifeless. Wiping his brow, smearing himself with more blood, the leader strode back to the wagons.

Wethersby Jnr assessed their casualties. Five dead, four wounded, including Mayling.

"You did well. What is your name?" asked Wethersby Jnr.

"I am Colonel Gamangerj Itis Ghirt; I go by the name Gamny. How is the woman?" he replied.

"Her bleeding has been stemmed. She will live as long as the wound is kept clean. The arrow went straight through the leg and speared her to the cart."

"Your cousin likes her. I do not blame him; she is a treasure to behold. The young maharaja got outplayed there by the old woman," laughed Gamny. "He wants her for himself. Maybe it is too late for that."

Gamny and Wethersby Jnr checked each fallen marauder, stabbing each one to ensure they would not move again. All told, they counted twenty-two.

The attackers, two fallen mares and the five dead maharaja's soldiers lay exposed on the arid land, all stripped of their clothes and a handful of personal items. Wethersby Jnr pocketed five large gold rings off the riders. The Southwold men distributed the extra swords and knives between themselves; the maharaja's men would have nothing to do with them.

Large birds circled for a huge feast. Soon a flock of well over two hundred, Rayleigh estimated, descended and squawked noisily as the caravan slowly moved on. Wethersby Jnr gained four fine horses from the fight; one had a significant wound to its shoulder. The other three were surprisingly unscathed. Rayleigh and Wethersby Jnr rode upfront with Gamny on their new mounts for the rest of that day. Gamny said nothing, nor did he reveal any emotion. Wethersby Jnr was apprehensive. They had been lucky there were not more assailants.

"Rayleigh, we need to cover more ground, but we are not going to change the animals' pace. We need to set up camp after sundown and set off before sunrise. That could gain us almost two hours each day," illustrated Wethersby Jnr. "When the attackers fail to return, others may come looking for them and us."

"I agree, but we would risk a dusk attack," replied Rayleigh as Wethersby Jnr bobbed.

"Gamny, let us set up tonight's camp after sun dip until there is no light left in the sky. The further we travel each day, the better," said Wethersby Jnr.

Gamny just nodded.

For the next seven nights, a dozen soldiers kept a rotating watch. Gamny inspected them every two hours each night. There were no slackers. There were no aggressors.

Mayling had taken Freya to travel with Fredrick and James in the middle of the convoy. Rayleigh chafed at first, knowing deep-down that his intoxicating affection towards Mayling was wrong. Now she was more like the sister he never had; he kept telling himself. He also saw the unmistakable glint in her eyes when she was in Fredrick's company. Freya had also taken to sit on Fredrick's lap, to Wethersby Jnr's disgruntlement too. He was still trying to deduce their relationship.

"Great, great-niece. No, that is not it," he muttered on several occasions while trying to focus his frustrated mind.

While they did not know it, they were only one night from Fatehpur Sikri when the attack happened.

The sentries were alert despite the early hour, but they did not hear nor see the arrows raining down on them until the first wail went out, followed by several thuds and many cries. Gamny was walking behind his men, ensuring they were awake and looking ahead. He was the first to be struck. An arrow pierced both sides of his neck. He made no sound, dying instantly; his wound rained blood over the startled soldier next to him.

The camp woke to the cries as more men were struck. The initial barrage was followed by two more. Four soldiers were dead, ten more injured. Then it stopped.

They did not see their assailants for another hour until the next wave, a running pitch, hit them. Wethersby Jnr was expecting something like this and was ready with large poles hidden behind the carts and animals.

"Pikes out, now," he boomed.

A mass of ten-foot wooden spikes came from out of the camp.

"Hold firm," shouted Wethersby Jnr. "Draw."

From behind the pikes, a short volley of arrows arched through the air.

"Again," shouted Wethersby Jnr, above the aggressors' roar and Mayling's incessant screaming.

Men were impaled by pikes, but more kept coming.

"Hold your ground," he yelled. "Make ready your muskets."

Two fighters had pushed through and were climbing over a cart. Fredrick speared one, and James slashed at the other; both foes fell in a heap. Fredrick grabbed a pike and held it steady as another attacker ran screaming at him. The heavy wooden pole briefly lurched upwards with the man's momentum. Fredrick caught him in the groin, and the man stopped yelling immediately. Fredrick frantically tried to release the shaft, but it was jammed.

One low salvo of the soldiers' arrows struck lucky, quickly cutting through a core group of attackers. The volley of musket fire surprised the remaining small band; they retreated quickly. Wethersby Jnr could not see how many ran away; perhaps a dozen, he guessed.

The camp remained apprehensive for the rest of that early morning. The horizon started to turn dark blue ahead of them. They moved forward towards the ever-rising sun.

They spotted the sandstone-walled palace fort of Fatehpur Sikri by early afternoon, elevated on a rocky ridge. As they approached the colossal entranceway and double wooden gate, a mob of children greeted them, holding out their hands, cheering. An elephant's hoof almost trampled one girl, but she did not seem to care and kept running alongside them.

The horses, camels and elephants had marched harshly that day and were now in desperate need of a long rest. Fortunately, the gates opened without any request, surprising Rayleigh and Wethersby Jnr.

Then a sentry shouted, "Horsemen only."

They moved into the courtyard and dismounted, and their two cavalrymen followed their lead.

"We come in peace. My, this was once a truly magnificent palace," announced Wethersby Jnr. "We must meet with your ruler urgently."

"He is always busy in the afternoon," said the cheerful warden. "You best wait. Rest in here while your caravan stays outside. How many of you are there?"

Wethersby Jnr thought for a moment as Rayleigh said, "Sixty Singh soldiers, some Englishmen, us two, a woman and a girl. We seek jackfruit."

The perplexed old gatekeeper said, "That is many a troop you have. What do you want with the ruler of Fatehpur Sikri?"

"Great fortune," replied Rayleigh. "Now get us some clean water, will you? We have been travelling for a long time and encountered many a fighting man."

The three men walked together towards a plain square building with an unusual roof.

"I am Nerway. In here, out of the sun, you can wait. Help yourselves but take care with that water; it is in short supply in these parts," said the guard. "If you need anything, ask for me. One of my men will be standing outside this door."

Nerway left.

Rayleigh surveyed the splendid room. Brightly coloured murals covered the four walls, and the ceiling glistened with gold leaf. A sizeable octagonal pillar dominated the centre of the room.

Sliced pineapples, bananas and partially open young coconuts lay on a large bench. Rayleigh and Wethersby Jnr each picked up a clay cup and hastily drank water from a large pot. Then, they began to devour pieces of fresh fruit.

The floral designs around the centre pillar made way for thirty or more brackets supporting a large platform above the floor. Rayleigh was fascinated by the paintings; scenes of elephants carrying men and scantily clad women. He longed to understand the room's stories and their significance. He soon became lost in his thoughts, reminiscing about Wethersby Snr's study.

"It is eerily quiet in this place; so windswept and tired. Where is everyone, Junior?" asked Rayleigh.

"Yes, this is a strange place. It looks like it was left to the elements some years ago, judging by the state of the plant growth, peeling paint and lack of people," said Wethersby Jnr.

"So why the warm welcome?" probed Rayleigh.

"They want something. Maybe the animals?" replied Wethersby Jnr.

"Perhaps the wagons?" murmured Rayleigh.

"Yes. It is fine eating, drinking, and losing your mind within this room. But what about the others?" said Wethersby Jnr. "I do not wish to leave the wagons exposed for very much longer."

Rayleigh opened the door, only for a short sentry to block his path.

"We need Nerway and to go back to our caravan immediately," Rayleigh demanded.

The man did not move an inch. Wethersby Jnr pushed his way past, and they walked to the main gate with the guard trailing behind.

Freya instantly ran up to Rayleigh and hugged his legs. Mayling smiled while Fredrick cussed.

"Come now, Fredrick, she is only holding onto her uncle," said Mayling. "There is no need for any jealousy."

"What have you been doing?" asked Mayling of Rayleigh. "I was getting frantic. I do not care for this place. I have an uneasy feeling; ghosts. Apart from these children, we have seen no one else."

"There is no need to worry. We were left alone, eating fresh fruit and drinking water," replied Rayleigh, as he rummaged in his pocket. "Freya, would you like a banana?"

Wethersby Jnr found James and the newly assumed soldier's leader, who went by the name of Jackal. They were trying to communicate mainly using hand signals, looking back from the area they had just travelled.

A large cloud of dense fog covered the westerly horizon where the sun should have been. They all stood on the wagon, trying to guess the phenomenon.

Despite Nerway's minor protests, Rayleigh led Mayling, Freya, Fredrick, and James back through the main gate and into the square room.

The door flew open after about thirty minutes. There stood a majestic looking man, his hair covered in golden cloth. He had deep-set black eyes and a long thick beard. His shirt was crystal white, and he wore a dark yellow sari and gold shoes. Everyone stopped eating at the sight of the man, their mouths still full. Rayleigh guessed he was around forty years old.

"Welcome to my humble neighbourhood, Fatehpur Sikri. Please excuse the surroundings. Our most prodigious leader, Emperor Aurangzeb, left this area more than a decade ago; his administration went with him. We have faced demanding times. I hope you have enjoyed our modest welcome," said the regal-looking man. "My name is Azam Shah. For what do I owe your pleasure and welcome?"

Rayleigh rapidly finished his mouthful and replied, "We have travelled from England, although we were recently in the company of the Maharaja, Ajit Singh, of Jodhpur. We come in peace and trade."

"The maharaja, he has much to learn. I hear his harem are rather special to behold, though," winked Azam towards Mayling. "Did you escape his clutches, young lady?"

"No, he never got that opportunity," she winked back, to Rayleigh and Fredrick's surprise.

The spectacular room entranced Rayleigh. He visited it every day, often alone. Fresh fruit and water were always waiting for him; two large thin sheets of smooth leather, different coloured powders and bristles, too; he never saw who brought them.

Mayling and Freya joined him. The latter was deep in thought, slowly drawing while looking back up to the walls.

Rayleigh started to believe his own stories from the wall paintings after asking Nerway to explain part of their meaning. Great battles, with the emperor winning them all, of course. Rayleigh used his imagination for the rest.

"Where did you find this?" enquired Rayleigh, kneeling with Freya and pointing at her drawing.

"Round roof," she replied.

He looked but did not notice where Freya was pointing.

Mayling gently touched Rayleigh's shoulder and whispered, "She has a vivid imagination much like you, but better eyesight. Look to the top of the central pillar. I believe you will find what you have been looking for."

Still, he could not see it.

She took a spoonful of yellow and red powders, mixing it with a bit of liquid, brushing the mixture on another leather sheet, spotting the circle with black and yellow.

"Do you detect it now?" she giggled.

Rayleigh lay on his back, slowly shaking his head, frowning in annoyance. Then it appeared to him. On a large part of the ceiling, he found the same outline Freya and Mayling had drawn. The roof image was huge, covered mainly in yellow skulls, seemingly emitting light. And black elephants, several with two or three heads. The large green rounded image stood on top of a golden stupa surrounded by white-capped mountains and many bells. He could not discern the symbols below. He had looked at the skulls and elephant heads many times before, but he had not seen the broader vision.

"A huge jackfruit," he yelled. "Those symbols below, I want to get closer."

Balancing on top of a rickety platform of wood around the post, Rayleigh painstakingly retraced the script over the subsequent three visits to the room. A few pieces of what looked like crumbling plaster obscured part of the writing. As he rubbed at the ceiling, the yellowing powder disappeared, revealing more letters beneath. He drew the scripts three times, and to be sure, asked Mayling to climb the tower, despite her healing leg, to check which was his closest impression. She picked one and smiled.

"A temple far away, to the roof of the world," she declared excitedly. "Muktinath, in the Kingdom of Kaski."

Freya sat unmoving, staring for hours at her picture, her eyes damp. She had not made a sound for three days. She reminded Rayleigh of when he was a boy sitting silently deep in thought, willing himself not to speak.

They left Fatehpur Sikri, and Nerway joined them. He explained his reasoning during the weeks that followed. Most of his family got slain a year earlier. His son remained with him but had succumbed to a delirious fever and lack of clean water. The maharaja never returned, banning him from leaving the fort. He held his pride and maintained the stronghold to the best of his abilities, but the relentless drought was devastating. For the infrequent visitors, he would put on a show to portray no sign of foreboding. His fears of Maharaja Ajit Singh diminished over time, replaced by a deep dryness at the back of his throat.

They marched on in an arc to bypass the incredible city of Agra. Nerway warned Wethersby Jnr not to head directly towards the vast mountains, so they avoided Delhi too. He advised that they would not want to confront the powerful Mughal rulers and their soldiers, much to the Jodhpur company's relief. Instead, they circumnavigated east at first, along an ancient trading route, to the holy city of Varanasi before heading through old mountain passes to the northern edge of the Kingdom of Kaski.

When they descended on Varanasi and the great River Ganges, the sight and smell of burning bodies at the river's stepped edge astounded the Englishmen. The Indian men bathed daily in the river, smiling continually. Nerway explained the spiritual significance of the holy river and why they were awestruck being there. Pilgrims came from across India to bathe in its waters, for redemption, or cremate their dead and set them free to float. Wethersby Jnr was keen to move on before everyone got too settled. He relented after Mayling's unblinking stare when he suggested they begin their journey again the following day.

"Do you remember the first time you visited London?" she asked him. "Multiply that feeling a thousand-fold, and you are not even close to what we sense and feel right now. It is our most special place. Let us be for another week. Then I will encourage them to move on."

That day came and went without moving a mile. Their animals were rested, well-fed and watered, so were the men. Mayling commanded the squad to gather at the newly built Shah Ghat before sunrise. Two of the team were missing. After watching a body shrouded in white linen set alight on the pyre next to the river, Wethersby Jnr calmly informed everyone to make ready in an hour. They would ride east and then north into the foothills.

# 22

# Earthquake

An uneventful trek along flat dry land cultivated with rice, some maize, and little else, slowly made its way to undulating hills and greener surroundings. They snaked their way north under Nerway's welcomed guidance as the valleys became more erratic, and their pace began to slow.

Rayleigh had changed his look. He sported a thick black beard and a mixed coloured cloth covering his ever-lengthening braided hair. He could easily pass as a local, thought Nerway. Wethersby Jnr remained clean-shaven, nicking a spot on his chin so often that a white protruding scar had formed. He kept his hair in a long queue, which fascinated young Freya as she often sat on his lap. Mayling spent most days with Fredrick. Her leg healed well, but she often had a fever and sickness; her strength started to wane again. At night, she and Freya would always sleep alongside Wethersby Jnr and Rayleigh.

The style of buildings changed as they travelled towards the mountains. Temple domes were smaller and usually less ornate, made from wood rather than stone and clay. Rice straw huts littered the countryside, generally in small clusters, occasionally concentrated into villages. At last, they crossed over a pass overlooking a broad flat valley with mountains on all sides. They watched the smoke rising over brown buildings from their elevated position towards the far end of the valley.

"Pokhara," observed Nerway.

A large lake with a two-storey crystal white temple at its centre dominated the village. A soaring mountain, primarily covered in blue ice, looked down on the whole area.

The oasis of the town and its folk was a magical sight. The gang feasted on stewed and dried yak, with rice that stuck to their fingers. Recharging their bodies, they rested for more than a week.

The incredibly friendly villagers were also generous, which initially surprised Rayleigh, given the area's barren nature. However, he soon discovered that the settlement was a stopping point along a vital trading route. Numerous caravans ploughed the way between India, Kantipur, and, as old Wethersby coined it, *The Roof of the World*, Tibet.

Rayleigh explored the surroundings on his own, climbing one of the many hills. A sweeping vista of the village, lake and valley rewarded his efforts. One mountain dominated; he thought it resembled a fish's tail, formed from two snowy peaks.

Rayleigh was anxious about what lay ahead. The village head had given them directions for the trek to the temple, Muktinath. It would be at least ten days further and hard, as the trail rose towards the white-capped peaks.

Chief Putki was a heavily wrinkled, dark-skinned man, with thin wispy grey hair. He had the appearance of a man who had lived a hard life. His deep-set small eyes made for a powerful stare. He continuously smiled through his one remaining yellowed front tooth. The cousins guessed he was nearing a hundred years old, but equally, he may have been fifty. Putki would not tell them how long he had lived, for he did not remember his birth year.

He agreed to lend them a pack of mules in exchange for a horse, warning them that the winter season was fast approaching. They should not waste more time and limit their numbers in case of difficulties. Four local guides were to go with them. These men knew the route from memory, having traversed the same peaks scores of times, a path handed down from generation to generation. The local men would also soften reactions from those they would meet along the trail as they could be a troublesome lot, Chief Putki had said. He was curious about their destination; he vividly remembered being asked about it only once, several tens of years before. Rayleigh was the perfect likeness to that man, Putki thought.

Mayling and Freya remained in the village with most of the Jodhpur army men and a half from Southwold. Fredrick joined Wethersby Jnr and Rayleigh, despite Mayling's pleas. Seventeen men set out with five mules and two yaks carrying their provisions, together with multiple sacks of dried food and clothing gifts from chief Putki. They neared more prominent hills and a significant obstacle at the end of the gentle-paced day. About eighty yards across, a wooden roped bridge was balanced over a fast-flowing river below, either side of two small villages. A sherpa walked over it effortlessly, poking a plank occasionally. He ran back, beaming, but said nothing. They crossed the gap in groups of three, fearing too much weight would send them to the waters below. It would be the first of several such junctions.

They began to climb a well-worn path, up steep banks of steps, and down the other side, cornering hills, gradually gaining height. No sooner would they rise, but a descent would follow. The weather was kind. Each afternoon, the sherpas would gesture and stop at a stone-built hut to eat and rest for the night. One lodge refused them entry. A tense argument ensued with knives drawn, so they moved on to the next stay.

Rayleigh became very tired. His legs burned, knees jelly-like, and his missing big toe joint throbbed after knocking it four or five times on the steps. On the sixth afternoon, they stopped in a river valley. The sherpas stripped naked and jumped into a small pool fed by a stream. Their bodies steamed. Rayleigh felt the water.

"Junior, come here with us. It is a hot spring," exclaimed Rayleigh, as the waters soothed his pains.

They all bathed for an hour in the warm, soft water and slept soundly that night. They awoke to a low rumble, followed by crashing rocks and ice.

"An avalanche? Get out of here!" shouted Wethersby Jnr.

The gang watched as the hut disintegrated. There was no rock or ice fall off the mountain behind them. The hot pool bubbled and hissed furiously. They saw clouds of dust rising in the direction of where they had come from the previous day. The ground shook back and forth for a minute.

They heard Fredrick's faint cries soon after the shaking stopped. Looking around, Wethersby Jnr counted. They were also missing a sherpa, Nanii.

The team pulled the splintered door off its last hinge and methodically removed a stone and tile at a time. They found Nanii first, motionless, his legs at unnatural angles, and a large wooden stick protruded from his chest. Next to the dead man were more bloody feet. Fredrick hissed as Rayleigh removed a rock off his groin, and a jet of blood smacked Rayleigh's face.

He held his hand firmly against the leg wound, and Fredrick yelled out again.

"Junior, here. Fredrick's alive, but I need help to stem his blood," commanded Rayleigh, spinning his head.

Wethersby Jnr choked. He pulled off his leather belt and wrapped it around Fredrick's thigh, above the gash; the blood flow diminished. Fredrick passed out. Rayleigh thought he was dead until he saw his chest rise and fall. The hut keeper's wife wailed uncontrollably. They carefully dragged Fredrick out of the ruin and went in again to remove Nanii's body. Nerway explained later that Nanii was her nephew.

Mixing water from the now scalding pool with river water, they cleaned Fredrick of dust and blood. They carried him about three hundred yards further up the valley to another stone cottage. It had fared better than the last, only losing a handful of roof pieces.

Unable to walk, they agreed that Fredrick would remain close by the hot spring. They would bring him down from the trail on their return from the temple. He resisted meekly as the gang moved on once more.

They navigated a long deep crack, tens of yards across; it had altered the river's path. After several small tremors, fortunately, the next three days were calm. Despite the terrain rising, they mostly wandered alongside the river, following the valley, until they came to a spread-out village, Jomsom. Nerway and the three sherpas wasted no time entering the most significant temple. They prayed to the Lord Buddha, surrounded by deep red painted walls and a green ceiling.

Rayleigh felt energised. The warm water brought his legs back to life. His ankle was pain-free for the first time that he could remember. Only his toe stump was sore, as he had knocked it again earlier that morning. He urged Wethersby Jnr to rest just for a single night before heading to Muktinath. That night he lay awake in the silence as an almost full moon lit up the shared room.

They trekked another eight hours north, meandering along the pebbled river. They reached a modest temple, perched on a small rocky outcrop, surrounded by steeply rising white mountains. The small main building had white walls and at its centre a multi-layered roof. A golden stupa circled by bronze bells was close by. A solitary old monk, holding himself up by a wonky bamboo walking cane, welcomed them. His name was Gunhi.

--x--

"What, surely not? Could it be that simple?" Rayleigh exclaimed, alone.

He had studied the murals in every room of the Muktinath temple for the last week. His imagination ran wild, as usual, with great snowy battles, processions, and harem kingdoms. He looked again, with a frowning expression and slight smile, realising what he had missed since the first day.

The door carving was in fair condition; watermarked, a little worn and the paint faded. The door had been open most of the time, so shielding the images. Rayleigh traced his finger around a tear-drop contour and that of a feather fletching, pointing to the right. The arrow's head rested within a rounded green-brown shape. '*WLT*' was scripted lightly within the silhouette.

"Pa's map!" he blurted out.

Rayleigh recognised the island's shape instantly.

"Old Wethersby, you were a cunning fellow to focus us on our family's land, but it is not the resting place of the JackFruit now. Oh, my bullying cousins, you are in for a monstrous disappointment," he taunted as Wethersby Jnr entered the hall.

Both men laughed together, mesmerised by the door's features. Wethersby Jnr hid his tears. Three hours later,

Rayleigh had carefully drawn the door's carving on the blank back of one of the green inked maps. He redrew the arrow multiple times, for it did not face precisely due east.

"Cousin, we have a long way to go and should not delay any farther," said Wethersby Jnr briskly. "I am worried about the silver, yes, but more about the increasing chill in the air. Did you see the snow flurry this morning? If it snows heavily, it could trap us here for weeks. Let us give some merit to the ageing monk for our good fortune and ask for his guidance to return to the city of Kantipur."

"Your journey ahead is long, but you have come far already, just a couple of short hops more. The white powder comes soon. Go now, before it is too late. If not, you will be keeping me company for months, just like my friend Mister Wethersby," said Gunhi, startling the cousins.

"You knew him?" asked Rayleigh.

"Why, yes, of course," replied Gunhi. "Mister Wethersby and I are the same age. He spent four months with us. That was before the novice monks left me. Mister Wethersby spent weeks painstakingly carving this door. He never told me why, but I can see, from what you are not saying, this door means everything to you, yes?"

"It's a map," showed Rayleigh.

"Why, of course," said Gunhi.

"Please take this," said Wethersby Jnr, handing the kneeling man a bar of silver.

They talked about Wethersby Snr until midnight before Gunhi called time. He received them at daybreak, although the sun still had a way to go until it reached the hills.

The men forced themselves up each morning, feeling more tired than the last, knowing another day of walking and climbing awaited them. The wind chill was severe, their faces blueing. Walking was tough on the icy path and steps. Just as they thought they were making substantial progress downhill, turning another corner, they faced yet another steep climb upwards. Towards the end of each afternoon, they stopped for simple food and slept overnight at a hut. They eagerly greeted Fredrick and rested briefly at the hot springs, soothing their aches and pains. They arranged Fredrick on a mule. Another five days later, they arrived back at Pokhara, exhausted.

Chief Putki welcomed them, Mayling sobbed. Fredrick's leg was black, blue, and greenish. The wound was healing well, but slowly, in the cool air. Rayleigh carefully carried him off the mule with Wethersby Jnr's help and sat him on a thick rug in the stone shelter. The light snow had stopped falling. The whole troop and some of Putki's family came together, discussing the trek into the valleys and to the small temple of Muktinath. They sat around fires by the lake's edge for the rest of that afternoon until the light breeze became more robust and chilled them, despite the embers' heat.

"Did you find what you came for, young man?" asked Putki.

"Yes, and no. Only more clues to a far-off land," replied Rayleigh solemnly. "We lost one of your guides to the earth movement, crushed by stones. I am deeply sorry."

They had yet to break the news of their discovery to Mayling. The cousins had discussed what to do for hours on their way back from the temple. They had agreed; to leave and travel first to Kalikata, then sail to Kandy as soon as possible. Wethersby Jnr, though, wanted to rest the men first, then have provisions readied. Rayleigh was impatient and wanted to move on the next day, sensing the weather turning and heeding Gunhi's warning.

“I’m sorry, Mayling. We found another clue, to Kandy and then beyond to Siam. Look here, I made a copy,” said Rayleigh softly.

She stopped to mop Fredrick’s forehead and looked at Rayleigh, holding open his new green inked plot.

“Where was it?” she asked.

“On a door to the temple’s main hall,” replied Rayleigh. “We were lucky that the rumbling earth had not damaged the temple; it rang its bells, a bad omen, according to the old head monk, Gunhi. Can you believe he knew Mister Wethersby, the old one, not Junior?”

She nodded and frowned, tilting her head to one side.

“Hmm, that is a coincidence. Chief Putki knew him too!” she eventually answered.

Fredrick shifted his position, bringing himself upright, and said quietly, “What? How can it be that we are on the same path as your grandfather, Rayleigh?”

“Well, Fredrick. He left us some clues, but he came from the opposite direction,” said Rayleigh and then asked, “How is your leg?”

“I will live. It is mending well, so long as I put no pressure through it. I can still make a son or a daughter,” said Fredrick, smiling.

Mayling blushed.

Three days later, they said their goodbyes to the villagers. They thanked Chief Putki profusely for his hospitality and apologised again for losing one of his own. They loaded horses, mules and yaks with enough supplies of dried foods, rice and water to last at least a month. After two mules stumbled and fell down a steep ravine, they lost some stores.

It took only four days to reach the Kingdom of Kantipur and its old city.

Kantipur was a glorious sight; a smoky brown cloud floated above the city. As they drew closer, the scent of burnt incense and meats hit them at the back of their noses; sandalwood and jasmine mixed with fat. Tiny alleyways led to open squares of multiple-level pagodas made from wood and small red bricks. Some buildings had collapsed, Rayleigh assumed from the quake. He wanted to explore this fascinating place. Its people seemed so friendly, and no one begged. They found a warm welcome into numerous homes which was quite a feat, given their number. It was clear to the cousins that the city rarely saw visitors from the west. However, it was unmistakeably a vital staging post from India and China, as Chief Putki had told them, given the great mix of people they met.

They sat in the corner of the simple darkened room for over an hour, enchanted by the low sounds coming from several large horns. Inside, red-clothed monks knelt and sang chanting, almost humming. Dense incense filled the void, almost choking Rayleigh and Mayling as they watched in silence, lightheaded. Rayleigh found himself swaying gently to the haunting rhythm. Mayling smiled.

Every day for a week, they visited the temple before dusk. Naked flames on long sticks punctured the darkness when they returned to their temporary lodgings. The evenings were cold, Mayling complained.

"I wish to stay here," Nerway asserted. "It has everything I want - peace, serenity and kindness. And, of course, a good supply of food and water. Although I fear I will suffer from the hot pepper."

Wethersby Jnr nodded, "Yes. What do you need?"

"Nothing more, apart from your blessing," replied Nerway.

"Of course. We will, though, need guidance to Kalikata," requested Wethersby Jnr.

"I thought you had the map?" said Nerway dryly. "No matter, I shall seek a guide for you."

Nerway returned with a frail-looking man three days later, who went by the name of Chazy. He reminded Rayleigh of the monk, Gunhi, at Muktinath; the only discernable difference was his straight cane. After introductions, Chazy explained that he had travelled to Kalikata four times in the same number of years. It was a fine trading place, dominated most recently by the British East India Company. He had made a small fortune, enough to sustain his extended family for years to come. Wethersby Jnr quizzed Chazy on his reasons to return, concluding he was perhaps rather greedy and a gambler.

The troop moved on reluctantly, into another unknown trek across valleys, plateaus, streams and raging rivers. They soon pursued the well-trodden route southeast, following the Bagmati river and crossing numerous mountain passes. After a week, the landscape flattened. Spirits in the group were low; most were bored travelling. One night ten of the Jodhpur soldiers disappeared; Rayleigh assumed they wanted to return to Kantipur. Wethersby Jnr called his usual early morning gathering and questioned the remaining army men of their intentions.

"You must make up your minds whether to travel with us or go it alone," said Wethersby Jnr boldly. "According to Chazy, we are about halfway to the village of Kalikata. The route is easy and flat. Head back to Kantipur, and you will face the brunt of winter and the mountains again. Put up your hands if you wish to return."

No hands went up.

"Good. Let me be clear. If any of you desert from now on, I will find and kill you. Understood?" Wethersby Jnr continued.

"Aye," they replied in unison.

Over the next month, their carried stores diminished. However, by netting fish from the river and drinking its water, they were well sustained. No more of the men disappeared.

Freya, however, was sick again. She carried a high fever and was continuously wet from sweat, her exposed skin covered with small itchy red spots. Mayling sobbed while trying to ease the girl's suffering.

--x--

# 23

## Dirty Gerty

Constantly nagged by the ringing in his head, James kept playing with the holes in his mouth. He tried to replay what happened on the *Frostenden Nave*, but his mind was blank after watching Charles thrown overboard.

James sat silently and listened, simply nodding occasionally, surprised at the brutality of the multi-coloured men. But it was his appearance that drew attention; his jaw now locked at an angle. A wrinkled flap of skin was all that remained of his ear. His voice was hoarse and shriller than before. James found it difficult to talk. His biggest surprise came when Everett described when the slaver, Ohama, bought him but never treated him as a captive.

"Why had Ohama treated him with respect?" he thought.

"Everett, how are we going to get off this godforsaken island?" asked James.

Everett had not mentioned their ghost ship in the other bay.

Everett and Ohama talked most nights, out of earshot from James, about setting off to the Indian coast. As each day wore on, their urgency rose. The repairs were taking longer than expected. They restored the timbers three times, and the canvas tore twice in their hands. Ohama guessed the pirates had returned to their islands much further north to share their spoils. He was right, and he was wrong.

At the end of the second month mending the *Frostenden Nave*, another ship appeared early one morning. It was the same distinctive shape Everett had seen before his boat got blasted and boarded.

Ohama ignored the small man's threats; he had heard them all before.

"So, where is the one-eared sailor?" laughed the man.

"Solroy, you never learn. Slicing off his ear, why? Did you get perverse pleasure from it?" replied Ohama, as he continued to stare at Solroy.

"He is nothing; thinks he is a joker. Who's laughing now?" snorted Solroy.

"Thacker is still here with me. He has had even more misfortune than meeting you," laughed Ohama. "But he is lucky too. He got struck by a thunderbolt and learnt how to fly, briefly."

Both men tittered. They moved apart and sat facing the sea towards the *Frostenden Nave*.

"How is our ship?" asked Solroy.

"In remarkable condition, considering you torched it," cackled Ohama. "We repaired your cannon-made holes and salvaged canvas. The sail is small now; it will slow our progress."

"What have you learnt of their expedition?" quizzed Solroy.

"It's captain, Everett, says they were heading to Kandy. He thinks it is a Maldives island; it seemed a shame to disappoint him, so I have not told them how far south we are from them," lied Ohama.

"I thought Mister Thacker was the captain, no matter. Kandy. Why?" Solroy asked.

"The usual. Illegal trade, bypassing the Dutch, Portuguese, French and even the English Navy," came back Ohama. "It seems Mister Thacker and his brother, the one you threw overboard, owned that ship."

"Up until the point he lost his ear and sibling," bellowed Solroy. "Let us go and see our prize."

They walked to a small boat and rowed out to the ship, going around to inspect the repaired hull.

"Excellent job, I like. Now lose the name," stated Solroy.

"Whatever. What do we rename it?" invited Ohama.

Solroy did not answer. They rowed silently and repositioned the small boat facing the beach, climbed the ladder and walked around the deck.

Solroy had his hand on his chin and then chuckled, "We should name it *Panotii*."

Ohama had no idea what he meant. He asked, "Why?"

"A legend, from way back. It is the name of a tribe who had giant ears that were so big one could touch the other," howled Solroy. "Inappropriate, do you not think?"

The men sniggered back to the beach.

Everett watched the two men for over an hour, out of sight, surprised by their cooperation. He sat too far away to have heard anything they said, but he saw enough from their behaviour.

Solroy appeared through the shack's door, startling James, who veered backwards on his mat. He crouched with his arms over his head and legs tucked inwards.

"Get up, baby. Let me take you to one of my women. Dirty Gerty will be delighted to see you," said Solroy.

James remained curled up and said nothing. Solroy leaned over, grabbing James and propelled him out of the hut, then shoved him along the beach, dropping James next to the boat.

"Get in before she gives you a second bruising," winked Solroy.

Less than half an hour later, the three men were standing aboard the ship, facing a beautiful woman.

"This is Gerty," announced Solroy.

Everett's mouth wetted; James stared as a drip of blood ran from his lips to the base of his chin.

"Which one is Thacker?" cried Gerty.

"I told you, he has one ear!" replied Solroy.

"But look, he looks like he's seen a ghost," said Gerty.

"Get on with your seeding before I change my mind," pronounced Solroy.

She grabbed James's hand and led him to a small compartment. It was dark inside; the only light came from cracks through the door.

"I want you now," she demanded as she slowly undressed.

James stood in the middle of the room, speechless with a deep sense of foreboding.

"Well? Get undressed," she said coyly.

James wept afterwards.

"Do not let Solroy see your weakness, for he will cut your other ear off without blinking," she said softly.

James remained dumb. Gerty led him outside.

"Return tomorrow. Same time, Mister Thacker. Do not be late," she said loud enough for Solroy and Everett to hear.

James slept solidly that night. In the morning, his body ached all over, apart from his numb groin. He smiled as he briefly remembered his dream, then recoiled, knowing he had to perform again later that day. Never in his life had he wished for no lovemaking; despite the fleeting pleasure, the bindings and her sheer strength overwhelmed him.

"Gerty, she is so beautiful, though," he kept telling himself.

Everett sniggered as James limped towards him and asked sarcastically, "How was your afternoon yesterday, James?"

"Wonderful," he replied, forcing a smile.

He walked off and then swam as hard as he could against the fierce current. An hour later, he returned to his hut and slept.

In the afternoon, he walked unaided alongside Solroy but outside his arm's reach. His limp had reduced, but his body pained him all over.

Again, she tied him, his body tightly outstretched into a star. She was uncompromising. He lasted two minutes. She laughed, then began to attack him but relented after the first slap. She let him rest for an hour.

"Again, tomorrow. Do not be late," Gerty demanded.

His new routine continued for two weeks. Despite the pain she caused him, he regained some strength and started to enjoy their encounters, surprising himself, but he tried hard not to show her his pleasure.

--x--

Everyone on the island had thinned. Stores of corn and rice were desperately low, and the produce in the small garden fields was wilting yellow. The grains had not yet formed, and the spring-fed stream, now a mere trickle.

Ohama and Solroy sat around a small fire near their huts, planning the atoll's retreat. It has served them well as a refuge for the past year, but they had given up hope of self-sufficiency, despite Ohama's best efforts.

They agreed their risk of survival was decreasing daily. The biggest challenge was gathering enough stores for their trip east rather than travelling north to the Maldives. Solroy had brought enough supplies down on the *Risqué*, and what remained, he estimated sufficient for ten people for a month; but there were twenty here now. Fortunately, their large water pots were full from the infrequent, but heavy, downpours.

Gerty had slowly extracted the unbelievable story from James over the last few weeks, the JackFruit treasure of huge sapphires and diamonds. James embellished his grandfather's words, insisting the hoard was still in the cave where Wethersby Snr first discovered the casket.

A fever struck them all.

They wanted to tow the *Panotii* behind the *Risqué*, but their ropes were too short and thin; both ships would have to sail freely. Solroy had also brought back about half of the trading goods he had offloaded from the *Panotii*.

Everybody left the island; Solroy guessed it was early October. The crews split up, so each ship's gang was equal in numbers. Everett stayed on the *Panotii*.

James, however, travelled on the *Risqué* with Gerty and Solroy. Their daily afternoons of passion caused much excitement to the *Risqué's* original crew, who wagered how long it would take James to scream aloud. Leaving the island was bittersweet for Ohama. He had spent months tending his land amid the intense sun but for little reward. He longed for the warmth of a woman. Gerty flirted with him constantly, but she was out of reach. In any case, he had no desire to be tethered like a dog again.

The *Panotii* surprised Everett with its speed; the canvas repairs held up. The new timbers patching up the hull fared less well; there was outward movement from constant creaking.

On a northeast heading, the two ships drifted apart. The *Panotii* had started to take on water two days before. She had slowed down, despite the crew's constant bailing.

Solroy wanted to return to his home on his island in the Maldives, fearing the food and water would not sustain them to Kandy, given the *Panotii*'s progress. Then there was the secret cache.

With its silver bars and gold coins under Everett's cabin, Solroy could not lose the *Panotii* now. He wanted to take more, but not with the men all around him. He had not told Ohama; he only snatched bars and a bag of coins, now safely stowed under *his* cabin's floor. The current tried to push them north. He battled with the trim to keep their course, stashing surplus sail. The *Panotii* came back into sight. Three hours later, the ships were within heckling range, to everyone's relief.

Ohama scrutinized the *Panotii* gang, especially those from England. His father had once told him that England was full of beggars and rogues; never trust an Englishman. Nevertheless, Ohama longed to see his father's home, fascinated by his childhood tales of ice and snow. When he found the silver bars under Everett's floor, he smiled and held up his tankard.

Laughing, he said, "To you, William O. Boyce. Where are you now, father? How am I to get these ingots safely off this ship without allowing that madman Solroy to get his thieving hands on it first?"

The ships stayed close together for the next two weeks, their course unchanged. Fortunately, the weather was kind, a strong breeze and medium swell occasionally bouncing over the bow. They made satisfactory progress despite the quality of the sail. Solroy rationed supplies by half again; Another week, and they would run out.

Five English men on the *Risqué* had become unusually sick, two of them were already comatose. Solroy told the others to expect the worst for them; he was right.

Two bodies dropped off the plank into the ocean. Their mates watched on as a mass of fish frenzied around the corpses, tearing away chunks of flesh. The swarm intensified within five minutes; the remains sank. Three days later, another two men succumbed to the same course. Ten more became gravely ill.

Another week and all food on both ships had gone, only a tiny amount of water remained; the sickest men got none, Solroy insisted they were a lost cause.

A shout went out, “Ship!”

Half the deck men looked up; the rest looked towards the horizon. Up at the crow’s nest, George was pointing due north, waving frantically. Solroy climbed the mast like a feral cat. He smiled as he saw the boat.

“George has great sight but a poor perspective. That is a fishing boat, not a ship. Let us see what they have caught for our dinner,” he shouted before sliding down.

The three vessels drew close. Five menfolk and a young boy smiled, struggling to hold up a fat fish in his hands - its head touched the floor.

“Tuna. We have more like this one,” the boy shouted.

The crews feasted on the red and raw fish. James detested it but would have eaten anything. Since they left the island, he ventured outside of his modest cabin for the first time. Embarrassed, his body was now skeletal, skin heavily wrinkled with dark bruises, pus oozed from his wrists and ankles. Gerty had not stopped performing her cruel games on him, despite his pleas for mercy, but the more he implored, the harder she played until he would pass out.

Despite the meals, two more men were fish-food.

“Irony,” reflected Everett aloud.

They spotted four similar boats during the next three days before finally sighting the coast.

# 24

# Fortress

Somehow, James had expected a fanfare welcome; after all, he had travelled such a vast distance. He was disappointed. No one greeted them. Their only salute was the sight of twenty or so anchored ships surrounding a great fort protruding into the sea. Most of the vessels were more extensive than theirs and far better equipped, given the number of gunports.

With its patched-up hull gaping again, the *Panotii* looked a sorry state in comparison; a poor man's boat, he thought. At least they had arrived safely. His only thought now was for fresh food and drink but no fish. He longed for beer or anything more compelling.

"Most of these vessels are Dutch; those smaller two are English, none are Portuguese. Look at that flag," said Everett pointing towards a warship, "Unmistakably VOC, Dutch East India Company. I am surprised we did not get an armed escort."

"Given our size, battered state, and the volume of ships here, we pose little risk," stated Ohama. "It will be different when we step foot in the fort."

With the anchor dropped, Ohama, Everett, and James climbed down into their dinghy and rowed towards the pier, leaving Gerty and Solroy behind aboard the other ship.

A guard holding a twelve-foot pike, two swords by his side, with his chest covered in faded armour and owning a grim expression, blocked their way.

"And where d'ya think you're going?" he demanded.

"We come to make trade, not trouble," replied Ohama, almost interrupting the soldier.

"What ya got on ya sorry boat?" the guard invited.

"Apart from our strong men, it's our business," retorted Everett, winking back at James.

"What happened to ya man? Where's ya ear?" the lookout continued, steadfast.

"An Omani, who is still on that ship, cut it off," let out James.

They all laughed, except James.

"Well, ya betta' get going 'fore someone tramps on ya boat and snatches ya trade. There be many-a pirate 'ere, that be good at that, ya know," declared the sentry.

He moved to one side and let them through the giant gates.

On the other side of the fort's barrier, people went about their businesses. Female chai and market sellers, staggering drunk men with fancy hats, and similar Dutch soldiers carrying their pointed pikes.

James sensed the unmistakable whiff of burning pork; his mouth began watering as he wandered towards the smoke. Ohama and Everett followed for they were hungry for fresh food too. A small, butterflied pig's carcass hung across a smoking pit of wood. Globs of fat dripped, hissed, and smoked off the embers. James stopped suddenly and smiled for the first time in months; the golden pig reminded him of home.

After they gorged on enough roasted hog for ten men, they bartered for more, buying a whole sizzling one, then carried it on a pole back to the main gate.

James said to the guard as they passed, "This is good."

They got back to the *Panotii* accompanied by the pig and watched it disappear over the top deck.

"Enjoy," shouted Ohama.

Solroy ignored them in disgust. Once they had rowed back to the pier, they snubbed the sentry and went through the gate unchallenged.

"Solroy and his men will not touch the pig. Against their principles, sacred," said Ohama. "Here in Kandy, and much of India, the cow is holy too, so the only meat they eat is chicken or goat if they can get it."

Soon they came to a grand red and green painted two-storey building with large open wooden shutters and they walked through the entranceway.

"Got goods to trade, 'ave we?" boomed an invisible voice, coming from in front of them.

As they walked forward, James made out a tiny man behind a small desk.

"Yes. Let us see the governor without delay," stated Ohama.

"He's always busy in afternoons. What 'ave you got on that miserable looking boat that would bring him out of 'is fortune pit?" asked the small man as he stood in front of them.

Ignoring his six-inch hat, he was only four feet tall, shorter even than Solroy. He wore a monocle in his left eye but looked at them, with his head lowered slightly, over the glass.

"Well?" the man bellowed.

"Ivory, from great beasts slain in southern Africa, and bullion from London," replied Ohama.

James and Everett, both shocked, looked at one another.

"And what do you want?" said the man.

"Spice; cinnamon, clove, nutmeg, mace, and whole pepper," stated Ohama, and added, "and a lot of it."

"Wait here," replied the man and shuffled out.

"Bullion," laughed Everett, still unsure whether his cache remained safely hidden.

"We are parleying," said Ohama. "Let's see where this leads us."

"My coins," murmured James, more seriously worried now than he was when he lost his ear.

Everett almost choked again, guessing that James had not realised his mistake.

The short man made them wait in the airless room for well over an hour. Ohama thought that this was part of a ruse until the man returned along with two others. Both were six feet tall or more, dressed in baggy pure-white shirts, with brown breeches below their knees. They wore the same type of hat; one red, one green. Everett thought that their headwear made them seem taller; the tips almost hit the ceiling.

"Ya want to trade, do ya? Under whose authority?" asked the green-hat man.

"Our own," returned Ohama. "We do not represent any one country."

"Where have I seen ya before?" asked the red-hat man, pointing at James.

"Sir, have you been to Southwold England? If not, then you mistake me for someone else," smiled James.

The man tilted his head slightly to his left and said while looking sternly at James, "Are ya sure ya never been to Kandy or India 'fore?"

"Correct. Do you mean to tell me there is another one-eared toothless Englishman around these parts, who looks like me too?" said James, still smiling, although a knot started to form in his stomach as he puzzled over the man's comment.

"Well, ya cannot be too careful 'round 'ere. There be many a pirate eager to cut off ya bits," winked the red-hat man and bellowed with laughter.

Everyone in the room sniggered, even James.

"My man tells me ya 'ave ivory and bars. Now show us, and we will see what trade is possible," said the green-hat gent.

Ohama nodded towards Everett and James, and they made for the door.

"Where's ya gold?" demanded the green-hat man.

"Bullion. I never mentioned its colour," smirked Ohama.

Governor of Kali, Gerrit de Heere, met James and Solroy back in the grand warehouse office, insisting that all the other men, including Everett, stay away. On first learning about the one-eared Englishman and Omani pirate, de Heere was fascinated by the two men. He was impressed by James, especially by his willingness to forgive Solroy for the gruesome injury he had inflicted and for the loss of his brother. However, it was his name that intrigued him the most.

Solroy stood, looking up towards the taller man, with James by his side. The governor had not seen them separated for the past two weeks. After two hours of going back and forth, they settled on an acceptable deal. Both Solroy and James fought hard not to grin. The governor remained stone-faced throughout. He knew he would safely multiply this trade ten, or perhaps even twentyfold, within a year, depending on favourable winds sailing back to Holland. He would always take his private cut, but never too much, from the company. This one would be different, under the disguise of the English.

Part of the deal included lodgings for the two guests at the governor's residence within the fort; Governor de Heere wanted to keep James close. They left the warehouse, gathered their meagre clothes and possessions, and moved into the grand building.

Solroy could hardly believe their luck when the governor agreed to this part of the deal. James, though, was apprehensive. Despite the time it took to conclude, the agreement was a little too easy for his simple thinking.

"Perhaps Solroy has had enough of pirating and wants to settle in Kandy?" James asked himself. "But he has no woman or family here. Why stay?"

Their apartments were opulent, spacious, and neatly decorated with old furniture. One had green walls; James's was maroon. A door connected them, lockable from both sides with separate keys.

During the next month, they wined and dined with the governor and his entourage. Several Dutch women and maids drew James's attention, but they were far from drawn to him. The young twenty-something governor's wife, Johanna, was a regular distraction and a discreet tease. James grew increasingly jealous, often hearing laughter and wild screams of excitement from Solroy's room at night, as he was never too sure which woman was there.

James invited Gerty to the residency to stay a night, with the governor's permission, on just two occasions. James thought that would help muffle the sounds from the green room rather than for their satisfaction.

James and Solroy were in an enviable position, effectively under the governor's protection. They could do little wrong and knew it. The governor frowned upon seeing the men stagger back to their apartments, full of drink. He only saw them do so twice in a couple of months. He was surprised, especially by Solroy, as he thought that drinking was against his principles. The men rarely had a night without their favoured local drink. They always drank the cloudy and yeasty coconut spirit when they were together.

On the other hand, Everett and Ohama grew to despise them as their influence increased. Gradually Everett and Ohama were locked out of the deals when new vessels arrived in Kali, those not carrying the VOC flag, of course. Indeed, the only trade conducted with those ships was now organised solely by James and Solroy. James thrived on the attention and his rapid rise to power.

It was a wet and windy morning on 4th December 1697. James nursed his groggy head during breakfast. He sat at the same table with the governor and his wife. They made small talk, for he could not bear being in Johanna's company with the governor present. They were talking about James's passage from England, again.

"There must have been more reasons to come from England and specifically to Kandy, James?" probed Johanna. "It is your first voyage. Why not find your way somewhere closer to home?"

"We left with bullion to trade for spice. Frankly, going to India or Kandy makes little difference," replied James, word for word as he had done so on several occasions before when the same question was asked.

"Yes, but I hear you came to seek another fortune," grinned Johanna.

"Oh yes, a wife to bear me a son," he roared, winking at Johanna out of sight of the governor.

Johanna's face briefly turned crimson despite her heavily powdered face.

"No, I mean other riches. Diamonds, star sapphires and other gems," she said hurriedly.

James laughed openly, unsure of his next move and bluff.

"I have heard that Kandy holds great wealth in local gems, although cutting deals here is full of those who want to take their cut; too many middlemen," replied James, still laughing.

"And what about jackfruit?" she continued.

"It is a big ugly fruit which stinks when it rots. No point trying to get those back to England. They would not last," James said, feigning interest. "What has the ugly jackfruit got to do with gems?"

"Come now, darling, leave Mister Thacker to his breakfast," said the governor. "He is playing with you. He must know the legend; anyone, who is anyone in these parts, knows."

"Well, I haven't been here long enough, obviously," said James, nervously.

"It is a myth," laughed the governor. "It leads young men to leave their comfortable homes to travel across oceans, only to lose themselves to the sun-kissed women of Kandy."

James laughed.

De Heere choked on his rice pudding, then said. "Perhaps that, though, is the real treasure here? My dear, stop teasing Mister Thacker."

James stared at Johanna de Heere as he finished breakfast.

"Is this a trap?" he asked himself.

He had never heard anyone anywhere on Kandy talk about the JackFruit, other than the fruit itself. Not even in the *Sardine Tavern*. The jackfruit on the table was delicious though, tasting like banana and pineapple, combined with a bit of mango, he thought.

When the governor got up and left the room, Johanna moved next to James, touched the top of his leg and said, "I will see you tonight at eight, and we can talk more about the JackFruit."

She stood up and left.

James's mind was a fog for the rest of the busy day. The low stir within the *Sardine Tavern* soon became a torrent of volume; they had spied a new and unknown ship moving outside the harbour.

Taking their cue from hearing the signal, Solroy and James downed their coconut grog and marched outside. They were soon spying the ship from the fort's sea wall. The vessel looked similar to the *Panotii*, except the sails were in better condition.

As it drew closer, Solroy remarked, "Look at its low pitch in the water. It either has a leak or a heavy cargo."

James replied, "Or both, Solroy. Let us get into position."

Soon the men were at the main gate, next to the same guard James had met for the first time, all those months ago.

"Go easy, gentlemen. I see the Dutch gang approaching, maybe trying to steal your march," said the guard.

"Thanks," replied Solroy. "We can manage this ourselves. Please see the men from the new ship through and delay the troops. Our usual arrangement?"

Solroy handed the guard a cloth bag with three silver coins inside it.

James approached the three men from the new ship as they passed through the gate.

"Sirs, my name is James Thacker. I am pleased to meet you. This man is Solroy, an Omani pirate turned good," laughed James and then continued sternly, "From where have you travelled, and what do you trade?"

"A one-eared toothless fellow Englishman. Now that is a shock and a surprise," replied one of the men in a broad Cornish accent. "Captain Jack Robertson. Pleased to meet with you. These two men are my officers, Henry and Harry. Yes, we have travelled from Plymouth, England and intend to turn around with spices. We travel under no flag."

James led the group of men to the *Sardine Tavern*. They drank for the rest of the afternoon and discussed the sale. Their volume slowly increased. They agreed to go to the ship to confirm the bars. However, Solroy and James made it clear that Robinson may go to their spice store without other men.

James was tired. The silver briefly lit up his eyes, but he was thinking of the governor's wife and a much larger treasure.

They took Robertson to their secret store with his eyes covered. They agreed on many sacks of clove, cinnamon, pepper, mace, and some nutmeg inside the heavily scented room. The captain was beside himself; never had he seen so much spice in one place. He knew it would earn him an enormous profit if he could get it to England safely. After all, he had stumbled upon the stricken ghost ship and its bountiful cargo only a week earlier.

They headed towards the tavern and, once there, continued to drink. James, however, took his time and hardly drank. Despite his drunken state, even Solroy noticed James's lack of interest in his usually favourite tipple.

Solroy asked James, "What distracts you? It is our biggest haul yet, don't you think?"

"Yes," James replied and tucked into his liquor.

Robinson and Solroy kept their cups from drying out while James left his on the bench, occasionally sipping it.

By six in the evening, James left for the residency. He was surprised how much he wobbled up the grand steps to the entrance. James slept for two hours in his room. When he woke, Johanna was standing over him, naked.

"How did you...?" he asked, still in a daze.

"Shhh. We better not wake the whole house. Now, tell me everything about the JackFruit before I devour you. Do not hold back, for I won't," said Johanna sternly before giggling.

"How did you break into my locked maroon room?" grinned James. "I remember I turned the key."

"You seem to forget where you are and who owns this place," she said, waving a key in front of him.

She jumped onto the bed, ripped off his shirt and breeches without saying another word. She held one hand tight over his open mouth and toyed with him with the other.

"I thought you said you wanted to understand about the JackFruit first," muffled James.

"Well, we have all night. The governor is out with his pals, governing. No doubt creaming off the top as usual," she said.

Half an hour later, he almost dozed off again. Johanna lay next to him.

"JackFruit. I know you know more. Tell me everything," asserted Johanna.

"I don't recognise anything other than a legend handed down from my grandpa. I've heard nothing else since being on this island," replied James truthfully.

"Your grandfather, was his name Mister Wethersby?" said Johanna, smiling.

"Yes. How do you know?" answered James.

"Let me be clear with you. I am the one asking the questions here," said Johanna, stroking James's right ear. "Your grandfather thought he disappeared from Kandy with the JackFruit, but he left behind a trail of clues."

James looked into Johanna's eyes, and he leisurely moved his gaze down her pearl-white body to her toes.

"All I believe is that he pushed us to come to Kandy in a pointless mission to locate the JackFruit. Coming here was, and is, a dilemma," said James defiantly. "He took the two diamonds back to England, sold one and bought our Suffolk estate, and stored the other in a London vault for his great-grandchild."

"Oh, only two, indeed! I hear the casket was full of gems," Johanna declared.

James's head was beginning to spin again. He wanted to sleep but desperately wanted more time in bed with the voluptuous Johanna. He was so curious to hear about his grandfather too.

"Maybe, just maybe, this wasn't going to be a wasted journey after all," he muttered.

"You must tell me where the casket is. I will not tell a soul. We can share the contents and escape to Europe," panted Johanna, as she held her chest hard and wiggled her legs around his.

"It is in Kandy, several hours from Kali. I know nothing more," replied James. "Escape, you say. You are hardly a prisoner in this palace."

"That's what you think. I detest this place. It's too hot, and the red spots that come up each rainy season make me sick," whimpered Johanna.

They made love again. James felt like he was back in Southwold for the first time in months, except for the crazy humidity, he thought, as he mopped his forehead. An unnatural expression stayed on Johanna's face for the next hour.

"I want those diamonds, and my husband will not get a guilder," screamed Johanna.

She convinced herself that her charms had seduced James. They were a similar age; she was half the age of her husband. The governor bored her; he was always too busy trading. "Governing", as she would sarcastically say to her closest friends. He found little time for her, despite her beautiful looks and young, bubbly personality.

She had no idea where the treasure was, nor for that matter whether it even existed. She merely recounted the mysterious stories told for several generations amongst the Dutch elite, especially in Kali.

Occasionally, she would go off into the bush together with her husband, looking for the JackFruit. She would ride with him, more for her entertainment to relieve the boredom within the fort - and keep an eye on him.

The governor himself had spent many years scouring the countryside, trying to locate it.

--x--

They had been out of the fort on one such excursion for one night with two other couples. They came across the entrance to a cave containing a small shrine and many tiny naked lights. The governor attempted to go deep into the shelter, but the passage was narrow and partially blocked after fifty feet. Johanna only went in twenty feet or so before the ceiling lowered. She refused to go further for getting her clothes dirty. She was curious about an amber light emanating from further down the passage. Upon exiting the cave, they all glistened from yellow dust that covered them.

They camped in the overhang at the cavern's opening. Johanna woke from a disturbing nightmare, where the walls closed in on her, and a rockfall buried her husband. She woke in the darkness, startled and soaking wet. The governor was not by her side.

Johanna cried out, "Gerrit, Gerrit, where are you?"

The four other bodies stirred. Johanna took a flame lantern and went back into the tunnel. Her white blouse soon got filthy from the sand. She bumped her head several times as it narrowed. Calling out his name, she eventually heard a low moan. She scrambled further in and found the governor lying on his back, his legs covered with sand and rock.

"Please, Johanna, remove the rubble and drag me out of this godforsaken pit," exclaimed the governor. "These rocks are warm and getting hot. They are starting to burn through."

Johanna removed the rocks and sand, which were clouding their vision. She managed to drag him twenty yards before they could stand up.

Back at the camp, the governor quickly went to sleep, leaving Johanna to ponder what might have been.

Ever since that night, Governor de Heere masked the small dark scars on his legs.

--x--

# 25

# GET OUT

Johanna entered James's room without knocking. She knelt on his bed and began slowly unfastening her white blouse, tantalisingly revealing a figure-hugging red bodice beneath. She said nothing. He smiled and rubbed his scarred earhole unconsciously. He began to feel uncomfortable in her presence, a feeling he had had with only one woman before, Gerty. Something is different about her, he mused.

"To what do I owe this pleasure again?" asked James as he stepped in front of her, never breaking his stare.

"I just need a man to satisfy me, to help find the diamonds," she replied, as another white button popped.

"Hmm, that will be difficult," he laughed.

"I hope not," she giggled. "I am taking a huge risk being in here with you. You better not disappoint me, both for my satisfaction and curiosity. I adore diamonds."

"Well, let us see about the former and talk about the latter," he whispered.

With the last button gone, she removed her blouse and bounced on the bed.

“I think it is your turn to keep Solroy awake tonight. I will not make a sound,” she murmured. “Now get here and uncouple me from this wretched device before I change my mind.”

James obeyed her. True to her word, she did not make a noise other than whispering into his good ear. The bed rocked, sighed, and creaked loudly for half an hour. They rested briefly before the bed moved to their rhythm afresh.

Sitting aside her, James asked, “Why me?”

“Firstly, Gerrit would least expect me to go with a mutant. Second, we need to find the diamonds,” said Johanna, laughing softly but with an unnerving stare.

“Thanks for the compliment,” was all he could manage as they lay facing each other, legs entwined.

“Now you have had your fun, tell me where we are going, finding the gems?” she said, digging a fingernail into his chest and drawing a spot of blood.

“I reckon it was you who came for fun,” he said, removing her hand and licking it.

“Diamonds!” she repeated, her voice rising. “Where did your grandpa stash them?”

She immediately realised her mistake as he bit her thumb and froze for a second.

“He was a sick old man. A dreamer. A scammer. A liar. He instructed us to rediscover his treasure but never told us why he left it behind. It does not exist,” James started.

“Where did he find it, originally, I mean? Is that not a good a place as any to start, do you not think?” she recovered.

“Deep within a strangely lit grotto, about six hours out from the fort,” he said. “You know of such a place?”

She dug into his skin again, scratching a four-inch line down to his belly button as he winced and shuffled.

“Maybe,” she muffled, licking his new wound clean.

At breakfast the following morning, James watched Johanna enter the room with the governor. She feigned scratching her stomach, and grinned, “Good morning, James.”

After they had finished eating, Johanna suddenly announced, “Gerrit, I wish to take Mister Thacker on one of our bush trips for several days. He has not had time to explore this beautiful island, and we have not been out for months. The rains have stopped, and it is cooler now compared to the last time we went out. Please?”

“Mister Thacker is a busy man. He does not have time for frivolity,” replied the governor. “Besides, the cinnamon harvest is in full swing. I must make sure that the warehouses are secure to stop the crooks from taking samples unnoticed. It will have to wait.”

“Darling, I appreciate it is a busy time for you. I would like something else to do, other than get under your feet,” she said softly, not blinking her stare. “Mister Thacker, I am sure, will not get lost. We will, of course, take three housekeepers and guards for our safety.”

“Mister Thacker, was this your idea?” asked the governor, shifting his gaze off Johanna.

“Yes and no,” James replied guardedly. “Yes, because I would like to see other parts of this island. The harvest is important but is in your safe hands.”

It was seven days after the breakfast discussion when they set off early. The morning was chilly and windy, a pleasant change from the heat of the earlier season. Four ladened carts carried enough supplies for ten days. With noticeable reluctance, the governor agreed for an excursion of not more than five nights, even though Johanna would have been happy with three.

Inwardly smiling, James sat on the puffed-up covers in a cart. Johanna sat with one of the four guards and rider in a different wagon. The governor gave them extra protection, or was it for his own benefit?

Johanna deliberately steered the riders one way and then another for the first day. She did not want to raise suspicion that she had planned a destination. They camped around the wagons and tethered horses. Johanna had a remarkable memory and usually a keen sense of direction. She thought they were about an hour due east from her goal. The night was cool and refreshing again, but James was restless. That same unnerving feeling had started to creep over him.

Rising at dawn, the team packed the camp, which Johanna thought took much longer than necessary. They started towards that imperceptible marker where the sun had risen.

The terrain was full of small hills, and the bumps were more prominent than the day before. Multiple trees, a mix of mango, jack trees, and cinnamon created shadows covering the ground. A chilly air, from the little sunlight, broke through their passage.

After a couple of hours, Johanna stopped the horses and rested. She tried hard not to convey her concern.

"We should have found the tunnels by now," she muttered inaudibly. "Why has James been so quiet and shown me no attention?"

Three men appeared, each carrying machetes and a large sack over their shoulders. James was not sure who was startled the most; he knew his appearance had that effect. A three-way conversation ensued. James recognised Johanna speaking in Dutch with her servant. Her servants spoke to the knife-wielding men in their local dialect.

"What's the discussion?" asked James.

"These men have been collecting illegal wild cloves. They have shown us the way for our silence. I have concurred," Johanna replied.

"I would like to see the cloves," asserted James, surprising Johanna.

One of the foresters opened his bag. It was half-full of tiny green buds with a pink scattering.

"They look fine. Four or five days drying in the sun, they will be good," mused James. "At least they are telling the truth. You should have looked first before giving away where we want to go."

Johanna nodded and lowered her head.

The ground was rock-hard and unforgiving despite the brief night's rain.

James jumped from the wagon, rubbing and patting his bruised backside in an attempt to bring it back to life. He hobbled as his leg muscles pumped once again. It was less than an hour before sunset on what had been a breezy day with a brilliant clear blue sky. The land was not completely flat. A dozen or so large jack trees dominated the surroundings; hefty green knobby jackfruits hung, unnaturally, from the wide trunks. James guessed that the pods must have each weighed a hundred pounds or more on the most prominent tree. It shadowed the mouth of a small cave.

"Good heavens, could this be the one?" said James aloud.

Johanna studied the green lumps up close and called one of the guards, "Bring me a knife."

The knife slipped before he could stop her, and colossal fruit dropped onto the guard's foot. The jackfruit did not crumble while the short guard, named Meely, winced in agony, shaking his foot and head wildly.

"James, help me, please. I am ravenous," she said, ignoring the guard.

"That you are," laughed James and patted her rear.

James struggled to cut open the mass. He slipped with the knife several times before halving it.

A sticky pus-like substance oozed from the wedges and covered the blade. James extracted a whitish flower-like capsule and tasted it. The lump projected from his mouth at once.

"I don't know what Grandpa was thinking. What a bitter fruit," he spat.

Nevertheless, Johanna tried a piece.

"That's given me a furry mouth. Georgia, fetch me a water bottle," demanded Johanna.

They set up camp inside the cave entrance. Drips repeatedly bounced off James, to his frustration, despite him moving the wagon twice. He imagined that the water was following him.

Crystals shone all around, and the flashing lights disturbed him. Johanna came out of the water, naked but not wet. He held her. He woke, wiping his face from another droplet of water. An intense blue-white glow from the nearly full moon covered half the small area underneath the cave's roof. The moonlight dazzled James's eyes. In all his travels, he had never seen it so intense. Johanna was lying asleep in the next wagon. He watched her chest falling and rising to her breath. He felt an intense longing but knew not to take chances, given her protectors.

Soon after daybreak, Johanna dressed in clothes from one of her servants and led James into a tunnel. She only carried a bag with water bottles. She gave strict instructions to the guards to maintain their position and not follow.

They each held a naked flame lantern.

"I have been once before with Gerrit," she puffed, as the roof lowered.

James ignored her as his stomach pains got worse. They scrambled along the dusty track.

“I had an unnerving night’s sleep, too,” she mused. “I was swimming with you here. It is odd. I never thought my dreams were in colour but this was yellow.”

He frowned and then chuckled, remembering his fantasy. He wished Johanna would hurry up.

“That’s strange,” she said and added, “last time, this passage was sealed.”

James retched. His head throbbed. The annoying tingling and ringing began in his head, slowly rising in frequency. He hated the sensation and the claustrophobic walls surrounding him. On their knees, they struggled not to burn themselves while holding coconut-oiled torches.

Johanna gasped, “Here, it opens up. Oh my, it’s amazing.”

She shuffled through the hole and into the cavern. James followed her, breathless.

While he lay on the cold ground, his eyes focused on needle-like white rocks facing him.

“What happened?” he asked wearily, spitting out a glob of dust-ladened mucus from his dry mouth.

“Oh, James. Are you OK? That rock almost fell on your head,” she replied.

Another thud and another rock dropped on the ground. A high echo rang through James’s head, and the whining inside intensified.

James picked himself up and spun his head, trying to shake off the sensation, but it made no difference. His light flickered and went out. He tried re-lighting it with Johanna’s, but it would not burn again.

“*Look*!” she screamed.

Another much larger rock fell.

“*Stop*!” he yelled as another piece of stone crashed to the ground. “My head, My head!”

“What’s wrong. Calm yourself. Look at this!’ exclaimed Johanna.

On the wall, above the hole where they had come through, scratched into sandstone were the words:

***Get out***
***Not here***
***Thatchers***
***WLT 2176***

James nodded.

"See, I was right. The cunning old devil led us across many oceans, only for it to be at home all this time," said James.

"What? What does this message mean? And the number?" replied Johanna.

Another pinnacle thudded to the ground, its echo bouncing off the walls and making the water wave in the corner.

"We must get out of here," said James

She undressed and jumped feet first into the pool.

"That's better. You are going nowhere. We are alone. Now come join me before the guards get suspicious," she giggled.

He stared at the wall's message, treading water while she poured water on his head and tickled his earhole.

She stopped suddenly.

"I hear something. Better get dressed quickly," said Johanna, irritated.

James heard nothing other than the constant high-pitched jingle, but this was no music. It was driving him crazy.

No sooner had they dressed did Meely's head appear at the cavity.

"Are you alright? We heard tremendous thunder coming from below. I was worried for you, my lady," said Meely.

"She's fine. Some of these needles fell, that's all," replied James.

The guard sensed an atmosphere around them like he had interrupted something, but all he had found was the two of them sitting at the pool's edge with their feet in the water, talking. He frowned. Then he noticed her hair was sparkling wet and then saw James's too. He saw puddles outside the pool, but their clothes were not soaked.

"Most odd," shouted Meely.

The stalactite struck the centre of his head. He collapsed in a heap of dust. Blood, pieces of his skull, and other matter scattered; the single flame flickered briefly before going out. Meely was dead; they were in trouble.

Stepping out of the pool gingerly and holding Johanna's hand firmly, James stumbled towards the hollow. Feeling the hole with his other hand, he crawled first, feeling his hands against the walls as he went. Somehow, she kept up with his frantic pace. Then it happened.

James felt tiny pieces of stone stinging his face. It felt like pieces of wood splintering off an open fire. The rumbling subsided. He felt his way forward but only for ten feet more. Johanna bumped into his legs.

Within a minute, another deep roar and vibration came from behind Johanna. Fine sand covered her, but luckily nothing of significance hit her.

Trapped, they whispered for what seemed like hours. Johanna was unsure if he was reassuring her or himself. Their emotions were on a knife-edge. She cried while he kept smacking his head.

A scraping sound followed a dazzling yellow light.

James stirred and said," Where did that come from?"

"Who cares? We can at least see now. I heard something else too. Wait. Yes! Can you hear that too?" panted Johanna.

Two hands dragged James out quickly and without ceremony.

Back at the grotto's mouth, he sat gasping, wondering about his luck. The guard who rescued him had vanished outside the cave. Another went back in too.

Johanna appeared ten minutes later. She sat quietly next to James, holding him tightly and shaking uncontrollably. He thought that his head would explode, the ringing was almost deafening now, drowning out all sounds.

"Where's Meely?" asked the guard.

"Dead in the big cave. A rock smashed his head," sobbed Johanna.

The group returned to the fort in a sombre mood. Johanna explained to Gerrit what had happened to Meely. Soon after, the governor called James into his office and listened carefully to what James had to say about the trip and death. Later, the governor summoned one of the excursion's guards.

Johanna, her husband, and the guard visited Meely's widow that eve, informing her of her late husband's fate and expressing their condolences. They left the hysterical young woman feeding her two-month-old son.

James remained in the maroon room, pondering the letters scratched into the cave's wall, now splashed with Meely's blood. James decided to go back to England, but his greedy and evil thoughts kept his mind preoccupied.

"Here, I can become a wealthy man *and* return to Southwold richer than when I left," he thought aloud. "I know now where Grandpa's treasure is; home."

That night James planned his next six months, for the seasons would change again, and winds would be more favourable for the passage home. He would hitch a ride on any ship, except VOC flagged, taking his spice store with him. "I am sure other people, Everett, perhaps even Solroy, would undertake that venture with me," he muttered.

Johanna entered without knocking. James removed his gaze from his reflection in the dressing mirror and shifted to watch her come towards him. She kissed his lips firmly, then slapped his face hard, knocking him off the stool, shocked.

"You lied to me," she said.

"Not I, my grandpa lied to us all," he answered, wiping his mouth, adding blood to his shirt cuff.

"I will depart for England before this century is over. You will come with me," said James boldly.

"That's never going to happen. Gerrit wouldn't allow it," she conceded meekly.

"Of course, but what of you? Do you always follow your husband's instructions?" asked James.

Johanna stood in front of him, nodding.

"I cannot go with you. You are a liar and truly ugly," she eventually responded and stormed out of his room before he could see her tears.

--x--

# 26

# Shepherds Cove

Upon their arrival outside one of three villages, Kalikata, twenty surprised and heavily armed Englishmen met them near the east Indian coast. Wethersby Jnr and Rayleigh spoke to their leader; he could barely believe the story from where the caravan had travelled. Once escorted to a fortified garrison and permission granted, they set up camp inside. A stern man named Jenkins, dressed in a heavy green uniform and an awkward-looking cap, welcomed Wethersby Jnr and Rayleigh to dine with him and his staff at nightfall. Wethersby Jnr asked for Fredrick, Mayling and Freya to join them too. The wagons of silver were at last secure in the compound.

Jenkins asked no end of questions during the lavish evening. He was fascinated by the incredible journey they had been on and admired their luck surviving, without losing heaps of men, only the deserters.

"I have heard of so few foreigners travelling across India while traversing Kantipur along the way," Jenkins boomed. "Why?"

"We are following in our grandfather's footsteps. For trade, to increase our fortunes," replied Rayleigh.

"We have increased our family too," said Wethersby Jnr. "Mayling is our grandmother's sister's granddaughter! We met initially in Jodhpur."

"Our grandmother died in an inferno when we were young boys back in Southwold," acknowledged Rayleigh. "Our grandfather, Wethersby Snr, lived a remarkably long but pained life. He passed away just over a year ago. It is wonderful to find more of our family."

"What are your plans now?" inquired Jenkins.

"We would like to rest here briefly, then procure a passage to Kandy," replied Wethersby Jnr, adding, "to make a new home for Mayling and Freya."

Mayling nodded.

They continued to feast on the fine spicy food. Rayleigh declined the offer of wine. Wethersby Jnr got drunk.

In the morning, Jenkins looked on as Wethersby Jnr manoeuvred one of the wagons into a large wooden shed, untied its covers and unlocked a box. The glistering metal lit up Jenkins' face and his droll smile.

"We have more of this with us. The wagon's real contents are to be secret. Not even your officers must know," said Wethersby Jnr sternly. "Tell them we have ivory, which is no lie, and many religious relics and goods from Kantipur."

"Agreed, but no sooner have you secured a ship, word will get out where your wealth came from," said Jenkins tapping his cap. "Around these parts, whispers spread more quickly than the pox."

All three men nodded.

"We do not wish to stay here any longer than necessary. We will ensure your support will not go unnoticed," said Wethersby Jnr.

"That it won't. My price is ten from a hundred," demanded Jenkins.

"We will see, once we find an available and suitable vessel," said Rayleigh.

Jenkins took the cousins to the main harbour. Seven large English flagged ships were at anchor, together with copious small fishing boats.

"I will take you first to Captain Scythe. He is an interesting character; he has spent too much time at sea. However, he is always the one looking out for a special deal and bargain. A risk-taker, a gambler," laughed Jenkins. "I trust him, though, but do not be put off by his appearance. He is as shrewd as they come."

Scythe bounded over, hobbling with a severe limp. He was perhaps fifty years old, although Rayleigh thought it was hard to tell, such were his deep-set wrinkles and dark sun-baked skin. His long curly blond hair curled uncontrollably. He winked constantly with his one uncovered eye.

"What ye want?" shrieked Scythe, touching his red eye patch, wiping away a teardrop beneath it.

"Why, your ship, of course," responded Jenkins. "For these fine gentlemen are going to Kandy in it."

Scythe rebalanced himself then howled with laughter. The men smiled back.

"Mister Scythe. Your battered ship," snorted Wethersby Jnr, pointing to a ragged boat anchored a hundred yards in front of them, "It has seen better days. It must be ancient."

"Thirty years out at sea. One careful owner. Many a storm," continued Scythe in his deep tone.

"More like one hundred and thirty," laughed Jenkins, winking back at Rayleigh.

"Let us have a drink if you are interested. The *Shepherds Cove* will cost you a fortune or your life; perhaps both," said Scythe, as he slapped Rayleigh hard on his shoulder. "This way to my parlour."

He led them to an open brown palm-leaf hut perched above the tide mark.

Jenkins gave the local brew a wide berth. The forceful yeasty rice potion made Rayleigh hungry; his cousin drank in unison with Scythe. Slowly they came close to a deal before the liquor took hold, and a slurring of words was the best Wethersby Jnr could manage, wobbling on his stool.

"Scythe, are you selling or not?" asked Jenkins suddenly, interrupting the men's laughter.

"Not yet," responded Scythe.

"You can skipper the ship and command your men, but not mine," stumbled Wethersby Jnr. "We have bullion, but where will you store it?"

Rayleigh placed his compass on the desk in front of Scythe.

"Here, you can keep this once our journey is over," said Rayleigh, without losing one-eyed contact with Scythe.

"Interesting. Jenkins, do they have what they say?" inquired Scythe, nodding. "I hope you are not wasting my time again."

"Yes, and no," replied Jenkins. "You'll never get a better and more generous offer for your precious battered boat."

"Ship," he answered back.

One-quarter of Gooty's thinner weight for a ship, a limping one-eyed captain and motley crew; Wethersby Jnr was content, except for the crew's pact. Scythe would not, at first, accept any of the Indian soldiers on board. Wethersby Jnr asked the Jodhpur army whether they wanted to make the next part of the journey by sea. Wethersby Jnr desired the best but wanted none of the men to feel forced into going with him further. More rice spirit helped lubricate Scythe's judgement. In the end, Scythe and Wethersby agreed that all ten volunteers could go.

Slowly, they prepared the *Shepherds Cove*. It seemed sturdy enough to Wethersby Jnr, with only small areas of decay on the main deck and railings. Still, from what he and Rayleigh could figure out, the hull was in good condition. Eighteen cannon with a large quantity of nine-pound cannonballs were a significant bonus. The main area for attention and repair was the canvas; two mainsails were beyond repair. They made deals with fellow captains, who drew on their reserves. The remaining cloth took a month to mend. The patchwork was a remarkable sight, singling out the *Shepherds Cove*; although it still looked forlorn. The holds were now filled with the valuables from the wagons and enough provisions for two months. Scythe expected the journey to take three weeks, four if the weather was poor. He took his newly acquired silver on board with him, except for Jenkins' cut.

They left on 21st December 1697. A small crowd gathered at the river and sea junction, but the Jodhpur men who had stayed behind were nowhere in sight, surprising Rayleigh and Mayling. Jenkins had returned to his garrison.

Freya was bedridden again, with her fever alternating from exceedingly high to low, and back up again, every day.

Scythe explained his route to Wethersby Jnr, using a cluster of old maps and why he wanted to sail far away from the coastline.

"Pirates," he exclaimed. "It's too darn easy for them if we are a day or less from shore. I learnt that lesson long ago and lost this fine lady, temporarily. Jenkins helped me out on that occasion."

Rayleigh reflected on the old sea dog's tales. Scythe told stories with great enthusiasm at any and every opportunity.

Rayleigh thought back to his grandpa's study and hours of describing similar unlikely adventures and close encounters. After seven days, they spotted a faraway vessel that never got closer and quickly disappeared from their sights. Winds were favourable, and they met no storms.

Twenty days after leaving Kalikata, and no more than three days from Kandy, Scythe thought their luck changed. Late afternoon, with a cloudless cyan sky, a ship's tiny silhouette sat in front of the setting sun. Its image grew more extensive in the next two hours, forming a ghostly shadow in the moonlight.

Scythe tried to steer away to the southeast, but the separation appeared static as the moon arced over the night's sky. The gunners readied the ordnance. None of the crew slept, for it was a tense night.

A low thud, followed in seconds by an increasing whistle, hit the ship. A giant splash off the starboard side drenched the deck. The night's sky was beginning to switch from black to dark blue to the east, where the cannonball's sound came from. No one saw the first flash. Wethersby Jnr was on the bridge with Scythe and Rayleigh, desperately trying to decide where the other vessel was. They then saw a flash and heard the same sounds moments after. It missed again, this time falling short. Scythe spun the great wheel and shouted to the crew to drop the mainsail.

"Starboard. Be ready to shoot on my command," he hollered and watched another flash out of the blackness, clearly seeing the small ship's outline for a brief second. "Fire!"

The *Shepherds Cove* rocked and vibrated heavily from its discharge. They struck the other ship's stern. The attacking craft lit up from at least three direct hits, smashing its mainsail, and it began to burn.

"Fire!" yelled Scythe.

The gunners adjusted the cannon and reloaded below decks moments before the second order went out. One of the great guns recoiled with random violence and bounced off its wheels, crushing the gunner, and instantly killing the man.

"Starboard. Reload. Fire at will," bellowed Scythe.

The stricken vessel did not return shots. Now well and truly alight, it was too easy a target. Scythe did not hold back. Of the third rounds, only one exploded, shattering rails and decking. Despite the meagre light, men visibly tumbled through the air and into the water below.

Scythe steered the *Shepherds Cove* directly towards the second vessel. As they drew closer, they could see two smaller ships; one was moving away from them at speed, the other dead in the water.

"Most odd," said Scythe, adjusting his eye patch. "It looks like we have disturbed their fun."

"*Panotii*," said Rayleigh squinting at the newly gotten boat.

Rayleigh saw the burning ship being consumed while its crew desperately tried to douse the flames.

"Why don't they untie and disconnect?" asked Rayleigh.

"A good question, young man," replied Scythe. "I suspect one of them is pirating the other. We shall soon find out."

Black and brown smoke rose and caught in the wind; its trail streaked above the waves. The ship listed as the sea slowly consumed it. Giant bubbles erupted on the surface as the last of the vessel disappeared. Men bobbed in the ocean, shouting for help. The *Panotii* remained lightly smouldering but otherwise intact. Men scrambled up its rigging. Scythe ordered the crew to pick the remaining men out from the water; seventeen all told.

"You will stay on this deck. No talking. Understood?" shouted Scythe.

One man stood out, wearing a cap.

"Where's your captain. What's his name?" demanded Scythe of the capped man.

"Everett went over with the owner, Mister Thacker. A cruel storm caught us all unawares. The seas swallowed them," stuttered the man.

"Now that's a lie," replied Scythe. "Mister Thacker has been here all along."

The man shook his head and said nothing more.

Rayleigh overheard the exchange; his puzzled expression did not leave him for the rest of the day.

--x--

# 27

## Land Pirate

James's empire proliferated, with Solroy outwardly never in charge but permanently by his side. It was the fourth ship the pair had skimmed off the top under the watchful, if somewhat blinkered, company's eyes.

The Dutch team had grown large, their processes and security formidable. However, this created weaknesses in the inexperienced senior officers. Some had taken the company's power for granted and became somewhat complacent yet far from lazy. Still, a handful of them became open to payoffs for turning a blind eye, fed up with seeing the senior commanders' favourites live a prosperous life. At the same time, they scraped by on meagre pay, missing their genuine homes, and getting sick during the heavy raining seasons.

The large ship, *St Botolph*, on which the two men now stood, rocked gently in the rising swell. Its captain, Beamish, gave James a familiar, fearful look, despite trying to hold his stance. James had seen this before, but it was strange to hear how Beamish uttered those words – a very familiar accent.

"My dear man, Thacker, did you know it is Christmas Day?" asked Beamish, almost smiling. "How did you lose your ear?"

"It's a long story, but this here Omani pirate did that deed," replied James and paused for impact.

"Really? I find that hard to believe. You appear related," laughed Beamish, bowing his head slightly.

"Where do you come from, originally?" inquired James.

"A fellow Englishman, of course. Lowstuf'," chuckled Beamish.

"Oh! There's me, assuming you're from north of our border," retorted James. "Are you sure? Let me see your webbed feet!"

To the astonishment of Solroy, who was his usual quiet self, the two men continued their banter for another hour. Though he didn't let go of his sword handle.

James and Beamish were virtually inseparable for several days, spending time on the *St Botolph* in the morning and the *Sardine Tavern* in the afternoon. By sundown, both men were drunk and wobbling around the bar. Their voices sounded above all else.

"*St Botolph* has a fine bounty, Thacker. You can handle it for me. Do not let any Dutch make a guilder from it," announced Beamish.

He dropped his tankard for the second time.

"I will take lower than my customary cut for the privilege. Twenty-five from one hundred, seeing you and I come from the same neck of the woods, even though you've fish feet," replied James, laughing at the top of his voice.

"Steady on, lad, that is more than steep. That's outrageous," retorted Beamish.

"Take it or leave it, I do not negotiate," said James with a dead-straight face, holding his tankard high in the air. "My deal is off once I've finished this ale."

"Hmmm. What does your ear lobbing friend here say?" asked Beamish.

"Nothing," replied Solroy.

James finished his beer and said firmly, "What's it to be, the Dutch pilfering your ship or…."

Looking directly at James, Beamish slurred, "I'll take my chances and handle the sales myself. I do not need a middleman from Suffolk taking my profit. My crew and I have come a long way and intend to return rich men."

"You won't make it out of this harbour without your ship in flames; its contents sunk along with you and your crew. That can be arranged, just like the last Englishman to try it on here," James threatened.

"Ten from one hundred," whispered Beamish.

"That's a start," said James angrily and added, "but as I said already, it's twenty-five from one hundred or your ship's baked. These thieving locals will see to that."

"No!" replied Beamish. "Twenty from one hundred is as close as you will get from me."

"Twenty, both ways, then yes," replied James, as he held out his right hand. "Not a penny or a rupiya less. Agreed?"

"Or more, Thacker," winked Beamish, as a wry smile formed across his lips as he shook James's hand. "Agreed."

"As we have finally sorted that out, it is time for drinks all around," shouted James.

The *Sardine Tavern's* volume fell to a hush, only to grow loud as the three young servers came round with full pitchers. A man grasped one of the women's rears. She roundly slapped him viciously across his cheek, and he fell over in a heap on the floor, ruing his mistake and misfortune.

The uproar continued for another good two hours before James and Beamish staggered out of the rear door, only for the humidity and heat to hit them square in their faces. Beamish passed out within a minute. James soldiered on for five minutes more until he too collapsed by the quayside. Solroy was watching on, as usual, guarding the new richest man in port. He and another man carried Beamish back to the *St Botolph*, returning to find James unmoved. There he remained until morning, reeking of stale ale.

Solroy and James inspected below the hatches. The vessel was rammed full of animal skins, bones, and ivory. Several hundred wooden barrels were stored too, apparently full of colourful glass beads, according to Beamish. There was a stench of rotten corpses that James could not escape. Beamish explained that they had not prepared the animal carcasses well enough. Now the whole ship had been penetrated by their hosts' odour. Solroy thought he knew better, suspecting human remains may lie hidden under the animal skeletons. He had, after all, performed the same trick on several occasions to spread perceptions and the value of cargo.

At two the following morning, the pair were supervising movement off the ship of the largest prized white ivory. Huge, curved elephant tusks bled with a brown stain, well over a dozen feet long and as wide as James's head at their base.

"Before slaying them, those creatures must have been a powerful, formidable sight," mulled James.

Solroy rocked his head while Beamish tittered.

"Where did you kill them?" asked Solroy.

"At the base of Africa, about fifty or sixty miles inland, in an area of vast open plains, spotted with trees that appeared to have their roots spread out as branches at their heads. We got lucky at first and culled this vast herd. It took us four days to round them all up before finally toppling the last," said Beamish, as he touched the largest of the tusks.

"As we can see, on close inspection, many are cracked and badly stained. These ivories may be enormous, but their value is greatly diminished," justified James authoritatively, lying. "We must move them to our warehouse to view again in better light before splitting eighty-twenty. That decision won't be by weight alone."

At the modest, musty store, Beamish mused - it was hardly the grand warehouse he was expecting. Boards covered the windows, and little light got through. The whiff of cinnamon and cloves caught his nose; he did not stop sneezing for several minutes. He estimated that there were perhaps a hundred sacks of clove and several hundred large bundles of tightly wrapped cinnamon bark in two corners. The rest of the area was, he thought, empty.

"Let us move and examine your cargo in our store. It is more secure there than on your exposed boat. I'll arrange to remove these wood panels once it is all transferred so we can see better inside," remarked James.

"Ship," replied Beamish and slowly nodded.

He was not convinced about security. Then again, he had a blindfold around his head since leaving the pier and was somewhat disorientated.

"How well do you know this island?" asked James.

"I've been here before, ten years ago. We stayed only briefly to replenish supplies and moved on to Malacca. I remember the smell of these spices; it always makes me sneeze," laughed Beamish.

"I don't care for the stuff personally, but it makes for such a commanding profit in Europe, especially London town, apparently," chuckled James. "This load is the last I have. Its price has doubled since I first arrived, especially the pepper."

Beamish deliberately forgot to mention his last visit to the island two years earlier. After that excursion, he had returned to England a wealthy man, after filling his ship's holds with Kandyan spice and trading some of it for superb quality ivory, slain in southern Africa. Beamish had come back to do the same again, but not with the Dutch this time. Meeting James Thacker was a bonus, cutting out the trading companies who took such a formidable cut; and going independent, or so he supposed. He could not see any pepper in the warehouse, though.

James had other ideas for Beamish's stash. Greed had overtaken him these last months, as the number of ships not aligned or willing to associate with companies had dwindled. Solroy had encouraged him to take more and more, either through agreement or theft; it mattered not to James now. Seeing the massive bounty on board the *St Botolph*, all sense of respect disappeared. He wanted it all.

"Here, you should have these, store them on the *St Botolph*, and take them back to England. When we meet again, you can give me whatever proceeds you see fit," said James, holding out his hand.

"Of course. That is very trusting. Why the sudden change of spirit?" asked Beamish.

"There's no change. I'd rather have your cargo in my store here rather than allow these spices to rot in this relentless humidity," replied James, biting his lip as he kept his smile in check. "Anyway, I've made my profit from all of this, several times over. There's no need to be greedy on this island. There's plenty of wealth to go around if one looks for it and is prepared to work hard for those pleasures."

Beamish nodded but feared a ruse. "That was too easy and too generous. He could have stored the spice somewhere else," he murmured. "Surely the spice holds more value, pound for pound, than these old shiny stained tusks?"

"Solroy. How can we dispose of the *St Botolph* and her crew? Well, at least Beamish and his officers?" asked James.

"At sea, of course," laughed Solroy. "I'd be happy to slice him up, though you should have that honour; you make a good pirate - for an Englishman!"

"You have better aim, Solroy," said James stroking his earhole. "When?"

"Up to you. Don't you want to get your hands wet with Beamish's blood?" teased Solroy.

James nodded, sipping his ale slowly. Solroy drank water.

"Let's get the spice on the *St Botolph*, make the deal, hitch a ride to Negombo and chase him down from there. There are too many prying eyes and ears here, ha-ha," said Solroy, and then slapped James hard on the back. "I jest, my deaf friend, but you make a great-looking pirate."

"That may be so, but doing my plundering from land is so much easier," cackled James, winking.

Beamish was not amused. Looking down at the holds of his ship, he had a sinking feeling that all was not right with Thacker and his Omani partner. He went down and opened one of the sacks. The cloves smelt wonderfully fragrant. They were fresh, dry and of excellent quality and were double the size compared to the last shipment he made to London. The cinnamon was mixed, though, but would still fetch a great price back home. The sticks were a single piece of thick bark. His last cinnamon were multiple thin wafers.

"Why, Thacker? Why leave this load with me? Do you truly think you will see any profit?" Beamish whispered, laughing. "I don't think so, even if we do spring from the same county."

Beamish held out trust in James Thacker and had still not seen any pepper. The price of his ivories would be the ship's holds bursting full of the small strong corns – a spice fit for the King of England, William III, he thought.

"So where is the rest of it, Thacker?" he demanded.

"You are an impatient fellow, Beamish. I am going nowhere fast; neither are your whitish African tusks," said James. "I will share your spoils tomorrow. Come by the *Sardine Tavern* at four in the afternoon, and we can arrange all movements of spice to your ship."

"Why wait? Let's go there now," suggested Beamish.

"You do not know how things work on this island, do you?" asserted James.

"I am not so stupid," replied Beamish.

"Firstly, the Dutch run the main operation, and Governor de Heere wants all the proceeds to fill his coffers. Secondly, the Dutch are next if the governor and his team do not get ahold of all the merchandise. The farms around Kali are all controlled, or so they think. My partner and I work on the outside. We stay close to the governor and his rather pretty wife. I act on behalf of Governor de Heere and take a cut, just like everyone else," commanded James.

"Yes. That is all very well, but you did not answer my question," said an impatient Beamish. "Show me the spice now, or our little deal is off."

"Steady on, man. I leave you with a prize of the best quality clove and cinnamon you will ever see, and you fail to trust me!" bellowed James. "You have some cheek. Patience, my webbed-feet fellow. It will be delivered, starting tomorrow night."

"I demand all of it in one night so that my crew and I can leave this godforsaken, pirated island and never return," shouted Beamish.

James pointed his finger towards the *St Botolph* and said, "You can make all the demands you want. However, I have the spice, and we will move it to your ship from tomorrow night."

"Woe betide you, should you try to cheat me, Thacker, for you will lose your other ear in a flash," frowned Beamish.

"As I said, I have the spice. I have friends in the highest places. You need to reconsider your idle threats. You may lose your ship and your life in a rather bigger flash, Beamish," said James. "Enough of this banter. I need to go and reconfirm the arrangements for tomorrow evening, and no, before you ask, you are not coming along for that ride."

James left Beamish, Solroy followed.

Buffalo-led wagons moved the *St Botolph*'s cargo of enormous elephant tusks to the secret store. James knew from experience it was hard, if not impossible, for this to go unnoticed. Still, he allowed only one wagon at a time to be near the ship and had insisted that his and Beamish's teams were to keep entirely silent for the whole time. James scolded one of his men for banging a tusk against the hull. He smashed the man's nose to pieces with one punch; no one else made a sound after that. All told, a dozen fully loaded wagons left the ship that night and slowly made their way towards the outer edge of the town. All the carts were unloaded before sunrise under Solroy's gaze.

James estimated that it would take another three nights to empty the *St Botolph* of the colossal amount in her holds and scattered in every spare space across the ship. That morning, James reviewed the store's bounty on his own, marvelling at the incredible length, width and weight of the magnificent tusks. The tips were all in perfect, slightly off-white condition. The only staining was at the socket points.

"For only some stinking rotten spices, this is pure cream. I will return to England a wealthy man and build my private estate with this little lot," he mused.

"When we capture the *St Botolph*, not only will we get our spice but a fine ship to sail to England, too," said Solroy softly, surprising James so much that he jumped an inch in the air.

"Aha, that be so," laughed James.

Seven days later, the *St Botolph*'s holds were full of pepper, clove sacks and bales of low-quality cinnamon. Beamish laughed at the sight as the last was loaded.

"Well done, men," whispered Beamish. "Time for a short rest now. Then we must ready the ship to set sail within a week. I don't care for the feel of the air here any longer; far too humid and smelling of mould for my liking."

"But Captain, are the winds coming from the west, not the east?" replied Johns, one of the officers.

"At this time of the year, they will change back in our favour any day soon, and they will speed us to the horn of Africa. It may be bumpy, but nothing we have not encountered before," lied Beamish.

Beamish steered his ship west, watching his back the whole time. He ideally wanted nothing more to do with the dreadful culling of elephants and rhinos, but still, his greed took over. Beamish had retained a half of the ship's load for ivories he previously bargained for at the Bay of Natal. They would head back there for stores and rest until returning to England.

Progress was slow. The expected westerly had dropped off, and the sails barely moved for two days. The sky grew darker by the hour, but the sea remained flat calm. From Beamish's years of experience, he had witnessed the extremes of the sea, especially the great ocean between southern Africa and India. A dead calm, though, worried him more than gales and huge waves. He kept his thoughts to himself, instructing his officers to keep the team busy scrubbing the decks, staving off boredom and keeping them fit and healthy. There were few repairs to make after their work during the prolonged stay at Kali.

Beamish felt a twisting in his gut as he held the giant ship's wheel. It began to bounce between his palms; he could not rationalise the sensation. A colossal thud and shudder rocked her, throwing every standing man backwards, including Beamish. He stood at an angle - the ship was listing to port.

"Men, pick yourselves up. Gather everything that moves and get below, quickly," shouted Beamish. "Johns, look for damage and report back immediately."

For the next hour, the ship took on more water. The principal gash was parallel to the waterline. A chain of men established a link to the sea and bucketed out the water. At the same time, another group made repairs to the ten-foot hole and associated cracks, supervised by Beamish.

They failed to see the ship until the first shot boomed in the distance; an almighty thud at the stern rocked the *St Botolph* as huge splinters rained out in all directions.

Beamish had been careless, and he knew it. The scrape with the shallow reef had consumed his attention; the preoccupation with repairs had blindsided him. Another huge roar followed in five seconds by another crash. The direct hit on the mast shook the ship violently, and it came crashing down, narrowly missing Beamish. Two of his crew lay dead; their skulls smashed in.

Another shot hit the *St Botolph* at her bow. More pieces of deck and railings flew through the air randomly. One large section pierced Officer Johns through his stomach; he held his hands over the splinter, then slumped forward, unable to stop his momentum. He was dead before he hit the deck; the wooden spike slid through him and jutted out of his back.

Beamish was severely winded. A railing piece had sliced through his upper thigh. He desperately ripped his shirt and wrapped it around his wound in an attempt to stop the gushing blood. He lost consciousness soon after.

James and Solroy hooted. They could scarcely believe their luck as the *St Botolph* ran aground. It, and her crew, were sitting ducks. Solroy took his time in positioning and aiming their big guns, seemingly unseen, onboard the *Panotii*.

"I was perhaps talking to myself earlier," said James to Solroy, raising his voice above the din. "If you sink them, a huge profit will be gone. I want those spices back, and I need that ship!"

"Calm, my boy. All will be saved. We must get closer now that we have taken out their cannon and rudder," replied Solroy. "But be wary of that Englishman. He will be in a deadly rage."

"He does not bother me," cut in James.

"That may be so, but we need to dispatch him to the depths as a priority; his squad will soon give in once he is no longer breathing," laughed Solroy.

The two ships drew closer. Several musket volleys came from the *St Botolph*, cutting down two of Solroy's pirates and grazing a couple more. They were slow to reload. James saw the fear in the men's eyes. Beamish was still at the helm, his hands on the great wheel. A mass of ropes with grappling hooks carried over to the *St Botolph*. Several got cut before five of the *Panotii* crew switched ships, carrying curved sabres in their mouths. They began cutting down the English crew, laughing. James remembered those same sounds when he lost his ear and shuddered slightly before composing himself. Solroy joined his company on the *St Botolph*. Two officers in scruffy uniforms put up a brave but fruitless fight against him, their legs cut to shreds. He was soon at the wheel.

“No, for pity’s sake, man. We had a deal,’ bellowed Beamish holding his sword aloft.

Solroy ignored his pleas and lunged through the wheel.

“But our deal?” were the last words Beamish would utter.

The sword punctured his lung. Beamish hissed, then fell, slumped over the wheel.

A boy of perhaps ten years old ran from behind the captain and yelped, “Our captain’s *dead*!”

James jumped from the quarter galley and crashed into the boy before his feet had touched the deck. Surprised, Solroy ran after the boy and jumped from the higher tier to tackle him, only to lose his grip as he wriggled away. It took three men to hold the boy down, for he was unexplainably tricky and strong-willed. James turned the urchin’s face and swallowed hard.

“Are you following me, little guy? Where’s your master?” asked James.

Solroy was perplexed.

They moved their looted spice first to the *Panotii*, then to a warehouse near Negombo. The *St Botolph* was repaired under James’s watchful eye during the next six weeks, the mainsail made from three pieces of timber.

Solroy took the *Panotii* and a skeleton crew to Kali to avoid suspicion, leaving the *Risqué* in its usual hiding place not far from Negombo.

The store was brimming. James worried that air could not circulate over the spice, given how tightly packed it was. He urged the carpenters to work faster and harder, scolding them, despite working from dawn to dusk to daybreak again. James hatched his grand plan to return to England, but the essential aspect escaped him; who would command the *St Botolph*?

Johanna snuggled next to James. It was past midnight on Thursday 16th January 1698 and another sultry night of high heat and humidity. Their sweat mingled; James was unsure whether his perspiration was more about not finding a captain or from Johanna's energy. He knew they had gotten careless with their evenings together. They continued, nevertheless. The governor was seemingly either unaware or did not care.

They both sat up, startled at hearing a pronounced shuffling from behind the room's door.

"Quick, someone's outside," exclaimed James.

--x--

# 28

# Rimmers & Roony

Charles's rescue came a week later, although he did not know it for several more days. The small, but sturdy, single-masted Dutch ship was plying the passage between India and Kandy, with a forceful wind straining the canvas. They almost ran over the small dinghy, passing it by less than one hundred feet. The captain ordered the canvas to be dropped as he steered the ship about. After fifteen minutes, they were drifting alongside the small craft. They did not give much hope for the two bodies on board; the stench was unmissable.

Charles opened his eyes to a plain wooden ceiling and tried to cry out, but nothing came. He moved his tongue around in his mouth, desperate to wet it. A huge man wearing a pointed orange hat came in, towering over Charles, shaking his head.

"Well, sir, you're a fortunate man," said the tall gent. "Wha' d'ya go by."

"Water," was all Charles could manage.

"That's an unusual name," he exclaimed. "Wait 'ere."

He returned with a jug and clay cup.

"Drink, but slowly," he said.

Charles dribbled most of the cup on his face and chin, unable to take down more than a small mouthful.

"Where am I, and who are you?" Charles asked.

"Normally, the first question gets answered before a second, but seeing your state, I forgive you this time. My name is Captain Jos Rimmers, and now, who are you?" he said.

"Cha-Charles *Thatcher*," he mistakenly replied, unable to talk clearly.

"Cha-Charles, I am at your service onboard this fine but ancient ship the *Dam Plague*," said Rimmers. "Now get some rest. Ya mother we sent to the deep. She stank, sorry."

"Where are we?" struggled Charles.

"Rest. We talk more 'morrow, on Christmas Day," replied Rimmers and left.

Charles could not contain his vomit as he stood up, only to collapse again as the ship's pitching and yawing made his head spin. He ventured out of the tiny room and onto the main deck.

Rimmers laid out a feast of sorts; rice, fermented eggs, burnt meat and dried fish.

"At least the smell is no worse than old Por," Charles said aloud. "Almost."

Rimmers smiled, "How did ya come to be out in the passage?"

Charles, unable to answer with his mouth full, just nodded.

After a minute and several swallows, he managed to say, "I do not know. My boat was attacked many, many months ago. I got thrown over as shark bait."

He ate many mouthfuls more.

"Somehow, I survived, drifting to an island. The locals picked me up weeks later and took me to another atoll. The dead woman in the boat manipulated me for months. Then she decided we should leave. I have no idea how many days we were in that boat, maybe a dozen or more," said Charles an hour later, the food lifting his energy and spirits.

"Ya a lucky man. We almost ran the boat and thought you were dead. I could not feel your pulse initially but felt your faint breathing. How did you like the meat?" asked Rimmers.

"This beef is excellent. How long have you had that hanging?" asked Charles.

"Long enough," said Rimmers trying to hold his grin.

The sloop had a small crew of twenty, plus the captain and two officers. Charles was surprised by the team's size; his smaller ship had carried about forty, larger vessels sixty or more. The men appeared fit, healthy, and obedient. The Dutch East India Company vessel bore the initials VOC and the usual company flag. Charles explored the ship at will, and he felt respected for the first time since leaving London. Rimmers allowed Charles to dine with him and his officers every evening. They recounted tales of their long journey from Europe. The *Dam Plague* left Amsterdam three months after the *Frostenden Nave*. They were returning to Kandy after trading along the southwest Indian coast.

Rimmers estimated they were three days west of the island.

Their arrival was quiet. Two dozen or more small single-sail boats out at sea were catching fish, shrimp, and squid. Nearer the shore, they spied men on stilts within the water, waiting patiently for a catch. Several teams were boatbuilding, the regular knocking of mallet on wood ringing like dull church bells.

Rimmers steered the ship five hundred feet from shore and dropped anchor. A dozen small dinghies came to them, eager to be the first to try to climb up and sell their produce.

He warned his men, "Remember, never buy from the first - always too expensive."

Three of the boats smoked. Soon the *Dam Plague* and its men were surrounded by the smell of chicken and coconut.

"Captain, that smells wonderful. May we get some?" begged Charles.

"Charles, it's a good idea for all the gang," replied Rimmers.

They feasted on the boats' offerings, eating a bird each, sucking the bones dry before throwing the remains overboard to a fish frenzy. Rimmers bought a dozen birds from each boat, hauling one batch to his cabin for they were so deliciously sweet and aromatic.

Charles and the captain left the *Dam Plague* and headed to shore. Rimmers was keen to reintroduce himself to the local head merchant quickly. He worried about having his ship exposed, despite it being away from the harbour and beach. There were too many boats all around for his liking, despite the excellent food they provided.

Negombo had a long expanse of palm-fringed beach, a bustling market with boatbuilders and fishermen. The few sturdy wooden buildings were small, except two. Rimmers headed to one with orange shutters. They walked through the once-grand entrance. No one greeted them for ten minutes, then a tall man in an orange pointed hat came out of the shadows.

"Captain Rimmers, good to see you again. Did you enjoy your lunch?" said the man.

"Why, Mister Roony. Yes, my men and I had a chicken each and fed your fish," replied Rimmers, smiling at Charles.

"Shall we get to business? What have you brought me this time, and who is this?" asked Roony.

"My name is Charles from *Thatchers*, Southwold in England. Pleased to be acquainted with you, Mister Roony," said Charles.

"And I too, Mister *Thatcher*," said Roony with a puzzled look. "Now, Rimmers, what do you want? I am a busy man."

Charles ignored Roony's slip of his surname. Roony removed his hat, exposing his bald head.

"Ivory, and a lot of it. Top-quality from the southeastern tip of Africa," said Rimmers and added, "and a few other things I will show you, and only you, aboard my ship."

Roony held his rising concern over the *Thatcher* name coincidence.

"Another *Thatcher* in Kandy at the same time. How is this possible?" he mouthed to himself. "I must find out how he came here and why."

"We had better go and take a look at what you have to offer, but first tell me what you want in return, Rimmers," said Roony, trying to avoid eye contact with Charles.

"Spice that I can easily ship back to England," replied Rimmers.

Roony laughed, surprising Charles.

"It is never easy to sail to England from here; too many pirates and the Navy wanting to steal your trade and boats," said Roony, still smirking.

Roony inspected the ivories, trying hard to control his facial expression. The ivories were magnificent, both huge and with minimal cracking and staining. They were the best he had ever seen. Roony knew that he would have to work hard to secure a deal without allowing Rimmers an opportunity to reveal the tusks to others. Then again, he had a large stock of illegal spice he desperately wanted to offload, for concealment had grown harder these last two years.

"What else is there?" Roony said, pretending to be uninterested in the tusks.

"Come, I will prove to you. Charles can wait here," replied Rimmers, nodding to Charles.

Leaving him, the two men went to the captain's cabin. Once they were inside, Rimmers locked the door.

"And?" inquired Roony. "What have you got to show me? Silver. Gold, maybe?"

"It is not what I have to show, but what I can tell you. For we go back a long way, to when we were kids," said Rimmers, smiling. "*Thatcher* has come looking for the JackFruit!"

"You know as well as I do that's a myth. Although Charles has the surname. Is it, in truth, his?" asked Roony.

"I have no reason to doubt him. He was close to death when we picked him up drifting with a woman, dead. I guess they had been at sea for three weeks, so lying about who he is does not fit," said Rimmers. "He said his grandfather found gems on Kandy."

"His one-eared brother is on this island too," exclaimed Roony.

"What? He never mentioned he had a brother. That is very odd," said a flabbergasted Rimmers.

Little did the men know they had the Thacker brothers' name wrong.

"I can supply you with pepper, clove and, of course, the best cinnamon for your ivory. Enough for you to retire and never need to sail again. Prices are exceptionally high in London," said Roony.

"That may be, but this ivory is the best and will equally trade for the highest prices in London too. You had better show me how much you have and its condition since rotten spice will only attract rats," said Rimmers. "Of course, I then run the risk of meeting the Dutch before getting to England."

“What shall we do with *Thatcher*?” posed Roony. “He will find out about his brother soon enough.”

“Just bring him along. We’ll keep that surprise to ourselves for now. We need to give Kali a wide berth,” replied Rimmers. “Too many Dutchmen and ships to chase us down.”

The two men walked back on deck; Charles was waiting patiently.

“Charles, we will go and see my spice. The location is privileged. You will use these,” said Roony.

He took out two strips of heavy black cloth.

Rimmers nodded. He knew the procedure and did not need to argue. He could see Charles frowning.

“Don’t worry, I have known Roony for many a year; we have traded well on every occasion,” stated Rimmers. “Along the way, you can tell us more about your favoured jackfruit. Roony will bring some of the sweet fruit for us.”

Six men pulled the bone-shaking cart carrying the three men. They travelled for what seemed like an hour, but it was less than half that. They munched on a very ripe jackfruit, which must have weighed over fifty pounds, thought Charles before they tightened his headscarf. Roony extracted the yellow fruits, discarding the inner nuts, and handed them to the blindfolded men. It was the first time Charles had tasted jackfruit. He did not mind it initially, although it was strange to eat something without seeing what he was eating.

“This has the flavour of banana mixed with pineapple, but there’s something more to it. Very odd. Crunchy, yet smooth, almost slimy,” thought Charles, as he munched.

Charles was bloated. They got through only a fraction of the jackfruit between them when the cart stopped. Roony jumped off.

"You will wait here. Do not be tempted to remove your bandana just yet. My men are watching you closely," stated Roony.

He returned within five minutes. Charles and Rimmers were taken off the cart and marched into a small room.

"You can free your eyes now," said Roony.

The room was quite dark. It took some moments to adjust to the modest light. Charles felt the cold floor under his sandals, but the aroma was intoxicating. He and Rimmers began to sneeze and found it difficult to stop. Charles felt his chest tighten and began wheezing.

"It's a powerful scent, isn't it?" said Roony, laughing. "Oh, that combination of pepper, cinnamon and clove, I am never too sure which smell is best or worst."

After scanning the room and walking around, Charles estimated that there must have been over a thousand sacks of spice in the sizeable and tall room.

Roony pulled two sacks from the back of the pepper pile and made Rimmers open them. Sniffing the corns, Rimmers pretended to know what he was looking at, weighing them in his hand and rubbing the black balls together. They looked and smelt like pepper and showed no apparent signs of mould. He performed the same ritual with the cloves and finally the cinnamon, his favourite taste but least appreciated for trade. It was the bulkiest pound-for-pound and went mouldy readily in cooler, wet conditions.

"Roony, these all look and smell fine," said Rimmers, winking at Charles. "You don't have enough, though."

"Ha-ha," roared Roony. "You know there's not nearly enough ivory to dent this pile of gold."

"You forget that all this stuff is illegal. Expect a hanging when you get caught. The longer you have it, the worse its quality goes," bellowed Rimmers.

"And the ivory *is* legal?" laughed Roony. "These piles are all sound. How much do you want for the white sticks?"

"All of this and the same again," said Rimmers sternly. "The trade must be for more. The risk of taking on this load shifts to me. Getting caught by the Dutch will be my death-rope, not yours."

They stood in the dim room for another thirty minutes verbally hurling offers to each other, moving closer together then backwards, over and over. The dance amused Charles, remembering how he and James tried to secure the deal on the *Frostenden Nave*, only to see it burn and disappear along with his brother.

"That was so many months ago," Charles muttered.

"Charles, do you have anything to add?" said Rimmers, annoyed and puzzled by the interruption.

Charles replied, "Ah, no. Sorry. This scent is quite something. I care for some fresh…."

A sack of pepper cushioned his head as he fell in a heap onto the cold floor. He lay there for some minutes, despite Roony's attempts to revive him. Not even a handful of cloves stuffed under his nose made any difference; he did not flinch.

Four cart pullers carried him out and dumped him on the dirt outside without care.

"I say, he can't take his spice," howled Rimmers.

Rooney shook his head disparagingly, laughing too.

"Now that you have seen outside of my store, we will make this quick. I will take you and Charles back to the coast, bring the spice to your boat tonight, and exchange it for ivory. All or nothing. Then you must be on your way and never return here," said Roony carefully. "I suggest you visit his brother in Kali before heading to England. But watch Charles like a hawk, for you need to find out more about the gems."

Charles remained dazed on the dirt, still faking the fainting, scarcely believing. He heard it all.

They brought the goods on several wagons at a time. It was four in the morning before the spices and ivory were exchanged and loaded. Rooney knew that he was taking a considerable risk moving everything in one night. He wanted rid of the wretched spice; it had caused him too much worry, despite making him wealthy beyond his station. In Kandy, though, he could not show it. The ivory was different. He expected great suspicion. It could pass off as local or Indian, although the tusks were immense.

The *Dam Plague* set off from Negombo just before sunrise on 10th January 1698. They headed for Kali. Rimmers was excited with his newly found wealth, brimming his ship's holds. His apprehension only softened by chasing something potentially more significant, fabled tales of gems big enough to fill a man's hand.

Stories of the Kali treasure were well known to Rimmers, but only a handful of others knew from him. Jacques Rimmers, his late great-grandfather, told Jos bedtime stories of a green stone coffin full of yellow stones when he was a young boy. From what Rimmers remembered, an Englishman named *Thatcher* found it. Jacques met the Englishman and his woman in Kali. Jacques spent a week with them until they left the island for a long trek back to England. Jacques said the gems were massive, fit for a king, but he never saw them. He also foretold a new illness that spread within the local cinnamon farms soon after *Thatcher* left the island; a season lay in ruins. Some years later, Jacques heard, third or fourth-hand, that *Thatcher* became a landowner on the English coast, north of London.

Jos Rimmers named his ship in his great-grandfather's memory after Jacques somehow survived the traumatic near-death illness in Kandy and returned to Holland. Jacques never ventured onto the high seas again and lived in agony for years afterwards in Amsterdam. Finally, he succumbed at the age of eighty; the ends of his limbs were rotten and mutated, his torso covered by large dark spots. Jos was only seven.

Before the spice arrived, Rimmers purchased a large number of thick hardwood planks. He bought multiple bags of dried Portuguese pepper, raw and ripe jackfruits, and durian too. The durian was especially pungent and made the woodworking team sick. He worried that the extra weight would affect the ship's trim. The vessel was undoubtedly lower in the water, but he judged it acceptable. The team began concealing the new sacks behind the panelling once they were an hour away from Negombo.

Their timing could not have been much worse. After the first day of virtually no wind and little progress, a swell and squall soon spiralled out of control after darkness fell. The *Dam Plague* pitched and rolled violently, throwing the men around, adding to their sickness.

Rimmers had remained calm before dusk, but he wished he had not dealt with Roony again. Now he began to worry about his vessel; she was not behaving herself.

Charles had remained cabin-bound since leaving Negombo until a massive crash and shake launched him out of his hammock; he landed on the floor, bruised. Another clang and he dropped to his knees. The seawater doused him as soon as he opened the door, then he recoiled at the dark frothing mass ahead of him as the ship rolled and pitched. Water covered him repeatedly.

Rimmers shouted, "Get inside, now!"

Before moving, a roaring wave covered Charles. He slid headfirst towards the guardrail. His head went past the railings. Both shoulders cracked, and he yelled in pain, but no one heard him. Another surge smashed him into the posts again, and he passed out.

Rimmers let go of the wheel; such was the tussle with the tempest. He reckoned they were far from shore. He needed to save his ship.

He vaguely saw a figure sliding on deck, Charles. Rimmers skidded down from the bridge and tried to catch him, but high water buffered Rimmers too, and he lost balance.

He managed to drag Charles, unconscious, back to the steps of the bridge, calling for First Mate, Hendrick, to help against the booming spray. His calls went unanswered. Blood smudged Charles's contorted face. Rimmers held back both eyelids briefly but only saw the whites of Charles's eyes.

Rimmers held onto Charles. For thirty minutes or more, they slid uncontrollably until the storm briefly relented enough for Rimmers to try to haul Charles to the bridge.

He and Charles landed in the water. Rimmers only recollected stopping the spinning wheel and hearing a colossal thud before the ship's movement stopped. In his sights, Rimmers saw her bow ahead and sensed it was within touching distance, or so he thought. The ship listed to aft, but he could barely see it as they drifted away. Rimmers held Charles's head, trying, as best he could, to keep water away from his gaping mouth. Charles was breathing but remained unresponsive until sunrise. The *Dam Plague* was gone.

# 29

## Brief brothers

When Charles finally woke, he bit hard on his cracked lips and tasted metal. Still unsure if he was dreaming, he slowly focused on low grey and white clouds bouncing above him.

"Charles, where have you been?" exclaimed Rimmers. "You have been out cold all day."

"What? Where am I? Where are we?" stuttered Charles as he swallowed some water.

"Between Negombo and Kali. That is the best I can offer, but we are now drifting to land. I can see trees ahead, occasionally," replied Rimmers.

Within an hour before sunset, they were swimming towards a long beach fringed with coconut palms along its length. Rimmers was exhausted. He could barely keep his head above water, let alone hold Charles's out of it too. Charles appeared energised, much to Rimmers's surprise and slight annoyance. They both fell head over heels through the breaking surf, crawled to the beach, and collapsed on their backs. Both men laughed.

"I have been here before, many months ago," smiled Charles after a few minutes and added, "yet this is not the same beach. That one was also beautiful, yet forsaken."

Rimmers nodded in reply.

They moved up the beach above a rough line of seaweed and tiny shells and slept until daybreak.

After a rough night under palms, both men woke covered in red itching spots. They swam to soothe their skin.

"Rimmers, you are quite a sight. Red-raw from the sun and now these bloody spots," said Charles.

"Sandflies," he replied.

The sight of a ship entering the bay was astonishing and elating. A dinghy came towards them.

They were soon on board the Dutch warship under the VOC flag. Captain Van Mers, gesturing in his given tongue, offered Rimmers his condolences for the lost ship and spice. However, Charles pretended not to understand his meaning.

"What is the day today?" asked Charles.

"Wednesday," replied Van Mers.

"Really?" was all Charles could say in reply.

"Your brother, James, he's a sorry, yet powerful sight. He may have lost an ear and some teeth, but by god, he has risen in power in Kali these last months," said Van Mers.

"James, *here*?" shouted Charles in utter disbelief. "He is alive, you say?"

"Quite so," replied Van Mers. "A royal pain. His henchman Solroy, the Omani pirate, is someone you would not want to meet in a darkened alley. They are inseparable friends, but I gather Solroy is the one who lobbed his ear off. Remarkable!"

Charles stared at Van Mers, not knowing what to say next, remembering that fateful day when he last saw his brother, his ship, and his dreams go up in smoke.

They sailed towards Kali and arrived at the fort harbour early the following day, 16th January 1698.

Charles was bewildered and flabbergasted. His ship, the *Frostenden Nave*, sat in the harbour, battered, repaired, and renamed. Van Mers watched on as Charles shook his head repeatedly for an hour before they disembarked without saying a word.

Charles found his brother in the smoky *Sardine Tavern,* close to the VOC administration building. Charles had a cloth mask over his face.

James stood tall and smiling, dressed in an elegant colourful robe and a tall hat that masked his missing lobe. Charles thought James looked like a cross between a Dutchman and one of the Omani pirates, albeit with missing front teeth.

Solroy was by James's side, dressed in the same multicoloured cloth that Charles had last seen him in.

Charles walked up to Solroy, invading his personal space as their noses almost touched. Solroy smirked as he recognised the man in front of him despite his mask.

"I finally get to see the man who cast me adrift and burned my boat," said Charles.

Charles lunged his hidden sabre towards Solroy's ribcage. Solroy's eyes flared as he immediately twisted his body.

James instinctively lashed out with his dagger, catching Charles's arm and slicing his wrist. Charles screamed in agony as his sabre fell to the ground, followed by his hand. Charles waved his stump about, splattering Solroy and James's face with blood.

"James. *No*!" wailed Charles.

It was too late. James struck Charles's neck with his knife, and he fell on the cold stone floor, lifeless.

Swords drew all around. The other men stood their ground, waiting for the next deadly move. It never came.

"Gentlemen," shouted Van Mers. "Now there is only one *Thatcher* left on this island. Can we please get on with our business of drinking the finest Kali coconut spirit?"

"The name's *Thacker*!" laughed James.

Rimmers was unsure whether the single tear he saw from the corner of James's eye was for his brother. He was equally confused by James's announcement.

"So, you are not *Thatcher* from England, Mister *Thacker*?" said Rimmers, hoisting his clay cup in the air, almost smashing it against James's mug. "Why kill him, your flesh and blood?"

"My brother was a bounder. He never once helped me in his life, and especially not onboard the *Frostenden Nave*. Now when I return to England, I will have his pretty little wife all to myself," said James gleefully.

--x--

# 30

# DEATH TAVERN

Wethersby Jnr's captaincy skills remained stretched, not by the crew but by the raging seas, as he battled to hold the ship's great wheel without breaking his arms. Too many times to count, she had pitched and rolled as waves battered her. They lost two more of their crew that day, both from the original Singh regiment, by monster waves and loose feet. The losses now tallied twenty since leaving the Indian east coast.

Rayleigh swore he smelt smoky food as the *Shepherds Cove* neared the island's coast. He gagged as he whiffed burnt coconut.

They feasted hurriedly on the delicious meat, letting out a chorus of belches and hoots. Only Rayleigh held his nose while acknowledging his first full belly for a month.

Frequent landing trips later, everyone from the battered ship gathered on the shoreline. Wethersby Jnr decided he wanted none of the crew to remain on board, despite their precious cargo. After such a wild trip south, Wethersby Jnr knew they would loathe and resent him if he did not let them go. Only the captain stayed behind.

Rayleigh said openly, “Junior, let the men explore on their own. They can do little harm. They need rest and to recover. Some freedom for them will, I am sure, be rewarded in their further loyalty towards us as we proceed on Kandy.”

“You are, perhaps, overly trusting of them, Rayleigh. I understand your meaning,” replied Wethersby Jnr. “Yes, tell them to be back here before this sunset. That will give them all afternoon to unwind.”

“Good. Let us get through this mass of hawkers and find someone in authority,” said Rayleigh

Rayleigh pushed his way through the melee and the stench of dried fish waving in their faces. He held Freya upon his shoulders; she squealed with delight. Mayling kept ahold of Fredrick’s arm.

Wethersby Jnr did not ask Rayleigh any questions about Negombo village. Mayling warned Rayleigh, but he decided not to divulge what he had uncovered, despite his eagerness and sheer surprise.

--x--

They passed the port of Columbo, fearing the Dutch would hound them out, and continued south towards Kali. As they turned eastward, another sudden fierce storm battered the *Shepherds Cove*. Wethersby Jnr estimated thirty-foot waves crashing over the bow and decks. Fortunately, the tempest was brief, but the waves knocked one of the Indians off the deck, his screams drowned out by the frothing sea as he disappeared under a giant wave.

They arrived at Kali on 17th January 1697, after two more days at sea. It felt like a week to Rayleigh; his dizzy spells had returned, and his hand was numb and painful again.

They anchored the *Shepherds Cove* alongside a blackened vessel, the *Panotii*.

Wethersby Jnr gathered the ship's members on deck.

"Men and ladies. We have arrived at our destination, Kali. Please bear in mind the Portuguese also call this place Galle. Take great care," he shouted. "We will rest here for three or four weeks. This ship is your bed. Be careful not to nest with the locals, for you never know what pox you, or they, may catch. Remember, you represent Rayleigh and me. Do not let us down. Understood?"

"Aye!" they roared.

"Stop. Where you go?" asked the lookout.

Wethersby Jnr and Rayleigh marched up to the enormous gate, ignoring the guard.

His pike lowered; the man repeated his words.

"To the governor, to trade, of course," declared Wethersby Jnr. "Now, if you wouldn't mind, we are busy folk and wish to be on our way without delay."

"He is not in port," replied the guard, then laughed. "You are best staying on your boat. Many a pirate be in these parts, fellow Englishmen especially."

"That may be so, but we can take care of ourselves, thanks," said Rayleigh as he strolled past the sentry with Freya still perched on his shoulders.

They soon found the *Sardine Tavern*.

A dozen men wearing tall hats, and red and green uniforms, dominated the tavern. It was smoky, humid and reeked of stale beer and sweaty sailors. Nevertheless, Wethersby Jnr and Rayleigh ordered enough for everyone. Mayling sipped hers.

Freya drank some water, quenching her fever. The tavern's owner was none too pleased to have women in his place, but he needed all the custom he could get, given the week's events.

Rayleigh overheard a group of four Dutch soldiers and strained to hear their slurred conversations. He did not understand a word. However, their gestures were apparent; a man held his sword, pretending to lurch into another.

"Captain, they are talking about two Englishmen," exclaimed Scythe. "Allegedly, one Englishman killed the other, right here, only yesterday. All hell broke loose, and the killer fled with an Omani pirate."

"Scythe, seeing you know some Dutch, please find out more about the Englishman and the buccaneer," requested Wethersby Jnr. "There cannot be many in these parts. I didn't see any English, Omani or black-and-white-skull flagged vessels in the harbour. Ha-ha."

"Yes, Captain Thacker," replied Scythe. "You never know what you might hear."

In the farthest corner of the inn sat Everett, apparently senseless, but his ears worked overtime.

The *Shepherds Cove* gang stayed for several more hours, savouring beer and the local spirit, curious yet wary about the slaying.

Everett snuck out.

"They're here," said Everett breathlessly.

"Who?" replied Ohama.

"More men from Southwold," said Everett.

"You're drunk again. Get some rest, for goodness' sake," bellowed Ohama.

"But I heard them, loud and clear. One is called Junior, another Scythe," retorted Everett. "I only had four flagons, and I know what I heard. They left the *Sardine Tavern* a few minutes after me. I followed them to the harbour, where they boarded a ship, *Shepherds Cove*. It's an English vessel too, for sure."

"A fine story. But where is James? He is a dead man if we do not find him. It's not as if there's another one-eared toothless rich land pirate in these parts," laughed Ohama. "When I catch up with him, I have a mind for losing him his other ear. He has cost us our fortunes by his impulsive actions, killing his brother in cold blood. We must creep out of harbour tonight, with or without him."

--x--

Mayling hid it well. Her gradual swelling belly was unnoticed for the last four months, but that time would soon come. A baggy full-length sarong would only protect her for perhaps a week or two at best. She could not hide the daily sickness; mornings were the worst, constant vomiting for ten minutes, every day for the last month. Rayleigh seemed oblivious, perhaps some would say uncaring, as his mind focused on his one-eared and toothless cousin's whereabouts.

"He must know by now," she whispered. "His kin is inside me, growing strong. Do I tell him or let that surprise be for himself?"

She sat watching the glow of the reddish sun settle over the water on the horizon; another day was beginning. She felt alone there on the beach, deep within her thoughts, dreaming of what might become of her family. She imagined a small house by this beach, laughing and smiling, despite dark clouds overhead. She wanted to spend the rest of their lives here, making the island their home. Then she saw Fredrick, rather than Rayleigh, in her vision.

Mayling and Freya remained in Kali with a significant batch of silver, Rayleigh and Wethersby Jnr honouring their commitment to Gooty months ago. Fredrick and another Southwold man, George, and five of the Singh soldiers agreed to stay to watch over and take care of them.

James Thacker and the Omani pirate, Solroy, had disappeared, despite the best efforts of the Dutch forces to apprehend them. Rayleigh and Wethersby Jnr gave up looking for them too after a fruitless couple of weeks, assuming they had snuck off the island onboard the missing *Panotii*.

--x--

# 31

# Chao Phraya

The *Shepherds Cove* made landfall on 21st February 1698; Wethersby Jnr decided their journey was close enough to the main river that fell into the Gulf of Siam.

The men were hungry, as usual. They had been at sea for three weeks, having avoided several land bridges, for reasons known only to Wethersby Jnr. All had been dreaming of fresh meat rather than rice and the fish they caught. Provisions were low but by no means critical, except their sugarcane rum was long gone, and the rice and coconut spirits finished.

Wethersby Jnr wanted to take a small number of enormous rhino and elephant ivory to England. They had three large barrels of glass beads, another with Buddha artefacts remaining from the kingdoms of Kaski and Kantipur, and a fifth with various Hindu objects made from metal and wood from Kandy. These were their collateral for exchange. Rayleigh despised the trophies intensely, although he knew they would command a colossal price. Then there were the remaining silver crates.

From the ramblings of their grandfather, they knew the God Buddha dominated Siam. Many miles north of this large village, the city of Ayutthaya was the place to head to do their best trading and gather information. Here they sought to understand and help pinpoint islands in the Gulf for further exploration.

During the last months, he had excelled at seamanship, in Rayleigh's eyes, commanded the crew well with a firm but fair hand. Rayleigh felt Wethersby Jnr tended to overreact, though, mainly whenever anyone ignored his orders, or worse if someone blatantly did the opposite. Occasionally Wethersby Jnr could be brutal.

Arriving at a large village at the Chao Phraya river's mouth, Rayleigh was in the crow's nest for the grand view. Wethersby Jnr guided them with a thud against the wooden edge.

Throngs of market traders lined the pier, yelling, trying to catch attention.

"Lower the plank, but do not let one of them set foot on it. Do it now!" shouted Wethersby Jnr from the bridge.

Thomas dropped the plank with a thud as several men burst through and were almost on the ship.

Wethersby Jnr scorned, waving his dagger, "Be off with you. We buy nothing. Thomas, come here to my feet."

Rayleigh, observing the chaos, knew Thomas was in for some trouble. However, even he was surprised by what Wethersby Jnr did next.

"I have made myself abundantly clear. Since we set foot in India, you must follow my orders precisely. I will punish anyone disobeying me," Wethersby Jnr bellowed.

The captain turned and punched Thomas with a left hook, catching the base of his jaw. Several teeth went flying, along with trails of spit and dribble as Thomas dropped like a stone off the gangplank, headfirst into the water.

As two of the local men backed away quickly, another two behind them also fell, one on top of Thomas, the other caught his chin on the wood as he fell. Two men lay in the water motionless, head down, the other waving frantically.

Rayleigh instinctively jumped in and scooped up Thomas, turning his head upright. James followed Rayleigh, grabbed the local man's head, and turned his face up; the man coughed and splattered, much to James's relief. Thomas, though, remained unresponsive.

Several men threw ropes as James helped the two wet traders and pushed them up; another crewmember heaved them onto the deck.

James then swam over to help Rayleigh with Thomas. He punched Thomas's stomach five times, as hard as he could.

"Rayleigh, we need to get him out of this water, like in a hurry. He has probably swallowed some of this filth after the captain knocked him out," spluttered James.

Rayleigh was treading water but finding it tough to keep his mouth and nose above it, with Thomas's head now lying across his chest. Rayleigh pivoted as James pulled his legs, as the three of them bounced off the ship and next to the ropes.

Wethersby Jnr climbed down halfway and yelled, "Cousin, push Thomas's arms to me, and I will pull him up."

Thomas and Wethersby Jnr were soon joined on deck by James and finally Rayleigh. James repeatedly pushed on Thomas's stomach for over one minute, although it seemed to Rayleigh like five. Thomas finally emitted a short gurgle, and a thick brown liquid trickled from the side of his mouth. His eyes opened wide; he started to choke.

"Finally, you are back with us, young Thomas. Tell us, how did you come to be in the water?" said Rayleigh with much relief.

"The captain. He hit me," he stuttered, touching his mouth, and feeling inside. "My teeth; he's only gone and felled them too."

Rayleigh thought Thomas was grinning, for he was not a pretty sight. Thomas's front two teeth and one below were gone, and several strands of bright red gum skin were hanging off their holes. His top lip had turned outward. At least he had come round.

"Now then Thomas, and everyone," shouted Wethersby Jnr. "Have I made myself crystal clear over these months? My orders are to be strictly obeyed and never questioned. I will punish severely otherwise. Rayleigh, see to it none of these men board my boat. Leave James with Thomas. Get the bottle I left on my desk. Thomas needs its contents."

Rayleigh said nothing as he went to fetch the almost empty bottle.

"Thomas, sit up and take stock of this," demanded Rayleigh and added, "the last shot of the captain's finest liquor, no less."

Thomas's eyes almost popped again as he drank the thimbleful that remained. His face contorted as the liquid touched his opened gums, then he relaxed as the spirit melted into his chest.

For all this time, one of the local men who had fallen into the water stood silently on the pier, his foot touching the wooden plank. He was steaming from the sun in his wet clothes while smiling as if he was biting his teeth. Rayleigh thought he had not moved a muscle after he got off the ship.

"So much for an uneventful arrival, Junior. What on earth possessed you to hit out at Thomas? You almost killed him," blew Rayleigh. "These locals, and that wet man, are going to take some convincing that we come for peaceful trade. We need their help to arrange transport to Ayutthaya and pick their brains for the whereabouts of the three-headed elephant skull."

"Ah, Rayleigh, you think I did that in anger? No, that was deliberate for two reasons. Firstly, Thomas disobeyed an order, and I need the crew to understand there will always be consequences for doing so," said Wethersby Jnr.

"And the second?" asked Rayleigh.

"Simple. To show these locals who are in charge here and to instil respect.

Rayleigh thought Wethersby Jnr might have done the opposite with the local people but decided to keep his thoughts to himself. Wethersby Jnr rarely listened to any argument that contradicted his own.

"Rayleigh, let us see if we can find some elephant burners and coconut oil for you in this vast market?" he winked.

Wethersby Jnr was first to march down the wooden plank, past the still steaming man and into the crowd.

Four stayed on board the ship, including James and a sleeping Thomas. The rest of the crew followed Wethersby Jnr and Rayleigh through the market area. As they walked past purposefully, the mass of people ahead of them opened up slightly so as not to impede the band.

Rayleigh loved the sights and some of the smells from the market. He did not care for the whiff of rotten, dried fish nor clay pots full of fermented fish heads and innards. Rayleigh scanned the masses; his eyes caught some sellers to the ship's left, particularly women selling dried meats. His nose, though, was full of rotting onions; he wanted to vomit. Immediately a spiked green globe was thrust in his face, catching his chin.

"Good grief, man, rid me of that," Rayleigh gestured towards the seller. "What on earth?"

He showered sick over the trader's feet. The man howled with laughter and slapped Rayleigh hard on his back.

"*Do ran. Mat kin cow*," Rayleigh thought the man said.

The man offered a piece of slimy yellow fruit to Rayleigh's nose.

"This is not jackfruit. It has a different stench and quality," said Rayleigh.

The man shoved the walnut-sized piece into Rayleigh's open mouth. Rayleigh's eyes bulged as he tried to spit it out.

As the lump dropped, Rayleigh uttered, "I was right. It tastes of onions too. How and why do they eat this?"

"One pod duang, master," said the cheeky man and howled again.

Soon Rayleigh passed another hawker, a very old looking lady, her back fully bent over. She made up a leaf full of shavings from a large dark green fruit, discarding its white seeds. She then added more than a dozen tiny red Portuguese peppers, a large spoonful of fermented fish liquor and one little blue crab, then mashed everything together.

"Som-tom, mister," shouted the hunchback.

She thrust the banana leaf mixture into Rayleigh's hand and hurried to make another.

Wary of the sour fish soup, Rayleigh held the food near his nose and instantly coughed from the spicy peppers but stayed off vomiting from the odour. Without wishing to offend, he gingerly pinched some in his fingers and ate a mouthful, then another and another.

He was pleasantly surprised by the intensity of flavours, although the concoction burnt his lips. It tasted much better than its fumes suggested. The old lady cackled in Siamese whilst she made several more leaves full of the mixture.

"Som-tom," she shouted again before handing a leaf to Wethersby Jnr and another to Rayleigh, who had finished his first.

"You have to try this, Junior. First, perhaps hold your nose. It may not be to everyone's liking. Yet, it has a sensational taste," said Rayleigh as he started his second helping.

Wethersby Jnr looked at Rayleigh and laughed, "Young man, this must be hot; your lips are scarlet,"

He dabbed his finger into the mixture to taste it.

"It is great," replied Rayleigh.

"The food of the devil. Rayleigh, did you see how many peppers she used?" coughed Wethersby Jnr.

"A good handful in each, cousin," laughed Rayleigh. "We have been at sea for so long. Any fresh food is a godsend, is it not?"

"An acquired taste," replied Wethersby Jnr.

They walked on.

The som-tom lady followed them slowly. Her long grey hair almost touched the ground from behind her curved back. After Rayleigh had finished the contents of his second leaf, the old lady grabbed his hand and stopped him abruptly. Wethersby Jnr did not notice and carried on without him. The old lady held Rayleigh's arm tightly, and his veins swelled from her pressure. She led him to one side passing other hawkers sitting on the ground. They reached a stall of dried dark brown meat.

"My buffalo, here," she said, surprising Rayleigh by speaking with an English tongue. "My granddaughter, Chiranya, seeks you."

"Who? Where?" was all Rayleigh could muster in response.

In what seemed like a split second, the old lady vanished. The beautiful woman who sat next to him, motionless, stared into his eyes. Rayleigh warmed and melted inside, transfixed by her bright green eyes, glowing silk complexion and wide shining smile.

He then remembered his cousin James saying, "You will know love when it smacks you in the face."

It was an expression James often followed with, "But it has never happened to me, and doubtless ever will."

A speechless Rayleigh did not blink; he was unable to look away. He did not want to, either.

--x--

# 32

## Solemnly north

The cousins argued over the trip north. Rayleigh trumpeted stories from their grandfather; Wethersby Jnr heard many of them now for the first time. Rayleigh became fixated by their grandfather's most talked-about location but never exaggerated any Siam tales to his cousin. The green-inked map within the atlas clearly showed, Rayleigh thought, a diamond-like symbol similar to those on the Indian pages, and he convinced Wethersby Jnr despite lingering doubts.

Slowly, they made their way, skirting the river, following its meandering northwards. Rayleigh marvelled at the scenery; vast flat, barren plains and only a handful of small misty mountain peaks to the northeast. Their cargo team struggled to control the valuable carts as the sun beat down relentlessly.

Wethersby Jnr was far less interested in the surroundings and rather more on the lookout for warriors. They brought three local guides for their knowledge of the relatively short route to Ayutthaya. They reconfirmed his worries after what he had heard in Kandy. The Siam ruler had apparently all but closed his kingdom to foreigners, favouring only the Dutch. They had seen two ruined forts built by the French but no signs of trouble on their path so far. The only blessing, so Wethersby Jnr thought, was the lack of cover for an attack. Rayleigh, though, was more concerned about how conspicuous and open they were.

Early morning of the third day, Chiranya unexpectedly screamed. Rayleigh instantly raised the camp's signal, the low unmistakable drone from a metal Tibetan trumpet.

More than a dozen aggressors, dressed head to feet in shining metal, wailed with swords held high, their faces shielded by masks of monkeys, lions, and warriors with grotesque tusks.

The assailants targeted where Chiranya was hiding. Four of the Southwold gang who were shielding her were struck within a minute, two dying each from a single blow. The swords' clanging reverberated as the attackers gained the upper hand, downing three of Scythe's crew and seriously injuring two others. Rayleigh and Wethersby Jnr stayed in front of Chiranya, along with all the Suffolk men. They kept pushing.

"Junior. Quick, to the rear. The masked devils are going there too," yelled Rayleigh.

"James. Thomas. Here. *Now*!" thundered Wethersby Jnr. "Aim for their heads or legs."

The four moved swiftly behind the wagons just before the armoured men descended. Three attackers put up a fierce fight, clearly skilled with the sword, seemingly unperturbed by their body shields' weight.

Rayleigh got nicked first on his left arm above the elbow, and then a glancing blow caught him lightly on his right upper side.

However, for just a moment, his attacker let open his guard. Rayleigh seized the advantage and slashed at the man's leg, dropping him to the ground, screaming, and oozing blood.

Wethersby Jnr got stuck in a trough. Despite his extra height, he was positioned lower than the man in front of him and disadvantaged. They duelled hard for two minutes, each trading blows. Still, mercifully for Wethersby Jnr, he did not get struck directly by the attacker's sword. However, his wrist and arm ached from the constant coming together.

Thomas and James engaged the third and largest man. Thomas, still weak after his arrival at the village, let James take the lead. They worked exceptionally well as a tag team. James nicked the man several times on his sword arm, through his armour, as Thomas repeatedly drove at the raider's legs, ducking potential blows. After the man stepped back, James finally broke through the formidable man's guard. He slashed hard at the man's left leg, slicing through the scaled armour, leaving a deep clean cut across his open thigh. The man let out a dreadful screech and slumped to the ground. Thomas drove his sword through the man's protection and into his neck. The man's head hit the ground, and he never moved again. James and Thomas turned breathlessly; small but deep cuts on their arms bled out.

"Thomas, go to Rayleigh. I will help the captain," said James.

Thomas nodded, and they moved fifteen yards towards the two skirmishes.

James gashed his evenly-matched aggressor three times through heavy armour despite suffering cuts of his own.

Thomas joined Rayleigh. The two of them slowly drove the man back until he tripped and fell, his sword flailing aimlessly in the air. Thomas quickly sliced at the man's shiny feet as Rayleigh aimed at his eyes. They hit him at the same time. A dull groan came from the man's mouth, and the assailant stopped moving. Rayleigh struck him again in his other eye to ensure the lifeless man went no further.

Lacerated on both arms, Wethersby Jnr managed to move up from the gully. Now standing a foot taller than the man ahead of him, Wethersby Jnr switched the lead. The attacker saw his comrades fall in his peripheral vision; he knew the numbers stacked against him now. His immediate focus, though, was on the tall man ahead of him. He struck four rapid and successive blows across Wethersby Jnr's sword, missing his intended target. His next swipe, an uppercut, breached Wethersby Jnr's guard, skipping his torso by a fraction of an inch. Wethersby Jnr, catching the man off-balance, dealt two swift and hefty blows to his chest guard; the attacker visibly coiled. The reverberation from the sword strikes through Wethersby Jnr's arm pained him intensely. He felt his power waning just as James thrust his sword at the back of the assailant's legs, catching the man unawares. The outnumbered man dropped to his knees. Rayleigh also snared him, this time catching the attacker hard across the neck. The blow did not penetrate his armour, but the man still howled and withered in pain. Rayleigh dispatched the man the same way as his first.

The weary men turned towards Chiranya's wagon. Their men outnumbered their foe now, having downed six but lost three of their own. The attackers relentlessly pushed forward while Southwold and Scythe's exhausted men protected their positions. Chiranya cowered under the wagon as her protectors clashed swords. Rayleigh reached the wagon and gathered four small black powder bags primed with thick twine. He handed one each to Wethersby Jnr, Thomas, and James.

"Quick, remember what we planned. We have only ten seconds after the spark to throw it. Split up, aim straight, and drop it behind them. Ready!" shouted Rayleigh as he grabbed a smouldering torch.

After quickly lighting each fuse, the first black bag blasted three men off their feet before Rayleigh finally set his own. Two of the four explosions successfully felled four men, killing them instantly and mortally wounding six others. The last two bags fell too far behind the attacked to cause serious injury. However, the surprise of the four blasts was enough to distract the last of the attackers. The discharges injured four of the *Shepherds Cove* crew, one of whom was caught by an attacker and had his hand severed. The others rallied around him and fought back. Vastly outnumbered, the muggers did not relent. Each was picked off by the increasing disadvantage, one to three, then four, then five, until they all lay defenceless or motionless on the bloodied ground.

"Well done, gang," congratulated Wethersby Jnr wearily. "Those of you who can walk and can use your weapon must check each of the devils. Follow Rayleigh's lead and pierce them in their soft spot, deep in each eye. Do not hesitate, for they may still be alive, and in any case, they would have done the same to you and me. Everyone else, get washed and let us assess you one by one. Do not worry. Nobody gets left behind."

None of the group coveted the task ahead and walked towards the fallen men. They each carried out the captain's instruction.

Wethersby Jnr, Rayleigh, and Chiranya tended to the wounded. Chiranya and Rayleigh paid particular care to Alfred's wrist stump; they tried desperately to stop the bleeding from his lost hand. One of Alfred's friends, Mark, had stayed next to Alfred, wounded in the lower left leg. Mark tore long strands from his shirt, wrapping them around Alfred's stump. Chiranya removed several of the shirt pieces; Alfred fainted. She rapidly removed all the cloth. Rayleigh held more strands as she covered the stump three times greater this time. Blood oozed through the fabric. Slowly, the flow subsided.

After twenty gory minutes, the crew returned and gathered in three groups surrounding a wagon with a large pot. Stripping off their clothing, they cleansed their bodies of residual bloodshed and assessed themselves. Most of them shook uncontrollably; not one said a word.

Wethersby Jnr left and grimly counted the dead. Pausing next to each fallen man, he checked for a pulse; he felt no signs of life other than a lingering warmth, soon extinguished. He closed each man's eyes. Wethersby Jnr made the sign of a cross with his hands then bowed his head.

"May God have mercy on your soul, dear brother," pronounced Wethersby Jnr.

He removed the crewmembers' personal effects; the collection was tiny. Wethersby Jnr vowed to return all the articles to Suffolk, as he had promised himself for his fallen crew. He relieved the invaders of their weapons. Wethersby Jnr cut a finger off one of them and pocketed a significant gold ring.

Thomas and Rayleigh cleaned their wounds and assessed one another. Their cuts were clean and thankfully not bone-deep; Chiranya, still shaking, looked on with great apprehension.

"I was lucky. I did not need to run hard, and I am swift with a blade now," said Rayleigh. "Please look after Thomas first."

Chiranya smiled and dressed Thomas's cuts, then tended to Rayleigh.

Before laying the men to rest, they were stripped bare, and their clothes burned. The crew dug deep into the hard parched ground as best they could and buried George, Duncan, and Stephen, entombing ash from their clothes too. At the head of each grave, they formed a cross from small rocks. They bestowed the same treatment upon Scythe's men and the invaders too.

Wethersby Jnr instructed the men to cover the holes and pack the ground gradually and tightly. Finally, with branches and leaves, they concealed the newly dug earth. Significant pools of dried blood littered the battle area; they covered as much of it as possible.

Only ten of the original seventeen crew from Southwold remained; Wethersby Jnr's anxiety only tapered in the knowledge that Scythe's team were a hardy and ruthless bunch. It was their collective number that worried Wethersby Jnr the most. They were now only thirty-three, and that included Chiranya, Rayleigh and himself.

Solemnly, they moved northwards, leaving their departed companions behind. A trio rode half a mile ahead of the posse. Chiranya had fallen heavily on her ankle in the skirmish; three lumps protruded. Rayleigh comforted her, unsure whether her cries of pain were for her strained joint or the men protecting her. They held each other tightly; he felt her shaking all morning.

By late afternoon she no longer trembled but could not put weight on her swollen foot. Rayleigh carried her from the wagon in his arms, gazing into her emerald-green eyes without blinking, spellbound. Rayleigh was in love, not out of desire but from compassion and humility.

At that moment, Rayleigh knew he would marry Chiranya, either in that land or when they returned to England. Rayleigh kissed her lips ever so gently and carried her to nowhere in particular. Finally, he let her slip from his grasp as his arms shot with pain. She balanced, her hand on his shoulder, looked up to him, and with her other hand, stroked his face. She kissed him vigorously, surprising him once again. They were lost together within that long passionate embrace for many minutes, touching, caressing, and wanting.

Chiranya fainted. Despite a life handling constant heat, the humidity was oppressive near the river. Tiny flies buzzed in her ear. Rayleigh picked her up from the wagon's floor and held her sitting upright, firmly tapping her cheeks. He noticed many red spots covered her neck and the back of her ears. She came to, confused.

"Who are you?" she invited.

"Joy, Chiranya, it is me, Rayleigh," he answered, frowning, puzzled.

"How do I know you, Mister Rayleigh?" she asked.

"Joy? We met in the market. Your grandma sold us som-tom," replied Rayleigh. "My cousin, Wethersby Jnr, and the crew of the *Shepherds Cove* have journeyed to Siam to find the JackFruit."

She drifted to sleep. Rayleigh held her lightly, baffled by her memory loss.

Two hours later, the wagon train stopped; it was close to sundown, the heat of the day covered them with sweat. She lay in his lap. He hardly broke his stare towards her beauty and vulnerability.

As she opened her eyes, she asked him, "Mister Rayleigh, no other person calls me Joy. Why?"

He responded, "You bring joy to my heart and soul,"

She nodded slightly and beamed a smile.

"Now tell me, what do you want with the giant fruits of the jack tree?" she searched.

"It is not the fruit we seek. It is a jade box full of gems fit for a king. But cursed," Rayleigh replied.

"A fine tale. I prefer to eat it when ripe. The fruit is sweet and complex. I roast the nuts too. Delicious," said Chiranya. "Rayleigh, we had better get up from here. I need to bathe."

She kissed him gently and winked, “I remember now. Come.”

She led him limping to a fast-flowing tributary away from the main river’s edge, surrounded by old trees. Out of sight from the other men, she undressed and waded into the water, her head turned slightly, beckoning Rayleigh to follow. He hesitated as she lowered herself in the stream.

“Rayleigh. The only things here that bite are the flies,” she laughed.

He removed his clothes and joined her in the refreshing water. They kissed passionately and embraced for over an hour until there was barely any blueness left in the sky.

“So, Mister Rayleigh, where is this JackFruit?” she asked.

He did not answer.

They returned to camp, Rayleigh sweating more than before he entered the creek. The air’s temperature and humidity seemed to rise that evening. Rayleigh found sleep impossible, as he and Chiranya slept separately, under canvas strung up between three wagons. The itchy red spots on their bodies appeared more extensive than before.

“Chiranya, what causes these spots?” he asked, pointing at her reddened neck.

Another night and another raid, this time the surprised assailants were initially beaten back from the camp’s front, but three monkey-masked men got through.

Wethersby Jnr duelled hard for a quarter of an hour, singlehandedly keeping two attackers away from the camp’s centre. At the same time, Rayleigh held one other from Chiranya.

One lunge, though, pierced Wethersby Jnr’s left side just below his lowest rib. Badly winded, he tried to move forward, but the masked raiders kept going for him, nicking his right arm and then slicing across his left elbow. Wethersby Jnr felt his strength ebb as he dropped his long dagger, defenceless, waiting for the final moment.

"Rayleigh!" yelled Wethersby Jnr. "Help me."

The sky was a light cloudless blue, the overhead sun allowing him only the tiniest glimpse. He rocked from side to side to a regular rhythm, strung between two guards. He vomited violently, but the motion continued unabated. Wethersby Jnr saw a man ahead of him with two thick bamboo poles across each shoulder. Wethersby Jnr spun his aching head around, seeing an identical masked man also holding branches. The pain from his stomach was intense. He looked down and prodded gently, despite tied hands; he convulsed and fell into a deep sleep.

"How long have I been tied up?" asked Wethersby Jnr as he woke in darkness.

No one replied.

He heard muffled voices to his right but could not move without deep pains racking him from inside, nor was he able to free his wrists. Dried blood caked his pulsing elbow. A tremendous blow to his upper leg startled him. Intense pain followed.

"Stop your moaning," said an unseen kidnapper. "Your pains are nothing compared to what is in store."

Wethersby Jnr pretended to pass out, desperately trying to control any movement. Another blow hit the same place on his leg. He grunted.

--x--

# 33

## Orange Clad

Rayleigh watched as Wethersby Jnr was carried away, helpless to do anything except protect Chiranya and himself from the attackers in front of them.

He shouted frantically, “Junior, I will come for you.”

They lost another of the Southwold crew, and two more were slightly injured. Ten more aggressors were dead too. The last skirmish took well over an hour.

For three days, they moved northwards. Rayleigh noticed many broken branches ahead of them and hooves next to the river’s edge. He was unsure whether the markings were simply cows, deer or disguised attackers’ movements. Rayleigh assumed the latter. He was amazed the raiders had not continued pushing forward and killed his cousin when they had the chance. Their precious cargo of silver remained untouched.

“How much longer can we endure this journey?” he shouted aloud.

There was no answer.

Chiranya cried. Rayleigh tried in vain to soothe her. Her sickness returned each night; she became weaker each day.

Now barely able to stand without support, Rayleigh bathed her each morning in the river before they ventured onwards. He saw her thinning body and more red spots covering her back and legs. He wished to hold her, but she wanted to be left alone.

Some crew took to stalking water buffalo and crocodiles along the water's edge, using bows and arrows captured from their foe.

Two got lucky late in the afternoon and speared a young buffalo on solid land next to the water. They crept up to its mother and crying calf, only to watch the gory spectacle as a colossal crocodile pounced out from the edge. It buried its teeth into the young buffalo's neck, dragging it quickly into the water and rolling it over and over. The mother tried to dislodge the beast, but the water was too deep; her baby was gone. She hissed in pain as they sent a volley of arrows into her head.

Four more of the crew followed the dying mother for an hour before she succumbed to her wounds, fortunately away from the river. Fearing that another crocodile would smell death, they worked quickly to dissect the carcass. They carried lumps of flesh back to the encampment.

Chiranya, ignoring Rayleigh's pleas, supervised the butchery, stripping the meat into slithers while carefully demonstrating to the men what to do. They feasted on fresh meat for four days and some green plants from the river's edge. The remaining flesh was left to dry, held by a patchwork of thin bamboo strips over the wagons. Rayleigh decided he hated bamboo, despite its usefulness. Its branches contained many sharp teeth-like barbs that nicked and stung his legs and arms. The scratches festered in the heat and from his constant sweat.

Tense and anxious, he led the gang north, their bellies now filled, the pace slow. Chiranya's ankle had gone from black to purple to a dark yellow. The swelling had diminished, but she still struggled to put her weight on it. Her sickness continued on and off. The group kept together with no forward lookouts. Instead, Rayleigh held the lead wagon with Chiranya, Thomas and two others.

They thought their luck might be changing; the weather had cooled to more like a hot English summer's day. Continuing their meandering way and staying close to the river, the group came to a significant golden temple. Its ornate stupa dominated the surroundings upon a small hill amid an otherwise vast and flat plain.

Three orange-clad monks greeted, "Sawasdee Krupp."

The monks were old. One of them was bent and hunched over so much his head faced the ground permanently; he was barely four feet tall. He shifted his head slightly and looked at Rayleigh.

"We come in peace. My name is Rayleigh Edwards," he said. "We seek knowledge of Mister Wethersby."

"Welcome, to our humble home," the old man said, then ushered Rayleigh towards two tall, ornately carved doors and added, "You must hurry. Soldiers are less than an hour from here. Come in."

"Thank you," replied Rayleigh. "There are almost thirty of us. We do not wish to cause you any trouble."

They entered the temple complex, open-mouthed, surveying the numerous wooden buildings, three covered in gold leaf. Hundreds of tiny bells, dangling off roof edges, sang in the slight breeze. The stupa dominated the expansive courtyard, twenty pure white steps led to its base.

They followed the three monks into a small plain wooden building. Inside, filling the length of the longest wall of perhaps fifty yards, lay a reclining golden Buddha. Brightly coloured murals covered the two walls at either end and behind it. Rayleigh cranked his neck in wonder. Two sun, two full moons, and white fluffy clouds dominated the otherwise blue ceiling.

Rayleigh dropped to the floor suddenly, smiling, holding his hand under his chin. The scenes behind the reclining image were near-identical to those of the Muktinath temple.

The old monk interrupted Rayleigh's thoughts, "Mister Wethersby, you say. That is an unusual name. How do you know of him?"

"Family," was all Rayleigh could reply.

"Many moons ago, a young fellow, similar looking to you, came here," said the old monk, nodding towards Rayleigh, "He, too, fell to this floor. What do you see?"

"How is that possible? Wethersby, he was here? When?" gasped Rayleigh.

"As I said, countless moons ago, five or six hundred, I am unsure now. My memory is not what it once was," said the monk. "My name is Patike. Tell me, what do you see?"

Having a well-rested night's sleep on a cool stone floor, covered in rough blankets, Rayleigh stirred. Chiranya's legs entangled his. He looked at her, then closed his eyes, smiling. Her warmth made him shiver with joyfulness. Moments later, he heard shuffling footsteps and snapped out of his rapture.

"Good morning, Mister Edwards. Come to the great Buddha with me. I wish to know more about this temple in Muktinath," whispered Patike.

Rayleigh followed the monk outside. It was still dark; he had no idea of the time. Through open shutters, the wooden structure lit up from the inside. Rayleigh was dazzled as he entered the building again. He wished he had made a drawing of the murals in Muktinath, but his memory was clear and precise. The paintings ahead of him were not just similar; they were matching in every detail.

"How can I prove to you these scenes are the same?" asked Rayleigh.

"There is no need. I see, from your expression, you have seen these before," said Patike. "Pray, tell me, what else do you remember from the room in Muktinath?"

"My grandpa, Mister Wethersby, carved a map on the grand door," said Rayleigh, unable to contain himself. "He led us here to Siam and towards Ayutthaya."

"A map. Indeed!" said Patike. "Mister Wethersby was a cunning fellow. He loved to draw, paint and carve wood here too. Where do you think this map leads to?"

"Our family secret," replied Rayleigh.

"Your resemblance to Mister Wethersby is unmistakable. Very tall, long black tied hair, blue-green eyes, and dark skin for an Englishman. I didn't see those marks on his forehead, though," continued Patike.

"No. These are burns from an awful fire when I was a boy. It consumed my ma, pa, and grandma. Grandpa, your Mister Wethersby, took me in, grief-stricken," replied Rayleigh and added, "and I lost this toe on the journey here."

"Do you have a big brother, young man?" probed Patike.

"No, but I have three older cousins," clarified Rayleigh curiously. "Why do you ask?"

"Again, your similarities are unmissable. It was doubtless one of your cousins who passed through here four days ago, swinging from a hammock, beaten and appallingly bruised," continued Patike.

The men walked around the room in silence for twenty minutes or so.

The old monk finally pointed above the reclining Buddha's head and said, "Your grandfather sketched his murals. At first, I thought it was from his memory, but later I discovered he brought drawings with him. If you look very carefully, you will see his mark."

“Where?” pronounced Rayleigh, “And why here? It is not as if we are in the city of Ayutthaya.”

“Yes, it is a grand city, but one war too many, especially from the Burmese, has taken its toll,” said Patike. “As Englishmen, you are best to give it a wide berth, for you are likely to receive the king’s wrath, for he only favours the Dutch now, although preferences can and do change.”

“I still do not see any marks,” Rayleigh offered.

“You must study the wall more closely, for it is there. When you see it, you will see it there forever,” stated the monk.

Rayleigh stared at the long wall, lost in his thoughts and intimidated by the painting’s details. He sat cross-legged in front of Buddha’s face. Above the giant ear, a three-headed elephant sat on its hind legs, frozen in the act of trumpeting. He traced the image to its feet and back again. Still, he could not see the spot.

“I give up. You will show me?” searched Rayleigh.

“Are you more interested to know your cousin’s fate?” said the hunched old man, then left the single-roomed building.

Rayleigh followed, lightly shaking his head, and found Chiranya still sleeping on the smooth stone floor. Rayleigh sat next to her, watching her chest move to each breath. He was exhausted but could not sleep. Instead, he closed his eyes, picturing the murals in his mind, trying to delve into their peculiarities. Over and over, he went through the images. Each time his focus came back to the unusual elephant creature above the Buddha’s head. His body suddenly convulsed, jerking him from his deliberations. Chiranya stirred. She held out her hand.

“Rayleigh, you made me jump. What is it?” she asked.

--x--

# 34

## PYTHON

A warrior dragged the languid Wethersby Jnr off his hammock. His body ached from regular beatings, be it from sticks or feet. He tried to get upright, but his knees buckled, and he landed on his face in the dirt. He lay there for several minutes, with his mouth wide open, dribbling.

Another kick to his stomach stirred him as he groaned. He finally managed to kneel and studied his surroundings. In front of Wethersby Jnr stood three soldiers clad in metal armour. He watched sweat dripping off their masks and pooling in the dirt next to their feet. Behind them stood two colossal stone temple guardian figures, mimicking the soldiers' outfits. Were the soldiers a copy of the statues? Wethersby Jnr was unsure.

The ferocity of his guards shocked him. Long barbed bamboo sticks whipped through the air and onto his body hourly. His back was swollen and bloody. However, the pain in his feet and behind his knees was the worst he had ever experienced. He could not rationalise the sadistic nature of the beatings. The men smiled and giggled as they lashed out their punishment; the more he cried out, the worse the next stroke was.

He felt his energy drain over the next four days. Even at night, the beatings were relentless; they refused to let him rest. In any case, sleep was only possible from sheer exhaustion.

Wethersby Jnr crawled out of the wooden cage, ignoring the new cuts from his knees scraping the bare earth. One of his captors side-kicked dust directly into his face before he could shut his eyes. Blinded, he was unable to clear his cloudy eyes for several minutes.

A wet liquid showered his head and trickled down his chin, as a commotion behind him accelerated, and Wethersby Jnr tried to wipe his face clear. He vaguely saw a huge masked man, perhaps seven-foot-tall, lashing out at one of the brutal men. Blow after blow rained down on the cowering man and did not stop even after he had passed out. The giant continued his vicious battering as five more guards came cautiously towards him. Only one was left standing, wise enough not to challenge further. Wethersby Jnr remained kneeling on the ground, shaking uncontrollably, unsure when the large man would use the stick on his broken body. Instead, the man grabbed hold of Wethersby Jnr's underarm and hoisted him to his feet. Unable to hold his own weight, he crumpled back to the ground, surprised and confused.

"Up!" roared the giant.

Sometime later, he stuttered, "Thank you. But why are these men so savage towards me?"

The giant said nothing in reply. Wethersby Jnr could make out his deeply-yellowed teeth but few other features. He slashed a bamboo stick so close to Wethersby Jnr's head, that he felt his ear pop as air escaped. Wethersby Jnr slowly rose to his feet.

The huge man spoke softly but clearly to the last of the guards, who was less than ten feet away, “This stops now. You and your friends have had your fun; it is high time you all learnt a lesson. Bullying does not increase your popularity or self-worth. It may get you noticed but only shows you are weak and cowardly. Leave this Englishman alone with me. He is not going far now.”

Wethersby Jnr fainted and unknowingly rolled over and snored loudly, much to the amusement of the giant. When he came to, it was pitch dark. He felt like he had not moved an inch for goodness knows how many hours. His body ached all over, especially his back and legs. He sat up, wincing. A small fire, fifty yards away, was all he could see clearly. He crawled slowly towards the embers. The smell of garlic and Portuguese peppers hit his nostrils; he coughed uncontrollably for several minutes before passing out once more. Finally, he woke, adjusting his sight. A beam of warm light gradually inched across his face and into his left eye.

Despite the giant’s warning, the last of the guards caught Wethersby Jnr’s queue and dragged him by his hair, along the dusty earth, towards the temple and the two massive guardian statues. He thought the eyes of the stone devils were following him as he was unceremoniously hauled up the thirty or so steep steps.

“You may want to pray to your God now, Englishman,” bellowed the towering man. “Although our Lord Buddha would best serve you now. Do you have eyes in the back of your head?”

Wethersby Jnr flinched, realising the giant was again speaking almost perfect English, albeit with a strong accent, rather like Gaelic, he thought.

“How is it you speak such good English?” he asked.

“That’s a long story. Not telling,” replied the giant.

Wethersby Jnr, still uneasy, sensed the man might be softening,

"I can help you. I see you are captive here too," he said, pointing to the man's feet. "Why do you have heavy metal chains around your ankles?"

"You have nothing I want, not a pod duang, penny or guilder," laughed the man, and his expression soured. "When you talk, you will address me as Pike, like the fish, not the spear. Understood?"

"Yes, Fish, I mean Pike," replied Wethersby Jnr, inwardly laughing. "May I ask, Pike, where you got that interesting name?"

"You may ask. I may not answer," replied Pike.

With that, the conversation went no further.

Wethersby Jnr was at least thankful that the bamboo lashes had now stopped.

He lay on the cool stone floor inside the temple, wishing for the pain to be relieved. The back of his legs soothed slightly. He then focused on the ceiling, which reminded him of Muktinath; the painted style was familiar, although the images were different. He spotted a three-headed elephant, then another, and all the faces of the men and women, each covered in an animal's mask. Monkeys, tigers and elephants. The monkeys and tigers appeared to be worshipping the three-headed elephants.

"Most odd. Rayleigh would love it in here," he said aloud.

"What do you see?" asked Pike, as he slowly removed his mask.

"The elephant with three heads," Wethersby Jnr replied, pointing towards the ceiling. "What does it represent?"

"Three of our gods; the Creator, Keeper and Destroyer," replied Pike. "Now look closer again. What do you see?"

"A jackfruit island!" he gasped. "Oh my Lord, I have found it. A teardrop."

"And?" encouraged Pike.

"Scales," was all he could muster.

He spun his head and looked at the now bare-faced Pike. Mottled green and brown spots covered his face; they gave him a snakeskin appearance.

"Why did they not call you *Python*? That would have been more dramatic, don't you think?" asked Wethersby Jnr.

Pike did not reply. He knelt and awkwardly sat cross-legged, his chains jangling.

After a protracted silence, Pike uttered, "Now what do you see?"

"I see a goliath of a man, wearing an elephant mask with three heads," replied Wethersby Jnr, carefully selecting his words while still studying the images.

"That is better. That is me, Pike. The monk painted my image for eternity," he acknowledged and added, "until the paint fades or the rumbling earth destroys it."

"I prefer Python," whispered Wethersby Jnr.

"Be careful, Englishman. Call me Pike when you address me, or next time it will be me putting those bamboo sticks to your legs," threatened Pike.

Wethersby Jnr winced.

"Why did those men beat me? What is wrong with them?" he asked.

"I do not know. They merely seem to get pleasure from others' pain and the sight of blood. They rarely steal goods or possessions. They are cowards, though. They often come to this temple to seek refuge, to hide from their fellow countrymen. I guess they were part of a rogue army group. They beat me too. Look," he said, turning his back towards Wethersby Jnr.

White and red lacerations were clearly visible through his back's mass of black body hair.

Turning his head, Pike said, "They will not be doing that again."

"Why are you here?" posed Wethersby Jnr.

"I have lived here for as long as I can remember. The old man initially took care of me, but that changed as I grew so tall. He treats me as his slave," recounted Pike, and then added, "of late, though, he has become very frail. He still has a fierce temper and uses his walking stick, not only for keeping himself upright, if you know what I mean."

Wethersby Jnr nodded, sensing there was much more of this story to be told.

"It is time for me to leave here," continued Pike, and added, "He has become as bad as these men lately. Now there is only one of these rogues who can still stand and fight, so it is the best time to finally escape from the overseer's clutches. We must help each other now."

An old monk, clad in a dark orange robe, appeared at a side door, seemingly emerging from nowhere. Wethersby Jnr had not heard nor seen him in his peripheral vision.

The monk spoke quietly to Pike while balancing on a wooden cane. Wethersby Jnr thought it was an odd but worthy sight; a short monk standing over an ogre. It was clear who was in charge; age over height, he thought.

The monk gently tapped his cane on Wethersby Jnr's foot, and a crooked smile erupted across his face.

"I see that they have been playing with their sticks and damaging you. Do not worry. I only use this cane to keep my balance," uttered the old man.

He caught Wethersby Jnr's foot once more, a lot harder than, perhaps, was necessary.

"Yes," murmured Wethersby Jnr. "The old man is definitely in charge here."

--x--

Over several days, Pike gradually released Wethersby Jnr's strapped and chained wrists and legs, but the ghostly monk rarely left them alone. The last guard was now stationed outside the temple's door, in the shadow of the two stone guardians below. Two of his comrades lay dead; the others had disappeared.

"You didn't answer my earlier question," said Wethersby Jnr, so he repeated it. "How come you speak such clear English?"

"I learnt from the monk; he speaks it too," replied Pike. "He sometimes talks about an Englishman he met many moons ago; that man drew some of the temple's murals. I guess the old man acquired his language too. Shhh, he is behind the door, listening to us. He is always listening."

Wethersby Jnr was now free of his bindings, but Pike repeatedly tied them back, loosely, to maintain the pretence.

--x--

After a day grappling with chains and trying desperately to conceal his efforts, Wethersby Jnr managed to spring Pike's oversized leg irons. He guessed that the locks had gradually rusted and weakened due to their age and the humid air.

--x--

Pike cautiously led Wethersby Jnr out of the temple, but not before he swung his bamboo stick at the remaining guard standing by the entrance. They heard the man's head crack as he bounced down the steps, dead before he reached the bottom flight. Both wary, they scrambled into the bush; now it was their time to act like ghosts.

They roamed the land for seven days, slowly heading roughly south, trying to keep hidden. They came across several temples but gave them a wide berth. Wethersby Jnr's legs continued to cause him pain. He was deliriously hungry. Pike scavenged various bitter leaves from small trees and bushes; he seemed utterly content with his freedom, his new partner thought. The view from sitting aloft on Pike's shoulders gave Wethersby Jnr a commanding, if somewhat conspicuous, position. They must have looked a peculiar sight.

Finally, he spotted the wagons, all intact and their riders too.
"Junior? *Junior*? Is it really *you*?" shouted Rayleigh.
"An island, it's on an island," replied Wethersby Jnr.
"But, we know…" was all Rayleigh could say in return, as they hugged each other, much to Pike's amusement.

--x--

The group made their way back to the broad river's mouth as fast as they could muster, all the while planning their next move off the mainland and back out to sea. But would Scythe still be waiting for them, as they had agreed, along with the *Shepherds Cove*?

--x--

# 35

## THE ISLAND ARRIVAL

The deep golden sun glowed for its last moments before settling under the horizon for another night. The ocean waves had gone. A stillness filled the approaching dusk, punctured by cries of men chained to the wooden deck below, asking for their mothers. For ten days, the men had waited. Rayleigh was one of them, his left ankle raw to the bone due to the rasping chains, mixed with sweat and the salty air. New prickly spots covered his almost bare body. Rayleigh was weeping now.

Early that morning, a bellowing voice from above had shouted, "Land!"

All five men said the same, then crept back to their lament. The land was so close now; the men could smell it.

Rotting food was thrown down to them; a large jackfruit, green and black-skinned, with a strong sweet aroma. The mass weighing perhaps thirty pounds thumped and splattered into many golden pieces in front of them, with one lump hitting Rayleigh square on his nose.

“Why do they call it jackfruit?” cursed Rayleigh to no one in particular, perhaps to himself.

He thought the yellow segments were moving, bubbling in the heat. It mattered not. The men gorged themselves again, picking out the slippery, apparently inedible, nuts from the pulp. Within an hour, a small pile of sticky kernels and remains of the mouldy shell were all that was left.

“Is this all we get? No meat, only stinking fruit that will give us the runs. How many days has it been, Rayleigh?” William complained.

“Ten since we last set sail. I quite like this fruit, but too much, and it is the devil on my insides. It is odd, though. I feel stronger for eating it, despite our restrictions,” responded Rayleigh.

At least food distracted them from their confines aboard the *Shepherds Cove.*

They did not know all that separated their small ship from the island was a large coral reef, where breakers rose quickly out of nowhere then crunched down to the shoreline. They rocked to sleep from the gentle motion of waves. Rayleigh slept soundly, his dreams full and vivid.

At that moment, Rayleigh heard a different clank from above. He stood up, only to shrink down again, hurt, relieved, and feeling sick. His four companions were now awake too, having heard a commotion above their heads and hatches being unlocked.

“Why had his cousin Wethersby Jnr chained them in their coffin-like quarters? After all, they had only acted as men do.” thought Rayleigh aloud.

The heat was already intense, the humidity worse. The damp wood of the outside deck smoked from the sun’s rays. Below, the five men were steaming too, sweating, and cursing, longing for their first unfettered steps on crisp sand or rock.

Peck slowly lowered his bulk down the short steps, his favoured deadly blade in his mouth and keys dangling at his side. He unlocked the men's shackles. One by one, they rose with closed eyes, feeling their way step by step before reaching the blue sky. Rayleigh was last up.

"Fresh air," exclaimed Rayleigh at the first step.

He eagerly moved his sluggish foot onto the second stair but buckled and fell, cursing his pride.

"Get up on your toes before I lock your chains again," vowed Peck.

They adjusted themselves to new surroundings, eagerly surveying what lay ahead; a reef, rising waves, and the island.

They climbed down the ship's ladder with another fellow into a small wet wooden boat; Peck followed Rayleigh. They started to row, passing over the shallow white and red coral bank, almost close enough to touch, and were immediately thrown up three or four times their height by a wave. Tucking in oars, they rode to the shoreline. Before the boat rubbed the sandy bottom, they saw a dark blue chasm filled with hundreds of brilliant yellow and orange fish playing near the surface.

They got out of the boat. Rayleigh's first impression was that the island smelt of smoking coconut, that heady scent which he loathed. The sandy beach was white and soft, like fine talc, and warm between his toes. Coconut palms were swaying in the light breeze, browned husks littered the tide line, and small grey crabs scurried ahead of the men shooting down tiny holes in the sand. The island appeared to rise gently to a solo peak, perhaps five or six hundred feet above sea level.

They walked around the island's shore, occasionally climbing over jagged rocks or venturing a little inland. The hike took most of the morning, for Rayleigh's pace slowed the men down. He had fallen silent since leaving the ship. Rayleigh's mind focused once again on the reward for which he had endured chains; Chiranya, his Joy.

--x--

Almost two weeks earlier, they had bid an emotional farewell to the giant snake-skinned Pike. It came to pass that Pike had a deep-rooted fear of water and baulked at going further with them, despite Wethersby Jnr's coaxing and pleas.

The crew had prepared the *Shepherds Cove* for their next voyage back into the Gulf of Siam. The captain gave the team their standard orders. Not to be lured by local traders but to focus on procuring only essential foods, water, netting, some canvas, and to bargain hard.

About a thousand feet from the ship's mooring, a large fly-infested market hawked a wide variety of local fresh fruit and vegetables, whiffing dried fish, squid and meats, barrels, water, cloth, and all sorts of gold-painted wood carvings and much more besides. It was an oasis for the men.

Chiranya found a large stall of dried water buffalo meat for Rayleigh. He bought enough of the dark, toughened beef to last many months. Too much, but Rayleigh bought it all, preoccupied and hypnotised by Chiranya's incredible bright green eyes, wide smile, and her shiny jet-black hair that reached long past her back. His friends were also exploring the market, eyeing the available stores, but the young sellers more so.

After several hours five men and five women headed back to the ship with loaded carts. Peck supervised the unloading and loading. There was no sign of the captain. Four men eagerly disappeared, along with Scythe, to the market and the empty wagons and their merchants, leaving Rayleigh at the water's edge with Chiranya.

For an instant, Rayleigh and Chiranya embraced. His body shivered as they held each other tightly once again, and her lips and tongue eagerly found his. They hugged for several minutes before Rayleigh felt a rough hand on his shoulders. Wethersby

Jnr had witnessed it all. He summoned Rayleigh to hasten back to the ship.

Wethersby Jnr caught up slowly with Scythe and the four other lads through the winding market and watched from a distance as the men and women climbed some steps of a large wooden shuttered shack. After ten minutes, he moved up silently and barged in, catching them all in the one room, in various stages of undress. Embarrassed, they complied with his scorns and, with their heads down, swiftly returned to the ship.

The four men and Rayleigh were chained for disobeying his orders and acquiring too many supplies. Wethersby Jnr wanted to set an example to all the men, surprising them, especially Rayleigh. Despite Rayleigh's protests, he explained that he had let the team do as they pleased within the market rather than instructing them, thereby encouraging them.

They set sail at dawn the following day. Scythe stayed behind. He handed the silver compass, its needle still spinning, to Rayleigh. Scythe removed his red eye patch for the first time, revealing a jet-black eyeball and wiped away a tear, saying, "Here, you keep this now. You never know; one day, it may work again."

--x--

After walking around the island, they located their small boat once again. Peck summoned them to find a source of clean water; Rayleigh thought that this was odd.

"Why had they not been directed to find water before they encircled the island?" he asked.

He knew it was fruitless to argue; they had no choice, though they were free of chains.

Some distance in, they heard the whistling calls of unseen birds as they passed through a grove of large jack trees where oversize fruits hung. Peck was clearing a path ahead of them using his sabre.

After more than twenty minutes, he stopped unexpectedly before a small clearing and called, "Beware. I smell blood."

Rayleigh stumbled and fell.

The skinned mammal ahead of them, a small goat, was hanging low off the ground between two cut branches with a fierce expression. It appeared fresh, although the heat, humidity, and tiny flies had begun the process of decay.

Rayleigh showered vomit over Peck's leathered foot.

"Wipe your muck off my boot until it shines," uttered the irritated officer.

Rayleigh mopped the boot briefly while Peck cut the mammal down. Rayleigh tied the creature with vines at two ends of a sturdy branch, thinking of his supper.

They came upon another opening within the jungle, about four hundred steps further, containing some large flat rounded stones. To Rayleigh, the boulders resembled barley grinders, but there was no barley here. He noticed faint and unusual markings lining the sides of the rocks.

Peck went to one and exclaimed, "Here."

As the men gathered around Peck, they saw a brown pool of blood on the stone in front of him. All the men were very wary then; they knew the goat might have been killed in the previous day, two at most, and hung out to dry.

Rayleigh and William quickly hoisted the mammal's branch onto their shoulders and backtracked along Peck's path towards the shore. The low hum came from a big tree, high up and to their left. Within a minute, many hundreds of giant yellow and black bees cloaked them, each the size of Rayleigh's thumb. The men scattered, eager to outrun the swarm but they were stung, with each one feeling a sensation like the jab of a red-hot poker adding to their already spotted skin. Between them, they must have got branded a hundred times or more. They needed cover. They had long stopped whimpering; they wanted to screech like cats.

As they came towards the sea, something was different.

"Is this the same path?" puffed Rayleigh.

They could see cut leaves and an occasional dusty footprint. Rayleigh realised that the invisible birds sang no more as they approached the palm barrier, and the bees had gone.

"Was it a dislike of rotten flesh, either theirs or their host's?" thought Rayleigh; all he could sniff was coconut.

Passing the trees, Peck jumped into the boat. It swayed violently with his bulk. He grabbed an oar and signalled with his raised bushy eyebrows for the men to get in. Peck's face was beetroot and swollen from bee stings, his slender mouth now bulging, and his left eye squinting from a puncture under it.

They threw the mammal in the boat and assumed positions apart from Rayleigh, who took Peck's regular place. Peck, despite his obvious discomfort, counted aloud the timing of the waves. The men would eat well tonight; the thought of honey would encourage them to return the next day despite the risk of meeting the locals.

Then at once, he shouted, "Now. Row hard."

They passed through a slight gap between the surf, over the reef and to the ship beyond.

Time seemed to speed up. Storm clouds slowly rose behind the island to the east, billowing high white, grey, and black at their base.

Back onboard the *Shepherds Cove*, something had softened Peck's demeanour.

"Was it simply the pain caused by the bees or the fear of those who had strung up the goat, or had Peck simply had enough of the captain's quests for haunted riches?" pondered Rayleigh.

"Serves you, Peck," muttered William with a wry grin as the men filled their mouths with the raw goat.

For the first time, since setting sail from the bustling fishing village at the Chao Phraya river's mouth, all thirty men ate together.

It was the freshest meat they had eaten for many a day. They did not care for its taste but longed to fill their stomachs with something other than dried fish, buffalo, or jackfruit. The meal finished in an hour. They carefully packed what remained for another day. Rayleigh, still angry with his cousin, stayed with the same men in the lower deck area. Peck did not come after them, nor did Wethersby Jnr.

The ship slept early that night. All awoke by a sudden thunderclap that shook the vessel and a lightning flash that seemingly pierced the ship down her middle. What followed was an almighty crash from above. Rayleigh briefly forgot his wounds and was, unusually, first up the steps. Thomas and William pushed against the weight bearing down; it gave slightly. But the trapdoor had stuck fast.

"Peck, where are you? Clear our hatch. Get us out of here," Rayleigh exclaimed through the crack.

It was no use; another more distant thunderclap covered his voice. George came to help and, between them, opened a gap enough for Rayleigh to slip through, although his left ankle tore on the trap, and he yelped in agony again. Rayleigh found the creature's branch and prised the hatch further.

The five men stood close together on the deck, speechless and in darkness. Through another flash of lightning, they made out her three masts had all sheared off one-third up. What remained resembled jagged needles with fragments on the deck. A smell, not unlike roasting chestnuts, wafted around them. The new canvas sails were gone, overboard, they assumed. Tangled masses of rope littered the deck.

"Junior, Peck, where are you?" yelled Rayleigh, just before a fork of lightning lit up the island's silhouette, striking a beach palm that caught alight.

Rayleigh stumbled to the captain's cabin, pushed the free lock, only to find Wethersby Jnr slumped in his grand chair, laughing.

"Junior, I mean Captain," exclaimed Rayleigh. "Praise be our masts have gone. You are amused?"

Wethersby Jnr stood up slowly, his laughter lines changing to an evil grin as he did so.

"Well, young Rayleigh, we may soon be finding who killed last night's dinner," he roared.

Rayleigh had only seen his cousin laugh so heartily in his presence once before, but that was long ago back in Southwold. His anger towards his cousin lessened.

"But Junior, we are stranded next to an island that has no freshwater. It has giant stinging bees and men we cannot see who sacrifice goats," declared Rayleigh with the tone of a man twice his age. "We are going to end our days here."

"Rubbish," replied Wethersby Jnr. "We have everything we need, coconuts and milk, honey, jackfruits, and meat. There must be water too. There are plenty enough trees for makeshift posts and wood for our fires."

Rayleigh could not believe that his cousin was being so hopeful.

"But what of those invisible men who came and killed our goat?" said Rayleigh, rubbing his ankle.

"Ah, cousin, who said they, and who said they are *men*?" chuckled Wethersby Jnr and added, "And who bought us enough meat to last three months or more, Rayleigh?"

Rayleigh snorted, and both men embraced each other out of sight of the other men.

"Let us see the damage, young Rayleigh, and make a plan. There be a treasure to find here, make no mistake," smiled Wethersby Jnr.

Rayleigh shook his head as they went back on deck. He had heard those exact words many times that year.

The other men were astonished to hear laughter from within the captain's cabin. They had found two of their company with gashes to their legs, unable to walk unaided. Peck had a deep cut across his cheek that added to his increasingly grotesque appearance.

Young Thomas, the injured makeshift surgeon, and Wethersby Jnr tended to the injured men, dressing their wounds. He allowed a measure of rice spirit to cleanse them and two to swill to ease their sleep. The captain also offered a portion to the other men; no one refused, all recoiled downing it.

Several hours later, the night sky began to turn a dark red, and quite soon, the sun appeared beside the island. The same six men and their captain returned ashore. Peck, despite his wounds, came back later to the ship to collect the remaining walking men. He brought enough sabres and knives for each man, some netting, and a dozen large pails.

--x--

# 36

## SMUDGED CLUES

Rayleigh scanned the horizon, wondering their fate. He wished the year-long journey to be over and to remain on the island with his beloved Joy. He turned his head; her eyes pierced his heart once more. The pulse and kick within her stomach jolted his hand as his body twitched in surprise

"Come closer and feel your kin," said Chiranya, as she placed his hand on her bump.

"How much longer?" he asked.

"When she is ready, she will grace us. Be patient, Rayleigh. We have so much time and nowhere else to go," replied Chiranya.

"How can you be sure we will have a daughter, not a son?" asked Rayleigh, smiling.

"Why so many questions? And anyway, how can you be so sure she is yours?" laughed Chiranya.

Rayleigh's hand bounced off Chiranya's stomach as another kick came from within her. Chiranya let out a low groan.

"She's strong, no? Chiranya panted.

"A lioness, raring to be freed," was all Rayleigh could manage, shocked by the baby's strength.

It had been seven months, more or less, since they left the mainland. Rayleigh had initially grown weak from exhaustion and boredom on the island. However, after the first month, he got into a routine for exercise in the mornings and late afternoons. Sometimes he would join the crew fishing in the lagoon or simply spend the day nestled with Chiranya, watching her blossom and radiate while sheltered from the sun's rays.

By contrast, Wethersby Jnr spent weeks exploring. He and a small team would leave their makeshift but permanent camp to venture into the bush at sunrise. Over the months, trampled leaves and mud marked the well-trodden path, snaking its way up the mountainous peak.

Wethersby Jnr had changed since his brief, but violent, encounter near Ayutthaya. Rayleigh still could not understand nor justify Wethersby Jnr's actions after they departed the Siam mainland, chaining him and the men in ship's holds for a week. It seemed a hysterical overreaction to Rayleigh, but Wethersby Jnr would have nothing of it. It took all of Rayleigh's patience to calm Chiranya. The lightning storm, and ending up being stranded on the island, had perhaps saved him from a worse fate; Chiranya was never too sure. She made every effort to keep Wethersby Jnr out of her sight.

The cousins had many a bitter argument over the newly inked map. Its contours were accurate enough, copied from old Patike's temple walls. However, the interior was smudged due to a previous disagreement. Wethersby Jnr tried to convince Rayleigh that a treasure box symbol was on the mountain at the island's centre. Rayleigh thought otherwise and held this to himself. Old Wethersby's original atlas contained no such map.

A musky white mould covered the remaining buffalo meat. Wethersby Jnr struggled to keep the beef dry, but the humid air continued the decay regardless of his efforts. Everyone ate the meat with relish.

The seemingly never-ending supply of coconuts sustained them. Rayleigh especially enjoyed the brown oldest nuts. Chiranya preferred the milk from the greenest young ones, and she would cleanse her skin with it too, out of sight of the men, or so she thought.

Wethersby Jnr returned that morning, much earlier than usual. Each man, six in all, struggled to hold onto their giant jackfruit. The largest, Rayleigh estimated, must have been fifty pounds, similar to those they brought from the fishing village months ago. Thomas dropped his green mass, narrowly missing his toes. Chiranya flinched and wiped some of its yellow pulp off her legs. The scent from the fruit was intoxicating to Rayleigh; he and Thomas gorged on the yellow petalled fruit, popping out the kernels, burping and giggling wildly.

Chiranya stumbled as pain gripped her abdomen.

She fell awkwardly, rolling over her ankle, and shrieked, "Rayleigh!"

Rayleigh watched as if in slow motion as Chiranya collapsed in a heap only a few yards from him. His slow reaction was too late to arrest her fall, and she almost fell over the cliff.

Sobbing, Chiranya asked him, "Please pick me up, but slowly. My ankle."

He gradually got her to her feet, placing her arm over his shoulder for support. He did not understand why she was smiling.

"I love your smile, but I thought you said your ankle hurt?" he quizzed.

"It does, but I have seen what you could not. Take care over the edge, for it is mightily steep and a long way down to the rocks below," she winced.

Rayleigh moved forward several steps. This time they both nearly slipped.

"Rayleigh, put me down for a moment. I will live. I have only twisted it a little," she lied. "Go to the edge carefully and look down to your right. Can you see the opening, just above the tide mark?"

He moved his hand to his forehead, covering the sun's glare from his eyes, rubbed his scar and spied the cliff below. There it was, finally.

A small tree almost covered the entrance to the dark hole. The waves bumped against the rocks at its base. The tide was shallow now, the lowest Rayleigh had seen it during their time on the island. Rayleigh guessed the tiny cave was only visible because of the shallow sea.

"Let's go quickly before the water rises," he exclaimed.

"I'm sorry, Rayleigh. I cannot walk without your help. The path down to the rocks will be slow," she said.

"We are going to explore this together. We have been stranded here for too many months, looking; I will not go alone now," explained Rayleigh. "Come with me, and we will go gently."

Rayleigh braced Chiranya with her arm over his shoulder. They gradually snaked their way down the cliff and towards the rocks and cave's mouth. By the time they were thirty feet from the entrance, it was clear that the water had risen, blocking their way inside.

"Rayleigh, it is too late, and the water is too high. Let us go back to the camp," she said.

They returned to the camp after an hour of gentle walking. Rayleigh had his head down most of the way, concealing his smile. Still deep in thought, Chiranya pushed him heavily towards Wethersby Jnr, surprising both men.

"Where have you been? It is late, and you know what the ghosts of this island are like at dusk," laughed Wethersby Jnr. Pointing at Chiranya's foot, he said, "I see you have been playing around again."

"I slipped near the cliff, that is all," justified Chiranya, as Rayleigh helped her to sit on a palm leaf mat. "Nothing to see here."

"You need to take greater care of her and your unborn, Rayleigh. I think…," barked Wethersby Jnr.

Chiranya broke his flow by asking, "How is your quest on the mountain to find the casket?"

Wethersby Jnr took a step forward, invading Chiranya's personal space, and said, "Another week and I shall find what we have all been looking for. Be sure of that, young lady."

Rayleigh squeezed her hand softly; she said no more. It was not often that Rayleigh experienced his cousin's wrath. He knew Wethersby Jnr disliked Chiranya teasing and interrupting him. That night, Rayleigh held his hand on Chiranya's twitching abdomen. They spoke very little, both deep in exciting thoughts of what lay within the tidal cave.

By mid-morning, they reached the same spot from the day before. They lay on the grass at the clifftop, with Rayleigh resting on one elbow, looking down at the gentle waves, watching for the tops of the wet rocks to dry in the sun.

"I reckon we should go down now. I think the water is close to the same low point we saw yesterday. Can you make it down on your own?" Rayleigh asked.

"Yes, my foot is better, just a little sore. Let me go first," she requested.

At the limestone cliff's base, they clambered gingerly towards the small low-hanging entrance. They moved inside.

On the mountain, Wethersby Jnr and two of the crew became stuck on a small unchartered ridge. They saw a small hollow about fifty yards ahead of them, their path hindered by the narrow needle-like pathway. Covered in blood, Wethersby Jnr's makeshift reed shoes were no match for the sharp stones; the two men's feet bled too; neither was willing or able to walk further along the ridge.

"We must retreat to camp and come back with stronger footwear," said Wethersby Jnr and added, "Let's go, slowly, and get our feet tended to."

After climbing off the ridge, wincing and groaning, they made their way back to the camp. Finally, they bathed their feet in the salty water's edge, still grimacing.

Chiranya and Rayleigh got stuck, too; their way out blocked. The water was, by now, up to Rayleigh's knees and Chiranya's stomach. They had gone as far into the cave as they could. Their eyes adjusted to the differing light; it was almost pitch dark at its rear. A dead-end, or so they thought. A sudden ray of sunlight came through the shadows, temporarily blinding Rayleigh. The sun was less than ten minutes from setting, but an eerily soft orange glow now drenched the entire cave.

Rayleigh quickly moved around the back of the cave. He stumbled and fell into an opening and found himself neck-deep and needing to tread water.

"Quick, pull me out of here," he called breathlessly.

She tried to heave him from the wet hole, but he only got partway. With aching arms and pains in her stomach, she tried again. This time Rayleigh somehow gained purchase onto its edge with his foot and prised himself up.

"Phew. That hole is deep," spluttered Rayleigh. "We need to go quickly before the sun sets."

“But the water has risen too far, and the current is too strong for me to swim against it. I do not have enough energy,” said Chiranya, as she kissed him ever so gently.

His eagerness to move stopped for an instant. Her kisses always had that effect on him.

“But we must go now; otherwise, we’ll get trapped here. Look at this mark,” said Rayleigh hurriedly, touching the wall where it changed from light-grey to slimy green.

He moved to the other side of the small space, not seeing another hole ahead of him. This time he fell and stopped waist-deep. The hollow was about a yard in width with smooth edges; its water felt warm. He began to touch and fish below the water.

He broke into a broad smile and exclaimed, “Chiranya, come and put your hands here. What can you feel?”

“I am not sure,” she said, now on her knees and almost falling. “There is something warm, flat and slippery. Hold my hand with yours.”

“Quickly, look. Water is flowing in,” said Rayleigh.

Rayleigh pulled at the object hidden in the crevice. As he moved it towards him, his back pushed against the rear of the void - he felt trapped. The object’s weight pulled on his hands and into his upper thigh. He moved the entity forward into its original position.

“We may have finally found what we travelled all this way for. It is so heavy even within the water, just like Pa described,” lamented Rayleigh as he climbed out.

By now, the approaching sea was another inch deeper and rising. Looking at one another, they kissed again, both lost in thoughts and fears. The last faint orange glow from the dropping sun touched her face, then vanished, plunging them into sudden darkness. They held each other tightly, feeling the swirling water creep ever up their bodies.

“On my shoulders. Now,” commanded Rayleigh.

“But, how?” Chiranya responded

"I will crouch down, get onto my back. Do it before it's too late," Rayleigh shouted, surprising Chiranya with his demand.

After three attempts, she was wobbling uncomfortably on his shoulders, her feet just touching the water. The sea showed no signs of stopping its advance.

"Rayleigh. Are we going to die here?" she asked.

"If we do, I will be happy knowing we were together in our final moments," was all he could manage.

Wethersby Jnr fretted about his cousin and Chiranya. He paced along the beach, shouting out their names. As usual, it had gone pitch-dark within about thirty minutes from the sunset. A strange and desperate feeling of foreboding consumed him. He felt cold and shivered despite the warm, humid night's air. His mouth dry and hoarse, he retreated to the camp and cried.

"Rayleigh, my boy, my best friend. Where on God's earth are you?" he muttered.

A small campfire, lit from a tiny amount of black powder and flints, ebbed away. Wethersby Jnr bided his time, poking the embers and adding the occasional jack tree branch. Hours passed, but he did not sleep.

The sea had stopped short of the high tide mark and just below Rayleigh's shoulder tops. Chiranya had become noticeably heavier, but as the water rose, he felt her lightening. He knew that he could not put her down as the water would have covered her head. He also knew that they needed to stay in that position for many more hours. He thought it would be unlikely Chiranya could tread water for very long. He felt his legs tighten and cramp up. He forced and focused his mind back to the well at *Thatchers*; he began to relax.

She softly sang a mellow, yet enchanting, rhythm that deepened Rayleigh's trance-like state. He felt the weight lift off his shoulders, quite literally. As she sang, a strange green glow began to form around the hole where he found the object, and a halo of soft light beamed on the cave's ceiling. Chiranya moved her hand off Rayleigh's head and into the tube of light. Tingling enveloped her hand, and she felt movement up to her forearm. In an instant, she thought she saw the bones of her fingers, then the warmth disappeared. She continued chanting.

The embers flickered for a final time as the wind began to blow drifting sand into Wethersby's eyes. He sat still, mesmerised, snivelling. His feet still stung from the stone cuts. He thought hard about the ridge and how soon he would find what they were looking for, the JackFruit.

Chiranya drifted with her neck above the water, motionless, her head to one side. She looked at Rayleigh and smiled. He was on his back; he slept with his arms outstretched. For several hours, they lay in the same position until the water receded. As Rayleigh woke, he felt his arms once more; a small shaft of warm yellow-green light touched his face. Dazzled, he saw a yellowed silhouette of Chiranya within the tube of light, centred on the small pothole where they found the object. She was neck-deep in water and smiling.

"Rayleigh. Did you sleep well?" she asked.

"Ah, I do not remember," he replied. "Where is this light coming from?"

"The casket. I see it now," replied Chiranya. "We need to wait for the waters to wane further before we take it out."

Rayleigh dived down into the light and held onto Chiranya's leg. The casket was warm and made his fingers prickle. Pins and needles enveloped his hands with an intense pain he had not felt since the blaze at his parent's cottage. He surfaced and rubbed his hands, trying to remove the sensation. After several minutes, the burning feeling subsided, and he regained life back into his palm. His thumb and adjacent two fingers did not flex completely; he thought his hand looked like the claw of a sloth, and he chuckled to himself.

An hour later, they manoeuvred the casket out of its ledge. It then fell to the bottom, resting at an angle. Rayleigh jumped into the small pool, his legs astride the box and attempted to lift it to the ledge.

"My, this is so heavy. Wait, let me think a minute," he panted.

A dim glow from the cave's entrance grew brighter; their eyes adjusted slowly. The peculiar yellow light started to flicker, then disappeared altogether. A stillness briefly filled the hollow before the waves from outside began to echo.

"Let us try one more time. I will hoist the box up onto the inner ledge. Once there, you need to grab and lift it for all you are worth as I push it up. Got it?" explained Rayleigh.

"Let's get on with it. I have warm feelings about this cave, but the light is surreal and not of this world," said Chiranya as she got to her knees.

Rayleigh lifted the casket onto the small ledge. Chiranya grabbed both hands under it, just before it slipped again, and pulled hard.

Rayleigh's knees now held the box. They somehow brought it up to the pool's upper edge with one last pull. There, it balanced for what felt like an eternity before Rayleigh finally shoved it along the slippery limestone floor.

They howled with laughter as Rayleigh jumped out from the pothole and lay exhausted on his back. Chiranya gently caressed his brow.

"I think I may have broken my thumb and fingers," said Rayleigh, still smiling.

"Where's the key?" posed Chiranya as she tugged at the golden lock.

Wethersby Jnr woke before dawn after a restless night's sleep, with misty rain filling the air; the sea was almost a dead calm. He, young Thomas and William, returned to the ship. They took three crumbling leather books from his cabin and returned to shore. They trudged back up the mountain with the books. Within two hours, they again came to the narrow ridge with needle stones. They tied a book cover around their feet. Then they ventured further along the ledge and into the small cave. It was circular and barely eight yards across and less than four yards at its highest point.

Wethersby Jnr read the heavily scratched words on the wall.

***JackFruit***
***Sunset --x--***

Thomas and William were dumbfounded as his words echoed.

"What on earth?" searched Thomas.

Wethersby Jnr felt the cave's wall, tracing his finger around each deeply carved word. As he pressed around the '--x--' mark, he felt his fingers slip deeper into the sandy wall. A modest yellow key two inches in length lay inside.

Rayleigh and Chiranya returned to the camp.

"Captain will go mad when he returns," said one of the men with a puzzled look, "Where on earth have you two been?"

"Stuck in a cave. The water was too high and the current too strong for us to get out. We stayed inside all night. Chiranya needs to change her clothes, rest and recover," replied Rayleigh. "Bring me my musket and powder before the ghosts resume."

Wethersby Jnr, Thomas and William returned, unable to conceal their beaming smiles, despite their sorely cut feet.

Wethersby Jnr bellowed, "Rayleigh. Where?"

"In a cave. You must come and see it for yourself," interrupted Rayleigh. "But the tide will only give us a little time to remove the casket, and these low tides may only last another day."

"Did you open it?" chased Wethersby Jnr, covering his grin.

"No key. Once we get it out, we can smash it open," replied Rayleigh.

"No. That's not going to happen," teased Wethersby Jnr.

He placed the golden key in Chiranya's palm.

"Where?" asked Rayleigh.

"JackFruit sunset 'x', where the map pointed, obviously! In a small hollow above a ridge of needle stones. Look." said Wethersby Jnr, lifting his foot. "We were both right."

"Let me see to your scratches before we continue this conversation," said Chiranya and added, "in any case, we must wait for the morning's low tide."

Neither Chiranya nor Rayleigh mentioned the cave's strange radiance. No one slept well that night, despite their exhaustion.

Chiranya and nine men brought the casket out. Rayleigh feared the tide was turning even more quickly than the previous day, so they agreed to open the box at the camp and in a better light.

The entire crew gathered around the green-jade casket as Rayleigh and Wethersby Jnr joked about who was to open the box. Wethersby Jnr gave the key to Chiranya once again.

"We have come far on a perilous journey together, my dear friends. Now stand back two paces, men," commanded Wethersby Jnr.

As she turned the key, Chiranya's hand slightly jumped from the click of the lock.

"Amazing. They are still warm," she declared, wiping off a white sticky substance and holding in the air a large dull yellow misshaped rock. "Look, another, even bigger!"

A dark shadow suddenly cloaked them. Instinctively all the men and Chiranya looked to the sky. Half was deep blue, the other half dark grey and black, just hiding the sun.

She pulled out eighteen smaller yet brilliant stones from the casket and carefully wiped each one. The pile ranged in size from an acorn to a large walnut, thought Rayleigh. Chiranya believed the smallest looked more like a jackfruit nut and the more significant gems like the flowers of its fruit, almost teardrop-shaped.

As she held the most prominent stone, a shaft of sunlight lit the small pile of gems nestling on the upturned strongbox's lid. A hot blush grew in her hand, so much so, she unconsciously threw the rock upwards, and Wethersby Jnr caught it. She waved her hand around, frantically screaming as she rushed to the water's edge to soothe her pains. The hole in the clouds disappeared, and they bathed in shadow once more.

"Never let be it held by any one man or one woman…" whispered Wethersby Jnr.

"Why, Grandpa? Why?" demanded Rayleigh, as he ran to comfort Chiranya.

--x--

# 37

## MEETING ON DECK

Baby Sarah was born, they guessed, on or about 30th September 1698. Thankfully, it was an unremarkable birth; Chiranya, having the pains for only a couple of hours. Their beautiful daughter was aloof, rarely crying. However, Chiranya got used to her daughter's attention-seeking, primarily through her eyes and quivering lips. Sarah shared their black hair and green eyes. She was tiny, no more than four pounds. A small rose birthmark on her right palm mirrored that on Chiranya's hand. The similarity to her mother's mark was subject to many discussions between the crew.

Rayleigh doted on her.

Repairs to the *Shepherds Cove* were basic, but Wethersby Jnr expected, or rather hoped, they would withstand the cruel seas to get them to Kandy, at least. The patching-up took on far greater urgency since the JackFruit's discovery and Sarah's delivery. Wethersby Jnr was desperate to get home. Rayleigh, though, wanted to enjoy the island's freedom with his new family. They agreed to sail within two weeks of Sarah's birth.

They had almost exhausted their supply of dried buffalo meat. The tree fruits were gone; they only had some old coconuts and little of anything else. They never found another goat, dead or alive, nor indeed see any native people.

The team used the trunks of three unusually tall jack trees as masts. The trees had taken most of their time and strength to cut and shape. Rayleigh worried that the mainmast was too heavy and would collapse the ship. He relented, though, knowing nothing was available as solid or straight, only soft coconut and other short trees. They made the best they could from the once tangled ropes.

The inner workings of the ship reeked of rot. Water had continued to penetrate the hull until that is, they came across the white sticky sap from unripe jackfruits and sealed the cracks with it as best they could. The white pus-like substance ruined their sabres; such was its tackiness. They would never get those knives spotlessly clean again; Wethersby Jnr coined it the Devil's Snot.

--x--

On a windswept morning, they upped anchor and quickly drifted away from the shoreline. The *Shepherds Cove* timbers squealed as the waves buffeted her bow.

Once they rounded the strait of Malacca, Wethersby Jnr aimed the ship northwest and finally due west using the sun's arc as his only guide. He estimated they had supplies for three weeks and wanted to avoid the coast of Siam and Malaya at all costs.

"Many a pirate in and around Malacca. Best avoided, but a necessary sea strait," old Wethersby would often say to Rayleigh.

Fortunately, and surprisingly, they saw none and no VOC vessels either.

Their journey west to Kandy was unexceptional, and favourable winds allowed them an arrival within eleven days from Malaya. Although Rayleigh constantly looked at the mast, fearing it would drop through the ship at any moment, the vessel held together astonishingly well.

--x--

They did not see another craft until they were in sight of land. A welcome party clambered aboard, holding up cooked chicken, vegetables, fruits, and various inedible wares.

A man with a bandana, a long dark beard and missing front teeth followed.

"Welcome to *my* island," announced James to everyone's surprise.

"Ha-ha, I think you'll find the governor will argue that moot point," replied Wethersby Jnr, feigning laughter.

James came forward to embrace his older brother. Wethersby Jnr took one step back, signalling his distaste.

"What day is today, brother?" asked Wethersby Jnr.

"Thursday, of course. 23rd October 1698," replied James. "Long time no see, old brother. What on earth have you done to this fine ship? You have trashed it."

"Lightning repairs. Nothing we couldn't handle. These fine masts took many months," sneered Wethersby Jnr.

Rayleigh came out of his cabin, holding Sarah in his arms.

"I heard you had returned to England, James?" scorned Rayleigh and moved to shield Chiranya from James's gaze.

"Scarface, my, haven't you been a busy boy," leered James.

He moved his head to one side, then another, looking to catch the eyes of the woman behind Rayleigh.

"This is Chiranya, and our daughter, Sarah," announced Rayleigh as he held Chiranya's hand tightly. "Now, have a care. We have places to go and deals to seek. Move your rotten lug out of my sight and off our ship."

"Yes, it is time you left already, young brother," demanded Wethersby Jnr. "You can tell us what happened to Charles another time. See to it we get escorted safely to the fort."

"So be it, brethren," scoffed James.

He climbed down the rope ladder and back into a large fishing boat. After some posturing, the vessel began towing the *Shepherds Cove*, and James disappeared.

--x--

A week later, the crew were rested and somewhat renourished. A small troop of Dutch soldiers boarded the *Shepherds Cove*. Wethersby Jnr and Rayleigh were humbled. They were granted an invitation to dinner at Governor de Heere's residence on the following evening, on condition that Chiranya and Sarah came too. They agreed.

At the grand door, a stern-looking guard greeted them. Chiranya giggled at the man's amusing-looking hat, which made him look unnaturally tall.

They were held waiting for over an hour and paced around the splendidly ornate room, marvelling at the wall-hung carpets. There were many stuffed animal heads and a dazzling blue and white porcelain collection, which Rayleigh assumed were Dutch. The room reminded him of old Wethersby's study, and it had the same distinctive musty smell; he thought he could detect a light scent of burnt coconut too. He was distracted by the squeaking door, as in came the governor, his wife Johanna, followed by James to their bewilderment.

"Welcome to my humble home. I am Governor Gerrit de Heere. Let me introduce you to my wife, Johanna. And you know already, of course, my loyal friend of the family," beamed de Heere. "He's not allowed out much, you understand. Come, let me show you around the household before we dine."

Chiranya felt Rayleigh's grip tighten. Rayleigh's eyes met Wethersby Jnr's; they both shook their heads ever so slightly, then slowly followed.

During dinner, the conversation swung around from the state of the spice trade, the weather, pirates and the legend of buried treasure. James did little of the talking. Instead, he fixed his glare on Chiranya. Rayleigh thought this was by way of distracting him. Chiranya faced Johanna. James's gaze went largely unnoticed. Little Sarah kept spinning her head, seemingly enthralled by the gold inlaid ceiling.

"Have you heard about an Englishman called Fredrick Bunting? asked Johanna. "He was here with his newly married wife and children; after a long adventure across India."

"No," queried Wethersby Jnr. "Why?"

"He's dead," revealed James. "Of the pox, or so they say. Others say his wife strangled him in his sleep."

"What! That's awful and impossible. I mean…," blurted out Rayleigh.

"My soldiers are searching for his wife, Mayling," stated the governor, "She has disappeared along with her young son and daughter."

"Samuel," said Johanna. "I hear he had a birthmark on his forehead, much like yours, Rayleigh."

"*What*!" exclaimed Rayleigh, then composed himself before continuing, "It's not a birthmark; it was caused by flames."

Silence filled the room. Rayleigh felt his anger and hot bile rising while he looked at James's mocking face.

Noticing Rayleigh shuffle in his chair, Wethersby Jnr tried to change the subject and asked, "What happened to your ear and the man who hacked it off, brother?"

"Oh, the Omani pirate, Solroy? He's dead, too, just a day after Bunting. Of the pox, you understand. I saw him covered in red spots; he wouldn't stop scratching," winked James.

He moved his hands to his neck, clenched his remaining teeth, and said open-mouthed, "Then again, others say he died by the hands of another."

"You two were the best of friends, were you not?" declared the governor.

"I wouldn't go that far. Let's say we had mutual respect for pirating. We did some of that business together," chuckled James. "Best to keep your enemies close at hand, I say. Don't you agree, Rayleigh?"

A chime from a grandfather clock filled the void. After nine strikes, stillness pervaded the room afresh.

"If only I could find Mayling and Samuel," emphasised James, breaking the silence.

--x--

# 38

## BACK SLAP

Three days after the governor's grand dinner four soldiers, led by James and Johanna, accompanied Rayleigh, Chiranya, Sarah, and Wethersby Jnr to the forbidden cave. Rayleigh pressed Chiranya to stay behind for Sarah, but she was strong-willed and rarely took no for an answer. Wethersby Jnr insisted on an armed escort notwithstanding James's moderate protests.

--x--

Rayleigh and Wethersby Jnr were deeply suspicious when James divulged details of the cave he and Johanna had found. They winced at hearing the death of one of the governor's men. Johanna, however, backed up his story.

Wethersby Jnr mocked, "He must still believe the JackFruit is there. Let's go along for the ride, but we must be on guard at every turn; he probably killed our Fredrick, his nemesis of a pirate, and perhaps Mayling too. The pox is too convenient; my brother is never to be trusted, ever."

"Do you truly believe *he* could have killed Mayling?" supposed Rayleigh.

"Oh yes indeed," replied Wethersby Jnr.

But he was wrong.

--x--

They lodged on the *Shepherds Cove* within the harbour for their safety and that of their precious cargo. It was late afternoon; an unusual dark orange glow covered the vessel, despite the sunset ten minutes earlier.

Two elderly women rowed out to the ship and gingerly climbed up the ropes.

"We bring freshly smoked chicken," cackled one of them, adding, "Captain's favourite."

Looking around, she straightened her bent-over back and removed her disguise. As she unwound her headscarf , she beamed a huge smile.

"*Mayling*, you are alive," wailed Wethersby Jnr.

"But my Fredrick, he is dead. He had the pox but got killed with a sabre in the *Sardine Tavern*," she whimpered. "That evil place is the death tavern; your brother got killed there too."

Before Wethersby Jnr could respond, the other woman decloaked, revealing a baby boy strapped around her chest.

"This is my friend, Patcharapa. She is originally from Jodhpur too, what a coincidence. I could hardly believe it when we found each other," said Mayling.

"And who is this young lad?" asked Wethersby Jnr.

"Your kin, Samuel," announced Mayling facing them. "Here is your son."

Taking a deep breath, she continued, "We are in danger. Your evil brother nearly caught us soon after he killed Fredrick. It was a miracle that the pirate, Solroy, obstructed his path. We escaped and have been in hiding these last ten days. We heard he killed the Omani too."

"But how can he be my son? You and Fredrick...?" retorted Rayleigh shaking his head. "It is not possible."

"I know," is all Mayling replied.

Patcharapa handed Samuel to Wethersby Jnr. The last of the amber glow lit up his blue eyes, and his black hair shone.

"Pa, Pa," gargled Samuel.

--x--

Johanna ran in first. The cave walls flickered as the oil-soaked torch spat seal fat; she gagged from its overpowering odour. One of the soldiers carrying several wooden pails rushed to catch up with her.

"Where's the yellow glow Pa described?" asked Rayleigh, shivering, despite the warm afternoon.

Chiranya and baby Sarah stayed on one of the wagons with the remaining soldiers. James followed Wethersby Jnr, and Rayleigh came behind him with two more pails, holding a naked torch in his other hand.

Rayleigh's discomfort began to increase when James suddenly turned and whispered, "You like enclosed dark spaces, don't you, Rayleigh? Does it feel like your well? Ha-ha."

"You know, the first few times you pushed me down that well, I panicked, but over time I learnt to overcome my fears. It's funny; the more you pushed me in, the stronger I became," laughed Rayleigh.

He abruptly dropped the pails and shoved James hard on his nose. James stumbled, then continued into the grotto.

They spent several hot and dusty hours removing earth and rocks until Johanna cried, "I can see through. We are near the enchanted lagoon."

The shaft of light blinded her for some moments. Disorientated, she spun and bumped heads with Wethersby Jnr.

"Let me get through," demanded James.

Squeezing through a gap that was hardly there, passing Wethersby Jnr and Johanna, James ripped his shirt and scratched his back raw.

"I see it too. You're nearly there, Scarface," James mocked.

As James hunched lower, he suddenly felt a deep warmth between his shoulder blades. He was constrained by an intense pressure, the power of which he had never experienced before. His knees buckled as he fell flat on his stomach, his legs outstretched.

Johanna screamed, "What happened, James?"

Covering James's back was a rock of equal size. His left eye was wide open. Droplets of black blood trickled from his missing earhole, nose and mouth. She cried out again, but he said nothing.

Wethersby Jnr, still dazed by Johanna's head clash, looked beyond her shoulder and declared, "Oh brother. Your trap; it has failed *you*."

For an hour, Wethersby Jnr and Rayleigh took turns attempting to dislodge the boulder to free James. They finally gained traction using some hardwood logs the soldiers found outside the entrance. James occasionally groaned, but for the most part, he was silent. Finally, they dragged him out of the hollow and onto the wagon.

They slept on the wagons that night and returned to Kali fort the following morning. James was barely breathing and was a sorry-looking mess.

--x--

Four weeks later, James woke from his coma. A desperate realisation soon came to pass; a bone protruded slightly out from the middle of his back as his spine was broken. He could not move any part of his body nor feel anything from below his nipples. James would never leave his grandfather's island of discovery, nor would he walk again.

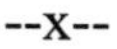

# 39

# Parting

Rayleigh, Wethersby Jnr, Chiranya, Mayling and their children, and all the enduring *Shepherds Cove* crew set off to circumnavigate the southern tip of India before heading north for the return to Ahmedabad.

They left James a week after he came out of his coma. They shed no tears, though; a life of bullying, and now murder, had seen to that. With Governor de Heere and Johanna's support, their acting surgeon, Thomas, agreed to stay as James's sentinel; Wethersby Jnr and Rayleigh pledged to reward Thomas admirably.

--x--

Three weeks later, they arrived at the great city again, just before midday. Lads on the quay caught the heavy ropes thrown to them.

"This ship is remarkable. How has the mainmast withstood the last storm? I can't see any new cracks whatsoever," said Rayleigh.

"They're firing at us!" shouted Chiranya.

"Aha, that cannon again. No, it's just gone noon," laughed Wethersby Jnr and added, "regular as clockwork."

A welcome party of thirty or more colourfully dressed hawkers shouted out their wares as Wethersby Jnr and Rayleigh disembarked. Mayling and Chiranya followed, with their children on their backs supported by a sarong. Gently pushing their way through the crowd, as wafts of pungent spices filled their nostrils, they saw three magnificent-looking men. One short, plump man, and two others standing guard, greeted them.

"Mister Wethersby, Mister Rayleigh. Welcome back to our kingdom," boomed the fat man. "Sultan Aurangzeb offers you the hospitality of his city again and, of course, a splendid banquet awaits you this evening. I expect you are all ravenous. Please come with me."

Sultan Aurangzeb of Ahmedabad was indeed an excellent and gracious host. He doted on Sarah and Samuel and showed great respect towards Chiranya and Mayling. Everyone stuffed themselves crazily with the lavish feast of food inside the grand room of the Azam Khan Sarai palace.

A cluster of snake charmers and a large troop of scantily clad female dancers entertained the over-a-hundred assembled guests, merchants and guards.

They were dumbfounded when Boyce entered the room.

Sultan Aurangzeb showed intense interest in their great adventure across the continents. Unusually, instead of sitting above his subjects, he knelt on a luxurious carpet alongside his guests. He listened with curiosity to Rayleigh and Wethersby Jnr taking turns sharing their experiences. The sultan nodded frequently and occasionally asked for extra details. He tried unsuccessfully to disguise his smile, then roared with pleasure as Rayleigh spoke about how they found Mayling and their previously unknown family in Jodhpur. Mayling could not help but notice the glint in his eyes as Rayleigh described the brilliance of the JackFruit crystal. Little did they know how his heart raced as Wethersby Jnr recounted their diplomacies with the sultan's arch-enemy, Maharaja Ajit Singh.

While Rayleigh conveyed a false account of Siam, where they were unable to find the remaining treasure, Mayling delicately whispered to Wethersby Jnr, "I wish to live in my home, Jodhpur. Please come with me, and care for my child. Samuel will be yours forever."

Wethersby Jnr shifted and stretched before resuming a cross-legged position. Slowly turning his head to her, he nodded as he brought his finger to her lips and held her gaze. They sat motionless, wordless, for several minutes, seemingly oblivious to a snake sliding towards them. The charmer abruptly dropped his pungi, grabbed the slithering snake, and placed it back in its basket. Their gaze broke and the reedy harmony restarted.

"Yes," he mouthed and kissed her tenderly on her cheek.

The evening's entertainment and adventure anecdotes continued well into the early morning.

--x--

Leaving his dear brother, Mayling, and Samuel behind in Ahmedabad was the hardest thing Rayleigh had ever done in his life. His solace was taking Chiranya and Sarah to England and sharing the treasures with his cousin.

The sultan generously provided camels, a team of soldiers and copious provisions for their second desert crossing. He also presented a carefully annotated map, a direct route to cut the journey, bypassing Jaisalmer by one hundred miles or more.

Wethersby Jnr offered Sultan Aurangzeb a cargo hoard of Kandyan spices.

"You owe me nothing more," smiled the sultan and added, "you have provided me with enough intelligence already."

--x--

On Christmas Day 1698, the cousins parted company. It was exactly two years since Joseph had read old Wethersby's will in the study.

Rayleigh agreed with Boyce to jointly skipper the *Shepherds Cove* back to England.

--x--

Wethersby Jnr, Mayling and Samuel confidently found their way to Jodhpur. They quickly reunited with Mayling's grandmother, Gooty, and mother, Mari, at a small but luxurious villa within the maharaja's palace walls. Recounting endless tales from their adventure became a regular evening ritual.

"Why did you leave the largest gemstones behind, Wethersby Junior?" asked Gooty.

"That's a good question and one I have asked myself countless times. Its rocks were warm, even hot to touch, with a golden glow. They seemed of another world," he replied and added, "and I remember my grandpa's last words. Goodness knows what hurt and ruin those stones bring."

He calmly held Mayling's weak hand.

From his pocket, Wethersby Jnr took a compact lead caddy and placed it in Gooty's palm. He looked into Mayling's deep green eyes, and they nodded together, acknowledging their promise. Gooty's inquisitive expression changed as she opened the box; a yellow radiance lit up her face.

"A replacement for you. It was Rayleigh's stone; he insisted. Please take it, for all the trust and faith you bestowed in us, but never touch it."

"*No*! See the maharaja's black spot where the JackFruit plunges, yes? He is a harmful man now," screamed Mari, startling her mother, quickly grabbing the box. "Look at my fingers. They pain me every day and will do so for the remainder of my long-haunted life."

"And mine too," acknowledged Mayling.

--x--

# 40

## GOLD ANGEL

Boyce and Rayleigh successfully navigated the *Shepherds Cove* back to England, landing on Rayleigh's twentieth birthday, 28th February 1699. Rayleigh's compass kept spinning.

Boyce, as agreed, took open ownership of the *Shepherds Cove* under one condition; if, or when, Rayleigh required his captaincy again, Boyce would provide it without hesitation or reward.

They traded the enormous cache of finest quality Kandyan spices at numerous Blackfriars' wharves. They held no ivory.

After all the trades concluded, Rayleigh returned to the Tower Mint with his family and crew. He deposited most of his bounty. Warden of the Mint, Newton, was mightily impressed. Rayleigh had replaced Wethersby's original inheritance of English gold sovereigns with a value of more than twentyfold and from his share alone.

Fortunately, after checking them all most carefully, Newton only confiscated two counterfeit coins; Rayleigh's cherished 1631 Gold Angel was not one of them.

The revelation of Wethersby Snr's firstborn grandchild astonished even the unflappable warden. Perhaps unsurprisingly, he initially assumed Sarah was the rightful heir. Newton's smile became wider and wider as Rayleigh narrated a brief account of their epic journey.

After over an hour of storytelling, Rayleigh concluded, "Wethersby Jnr, Mayling and Samuel are in Jodhpur, living in great comfort at Maharaja Ajit Singh's palace with Mayling's mother and grandma. We will retrace our sandy steps there one day. Perhaps, on another day, Samuel will come to England to claim his JackFruit."

Rayleigh pledged to meet the warden to release Wethersby Snr's Trust in two years. Rayleigh, though, had no intention of removing those unique coins from the Thackers' vault.

Soon after arriving at *Thatchers* with the enduring crew, they visited each of the dead men's families and Thomas's too, expressing sincere gratitude and remorse. Rayleigh offered each family their son's share of the bounty, honouring their original commitment; through tears, all accepted. He affirmed he would accompany them to the Tower Mint to collect their share whenever required.

Earlier, each of the surviving crew stored in the Thackers' vault, a one-seventeenth share from half of the trade.

They had feared an almighty ambush on the stages home should they bring it back all in one go, after Rayleigh pronounced, "Imagine *that!* After everything we have been through together and our friends we have left behind."

Rayleigh's great fortune was tempered as Chiranya's nausea deepened and expanded little by little, as did her palm's blemish.

Rayleigh vowed to reunite Sarah with her half-brother Samuel in Jodhpur. However, he knew that would be Chiranya's decision alone.

--x--

# 41

## A WILY PLAN

Five days after Rayleigh and Wethersby Jnr left *Thatchers*, for their adventure, Joseph made a surprise announcement.

Two weeks later, in March 1697, he married Jane Bunting, the Blakes' servant. Joseph was lonely without his boys, and Jane was a beautiful woman and had been discretely craving Joseph's attention. In late September that year, their first child was born, a son they named William James. He was a healthy and bubbly boy with jet-black hair, dark green eyes, and a black birthmark covering the back of his left ear. He was a noisy baby, constantly crying and had great difficulty sleeping, keeping Jane and Joseph awake almost every night, much to Joseph's annoyance.

Joseph struggled during that year with the upkeep of his estate. The harvest was a disaster again due to the dry spring and extremely wet summer; the estate managers could not pay their rents. Rose Thacker had moved back in with her mother and father after Joseph threw her out of his estate house immediately after his shock declaration. Not even Rose's parents were spared Joseph's demands for their payments.

He was hatching a wily plan to embezzle the JackFruit diamond from the Thackers' vault at The Mint.

--x--

After a noisy and challenging journey to London, he arrived with Jane and William in tow.

On Thursday 16th January 1698, the warden of the Mint, Newton, was ready and waiting for them. Dispensing quickly with introductions, they got down to business.

"Your child, you say?" said Newton quietly.

"Yes, born on 21st September 1697. Here is William's birth and our marriage papers. Everything is in order," replied Joseph.

"I see, I see," repeated Newton, holding his thumb across his chin.

"Please, can we move this along? William needs another feed," stressed Joseph.

"I read your letter with great interest. You have not heard from any of your sons or nephew?" asked Newton.

Joseph shuffled uneasily in his chair, sensing the warden was toying with him.

"No. Nothing. I have no idea where the boys are, nor indeed whether they are still alive, chasing after my father's eccentric dreams," responded Joseph.

"Let me get to the point. I have studied your late father's will and instructions most carefully these last weeks after receiving your letter. I have some material evidence that you will not enjoy," frowned Newton as his voice lowered.

"How so? The papers are in order, and you can see my wife, child and me here in the flesh," asserted Joseph, his tone rising.

A bead of sweat dripped from his brow and onto his lips.

"You should have read your father's will more carefully. The will indicates the JackFruit diamond is to be inherited by the firstborn of one of his *great*-grandsons," declared Newton with a disguised dry smile. "The birth paper states young William James Thacker is *your* child, Joseph, denoting William as your father's grandson. Your marriage paper states that this fine lady is, mercifully, *not* your daughter."

Joseph felt fiery acid rise from his chest and the blood drain from his face; ashen, he nearly fainted.

"What! How dare you block me from my inheritance," seethed Joseph.

"Come now, Mister Thacker, I have read that your late father has already given you his entire estate. It must be worth a fortune and generate a handsome annual income. In any case, your sons' or your nephew's firstborn inheritance will be theirs alone," articulated Newton. "Now, let us discuss the other more pressing matter, Rayleigh's Trust."

Joseph recovered his composure, although he was rendered almost speechless. Jane continued to tend to William, playing with him and distracting his attention from unfamiliar surroundings. She found their conversation fascinating, but she had an uneasy feeling that Joseph's fiery temper may soon reappear once they returned to Southwold.

They spent another hour at the Mint. Joseph agreed to everything Newton suggested for the maintenance of Rayleigh's Trust. He knew he must wait for Rayleigh's return before he could get his hands on those gold coins.

--x—

Sir Isaac Newton, the famous mathematician, physicist, astronomer, theologian and author, who formulated the theory of universal gravity, was promoted from Warden to Master of the Mint in 1699, a position he held until his death in 1727.

--x--

Jane held onto her secret, never telling a soul, despite the riches that her son would inherit later.

Little would Sir Isaac Newton, Joseph, or even James, ever know who, indeed, had fathered William James Thacker back at the Blakes' barn.

--x--

# THE END

# ACKNOWLEDGEMENTS

This book would not have happened if it were not for the inspiration, energy and unwavering commitment of Michael Heppell and his Write That Book programme.

*Thank you*, Michael.

To the Write That Book Stormsurfers and Boomerang teams: Jeannie Duncanson, Steve Kelly, Nichola Kingsbury, Sarah McGeough, Ian Pilbeam, Ildiko Spinfisher, Sheila Starr, Richard Thomas, Gillian Westlake, Diane Wyatt, and especially Christine Beech and Nick Finney for reviewing the whole book!

In faraway lands, Elizabeth Chandler and Philippa Mathewson.

*Thank you* all for your unyielding support, massive encouragement, critical feedback and for your friendship. May we meet some day - not only virtually.

To Duncan Mirylees, my ex-neighbour in Godalming, England, for managing the book samples, for your advice, suggestions, historical editing, and your considerable patience.

To my brother Andrew, for handling a lot of books' shipping from Ipswich, England.

--x--